On a
Caribbean Tide

To Ted happy sailing

DB Lawhon
X

D. B. LAWHON

To learn more about the author visit; dblawhon.com

NEWMAN SPRINGS PUBLISHING
320 Broad Street
Red Bank, NJ 07701

First originally published by Newman Springs Publishing 2022

ISBN 979-8-88763-019-9 (Paperback)
ISBN 978-1-68498-482-4 (Hardcover)
ISBN 978-1-68498-483-1 (Digital)

Printed in the United States of America

Dedication

Throughout my life I have been blessed to have had a number of strong independent women around me. This included my own mother, three aunts, my grandmother, my sister and coworkers as well. Because of this, the women of my stories are built from the strengths I came to see in them, and how they dealt with life, and this story is no exception.

And for the last twenty-three years I've been blessed and proud to be married to the most incredible woman I've ever known. I have never come across anyone that's as together, confident and comfortable with who they are and what they believe as my wife. She exudes a rare magnetism and positivity that all who know her benefit from in one way or another.

I therefore dedicate this book to my wife Darlene, who continues to amaze and inspire me.

Acknowledgements

It has been a habit of mine throughout my life to challenge accepted thought, methods, and the so-called conventional wisdom on how to accomplish a goal, whether with my work or in my personal life.

One of the things I came across while reading several books on the art and science of writing was that you never want to use friends or relatives to do things like editing, proofreading etc. I didn't heed that scholarly advice, in fact I metaphorically ripped it out of that self-help book, wadded it up, stepped on it, and tossed it unceremoniously in the waste basket. For the following acknowledgements reads like the guest list to my family reunion.

While not everyone listed here is a family member, they are through the connections we all have of one person to another in the great family of mankind. So, without further ado, these folks, are all family in one way or another and all contributed something to this novel.

Gina Hamilton, my dear cousin, it gives me great pleasure to be thanking you once again. You were so instrumental in helping me get the Navajo Sign out as a published work. And now this time, you have been on the whole cruise with me for On a Caribbean Tide. You have been so good at catching errors of punctuation, grammar and story critiques, not the least of which was understanding the very complicated game of poker, (which I have never learned) pointing out what can and cannot happen in the game. I must admit to being surprised to find this out about you. Yet another reason you remain a riddle, wrapped in mystery, inside an enigma for me.

And while I'm on the subject of the game of poker, (which figures prominently in the story) I have to thank another cousin of mine, Brent Lawhon. Thanks, Brent, for helping me to war game how the poker game could go, a critical component to the end of the story. Brent, it's a funny thing about life, you just never know when something you have learned and mastered earlier in life will be of help to someone else later on in life. Now while you are not a master of the game of poker, (so you say) you were, in your younger years, a master magician. As a consequence, you know very well how to handle a deck of cards, and sometimes two decks. I remember watching you many years ago, simultaneously fan out two decks of cards in one hand, so that all cards could be seen, I've never forgot that.

And to the youngest of my five sons, John, who sat with me years ago when I started to write a short story for a writing contest, which became the opening chapter to this story. I believe you were about ten years old at the time. I asked you what the main character's name should be, and with no hesitation you blurted out Caleb Arnold. So, Cal was born that evening almost ten years ago.

To continue with this little family reunion, my #3 son Kyle, who at ten years old, and on a trip with family friends in the Florida Keys, snapped the amazing picture that graces this book's cover, and he did it with a little throwaway Kodak camera on Key West. Talk about being at the right place at the right time, it is a perfect picture, and I am so proud to have something he did as the books cover.

To my amazing sister Denise, who I bestowed the unenviable task of marketing my work. You took up this task at a very difficult time in your life and have gone after it with the same zeal and confidence that you have shown in beating back your cancer. You have shown me and all whom you touched during the last year your incredible strength and the compassion you have for others who are in this same battle.

I want to thank David Grey at Flame Productions for developing, creating and launching my new author website, dblawhon.com. You and all your staff did an exemplary job, both during and after its launch and your readiness to help even after its launch is both refreshing and appreciated.

To James Gordon at Newman Springs, you and I have been working together for almost three years now. You have never failed to be there when I've had questions, no matter what they were, even through a pandemic. You always came through with answers on everything, not only from the publishing side, but also on the business side of things. Thanks, and I'm looking forward to the next adventure with you and Newman Springs Publishing.

And last but not least, I need to give a shout out to Chris Dorn-Rusham. While you are not family you have encouraged me like any good family member would do. Chris and I were working together at a general contracting firm, when I began my first novel. Chris was brave enough to be the very first person to see, critique and encourage me to keep writing. Chris I'm happy to see that your eyes have finally stopped bleeding from that experience.

Chapter 1

Caleb Arnold, known simply as Cal, was a man who came from a difficult background, having become the "man of the house" in his early teens. It was during those formative years that he developed a particular talent for persuasion. In 1943, he found himself aboard a Navy aircraft carrier as the ship's purser, a position that suited him well. Along with his powers of persuasion were his skills at playing poker and billiards, all learned at an early age.

In 1946, with the war and his time in the Navy behind him, Cal found himself with no job and no particular skill or desire for manual labor. Sitting alone in a dingy diner on the outskirts of Newark, he watched passenger planes take off through the low clouds of the next snowstorm. Thoughts of his current situation and the gloomy weather had him feeling lower than he ever had in his life. He was going nowhere, and fast.

However, taking a sip of his coffee, fate, as it often does, stepped in. Right in front of him he spied an ad on the back of a newspaper being read by the faceless patron in the next booth. The headline of the ad said, "Make Money Selling Florida." The ad was aptly bordered by big dollar signs, and as if to drive the Florida point home, a smiling sun brightly shone down from an upper corner of the ad.

Cal's dark brown eyes widened with newfound promise. "That's it!" he confidently stated to himself. Rereading the ad, he thought, *Who better than me to sell land?* Or anything else for that matter.

Casting a slow gaze around his immediate surroundings, then back to the ad, he read it again, took note of the phone number, and with a confident nod, decided right then to leave the snow-bound cities of the northeast. With nothing or no one to hold him there, he confidently decided he was done. It was time for Caleb Arnold to make it big! With fifty bucks and a bus ticket in his pocket, he set out for Florida, intent on making it big in the burgeoning Florida real estate market, but good intentions and good results are seldom bedmates.

Along the way to making his fortunes in Florida real estate, he found he wasn't the only one who had the same idea. The stiff competition in the real estate business often caused interruptions in his cash flow. To remedy his feast-or-famine monetary troubles, he used his gift of gab to augment his income in somewhat less than honorable ways. Those ways ranged from card tricks done in local bars to selling "rare" jewelry to the gullible passersby on street corners and bus stations. He managed to use his luck and talent to keep one step ahead of the law…well, most times.

Currently though, Cal had to rely on his talents of persuasion once again. For a short distance away, the sound of Jacob Haines Walker, the local sheriff, and his deputy, Miles Dempsdale, could be heard working their way through the thick south Florida underbrush.

He heard them coming long before he saw them, cussing and fussing about the heat and humidity while slapping at the mosquitoes that peppered them relentlessly with unforgiving viciousness. Cal also heard the sheriff questioning his deputy about the accuracy of his informant as they trudged and fought their way through the underbrush.

"Miles," he scoffed. "You sure that we're on the right trail? This is a long way off the beaten path if you ask me."

Miles stopped, turned, and looked back at Jacob with sweaty exasperation. Removing a handkerchief from his shirt pocket, he dabbed his brow while confidently stating, "It dang sure is. Ole Juky wouldn't lie 'bout a thang like this, no sir. He wouldn't lie 'bout this a-tall."

Jacob glared at his deputy for a long moment. He then turned his gaze up through their surroundings. Jacob shook his head. Seeing only a wink of sky through the vine-laden overgrowth of palmettos and the sentinel-like stance of pine trees, he grudgingly barked at his deputy, "Well, get going. We don't have all day."

Acknowledging the sheriff's terse order with a short nod, Miles pressed on shoving the bramble and thorny vines out of his way, hoping that his informant had indeed told the truth.

They hadn't gone far when Jacob decided he could take no more. He was about to call off what was looking more and more like a wild goose chase when they came upon a small clearing. Stopping at the edge of the clearing, and thankful for the moment just to be able to straighten up, both men cautiously surveyed their surroundings. They stood for a moment more wiping sweat from their faces and struggling to catch their breath in the humidity choked air.

In the distance, a thunderstorm rumbled low across the landscape giving the sheriff another reason to end this and head back. Seeing nothing unusual at first glance among the twisted vines and gnarled branches of Brazilian pepper that encircled them, the sheriff let out a huff of exasperation and was about to turn and start back the way they had come.

Suddenly, almost at the same instant, their eyes landed on it. A short distance away, there sat the object of their sweat-soaked toils. Practically invisible at first glance sitting tucked into a cove cut into the thick vegetation, a soft fire licked at the sides of a boiler. The unmistakable copper coil and collection jug told them they had indeed found a still!

"Well I'll be danged, ole Juky was right about a still being out here after all," Jacob exclaimed.

"We musta scared off whoever was tending this thang, Sheriff. They wouldn't leave it just sitting here a-filling up a jug," Miles said, walking in for a closer look.

Sheriff Walker impatiently glanced around then down at his watch. "It's get'n' late, Miles, and that storm sounds like it might be moving our direction. Since there ain't no one here to arrest in connection with this here still, we'll just have to take it out of commission and git on back to town. This ain't no place to be caught in after dark."

Smacking another mosquito on his neck, Miles questioned, "How we gonna do that, Sheriff? We didn't bring no axes ta bust it up with."

Jacob gave a wry smile while sliding his gun from its holster. "That's easy, Deputy," the sheriff said, pointing with his drawn gun. "You get a bucket of water from that artesian well over there and douse the fire. Then you and me is gonna put so many holes in that there boiler it's gonna look like a damn cheese grater."

Laughing out loud, Miles started for the well. Scooping up a bucket full of water from the free-flowing spring, Miles trudged his way back to the still. Gripping the bucket with both hands, he reared back to douse the fire. Just before Miles sent the water cascading from the bucket, a voice called out from the thick brush commanding Miles to stop. The sheriff and Miles quickly turned to see Cal step from out of the thicket where he had been hiding.

Jacob pointed his drawn gun right at Cal. "Just who the hell are you, boy?" he demanded. "This *your* still, boy?"

Holding out the palm of his hand in a halting motion, Cal anxiously asked, "What's going on here, Sheriff?"

"I ask the questions here, boy. Now who are you? And *is* this your still?"

"Look, Sheriff, my name is Cal. And this isn't a still. *Well,* not the kind you think it is, Sheriff."

Raising a suspicious eyebrow, the sheriff studied this stranger with a good deal of skepticism. However, seeing no sign of a weapon or aggression, the sheriff slowly lowered his revolver but kept a wary eye on this stranger.

Cal, however, being a man of quick wit and grand imagination, seized the moment. He quickly began to weave a story so fantastic that it would surely have made Mark Twain proud. Artfully he told of how the Calusa Indians had used the rendered sap of the gumbo-limbo tree to rid themselves of all manner of ills. And he was simply out there trying to recreate that same magic elixir.

Cal's smooth voice and glib tongue were in fine form this day as he spun a tale of the elixir's benefits of incredible health and vitality to the sheriff and his spellbound deputy. Soon, Cal had replaced the sheriff's earlier skepticism with feline-like curiosity. With the smoothness of a well-polished car salesman, Cal could see he had them right where he wanted them. He convinced them to take not just one sip but several of his mysterious magic elixir.

The whole time they drank Cal continued embellishing the story more and more, regaling them with tales of great Calusa Indian conquests—conquests not only over their enemies but also over women! Miles and Jacob both smiled broadly upon hearing this. Hoisting their tin cups high, they shouted "Look out, women, here we come!" then tossed back yet another slug of magic elixir.

By this time, Jacob and Miles were quite drunk, laughing and singing aloud. Cal, on the other hand, was ready to get going. So in a gesture of good will, and to move things along, he poured himself a little of the crystal-clear liquid then offered up a grand and verbose toast to the sheriff and his deputy.

At the conclusion, they each tossed back their drinks. Both lawmen quavered on wobbly legs. The sheriff slowly pointed at Cal while trying to utter a complement on such a fine toast. However, not a single word left his lips. Jacob's eyes rolled back, and his legs melted out from under him. The good sheriff dropped to the ground like so much wet laundry.

Miles looked down at his boss, and through spittle-slurred speech and wobbling in ever widening circles himself, he asked, "Jacob, are…are…we…gonna…live fer ever now?"

Hiccupping, Miles looked back to Cal, saying, "He looks happy…don't he?" He then spun part way 'round dropping like ripe fruit in a banana wind, sprawling right across the motionless sheriff.

Cal stared down at the pile of the county's finest laying passed out with smiles on their faces. "You boys almost had me. But it's time for this sailor to weigh anchor and hightail it outta here. I need to find this Juky fellow, and how he knew about my little operation, and *why* he'd rat me out."

*****

Suddenly Cal heard, "Dad, are you telling that same old story again? That poor man didn't come in here for that. He just wants a cold beer and a cool place to sit. Am I right?" he asked, giving the smiling black man at the bar a sympathetic look.

A hearty deep laugh burst through perfect white teeth and the large mouth that held them. Deep wrinkles rode on the smile that wrapped the eyes of the balding man's round face as he spoke. His Caribbean accent resounded deep against the cypress wood walls of the Salty Anchor bar and grill.

"Ah…no…dis is exactly what I hoped to find in he-ah. And yo-ah father is an excellent storyteller. A cold beer a maun can find anywhere. But a good story…well, that is indeed refreshing."

Cal gave a smug look back over his shoulder at his son, "There, you see, son—someone who appreciates a good tale, especially one that's true!" Not waiting or wanting a reply from his son, Cal turned back to face this new customer, who was finishing the last of his beer and setting the mug down on the bar. Cal swiped the mug off the bar filling it again, saying, "Here, this one is on the house. What's your name, friend? Mine is Caleb Arnold, but most everybody calls me Cal."

Taking the frosted mug, he held it up letting the foamy head run down the sides and drip on the thick wooden bar top. Smiling broadly, he said, "Here's to making friends, new aund old." Hesitating a moment, he looked deeply into Cal's eyes as his smile slowly melted away and said, "As fo-ah my name, et es Julius Kerns Youssaint."

Cal gave a chuckle. "That's a lot of vowels and consonants piled together—what do your friends call you?"

Holding an expressionless stare on Cal's smiling face, he said, "Mah friends…deh call me…Juky."

Chapter 2

Time froze. Cal's smile evaporated instantly from his face. Kevin saw what was coming. He had seen that look before. Rushing to get between his dad and the somber-looking Juky, Kevin nervously spoke to his dad.

"Dad, Dad. Don't go getting all crazy here."

"Son, this has nothing to do with you. Now step aside!"

"No, Dad, not until you calm down."

Cal pitched his head sideways while rolling his eyes. "Kevin! I said step aside, dammit! Look, I'm not going to hit him, son. I just have to find out a few things."

Remaining steadfastly between his dad and the stone-quiet Juky, Kevin stared long into his father's eyes. "What is it that's so important that you have to know, Dad, that some hick cops found out about a damn still you had in 1952? Dad! It's 1983, that was over thirty years ago. Who cares? It's not important now."

Cal's eyes widened, then squinted in renewed anger. Pointing around Kevin, he exclaimed, "That guy changed my life. I did ninety days in jail because of him." Rubbing both hands over his head in frustration, Cal continued. "Not important! I lost my job with the real estate company because of him."

"Yeah, yeah, you did. But look at what all you've gained," Kevin said, pointing around the room.

In disbelief, Cal looked at his son. "What? This? A stinking bar and bait shop?"

"Dad, this place is a lot more than a 'stinking bar and bait shop,' and you know it. This place has made you a pretty good living, and an honest one too. Besides, it's where you met Mom, remember?"

Cal's whole demeanor softened at the mention of Kevin's mother.

"Of course, I remember. But you got no business bringing your mom into this. She has nothing to do with this."

"Dad! Think for just a second," Kevin pleaded. "You told me once that a person's life is like the links in a chain. That every event in a person's life connects like the links of a chain all the way back to the day you were born."

Cal's head dropped. He then peered around his son at Juky who sat quietly with his hands folded on the bar. Juky held his gaze on Cal for a long moment. A smile returned to Juky as he calmly said, "Yo-ah son is quite wise for his age, Cal. Are you *still* Cal to me?"

Cal shook his head a couple of times as if trying shake out years of pent-up resentment. Exhaling through puffed cheeks, he cut his eyes up the meet Juky's. "Yeah, I suppose so." But then sternly added, "But not before you tell me why you told the cops about my still."

Juky nodded, his face held a warm smile as he said, "Okay. But only after you listen to a proposition I have for you."

With one arm motion, Cal swiped his way past his son right up to the bar, practically shouting, "What? Why in the world would I consider a proposition, or anything else from you? Hellfire and damnation, until you came in here, I didn't think you were within a thousand miles of here."

Another boisterous laugh erupted from Juky. His eyes brightened. Slapping the bar, he said, "Why would that be so, Cal, because I'd be scared dat you would still be looking fo-ah me?"

Cal smashed his lips tight. He never much cared for being the butt of a joke. And this one, he particularly didn't care for. Raising a pointed finger at Juky, he barked, "Okay, okay, you've had a good laugh and a free beer, so why don't you just weigh anchor and shove off. I don't need or want anything you've got to offer."

Juky quickly spoke through waning laughter. "No, no, please wait, mah friend. Can we take a walk out on de dock, just you and me? I think I might be able to change yo-ah mind once you hear my proposition."

"*No!* Nothing is going to get me to listen to anything you have to say." Cal swiped the empty beer mug off the bar as if Juky might steal it and began brusquely washing it in the under-counter sink.

Juky's face went straight before he spoke. His deep voice was hushed as he said, "Even if it means making a great deal of money?"

Ceasing his washing of the mug, he looked up at Juky. His expression told Juky he had Cal's attention. Easy money always did the trick, Juky thought.

Suddenly Cal's face went sullen as he returned to washing and rinsing the mug. Cal, though, was fighting the urge to ask how much money. He knew all too well that this was the oldest con-man lead-in in the world. He should know. He had used it enough himself.

Juky drew his eyes around the bar. At eleven in the morning, the bar was mostly empty. Only a couple of other people were in there, and they were sitting well away from them. Kevin, in fact, had taken a portly man another beer and was making small talk with him.

Retrieving an ink pen from his shirt pocket, Juky quickly jotted something on the bar napkin, spun it around, and slid it across the bar so Cal could see what he had written. Returning the pen to his pocket, Juky leaned well back in the cane-backed barstool, smiled, and waited.

Cal cast a quick look at Juky then down at the napkin. Cal stopped his drying of the beer mug, almost dropping it as he fumbled to set it down. His eyes narrowed under a deeply furrowed brow. He looked back and forth at the napkin and Juky, who remained smiling and silent.

Finally, Cal spun the napkin around and pushed it back in front of Juky. "That's bullshit. Where is Rum Cay? You haven't got any idea of where the Atocha is. Even if you do, why would you be willing to share it? What is it you really want? I ain't no hit man, and I don't run no drugs for any amount of money."

Juky leaned across the bar getting almost face-to-face with Cal. "That, mah friend, es why we need to take a walk on de dock. I want to show you something."

Cal looked long and hard into Juky's face. Then without looking around, he called out to his son, "Kevin, I'm going out for a walk on the dock. I won't be long." He then motioned to Juky. "I'll take a walk, but not for that bullshit on the napkin. I'm just curious what kinda crap you're trying to sell."

Taking the napkin off the bar, Juky folded it twice and poked it in his shirt pocket. He then eased his way to a pair of doors that led out onto to the long wooden docks directly behind the bar, pushing one open. As Cal shouldered his way past, he calmly said, "Mista Cal, mah friend, I would hardly call millions in Spanish doubloons crap." Juky then palmed three gold doubloons in his hand so only Cal could see.

"You're right, it isn't. But what you just showed me is just a loser's bet. This better be good."

Ten minutes or so passed, Kevin was busy replenishing the bottled beer case when his father burst back through the door. "Son, I'm taking off the rest of the afternoon. I've got to outfit the *Donna Marie* and get her ready to sail."

Grabbing his lucky ball cap and his jeep keys, he headed for the small office and the safe it held. "Gonna need some cash too, son. You know how you have to bribe them sons of bitches down there."

Kevin dropped what he was doing and headed to the office but had to stop to wait on another customer who had just sat down. Frustrated, he called out to his dad. "Wait a minute, Dad, what the hell is going on?"

Hurriedly snapping the cap off a bottle of beer, Kevin slid it down the bar to the bewildered patron, then raced for the office. Kevin slid through the open door like Tom Cruise in *Risky Business*, only to find the back door, like the safe, hanging wide open. And his father…well, he was nowhere in sight.

Chapter 3

The next morning Kevin wheeled into in the shell parking lot of the Salty Anchor, parking next to his dad's jeep. Looking over at it, he felt good that he was able to talk some sense into his father last night.

Entering the back door of the office, he smiled. Everything was normal with none of the craziness of yesterday afternoon. Tossing his keys on the desk, he glanced around the small office. Several photographs graced the rough-hewn cypress wood walls, some in frames, others simply push-pinned to the wood. One picture always gave him a melancholic smile.

That particular picture was the day they had christened the new schooner his dad had bought as the *Donna Marie*. Named for his mother, he always remembered how she cried when his dad unveiled the name on the stern that day. Holding the photograph in his hands, a soft smile and laugh came, recalling how mad she later got when she found out that he hadn't bought the boat at all but had in fact won it in a card game right here in this very bar.

She said she wouldn't ever go on a boat gained through the sin of gambling. And especially not on one with her name on it. Things changed when his dad had brought the former owner into the bar and paid him for the boat right in front of her. Kevin laughed again, setting the picture on the desk. He spoke out, "Never could figure out how someone could be so adamantly against gambling yet have no problem with being married to a guy who owned a bar."

If you asked her about that, she would always correct you by saying it's a bar *and* restaurant, then further qualify her rationale by adding, "Folks have to have something to drink when they eat."

His dad always called her the queen of pragmatism, which made her roll her eyes and immediately steer the conversation away to something she wanted done; it worked every time. His dad, though, wasn't a fan of being told what to do, so he would snap back that it would get done when he was good and ready, and always followed by a firm nod.

Kevin's fond recollections were abruptly blown apart by yelling and a door being slammed out in the bar area. Jumping up, he jerked open the office door to the bar area to see his dad practically running through the dining room throwing his arms and expletives in every direction.

"Dad, Dad, what the heck is the problem? What's wrong?"

"What's wrong?" Cal shouted back, stopping five feet short of his son. "I'll tell you what's wrong. That no good son-of-a-bitch stole my boat! That's what's wrong!"

"What the heck are you talking about, Dad?

"The *Donna Marie*! That SOB stole her!"

Chapter 4

Kevin glared at his dad then shoved his way past him, pushing chairs out of his way, hurrying to large plate-glass windows facing the docks. Pressing in close to the window, his mouth dropped open. Glancing back over his shoulder at his dad then back out the window, he asked, "Are you sure *he* took it? Why would he do that?"

"How the hell should I know? All I know is the *Donna Marie* is gone, and so is he."

"He couldn't have been gone long. We've got to call the police or the Coast Guard—we can't let him get away."

Cal paced the floor rubbing his hands over his head in frustrated thought. "No, that's exactly what we are *not* doing."

Kevin turned from the windows glaring in disbelief at his father. Walking briskly toward his dad, he spoke to him as he went. "What? Of course we're calling the authorities. We want him caught and the *Donna Marie* back!" Moving past his dad, he added, "Now come on, we're calling the cops."

"I said *no!*" Cal barked while grabbing his son's arm.

The two men froze for a moment glaring eye to eye. They had not been at odds with one another since Kevin was a teenager. Kevin then reached and snatched his father's hand off. Even though he was younger and stronger, he was not going to challenge his father any further. Instead, he calmly asked, "So what *are* you going to do, Dad?"

Cal stepped away from his son and resumed his pacing. His mind was going a million miles a second trying to weigh all the options. He had walked a few feet from Kevin then stopped. Snapping his fingers, he turned to face Kevin. "That's it!" Cal practically shouted. "We're going to call someone, all right." Cal then raced for the office.

Kevin quickly fell in behind his. "Call who? You're calling the Coast Guard, right?"

Without looking back, Cal said. "Oh hell no. I'm calling Artie Thomas."

"Artie Thomas! Why? What the heck is he going to be able to do? He's just some guy who lives off remittance from his super rich dad. He doesn't do anything except hang out at the bars in town and spend the monthly check he gets. Honestly, what can he do to get the boat back, Dad?"

Cal stopped in his tracks turned to look back at his son. "It's not what he can *do*, it's what he *has*, son."

"What? A butt load of money."

"No, dummy, a fast-ass boat, one of those Scarabs, that's what he's got."

Kevin looked at his dad like he had lost his mind. "Are you crazy! So he has a really fast boat. So what! You don't know what direction the *Donna Marie* went. You could wind up going *really fast* in the wrong goddamned direction, Dad."

Cal's eyes widened at hearing his son's rare use of foul language. It was his mother's influence that made those times rare, so it was pretty clear how upset his son was at the moment.

Cal raised an eyebrow at his son before stepping into the office. "Do you kiss your mama with that mouth, boy? Look, don't worry. That isn't going to happen. I'll find that worthless Juky and the *Donna Marie* too."

"How can you be so sure?"

"Look, Artie's boat *is* very fast. But speed isn't the only thing it has." Cal gave Kevin a shrewd smile then added, "It's fast, *and* it has radar on board."

A bewildered look came to Kevin. "Radar? Why in the world would he have that?"

"Look, son, he has it because he wants it, okay. Besides, running a fast boat at night, you need it."

Kevin shook his head trying to follow the logic. "But why would he be going that fast at night…" Kevin stopped in mid-sentence as the reason became glaringly apparent to him.

"Oh my god! Dad, that's even more of a reason to call the Coast Guard and let them handle it instead of some two-bit drug runner. Besides, the Coast Guard has radar, plus they have guns—really big ones too."

Cal had sat down at the desk and popped his head back to look out the office door at Kevin, dryly stating, "Oh, Artie has those too, son…well, except for the .50 caliber on the bow. But I think we can get the message across without that."

Kevin shot through the office door. "Look, Dad, you are fifty-six years old. I'm not going to let you go off on some wild goose chase. We are calling the Coast Guard."

With the phone to his ear, he spun the office chair back around and put his finger to his lips. "Shh. I got Artie on the phone, son."

Kevin threw his hands up in utter frustration and stormed his way back out the office door. "Oh my god, this just went from crazy to insane!"

Chapter 5

Kevin left his dad in the office. He had to open this place up soon, and things needed to be done. The cook and one of the waitresses were due in here shortly to help with getting things ready to open. It was Friday, and even though it was summertime, it still got busy earlier in the day than it did in the middle of the week.

During season, this place was a zoo all the time. Being two-thirds of the way to Key West, Ramrod Key made it an ideal place for tourists to hole up. The Salty Anchor also had a dozen small one-room cottages they rented out mostly to weekend scuba divers and sport fisherman who liked Ramrod Key for being close to Key West, but not too close.

What his dad flippantly called a bar and bait shop was in fact a full-service marina. While it may have started out as just a bar and bait shop back in the fifties, it now had fifteen full-time employees; that number doubled during the winter months when northeastern-ers descended on the island chain like a swarm of sun and fun-starved locust.

Kevin and his wife Tammy did most of the "heavy lifting" when it came to managing this place. Besides the cottages, the Salty Anchor consisted of a bait, tackle, dive, and gift shops, along with boat rental and repair shop, all of which kept things hopping most of the time.

Retrieving a ring of keys from a hook off the side of the bar cash register, Kevin headed outside to unlock the icebox. The sound of small shells and sand crunched on the old-west-like boardwalk that rimmed all the buildings of the Salty Anchor.

He had no sooner unlocked the second door of the icebox when a "Good morning" was called out to him from behind. Kevin didn't look around; the accent told him who it was, Angus, their boat mechanic coming to get his daily bag of ice for his cooler.

"Hey, good morning, Angus. Gonna be a hot one today, isn't it?" Kevin commented while handing him the bag of ice.

"Aye, that it is, Kevin my boy. If it weren't for ice and air-conditioning, I'm thinking I couldn't stay on this sunbaked patch of dirt we be flo'tin' on."

Angus's Scottish accent had temper to go with it that would flare when things weren't going well in the repair shop. At times this provided for some good entertainment when a wrench would go flying out of the shop right into the canal just a few yards away all accompanied by a string of indecipherable expletives.

Rags, his black Lab, convinced it was a game, would immediately jump off the dock and dive for whatever just hit the water. The amazing thing was Rags always found whatever was hurled into the drink in mere seconds.

The two men made some small talk about parts and supplies Angus needed in the shop. Angus turned to leave but abruptly stopped, asking Kevin, "Say, where might your father be heading in the *Donna Marie* so early in the morning?"

Kevin tossed the padlocks on top of the icebox and turned to face him. "Wait, you saw the *Donna Marie* leaving this morning?"

"Aye, that I did. Saw her heading under the Niles Channel Bridge as I was coming over this morning. He hadn't hung any canvas yet."

"You sure it was the *Donna Marie?*"

"Aye, Kevin, you can't miss the prettiest schooner around. Why? Something wrong?"

Kevin gave him worried glance. "No, uh, nothing's wrong. Listen, Angus, I gotta finish opening up. I'll uh…see you later."

Kevin hurried through the rest of his early morning duties then strode quickly back to the office. He felt he at least had a time line on how long ago Juky left. With this information, he felt he could talk some sense into his dad before he took off on some kind of high-speed Don Quixote quest.

Shoving open the office door, Kevin's shoulders immediately dropped. His dad was nowhere in sight! He knew too, without going to look, his jeep was gone as well. Glancing down at the desk, he saw a notepad on which his dad had scratched Artie's phone number. Without hesitation, he sat down and made the call. Hopefully his dad had not gotten to Artie's place yet. He further hoped to talk Artie out of taking his dad anywhere and to let the police handle things.

On the third ring, Artie picked up. "City morgue, you stab 'em, we slab 'em."

Confused, Kevin answered, "What? I'm sorry, I must have the wrong number."

"Maybe, who you looking for?"

"Artie Thomas."

"You got him. Who's this?"

"Dammit, Artie, it's me, Kevin. Look, I don't have time for this. My dad is on his way over there. Whatever you do, don't let him talk you into taking him in your boat, all right?"

"Well, that shouldn't be too difficult."

"No, he's pretty fired up, Artie, and you know how he is when he gets an idea in his head."

"Yeah, I know. But he won't be going anywhere on my boat today or even the next two weeks. I'm overhauling the engines. The *Stiletto* is dry-docked, baby."

Sounding even more confused, Kevin asked, "Didn't you tell him that when he called you?"

"Yeah, sure I did. I also told him about a guy with a sea plane who might be able to help him out."

Dragging his hand down his face, Kevin said, "Crap, you didn't."

"Yeah, he sounded pretty desperate. What's this all about anyway?"

"He didn't tell you?"

"No, not really, kind of muttered something about needing to make a quick trip to Rum Cay in the Bahamas maybe."

The words had barely left Artie's mouth when a loud deep roar shot straight overhead shaking dust from the cypress pole rafters. "What the hell!" Kevin dropped the phone and raced out the back door just in time to see a blue-and-white Grumman Albatross banking hard out over Florida Bay to make another low pass.

Kevin stood in the shell parking lot watching the sun glint off the fuselage of the twin-engine aircraft as it banked to line up on the Salty Anchor. Several of the arriving employees had gathered near Kevin watching with him including his wife, Tammy.

"Kev, who the heck is in that plane?" she shouted out just as the big plane roared right over again even lower than before.

Without looking at Tammy, he shouted back, "My crazy-ass dad."

Tammy turned back from watching the plane. "Your dad's flying that plane?"

"No, but he may as well be."

"What the heck is going on, Kev?"

Putting his arm around her shoulder, he said, "C'mon, let's get this place opened up and I'll tell what I know, which isn't much."

Having taken only a few steps, Kevin spotted something lying in the middle of the parking lot.

Picking up the small orange plastic canister, he saw that it had a screw-on lid. He knew it wasn't there when he came outside just now. It took a minute for him to realize it had been dropped from the plane.

Peering past his shoulder, Tammy asked, "What is it, Kevin?"

"I think it got dropped on that last pass, probably why they came in so low," he said, shaking the canister, hearing something rattling inside.

Unscrewing the lid as they walked, he shook out the contents, which was a bag of small bolts. Looking inside, he saw a piece of notebook paper lining the interior of the canister. Fingering it out, he unfolded it to see his father's near-perfect handwriting. Tammy looked over his arm and read along in silence with him.

> *Kevin, if you are reading this, then my air-drop was a success. Of course, it helps when you have an old bomber pilot helping time the drop. This shouldn't take long. Searching by air is much better*

than by boat. I'll find the Donna Marie *and be back before lunch. And in the process kick that Juky's ass like I should have done thirty years ago.*

Oh, if you are wondering about the bag of bolts, they were just in there for weight so the prop wash wouldn't shoot this out into the mangroves. Hope it didn't hit you in the head.

Oh yeah, and this is important, do not call the Coast Guard, the cops, or anyone else…understand! I can handle this.

Besides, this is fun.

Later, Dad

Kevin folded the note back up. Tammy, worried and confused, again asked, "Kevin, what the hell is going on? Who is this, this Juky, and why is your dad going to kick his ass? And where is the *Donna Marie?*"

The stress was apparent on his face as he looked around. "Tam, we gotta get this place opened up. I'll fill you in after things are up and running. It's the start of lobster season this weekend. You know how crazy it can get." He repeated "crazy" again, then looked up in the sky. "Damn it, Dad!"

Nearing the back door to the office, the sound of a car skidding to a stop a few feet behind them startled them both. Both quickly turned to see a gray Volvo grind to an abrupt halt amid billowing clouds of dust.

Both Kevin and Tammy's mouths dropped open saying the same thing, "Mom?"

Chapter 6

Cal smiled broadly gazing out the cockpit window of the big seaplane; he was thoroughly enjoying the rumble of the engines and the sound of air rushing over the fuselage. Glancing around the cockpit at the instrument panel and flight controls, it reminded him of his days in the navy. Cal always loved it whenever he got the opportunity to fly. He then wondered why he never took up flying instead of sailing. He mused to himself it was probably only because he won a sailboat in a game of poker instead of plane. Suddenly his headset crackled on with Jim Abbot, the pilot, asking him what direction he wanted go.

"Rum Cay in the southern Bahamas," Cal said, pointing at a folded nautical map he held on his lap. He then added, "We aren't going there. I'm just looking for someone who is."

"I take it that they're on a boat of some kind?"

"Yeah, my sailboat, the *Donna Marie.*"

"How big is she? The reason I ask is we might need to lose some altitude. Small boats tend to look a lot alike at this height."

Cal frowned a bit at his assumption. "Don't worry about that. I'm fairly certain she'll be the only forty-five-foot navy blue and white two-masted schooner cruising an hour out of port."

Jim gave him an approving nod then asked, "You sure about the direction, Cal? The southern Atlantic is a lot of water to cover."

Cal gave him a pensive look then answered, "No, just gut feeling."

Jim nodded again then said, "Look, I can fly a search pattern we used for downed pilots when they crashed or ditched in the drink."

"Great, let's do it."

"What do you want to do when we find her?"

"You are going to set this thing down, and I'm going to take my ship back from the asshole that stole her."

Jim's eyes abruptly widened. "Whoa! Hold on, I didn't know we were going after boat thieves. Those guys carry guns…lots of them. I got shot at enough during the big war, and I have no intention of having my plane shot up by a pack of dope smugglers. I'm turning us around right now!"

Cal placed his hand on Jim's arm to stop him from making the turn. "Hold on, hold on. It's not a bunch of dope-smuggling pirates that took my ship. It's just one guy, that's all, and he's not even armed…as far as I know."

Jim stared hard into Cal's eyes. Pressing his lips tight, he then said, "All right. But if I get even one bullet hole in my plane, you are going to pay big for this little trip. You hear me?"

Cal quickly nodded, adding, "It will be fine, I promise."

Jim gave him a slight nod then pushed the wheel forward. "We need to lose a bit more altitude. You say she's a forty-five-footer?"

"Forty-seven feet seven inches to be exact. She'll be flying the flag Stella Maris from her mainsail, the Star of the Sea."

As soon as he said that, he thought of Donna, his wife. She was the one who had insisted the *Donna Marie* sail under the protection of the patron saint of the seas, the Virgin Mary. He wondered too if her father had given her the message when he called this morning before taking off.

He recalled how mad she was when she tossed a couple of suitcases into the Volvo and said she needed a break and was driving up to her parents in North Carolina. That was a week ago and not a word from her. She wouldn't take any of his calls either. He hoped the nonspecific message about a family emergency might at least get her to call him. He'd soon know if that worked when he got back to Ramrod Key.

The search dragged on, and Cal's frustrations grew. The search pattern they had been flying had turned up practically nothing. Only two vessels were spotted about thirty miles out that were worthy of dropping down for a closer look. However, both were sailing north paralleling the coast and were not the *Donna Marie*.

Jim reached over and tapped Cal on the arm then tapped the fuel gage. "We can't stay out much longer, Cal."

Cal dejectedly asked, "How much longer?"

"'Bout fifteen minutes."

Cal took one long last look out at the calm waters of the southern Atlantic and wondered how in the hell Juky could have gotten out of sight so quick with a vessel as easy to spot as the *Donna Marie*.

Shaking his head, he said, "Let's head back. No point in burning any more fuel just to look at water. I need to do some thinking. Something's not right here."

Jim simply nodded, then made a long sweeping turn and pointed the big Albatross he dubbed the Water Lily back to Marathon. This search was over. Jim briefly thought about asking Cal why he hadn't involved the Coast Guard. However, seeing Cal's somber mood at the moment, he thought it best to just let it slide.

Jim gave Cal an apologetic look. "Sorry, Cal, wish we could have found her. But she's just not out here, at least in our search area." As if to help keep hope alive, he added, "Cal, are you positive about the direction he went?"

Cal simply shrugged his shoulders. "Jim," Cal began, "I'm not sure of anything right at the moment. I need to stew on this for a while."

He had a lot to think about. His wife of thirty-two years had left a week ago to do some thinking herself because he wanted to sell the marina to some northeast investors—something she was adamantly against. The cold realization hit him that he had now managed to lose the *Donna Marie* too. How was he going to tell her that? He loved his wife more than life itself.

He wanted her back in his life in the worst way. But now his letting some guy he didn't even know walk into the bar and talk him into some cockamamie scheme about a sunken treasure and *then* have him steal the *Donna Marie* right from under his nose wasn't going to help matters at all.

They had flown back in silence and were within sight of Marathon when Cal snapped his fingers and excitedly cried out, "That's it!"

Jim, who had been lost in his own thoughts, barked back, "Geez, Cal, you scared the shit outta me. Whaddya mean, that's it?"

Cal eagerly explained. "Jim, that son-of-a-bitch never left the Keys. He has hidden her somewhere."

"Hidden! How do you hide a sailboat that size?"

"Look out there, Jim," Cal said, pointing to the panorama of islands. "These islands stretch all along the overseas highway but also hundreds of small mangrove islands that are scattered throughout the whole length of the chain. Cal continued, "She could be sitting tucked in between a couple of those mangrove islands, and you'd have to be right on top of her to see her."

Jim nodded his agreement while scanning the horizon. "We can refuel and make a quick run down island to see if we can spot her if you want."

Cal thought about that for a second then shook his head. "No, I think it would be a waste of time. I think I need to put this out on the ship-to-shore radio. That way instead of just me looking for her, I'll have every SOB with a radio in their boat keeping an eye out for her."

Cal turned his gaze back out the window and said, "If she's anywhere in this pile of coral and crabs, someone is bound to see her, especially since its lobster season."

Cal was sure he would find the *Donna Marie* and bring her back safe and sound. However, he wasn't so sure if he could do the same for its namesake. His strong-willed Irish wife was another matter altogether.

Unknown to him, one part of his conundrum of missing wives and boats had already been resolved. Furthermore, he had no idea that things were going to change in the Arnold household in a way that no one could expect. But change it would.

*****

24

Leaning back in the padded deck chair, smiling broadly, Juky gazed up into a perfect cloudless azure sky. He had carefully tucked the *Donna Marie* into a horseshoe-shaped cove of mangroves that followed the contour of a large oyster bed that grew beyond—a risky maneuver considering the depth of the surrounding waters coupled with the fact that he was operating the *Donna Marie* all by himself.

However, the channel that ran a quarter mile away from the cove of mangroves moved a great deal of tidal water in and out of the bay. Because of this, a strong back eddy of water had scalloped out a natural deep water cut into an area of the bay that would otherwise be too shallow for the draft of the *Donna Marie*.

Juky snapped the cap off a bottle of beer that Cal had stocked in the "fridge" along with all manner of food and gear the night before. He was feeling quite pleased with himself. Taking a long pull on the long-neck Budweiser, he took in his surroundings. The decades of tides had piled up a large amount of sand in which the mangroves thickly grew. The roots filtered much of the sand out to help form the perfect environment for the massive oyster bed that surrounded the old stand of mangroves.

A half-dozen brown pelicans cast a V-shaped shadow as they flew low over the *Donna Marie*. Juky turned to watch them as they headed directly for the channel. Suddenly, the lead pelican rose up sharply. It arched over with wings tucked in tight and plummeted straight into the water thrusting its long beak forward at the last second.

Juky held the beer up in a mock toast to the pelican, saying, "Touché, mah friend. Timing is everything for de hunter just as it is for the hunted. Mah own pelican no doubt searches for me now, and *that*, mah feathered friend, is what Juky is counting on."

Chugging this last of the beer, he then thrust the bottle up high and laughed out loud. "Yes, come aund find me, Mista Cal, for adventure she calls!"

Chapter 7

Driving back to Ramrod Key, Cal stewed on all that had occurred. Not just on the last twenty-four hours but also about his wife and the disagreement they had over selling the Salty Anchor. His thoughts trailed to the day they both sat at one of the tables in the dining room listening to a couple of northeast developers make a very lucrative offer to buy their whole operation. Cal liked the idea of being retired at fifty-seven. Donna was far more skeptical of the developers and their deal.

Their offer was deep into seven figures—it was more money than they could hope to make running this place for years to come. Donna though was not of the same mindset. She saw the Salty Anchor as a family heirloom to be passed down to the kids. It had, after all, been part of their lives for twenty-five years. The money didn't matter much to her. To her, the Salty Anchor was purpose and permanence. She loved the place and all the craziness that came with running a tourist stop.

A sad smile spread on Cal's face as he thought of how no one left a stranger if Donna was anywhere around. She loved meeting and talking to people. She had way of putting folks at ease no matter what the situation. The spark and zest for life that she possessed positively bubbled from her. She was the perfect positive yin to his pessimistic yang.

Still lost in his thoughts, he suddenly smacked the jeep's steering wheel with the palm of his hand, like he figured it was time to get his wife and bring her home. "That's it! When I get back to the Salty Anchor, I'm calling her parents' house, and if I get told that she's not taking any calls again, I'm flying up there and bringing her home where she belongs."

Having settled that in his mind, he felt he could focus more on the immediate problem of where their sailboat had been taken. Driving along the seven-mile bridge, the familiar clip-clop sound of the tires striking the bridge expansion joints had a sort of metronomic effect on the tempo of his thoughts. He took glances out at the expanse of Florida Bay to his right and then the Atlantic to his left. The sheer volume of water that surrounded him drove home the enormity of what he was trying accomplish. For a moment he considered just turning it all over to the authorities.

Something kept gnawing at him and the way Juky had put it when he said why they were going to Rum Cay. He slapped the jeep's steering wheel again. "Damn it! I let that son-of-a-bitch snooker me with that pipe dream about the *Atocha*."

Shaking his head, he cursed, "Damn it! I have really lost my touch. I use to do that to gullible schleps all the time when I was young." Looking out at the waters of the gulf, he continued his solo conversation. "I can't believe that after thirty years, I'm still trying track down that SOB." This time would be different, he thought. *That guy isn't making me a fool again.*

Thirty minutes later Cal wheeled into the Salty Anchor's parking lot tired and irritated from the slow ride along US 1. Seeing the parking lot full of cars didn't help; he was in no mood to deal with customers right now. Parking the jeep, he reached to grab his binoculars off the seat and glanced out the passenger window before turning to get out, but froze. Sitting there like usual was his wife's Volvo, big as life. A wave of relief washed over him, and just to be sure, he looked for her little good luck crucifix that hung from the rearview mirror. Yup, he thought, it's hers.

A smile spread across his face, but then quickly disappeared remembering the phone call to her parents the night before. Grousing to himself, he said, "There ain't no way that girl could've driven all the way back from North Carolina that quick. Just where the hell *has* she been?"

Exiting the jeep, he marched for the office door. He wanted answers, and by golly he was going to get them. Reaching to open the door, it was suddenly thrust open. Cal grabbed the edge of the door to keep it from hitting him while calling out, "Whoa! Slow down, Mario." He then yanked it on open, pulling Donna right up into him.

Startled, Donna let go a small yelp, putting her fingers to her lips. Freezing in the open doorway, they each called out the other's name. In the next moment, Donna had her face planted in his chest and her arms wrapped tightly around his waist.

"I came as quickly as I could, Cal."

He hesitated only a second before putting his arms around her, settling his cheek in the softness of her auburn hair and inhaling her scent. Practically at the same moment, they both remembered their irritation with one another. Pushing back from each other but still holding to each other's forearms, they started peppering each other with questions.

"Cal, what is going here? The kids won't tell me anything."

"Donna, just where the heck have you been? And don't bullshit me about being at your parents."

"Walter Caleb Arnold, don't you talk to me using that kind of language! I want to know what's going on and right now!"

"Now you hold on just a darn second, Donna. You have been gone for a whole week, supposedly staying at your parents. Now I may not be Einstein when it comes to math, but I am smart enough to figure you can't drive from North Carolina to Ram Rod Key in twelve hours."

Donna gave Cal a sharp look, then lit into him again. "Listen here, you call my parents' house and scare the heck out of me and them with some ominous message about a family emergency. And then I pull into the parking lot in time see a plane buzzing the roof off this place, so I don't want to hear another word about where I have been. Now what is going on here?"

Cal let go of her arms and took a step back. Taking a deep breath, he tried to ready himself for the ass burning he felt was coming when he told her that the *Donna Marie* was gone and why. As calmly as he could, he said. "Come on, it's hot standing out here. Let's go into the office and I'll fill you in."

Donna suddenly felt a twinge in the pit of her stomach. Silently she wondered if he was going to tell her that he was seriously ill or someone had died instead of what she was expecting to hear. Briefly she stared up into his dark brown eyes trying to read them. Opening the door, he motioned her in. Closing the door behind them, he turned and locked it, then went and closed the door that led out into the bar area. Facing her again, he said, "Have a seat, this isn't going to be easy."

Now she was really getting worried. Sitting down, she never took her eyes off him. She had seen him this way one other time when a favorite uncle had passed away. She was becoming more convinced there was something seriously wrong with the man she had been in love with for more than thirty years. Cal spun the high-backed office chair around to face his somber-faced wife and sat down. He took a breath, pressed his lips together for a second, then began.

"Donna, sweetheart, I hate to have to tell you this, but...she's gone, and it's my fault."

Donnas' face went from being on the brink of tears to perplexity. "Cal, who's gone? What's your fault? What in the heck are trying to tell me? Heaven's sake, Cal, just spit it out. You got me all twisted up in knots with all this drama."

Cal held his eyes in hers for a second then quietly said, "I lost the *Donna Marie*."

Ahh, there she thought, this was what she had been expecting to hear; however, it came with a lot more drama than she was expecting. But she had to rapidly roll into what she thought he would expect from her. Cal watched her face morph from deep concern to one of a steaming pot about to boil over. When she spoke, her voice quavered as if she was doing all she could to maintain her composure.

"Cal...you lost the *Donna Marie*? What exactly do you mean? You better not have gambled her away."

Cal let go a nervous laugh hoping that the fact that he hadn't lost her in a card game would soften the truth. "No, of course not, I would never risk her that way. You know that."

"Then what happened to her—you sank her then."

"No."

"Dammit, Cal, stop beating around the bushes. You're pissing me off."

Now I've done it, he thought. For her to use any bad language meant she had had enough. So he quickly began to give her the low-down on what happened.

"Listen," he began. "You've heard me tell that story about that Juky guy that ratted me out years ago, right?"

With skepticism riding high in her voice, she said, "Only about a thousand times."

Cal cut his eyes at her then said, "Be that as it may, it was Juky that stole her, and right from the dock last night sometime."

Donnas' eyes flew wide open. "What? Cal, how can that be? I always thought that story was just your imagination. Just your folksy way to entertain the tourists while they drank beer. You mean this guy is a real person?"

Trying not to sound hurt about her not believing his story, he said, "Yes, of course he's real. He's damn real enough to steal a forty-seven-foot sailboat, that's for sure."

"You called the police and the Coast Guard, didn't you? He can't have gotten very far if he sailed out sometime during the night."

"Actually, it was just before dawn, Donna."

Glancing at her watch then up at Cal, she said, "Its two o-clock. You did call the authorities, right?"

"Not exactly."

"Walter Caleb—" He stopped her before she finished doing that a second time.

"Hold on, hold on. Let's take a walk out on the docks and I'll fill you in on everything, okay?"

Donna glared at him for a long moment before replying in a less than warm tone. "Okay, let's go!" She then promptly stood and headed straight to the office door. Cal watched her yank the door open before he stood to follow. He wondered just how in the hell he was going to keep that Irish temper of hers in check. He smirked as he stood mumbling out of the corner of his mouth. "Been trying to figure that out for years."

"Are you speaking to me, Cal?"

"What? Oh, just marveling at how good your ass still looks in those jeans."

"Stop trying to soften me up, Cal. I'm not one of your marks. And watch your mouth when you're in the dining area."

Falling in behind her, he thought telling her about the *Donna Marie* was going to be tough enough. However, that paled in comparison as to why it was gone. He was certain this was going to make her go ballistic on him. He was just glad she agreed to walk on the dock. He knew she would contain her emotions in public. No surprise there. All bets were off though once they were behind closed doors.

Being a deeply passionate woman, she seldom hid her feelings. Cal always knew where she stood. This made her easy for him to predict most times. But even after years of martial familiarity, husbands and wives can still bring a surprise or two. And Cal was soon to be reminded of that fact.

Chapter 8

Kevin and Tammy both stopped for a moment and stared out one of the big windows facing the docks.

"What do you suppose he's telling her?" Kevin asked, watching his mother and father walking slowly by all the boat slips.

"Well," Tammy began. "If I know your dad, he is putting his best true politician-style spin on a bad situation."

Kevin snorted out a quick laugh. "No doubt. But Mom can read him like a book. She'll cut right through the fluff and pretty bows he likes to put on things."

Tammy smirked and laughed too while thinking of all the times she had watched him try to pull the wool over her mother-in-law's eyes. "Yeah, but I don't see him talking his way out of this one. Mom isn't going to buy anything Dad has to say."

Kevin gave Tammy an impish look. "We might better go make sure our fire extinguishers are ready to go. I have a feeling that when Mom finds out that Dad let himself get talked into some cockamamie scheme, she is really going to heat things up around here." Each gave a knowing nod then turned and headed for the office. In spite of what might be happening out on the dock right now, they still had a business to run.

Tammy was seated at the desk talking on the phone to their fresh seafood supplier while Kevin sat opposite her quietly reviewing the accountant's profit and loss statement for the past month. Without warning, the office door suddenly flung open wide. In stormed Donna with Cal in tow. "Kids, Dad and I have to leave. We are going to get our sailboat back. Right, honey?"

Cal, stumbling over his words, said, "Uh, yeah, that's, that's r-right." Cal glanced over to his son, shrugging his shoulders.

Tammy finished her call. Hanging up, she gave them both a confused look. "Wait a second. What did you just say?"

"I said, Dad and I are going to get our boat back."

Kevin abruptly stood. "Mom, Mom, just hold it a second. What do you mean get our boat back? You're calling the cops, right?

Donna shook her head no. "Wrong. We know where she is... well, sort of."

Kevin looked over at his dad hoping for more information. "Dad, what's Mom talking about? You can't go traipsing all over looking for the *Donna Marie*. That thing is probably halfway to the Bahamas by now. Do you know where she is or not?"

Cal looked nervously at his wife then back at Kevin. "Well, not exactly."

Donna interrupted. "Look, Kevin honey. One of the dive boat captains thinks he saw it south of here in Florida Bay. It was tucked back in some mangroves."

"Wait," Kevin said, holding up the palm of his hand. "You said he *thinks* it was the *Donna Marie*? Look, Mom, Dad, just calm down. Call the police for heaven's sake—they will handle it."

"Yeah, Mom, Dad—listen to Kevin," Tammy interjected. "If it is the *Donna Marie*, you'll have her back by tomorrow."

"Nope, that's where you're wrong," Cal began. "We don't know anything about Juky or why he took her, or what kind of story he's going to fabricate to save his ass. So there's a good chance they'll impound her for God knows how long."

"That's right kids, and if they have any suspicion that it was involved in drug smuggling, they will tear her apart looking for evidence. I'm not letting anybody tear her apart, and I don't care who they are," Donna added with a sharp nod.

Cal chimed in. "Look, we are wasting time talking. I'm going over to the boat rental and grab one of our runabouts. Mom and I will scoot down there and take a cautious look. If we don't find her, then we'll call the police. I'm not anxious to get my ass shot off either, son."

Kevin looked at his mom standing next to his dad, each with looks of determination.

"Mom, this is crazy. I thought you'd be the one to talk some sense into Dad, not go off on some wild goose chase *with* him for Christ's sake."

Donna angrily snapped her fingers, pointing her index finger right at Kevin. "Don't you use the Lord's name like that, you hear me? Kids, this isn't a wild goose chase. We are simply going to get back what belongs to us."

Cal moved in close to Donna, throwing his arm around her shoulders. "Yeah, that's right. And if we have to kick a little ass while we're at it, well, that'll teach that sneaky-ass thief a lesson."

Reaching for the phone, Kevin's eyes flashed with anger. "No! I'm not going to let you two do this. I'm calling the cops like I should've done first thing this morning."

Suddenly Donna thrust her hand right down on top of Kevin's stopping him from picking up the receiver. "You'll do no such thing, young man! Do you hear me? Your father and I are not stupid, Kevin. Despite what your father just said, we are going to get the *Donna Marie* back, and we are *not* kicking anyone's butt to do it."

Cal leaned in close to Donna, almost whispering, "Ah, just for the record, dear, I said 'ass,' not 'butt.'"

Donna gave him a quick elbow to the ribs and eye cut but said nothing.

Kevin slid his hand from underneath his mother's, fixing his eyes in hers, then quietly said, "Okay, Mom. Just remember—a boat can be replaced. You two can't be."

Donna smiled, her eyes squinting with the love she felt for her oldest son. She then looked at her daughter-in-law. "Tammy honey, don't you worry either. We'll be back by dinnertime with or without the *Donna Marie*."

Cal quickly interjected, "Oh, we're coming back with her. That's for sure. And we'll have a boat thief hanging from the yardarms when we do."

Donna spun out from under Cal's arm glaring at him as she retorted, "Caleb Arnold! Will you stop saying stuff like that—you're scaring the kids. You're not Captain Bligh for heaven's sake."

Kevin shook his head listening to his parents squabbling. He then put his hand on his mother's shoulder and laughed, saying, "Don't worry, Mom. Dad has talked his way out of more fights than he's ever been in. Besides, the last time he took a swing at anybody, Eisenhower was president."

The three of them burst out laughing. Feeling a little hurt, Cal pointed a finger around at the three of them. "That's right, go ahead and laugh. I'll have you know, son, I was our ship's boxing champ during the War."

Kevin let go another burst of laughter. "Oh, I'm sorry. It was when Truman was president, or maybe even Roosevelt."

Cal was almost to the office door when he turned back to say, "All right, all right, son, you've had your fun. C'mon, Donna, let's get going before he laughs himself to death."

Donna looked at her husband and couldn't help but smile at his thinly-veiled attempt to prove he could still take care of things. She knew he was no wimp. After all, she knew him before he had settled down. The kids, of course, never did. They only knew him as Dad—the man who owned the Salty Anchor who told lots of old stories of days gone by. But with being sixty years old staring him in the face now, she knew he had been feeling a lot less needed and maybe even little like life had passed him by.

Every now and then at night at the end of a long day, he would let his guard down a little. Their pillow talk would turn to what was next for them, which entailed the possibility of selling the Salty Anchor. His wanting to sell the family business had scared her. She knew if she let that happen, the man she knew and loved would, over time, only feel more and more useless.

She had watched this happen to her own father after stepping down from his life as CEO of a worldwide shipping concern. He became rudderless. His reason to put his feet on the floor each morning to start a new day had been dulled. He had told her once that he would do his old job for free now just so he could have that sense of purpose again. She had made numerous suggestions of things he could involve himself with that would do that and that might help someone along the way.

But each suggestion was met with the usual tepid response. She watched her father age more in the ten years after his retirement than he had in the thirty years prior. Seeing that is what had really terrified her about selling the Salty Anchor and her week's hiatus was the kick off to her doing something about it. She knew that Cal needed this place. She just needed him to see that.

Cal called anxiously to her again, "C'mon, sweetheart, times a-wasting."

"Aye, aye, Captain," she said, saluting him. Giving him a bright smile, she strode to his side and thought, *There. Now that's the man I married.* At that moment, Donna was feeling pretty good about how her little plan was coming together. But the winds of fate, as it often does, can change things in the wink of an eye. And plans, no matter how well laid out, can run aground.

Kevin and Tammy stood there speechless, watching the two of them push through the office door.

Kevin spoke out to no one in particular, "What the hell is going on here, can anybody tell me?"

Tammy gave a tilted look at Kevin. "I have no idea. But something's up. I've never seen Mom go along so easily with one of Dad's crazy ideas."

"Yeah, I know. Something about this whole thing is off kilter," Kevin said, rubbing his neck. "This Juky guy shows up out of the blue, tells Dad something to get him all fired up to sail off to the Bahamas, for what, I still don't know. Then the *Donna Marie* turns up missing, and Dad is convinced this Juky guy took it."

Tammy added, "Yeah, and Mom showing back up just in time to get mixed up in all of this is very odd."

"Hell, her even being gone like she was is not right. Mom has never done anything like that before. I know she was upset that Dad wanted sell the place. But to leave for a whole week—heck, she was a lot more pissed at him when she found out he had won the *Donna Marie* in that card game."

Tammy nodded agreement then said, "You don't suppose your mom had something to do with all of this do you?"

Kevin's eyes darted back and forth in thought. He then burst out laughing. "You know, you just might have something there. My dear, saintly mother just might be running a con game on my unsuspecting *dad*."

"You think so?"

"Yeah, maybe. It's the only thing that makes any sense…in a crazy sort of way."

"Well, I must say it does fit your parents. They've always been a little on the wacky side."

Kevin turned to look at Tammy. "Oh, so they're just *my* wacky parents, huh?"

"Sure. My dad and mom would never do anything like this. Especially Dad. Heck, Dad barely goes outside, let alone take off looking for a stolen sailboat."

Suddenly, Kevin snapped his fingers then grabbed Tammy by the shoulders.

"That's it! Don't you see? It *is* Mom that's set this all up—she's trying to put some adventure back in Dad's life."

"Really?"

"Sure, you know how Dad's been talking around here—about his needing to do something different. And that offer to buy this place only exaggerated that."

Tammy nodded thoughtfully. "Yeah, and the idea of selling this place really shook Mom up too."

"Yes, it did." Kevin looked back at the office door and smiled. "How do you like that. My strait-laced saintly little mother has cooked up some scheme to deal with Dad's doldrums and show him that we need to keep this place."

"What do think she has planned?"

Kevin shook his head. "I have no idea. But with those two on the loose, the entire Caribbean is in trouble."

Tammy moved up beside Kevin, threading her arm around his waist. Looking up into his eyes, she said, "I think it's romantic—

wacky, but very romantic. Would you do something like this for me someday?"

Sporting a devilish grin, he asked, "You mean do something wacky and romantic?"

"Yeah. Would you?"

"I already have. I married you." He then began giving her little pinches to her ribs and laughing.

Tammy's eyes flashed open, trying to sound hurt. "Oh, you big turd. You think you're so funny, don't you?"

"I do, plus I'm cute too," he said, laughing, while continuing to poke and pinch her.

"Stop it, Kev, I'm mad at you."

"Then why are you smiling?" he asked, ceasing his pokes and prods. He then took her by the shoulders, looked her right in the eyes. "Guess I better do something to change your mood." Leaning down, he gave her a quick kiss, surprising her.

Holding his gaze, she said, "One little peck ain't gonna change much, mister."

"Oh, I see. Well, how about this?" Placing a hand along her cheek, he stroked her soft brown hair back, then slowly bent to meet her lips, giving her the kind of kiss that always made her weak in the knees.

Suddenly the phone rang. Simultaneously, a knock came at the back door, breaking off their moment of quiet passion. Both let out sighs still holding their gaze on each other.

"The Salty Anchor beckons," Kevin said.

"Yes, she does," Tammy agreed with exasperation.

Chapter 9

Cal had brought along a chart of Florida Bay marked with the dive captain's location and description of where he saw the sailboat. Donna, with her sharp eyes, saw a large stand of mangroves ahead that fit the description perfectly. Anxiously, she tapped Cal on the shoulder and pointed in the direction of the mangroves.

Cal glanced down at the chart he had marked up, nodded, and shoved the throttle forward. Donna grabbed onto Cal and the windshield. They looked at each other as the boat's speed quickly increased. Nervous excitement built in them both but for different reasons. Cal's was about not knowing exactly what they were heading into, and Donna's, well, she was hoping that her husband wasn't going to blow his stack when all he was going to find was a note and not the *Donna Marie*.

Nearing the mangrove island, Cal abruptly slowed the boat, bringing it down to a slow idle. Cautiously, he scanned the whole scene. *Something's wrong*, he thought. Shouting over the sound of the outboard motor, Cal angrily pointed out. "There's no mast!"

"What?" Donna said, feigning her surprise.

"Those mangroves are pretty high, Cal—let's go on up there and check things out."

Cal gave her a look of skepticism, then bumped the throttle up a bit more. Fortunately, it was high tide, so he wasn't too concerned about getting out of the channel to start circling the lush island of the "walking trees" known as mangrove.

Easing the boat around to an opening in the island, he quickly saw that it was a perfect place to hide a sailboat, *if* one had been in there. Cal pounded the windshield frame with his hands. He started to turn the boat to leave when Donna urged him to go on into the cut to look for any evidence that the *Donna Marie* had been there.

"What for? We aren't going to find anything in there."

"Don't be hardheaded, Cal—it will only take a minute. Besides, we've come this far."

Grudgingly, he relented. "All right."

Turning the bow toward the opening, he eased their way slowly in the thick U-shaped wall of greenery. Several brown pelicans took flight from their roost among the tangled branches. Cal placed the boat in neutral. The incoming tide swirled them in a slow circle within the mangroves. It was remarkably peaceful in this spot—giving one the illusion that you were much farther away from civilization than you actually were.

"See, Donna honey? I told you we wouldn't find anything."

Donna worriedly scanned the mangrove branches. *Where is it?* she thought. "Something is wrong, Cal," she said.

Cal gave her a curious look then said, "Hell yeah, there is. Our sailboat isn't here."

Donna's heart sank as the cold realization took hold that she may have made a big mistake with what she was attempting to do. After all, she had trusted a man that she really didn't know very well, relying on her woman's intuition and a few references. She had planned this little adventure to put some spark back in her man's life—hers too, for that matter.

Feverously, she scanned the wall of mangroves. It had to be here. Juky was supposed to leave one of the red-and-white life preservers on one of the branches with a clue pinned to it on where he was heading next.

Donna dropped heavily down onto the seat. How was she going to tell the man she loved that it was his own wife who had managed to lose the *Donna Marie*? At that moment, she burst out crying. Cal looked down at his sobbing wife and shut the boat off, letting the current push them to the back of the cut. Sitting down beside her, he put his arm around her and brushed back a few strands of her hair.

"Don't worry, sweetheart. I'll find her somehow. I guess we'll have to get the authorities involved now."

With tears flowing down her cheeks, she looked straight at Cal. "Cal, I'm so sorry. I…I thought—"

Donna's confession was suddenly interrupted by Cal. "Donna, look! There!" Cal shouted. "It's a life preserver up in the mangroves. Maybe it's one of the *Donna Marie's*!" Cal immediately stood trying to get a better look through the branches.

Donna shot to her feet while pawing the tears from her face. "What, where?"

Cal then spied a length of rope swirling in the water that ran up to the preserver.

"I'm going to retrieve it. Stay here, Donna." And with that, Cal jumped in the water grabbing for the rope as he went.

Chapter 10

Donna nervously watched Cal swim the short distance to the edge of the mangroves. Nearing them, he reached for a short length of rope that swirled snake-like in the tidal back-eddies. Grabbing the line, he quickly spun a couple of loops around his hand and pulled. At the other end, the life ring slipped in the tangle of branches. Cal gave it another hard yank. It slipped again then wedged between two heavy limbs.

He then pulled himself to the edge of the mangrove island. Just as he reached for a low overhanging branch, the water in front of him exploded, sending a sheet of frothy saltwater cascading over him. Startled, he cussed out loud.

"Jesus! That dammed snook scared the shit out me!"

Donna had let out a short scream herself when the big fish took off. But she still managed to scold Cal for his language.

"Cal, don't use the Lord's name like that!"

Still holding onto the rope, Cal mopped the saltwater off his face with his free hand while sarcastically replying, "Yes, Sister Marie." He would call her that to annoy her for nagging him about his language.

"You don't have to be a wiseass about it, Mister Arnold." Referring to him as Mister Arnold was her jab back at him. She knew it reminded him of the captain of the ship he was on in the navy.

"Well, now wait a minute, you just said ass. How come—"

She cut him off before he could finish. "Just don't you worry about what I said. I was referring to the animal. But you should respect the Lord's name."

Pulling himself back to edge of the mangroves, he said, "So 'ass' is okay to say? Do you have a bad word rule book from the pope or something, 'cause I'm confused," he said, laughing out loud.

"Yes, it's called the Bible. You should read it more often."

Grabbing for the same low branch as before, he looked back at her standing on the bow with her hands on her hips glaring at him with a look of indignation.

"Don't think I need to, Donna. You tell me what's in it all the time."

"You just never mind that now and see about getting that life ring. It looks like the tide is starting to shift."

Cal saluted her. "Aye, aye, sir...uh, ma'am."

"Cal, do you always have to be a wiseass?"

"Only when it's necessary, sweetheart."

"Cal, just get the darn ring, will ya?"

Smiling to himself, he began pulling himself up into the stand of mangroves. He had kept his deck shoes on when he jumped in due to the razor-sharp edges of the oysters and barnacles that grew in and around the mangrove's exposed root system.

Donna watched Cal weave his way farther into the thicket of roots and branches. Cal, even at his age, was still able handle himself. However, she knew that the water was filled with danger. Besides, the risk of his getting sliced open on the oysters and barnacles, alligators like to frequent spots just such as this.

"How much further, honey?"

"Almost there."

Cal contorted his way through a couple more branches and finally was close enough to grab the life ring. Wresting it from the branches it was wedged between, his eyes widened at what he saw.

"What is it, Cal? Is it the *Donna Marie's*?"

"Yes, looks like a message is scrawled on it."

Donna breathed a sigh of relief at hearing that. She hadn't counted on Juky going to so much trouble to leave the next clue. But she quickly fell in with her original plan.

"A message? What does it say?"

"Fire up the boat and swing it around to this side. I don't want to trudge through that quagmire again. Hurry it up, the tide is starting to run out pretty fast. The water is going to get skinny quick on the backside of these mangroves."

"I am, I am. Keep your shirt on, old man." Donna fired up the boat's engine effectively muffling Cal's retort to her.

Donna skillfully maneuvered the center console runabout out of the U-shaped cut and out over the oyster bar. With only three feet of water and a fast-moving current, she had to be vigilant. The bottom was not flat and could rise up very rapidly, leaving only inches of water covering the oyster bar.

Cal coached her from where he was. Right in front of him the daily tidal currents had washed out a rather deep but narrow trough in the sandy bottom immediately past the overhanging mangrove branches. Slowly she nudged the bow of the boat right up to where Cal stood on a large tree root. Grabbing the bow rail, he steadied the boat, tossed in the life ring, then jumped aboard.

Donna started to relinquish the helm, but Cal quickly stopped her. "No, no, you stay there and drive the boat—I'm going to keep an eye on the water depth. I'm hoping this trough runs all the way around so we can get back to the channel."

Donna nodded and eased the boat forward while he leaned over the bow giving her hand signals on direction. Together they skillfully maneuvered their way back to deeper water. Satisfied they were in deep enough water, Cal turned and plopped down in the front of the boat. Plucking the end of the rope off the bottom of the boat, he pulled the life ring back to where he sat in the bow.

"Donna baby, idle the motor—let's drift with the tide a minute and see what the heck is written on this life ring."

Donna pointed the bow into the outgoing tide and idled the motor. She then stepped into the bow and sat down beside Cal.

"What does it say, honey?"

Without a word, he handed the life ring to her. Reading it, her eyes widened. "Boat boarded…taken as hostage Pirates Well." Donna looked from the ring to Cal. She was genuinely confused. Her stomach knotted. This was *not* the message that was supposed to be on the ring, she thought. Once again, she was confronted with having to tell Cal what she had done. Tears came to her eyes as she began. "Cal…honey, I'm so sorry. I had no idea this would happen."

Intently focused on the last thing written on the life ring, Cal didn't pick up fully on what she had just said. He sat repeating the words *Pirates Well* out loud, effectively interrupting Donna's preamble to her confession.

Emotional and frustrated, she blurted out, "Caleb Arnold, did you hear what I just said?"

Cal looked back and forth from the life ring to Donna a couple of times then said, "Yes, yes, I did, dear. I'm sorry the *Donna Marie* is gone too. But look, I think 'Pirates Well' may be where she's headed."

Donna was on the brink of just spitting out her confession when she stopped to listen to Cal who stood up in the bow holding the life ring out in front of him. Looking for all intents and purposes like Sherlock Holmes decoding a clue at murder scene, she listened to him expound on what his deductions were.

"Look, dear," he said, pointing to the message. "Juky has told us he was boarded by someone, or more likely several someones, and are likely using him as a shield for safe passage into international waters in case the authorities get nosy."

"But what in the world does 'Pirates Well' mean, Cal?"

"That, my dear, is where I believe they are headed."

"You know where this place is?"

"No. Never heard of it. But it's the only thing that makes sense. Without that bit of information, he's good as dead. Might be anyway once they hit international waters."

Hearing that, Donna became panicky. "Cal, we have to do something. We have to find Juky. I couldn't live with myself if something happens to that poor man because of me."

Cal was lost in thought again staring at the life ring, thinking about where he might have heard the name Pirates Well before. Suddenly, the last of what Donna had said finally registered with him. Looking up from the ring at his wife's tortured, tear-stained face, he cautiously asked, "Wait, what did you say? Why would any of this be your fault? I'm the one that went off half-cocked on some harebrained scheme."

"Yes, you did, Cal. But the harebrained scheme was mine…and Juky's idea."

Cal's eyes narrowed sharply as he glared at Donna. "Donna, what the Sam hell are you talking about? You don't even know the man. In fact, up until yesterday, I didn't know he was even alive. You weren't even here when he came traipsing in the bar like he did—" Cal suddenly stopped. Placing his hands on her shoulders, he looked her hard in the eyes. "Donna Marie, you better start spitting out what's going on and right now!"

"No. Not now."

"What? What do ya mean, not now!"

"Calm down, Cal! Remember there is a man's life at stake right now, and we need to help him. We need to get back to the marina and fast."

Cal, still quite angry, hesitated a moment then without another word, he spun around and took a seat at the helm then barked, "Sit down and hold on. We're heading back and fast. I'm going to call the authorities and then you are going to tell me exactly what the Sam hell is going here."

Donna gave him a nod and quickly sat down on the seat immediately in front of the console. Right then she wanted to die. She had never in all the years of their marriage seen him this angry with her. And for good reason, she thought. She had really messed things up, and now a man's life was in jeopardy.

Cal engaged the boat's motor then gruffly shoved the throttle wide open. The bow of the boat practically leapt out of the water. Glancing down at the back of Donna's head, he cursed out loud again. "Damn it, Donna, how the hell am I going to fix this?" As the wind began streaking through her hair, he shook his head in disbelief then added, "Don't even think about giving me any shit about my language either."

Right then she didn't care. She was completely devastated by what was happening. Gaining speed rapidly, the boat's bow skimmed low over the water. The roar of the wind and the engine drowned out any other sound. Unfortunately, it couldn't drown out how she was feeling. Unable to contain her emotions any longer, she dropped her head in her hands and began sobbing.

Cal glanced down seeing her crying and immediately felt awful for having been so hard on her. Deep down he knew that whatever she had done, she in her own way was only trying to do something good. Reaching over the short windshield, he placed a hand on her shoulder giving it a gentle squeeze, then stroked the side of her face with the back of his fingers. She quickly cupped his hand to her tear-streaked cheek. Right then, contained in something as simple as a touch, each knew they were okay with each other. And each felt the same sense of relief that came with that small gesture.

Cal looked to the west. The sun was settling ever closer to the horizon. *Not much time left to this day*, he thought. He then thought, *May not be much time for Juky either*, glancing down at Donna and then up at the orange and pink sky of the looming sunset. Under his breath, he said. "Lord, if you got time, I'm gonna need your help on this one."

Making a sweeping turn, they headed under the Bahia Honda bridge. Ramrod Key would soon be in sight. Something was gnawing at Cal. He had never seen or heard of Pirate's Well before. He was sure it was a destination. But where?

The Caribbean is littered with small coves and inlets and such, each with their own name. Some of those names make it on nautical charts; many don't. Sometimes locals refer to places as one thing while a map will use a different name entirely. Was it a settlement—perhaps the name of a small island? He just didn't know. Time wasn't on their side to be pouring over dozens of charts and maps.

Donna sat in silence the whole way back. She couldn't believe that something she wanted to do for her husband could go so wrong. She had never even remotely considered the possibility that modern-day pirates would commandeer their beloved sailboat. And now a man's life hung in the balance. She said her prayers nearly all the way back. Soon the lights of the Salty Anchor lay just ahead. Her stomach tightened; a man's fate rested in what they did next. They just had to find Juky and soon.

Cal slowed the boat to an idle as they neared the dock. Though the sun had just set, enough dusky light remained to see. Without either one saying a word, Donna stood and prepared to grab a hold of a dock piling. Inches away, Cal slipped the motor into neutral just as Donna grabbed a piling. She eased the boat to a complete stop, then slipped the bow rope around the piling quickly, tying a double bowline knot.

Cal smiled watching her. He thought about when they were dating. He would take her out sailing on his first little sloop. He taught her how to sail and about navigation. But the thing he enjoyed teaching her the most was tying knots. He marveled at how her small delicate hands, nail polish and all, could so deftly tie even the most difficult of knots. *She is the best first mate a guy could ever have*, he thought. Stepping to the back of the boat, he grabbed a rope and tied off the stern.

Slowly tying the knot, his thoughts drifted back to their present situation and what he could possibly do other than calling the authorities and hope that they could find the *Donna Marie* before they left U.S. territorial waters. Cinching the knot tight, he tossed a sideways glance up at the darkening cloudless sky. The evening stars shone prominently in the eastern sky. Under his breath, he said, "Sure hope you were listening back there, big guy."

He then looked back at Donna. He had to find a way to fix this. She was so upset, and with good reason. He truly worried that if something bad happened, the woman he had married and loved for all these years would never be the same. He was bound and determined to not let that happen. At the moment he was fresh out of ideas.

Cal stepped out of the boat first onto the dock and went promptly to the bow to assist Donna up. She still hadn't said a word since heading back. Cal reached for her hand when she turned back from grabbing her purse and hat. Looking Cal in the eyes, she hesitated a second before reaching for his hand.

He knew what she was thinking. Clasping her hand, he helped her out of the boat. Pulling her up onto the dock, he said, "Donna sweetheart, we will find him. Don't worry."

Looking him in the eyes, she said, "But how, Cal? We have no idea where he is."

Placing both hands on her shoulders, his words came soft and tender. "Donna, I won't let this happen."

"But how, Cal?" she asked, her eyes welling with tears.

Cal gave her a crooked smile as he said, "Sweetheart, don't you always say that miracles happen when you least expect them?"

Hearing that, she dropped her purse and hat on the dock and buried her face in his chest and cried. Cal wrapped his arms around her slowly stroking the back of her head. He glanced back up at the evening star, no longer alone in the sky now.

He thought, *I need a miracle right now so I don't lose two people.*

Cal started them walking toward the restaurant. For the first time in his life, he couldn't conjure up a quick solution for a tough situation. Something that had been second nature for him all his life now eluded him. They had gone only a few feet down the dock when, from out of the darkness, a voice called out to them. It took a second for them both to make the connection of who it was. Mildly annoyed at the interruption, Cal turned to face the shadowed figure walking toward them. A small dock light perched on top of a piling illuminated the face of a man they both knew. Cal called him by name, "Johnny Mac. What brings you into our neck of the woods?"

Johnny Mac stopped by the light. The corners of his smile pressed into the scars that littered his face. "Ah, what brings any of us anywhere but the winds of fate. And so it is, my good friends, that fate has blown me here."

Cal and Donna both looked at each other not quite sure what to say. One thing they both knew was that right now was not the time to chitchat with the Key West prophet.

"Johnny Mac, we'd love to sit and talk, but we have an emergency on our hands that needs to be dealt with immediately. So if you'll please excuse us." Cal normally would not have been so dismissive of Johnny Mac, especially since he was a veteran too. But he had just one thing on his mind right now.

Cal cupped Donna's elbow in his hand and started them walking down the dock. They hadn't gone but a few steps when Johnny Mac called after them again.

"The namesake you seek is no longer guided by the earth's magnet. The one from your past now guides it by the stars. Whom scoundrels of the sea must now trust."

Cal instantly stopped them in their tracks and turned back to face Johnny Mac. Cal's eyes narrowed as he questioned him, "What do you mean by 'namesake,' Johnny Mac?"

Slowly Johnny Mac lifted his arm straight out and pointed what was left of his index finger straight at Donna and softly said, "Her, the namesake of what you seek."

Chapter 11

To say that Johnny Mac was an unusual person would be a grand understatement. His usual attire consisted of a baggy floral print shirt, a Dodgers ball cap of which long white hair flowed out from under it to well past his shoulders. All of that being topped off by a pair of tan khaki shorts and leather sandals. The visual effect gave him an odd Tibetan shaman on vacation look.

Cal, as did most of the locals, knew him as Johnny Mac or J-Mac. It was the snowbirds and seasonal residents that would often refer to him as the Key West prophet. However, his real name was John McKenzie Daniels. His being referred to as the Key West prophet was due to his uncanny knack at being able to accurately tell people about their lives, most times without their ever saying a word to him. The accuracy of his revelations and predictions were stunning, to say the least. But as to how an average kid born in Budd Lake, New Jersey, wound up in the Florida Keys telling strangers about their past, present, and future was just as stunning, if not miraculous. Cal knew his story. Donna did not.

Johnny Mac had told Cal one late sunny summer day when the two military vets sat in the shade of a lone beachside chikee hut. A gentle tide lapped the shore chasing sandpipers back and forth over the wet sand. A cool surf-side breeze rustled the fronds of the chikee's thatched roof they lounged under. Johnny Mac, in a rare moment, talked of his time in Nam, and Cal, a WWII vet, just sat and listened. What he heard was sad, crazy, and a bit humorous.

Johnny Mac was inducted into the army shortly before the Tet Offensive of sixty-eight. Eighteen and green as a summer frog as he said. His time though in Nam was wretchedly brief. During the battle for Saigon, he was severely wounded; his injuries were many and grave in nature.

A local man by the name Bao Hoang found him unconscious and bleeding profusely amongst the rubble of a bombed-out building near the edge of the city. Whether it was Bao's hatred for the Communists or a sense of pity for the wounded man, or both that drove him, he elected to hide Johnny Mac in a dirt pit in the jungle a short distance behind his home.

It was an enormous risk not only for himself but for his entire family. If they were discovered to be hiding and caring for an American soldier, it would mean instant death. Still, he and his wife cared for him as best as they could. But infection soon set in making a bad situation worse.

To help combat his intense pain and to keep him quiet, they gave him copious amounts of opium. Even after control of Saigon had been wrested from the Communists, they continued to hide Johnny Mac in the jungle, mostly because they didn't really know who to trust even among their own people.

Finally, the South Vietnamese authorities were told of a "round eye" that was being hidden in the jungle by a local family. The moment of truth had arrived for Bao and his family. A detachment of South Vietnamese and American troops were dispatched to the family's home on the outskirts of town.

A sharp rap came to the door of their humble home. Bao opened the door only a crack, but a south Vietnamese officer shoved it open and stepped quickly in startling Thien, Bao's wife, and two small children who sat huddled on a worn couch. Thien instinctively drew her daughters close.

The Vietnamese officer spoke quickly and tersely to Bao. Bao, fearing that he was going to be arrested, only gave vague references and short replies. This agitated the officer to the point where he raised his hand to back slap Bao. A sergeant with the American contingent stopped him and asked if he could try something. The officer gave a rapid nod and stepped aside.

The sounds of the jungle mingled with the humidity and the smell of a nearby hog pen thickening the air in an otherwise silent room. The sergeant nodded toward Bao then stepped around him to his wife. Thien pulled her daughters even closer. Tears began to stream down her face as she looked up at the American who was twice her husband's size.

The sergeant unsnapped a pouch on his gun belt and fingered out something concealing it in his large gloved hand. Looking down at the smallest child, he knelt down in front of her. The little girl like her sister sat barefooted and clad only in a threadbare dresses. Both shrunk back even farther in their mother's grasp.

The sound of the sergeant's gear creaked and groaned as he settled on one knee. Holding out his clenched hand, he slowly turned it over. Opening his hand, a chocolate bar was revealed to the little girl. Looking to Thien, he spoke out to the Vietnamese officer.

"Tell her we just want to take care of our family too."

Even before the translated words had dissipated into the din of cicadas emanating from the surrounding jungle, Thien, in that split second of time, saw in the sergeant's eyes that it was all going to be okay. The little girl looked up at her mother for approval to take the candy. Thien nodded as she wiped the tears from her cheeks. Thien spoke to her husband who nodded reluctantly. They were then cautiously led to where Johnny Mac lay in a thatch-covered pit in the ground.

He was near death and not even expected to survive the short chopper flight to the base hospital, let alone back stateside. But survive he did. It was during his months of repeated surgeries and recuperation at Walter Reed that he began to notice that something different was going on with him. The difference went far beyond being eighteen and his shaved-off hair growing back in stark white.

The bigger and more disturbing clue that the same person that went to Nam didn't return from there was that whenever the nurses or doctors or anyone else came near him, he would suddenly have personal knowledge about that person or people close to them. As time went on, this ability became much stronger to the point that it wasn't always necessary for someone to be near or touch him for things to be revealed to him.

Finally, after remaining silent about this and thinking he might be going crazy, he mentioned it to the one of the doctors. This quickly landed him in the psychiatric ward for evaluation. He tried to retract his story when it became apparent that the chief of staff was going to make him the guinea pig for a research paper. This was going to mean even more time in this place.

It was then that Johnny Mac decided to use his newfound ability to "buy" his way out of his predicament with a clean record—where it concerned his mental state anyway. He did this by revealing to the good doctor during one of their hour-long sessions that he knew about the affair he was having with a woman who lived more than fifty miles from his home outside of Bethesda, Maryland.

The doctor remained skeptical about Johnny Mac's psychic ability. He believed him to be just making deductive lucky guesses. That is until Johnny Mac described his long-distance lover to a tee, even describing the inside of the restaurant they frequented when they would meet up. This had the desired effect that he hoped for. He was quickly released from the mental ward with a clean bill of health from the good doctor. As for the doctor, well, he had a mystery that he didn't *ever* want to know the answer to.

These days when Johnny Mac wasn't giving readings to visiting snowbirds while sitting under the fronds of a large plastic palm tree, he worked part-time as a bridge tender. The solitude of operating a drawbridge was the only job he could do, not only for physical reasons but also for the psychological rest and peace it brought to his mind.

Cal knew all of this about Johnny Mac. But Donna did not. She too had seen his abilities firsthand and had no doubt that it was legit. What bothered her about Johnny Mac was that she didn't know from which side of the spiritual fence his remarkable abilities were coming from. Because of that, she was always polite to him but kept her distance from him.

Again, Cal asked if he knew where the *Donna Marie* was going.

Johnny Mac smiled then said, "The dark man who guides by the stars has the advantage for now. When the namesake arrives not in the place of intent, the scoundrel's anger they will vent.

Cal rolled his eyes in frustration. "J-Mac, I don't need you to be the Key West prophet right now. I need the guy from Budd Lake, New Jersey, to tell me what the hell is going on. A man's life is in danger for Christ's sake. Now come into the office and let's talk."

Donna jerked on Cal's arm. Through gritted teeth, she hissed, "I don't think that's a good idea! And don't bring Christ's name into this."

"Relax, Donna. If Johnny Mac can tell us something, then I'm ready to listen. Besides, how do you know the Lord didn't bring him here?"

Donna turned back to start walking toward the restaurant mumbling just loud enough for only Cal to hear her, or so she thought. "I doubt Christ has anything to with him or this."

Cal looked apologetically at Johnny Mac shaking his head. Johnny Mac then spoke up with none of his usual lyrical inverted manner but instead as the New Jersey kid that still lived in his heart. Knowing her suspicions as to where his abilities came from, he said, "Mrs. Arnold, I promise I'll leave my band of demons outside. I only want to help you find Juky and the *Donna Marie*."

Donna froze in her tracks. Turning back to face Cal and Johnny Mac, she stared at him for a moment then quietly asked, "How did you know his name was Juky?"

Johnny Mac smiled a crooked smile, the only kind Nam had left him able to make, and said, "It's who I am now, dear lady."

Chapter 12

The *Donna Marie* slipped gracefully through the dark waters of the moonless night. The multitude of stars ran down the night sky to lay right on top of the calm seas making it easy for Juky to chart his course. Juky cut his eyes to the man assigned to keep an eye on him while he was at the helm. Since none of the three men who boarded the *Donna Marie* at gunpoint knew how to use a sextant and reckon by the stars, they were dependent on him to take them where they wanted, and they were none too happy about it.

Juky had seen to this happening shortly after they had taken control of the *Donna Marie* and forced him below deck. With his captors preoccupied above and no one watching him, Juky had hurriedly searched the ship's storage compartments for anything he thought could change the current situation. He found the flare gun quick enough but reasoned that with only one shot and three armed men plus the risk of starting a fire onboard, using it was out of the question. While placing the flare gun back in the storage cabinet, he noticed some speaker wire.

Looking up above his head, he saw a rather large stereo speaker in the face of the cabinet. It only took a couple of minutes for him to remove the speaker. Going back to the tool box, he found a roll of duct tape and made his way to a compartment at the underside of the helm above. Opening the doors to the compartment, he carefully taped the speaker directly underneath the ship's compass.

It was a tight space; he had to be careful not interfere with the control rods that ran from the ship's wheel to the rudder. Working quickly, he taped the large magnet on the back of the speaker as close to the compass's location above as he could. This had an immediate effect on the compass. Finishing up, he hurried to take a seat and wait to see what happened next.

It didn't take long for them to notice that the compass was no longer remaining on a fixed heading. Hearing shouting about it above and what to do about it, Juky took the opportunity and shouted through the cabin door, saying it was because they were sailing through the Devil's Triangle that they need to use a sextant to plot their course now. That's when they revealed what Juky had banked on, their inability to do that.

After a few more tense words through the cabin door, he again found himself up on deck at the helm of the *Donna Marie*. Juky was given the heading of the location the pirates wanted to go. Juky made a big extended display of using the sextant and plotting lines on the map. He then plotted a course for Pirates Well, at least that's where he had his captors believing they were headed. Instead had them heading west and well north of Pirates Well to a place called Rokers Point. Rokers Point, unlike Pirates Well, was a resort with lots of people around. Getting there was not the big challenge. The big challenge was staying alive once his captors realized they had been snookered.

*****

Instead of going into the office, Cal, Donna, and Johnny Mac sat at a lone table outside the restaurant. Kevin had spotted his mom and dad walking with Johnny Mac as they reached the table. Kevin was already heading out to intercept them and find out what was going on, but before he reached the door, he was accosted by one of the regulars who wanted to chitchat about his day of fishing. Kevin, being the good host, obliged but kept glancing out the window at the three of them. Between giving feigned nods of interest to the slightly inebriated patron's lengthy story, he noticed that Johnny Mac was doing most of the talking. *Not too unusual*, he thought.

What was unusual was for his mother to be sitting there with Johnny Mac. And on top of that, she appeared to be very interested in what he was saying as well. He had never known his mother to give Johnny-Mac much more than polite small talk, let alone sit at a table in what appeared to be a serious conversation with the man.

He was dying to get out there to find out what the heck was going on. He finally found a break in the man's rambling story to politely excuse himself. But before he got halfway to the door, Tammy called for him in a panic from the kitchen door waving frantically for him to come over.

Rolling his eyes, he spun around to go see what was on fire. Nearing her, he pointed back toward the windows, saying, "Tammy honey, what is it? Mom and Dad are back, and they're outside talking to Johnny Mac. I want to go see what the heck is going on."

Tammy pressed her lips together looking around Kevin to see what he was talking about. She quickly waved her hand dismissively in the air, saying, "Kevin, that can wait—we have a bigger issue right now. The walk-in freezer is on the fritz."

"What? Are you sure? It might be in defrost right now."

"No, I don't think it is. It has been off for a while now."

"Great. I'll go take a look at the compressor and see if I can figure out what's wrong. Meanwhile, you go see if you can find out what is going on out there," he said, pointing a thumb over his shoulder.

"Okay. But can I wait until *he* leaves?"

"Who leaves?"

"Johnny Mac—he kinda creeps me out a little."

"Why? He's okay. A bit quirky and mysterious, but I like him."

"I don't know. Maybe I'm just this way because your mom is so standoffish with him."

"Don't look now, but she and Dad are both in a deep conversation with him right now."

Tammy looked around and saw Donna and Cal both carrying on what appeared to be a very serious conversation about something.

"Huh. That *is* a bit unusual, not for Dad. But Mom, now that's a different story. Okay, I'm in. Even I have to know what is going on with that."

Tammy looked back at Kevin before heading out. "You don't think they are consulting him on where the *Donna Marie* is, do you?"

Kevin cut his eyes to again look out the window. "That has been the big story of the day, and Dad hasn't done anything normal since this all started. So yeah, I think that's exactly what's going on. What I can't figure out is why Mom is sitting there listening to anything Johnny Mac has to say. You know how she is about that mysticism stuff."

"Boy, don't I. She does the sign of the cross every time he stops in here."

Kevin chuckled, adding, "Yeah, then and any time tools and cuss words are flying out of the boat shop."

Both snickered and headed off to deal with the tasks at hand.

All talk stopped as Tammy approached the table; however, she immediately filled the silence. "Mom, Dad, Johnny Mac. Is everything okay? I saw you all talking out here and came to see if there was any news about…" She stopped, unsure if they had said anything to Johnny Mac about the *Donna Marie*.

Johnny Mac didn't have to be a mind reader to know why she had stopped talking. So he eased her mind on the matter. "Tammy my dear, I have come to help your in-laws find the *Donna Marie*."

Tammy was taken aback a bit hearing him talk like a normal person. It wasn't that he never did that around them, but he just didn't do it a lot, mostly because of strangers being around the Salty Anchor all the time. He'd always say he needed to maintain his image.

Johnny Mac patted a spot on the bench next him telling her to have a seat. Tammy looked nervously at Cal and Donna then took a seat at the end of the bench keeping as much space as she could between them.

Johnny Mac took no offense to her cautious manner and laughed, telling her, "Relax, Tammy, I promise you I'm not going to turn into that monster from the movie *Alien*. I don't have enough saliva for that. I'm more like the *Man from Planet X*," he said, making reference to an old '50s era movie.

Tammy wanted to move the conversation away from her and back to the *Donna Marie*. Looking across the big wooden table, she asked, "So Dad, Mom, what is going on? I take it you didn't find her or the man who took her."

Both grimly shook their heads no. Then Donna added, "It's even worse than we thought."

"What?" Tammy's eyes darted between the two of them. "What do you mean?"

"Tammy honey, it looks like boat thieves have taken the *Donna Marie.*"

"Boat thieves? I thought that was who took her already…that, that Juky guy Dad's always telling that story about."

Cal then interjected, "No, he wasn't a boat thief…well, *maybe* not. It looks like Juky took the *Donna Marie* for reasons Mom here has yet to explain. We found where Juky had her hidden, but it looks like some drug smugglers or boat thieves found him and taken the *Donna Marie.*"

"You called the Coast Guard, right?"

Cal and Donna looked sheepishly at each other. Cal spoke up again. "Well, not yet. We *are*…just not yet."

"What! why are you waiting?"

Donna answered her, "Because we have a good idea of where they are taking her."

"Yeah, and it's not where the thieves think they're going," Cal added.

"Wait a minute. How is it that you know all of this? You just got back twenty minutes ago."

Looking more like two embarrassed school kids having to rat out a student to their teacher, they cautiously looked over at Johnny Mac. Tammy shot to her feet. "Oh my god! Mom, Dad, you have got to be kidding me. And Mom, I'm especially shocked at you. Are you two seriously thinking of going wherever the hell *he's* told you to go?" she asked, pointing a finger at Johnny Mac. "Have you both lost your marbles? Dammit that's as crazy as he—," she stopped in mid-sentence.

"As crazy as me," Johnny Mac said, smiling at her.

"I'm sorry, Johnny Mac. I didn't mean to insult you. It's just that…well, this is all so messed up. And, well, I've been a little out of whack lately too."

Johnny Mac gave her a warm smile then said something else that was going to rock all their worlds. "I understand. You don't need to apologize. All of this can be very disquieting for someone in your condition."

Perplexed, they all three shot him brow furrowed stares. Not having any idea of what he was talking about, Tammy tentatively asked, "What do you mean 'in my condition'? I'm not sick am I?"

Still smiling, he said, "Have you not been feeling ill recently?"

"Well, yes, in the mornings. But I figure I'm just coming down with…wait, how do you know that?"

Johnny Mac said nothing, just tilted his head, giving her a "well duh" expression.

Looking a little embarrassed, Tammy said, "Oh yeah." Her face went suddenly straight. "Wait, is it something bad? Is that why I've been sick these past few mornings?"

Suddenly Donna let out a shriek. "Oh my god, Tammy honey—you're not sick because of something bad."

Tammy fixed her eyes on her mother-in-law's brightly beaming face. Her jaw dropped as she plopped back down bedside Johnny Mac. Donna, unable to contain herself, practically squealed it out, "You're pregnant, sweetheart."

Cal looked over at Donna, then at his in-shock daughter-in-law, then at Johnny Mac, asking, "Are you sure?"

"As sure as I am of where her namesake is heading," he said, pointing at Donna.

This brought Cal's focus back to their original reason for talking with Johnny Mac. Cal was in the middle of asking Johnny Mac where the *Donna Marie* might be headed when Kevin strolled up to the table.

"Hey, Mom, you sure are smiling big. You guys know where the *Donna Marie* is now?"

"No," Cal began, "but you might want to sit down, son."

Johnny Mac slid down the long bench to make room for Tammy and Kevin to sit.

Sitting slowly down, Kevin looked at Tammy. Her face was contorted with a confused smile. Tears rimmed her blue eyes.

"What's going on? That Juky guy—he sank the boat didn't he?"

"No, silly." Tammy then held her gaze in her husband's eyes. "Kevin, you know how I have been getting sick over the last few mornings?"

Cautiously, he answered her, "Yeah," he then cut his eyes over at his mother who sat smiling bigger than he had ever seen her do before. His jaw suddenly dropped; his eyes widened as the implications of her morning sickness hit him.

Kevin stared at his wife of just three years. And though she was smiling, Kevin saw trepidation in her eyes. Putting his arm around her, he pulled her close and kissed her on top of her head. "Sweetheart, don't you worry. You are going to be a great mother. I know it. Heck, look at the way you boss all of us around. A little baby should be easy, right?"

Cal watched as Tammy pulled away a bit, giving Kevin a look of disbelief. "Uh-oh. You've stepped in it now, son."

In the next second, Donna was on him like a Kodiak bear on a salmon. "Easy! You think it's easy! I'll tell you about how easy it is, young man." Just as she was about to inform her naïve son of all the rigors of raising a child from birth, she caught a glimpse of the worry on her daughter-in-law's face.

Donna reached across the table and cupped her hands around Tammy's hands. "Look, if this guy sitting next to me can do it, you two will be able to ace this. Just be there for each other and you'll be fine. Besides, you two will have the best grandparents right here with you. Okay, well, maybe not the best, but you know what I mean."

The Salty Anchor, as it usually did, kept family moments like this short. Kevin was informed by one of the kitchen staff that the refrigeration service company had arrived. No sooner had he left to deal with that than Tammy had to go and see why the new Casio electronic cash register was acting up…again.

Cal and Donna were alone once again with Johnny Mac. Johnny Mac looked at them and smiled. "It makes me happy when I can bring good news such as this to people. However, we still have the difficult question of the *Donna Marie* and her two fates."

Cal's eyes shot to Johnny Mac's. "*Two* fates?"

Donna interjected, "What do you mean, how can the *Donna Marie* have two fates?"

Johnny Mac's eyes held a tender look as he answered her. "Dear lady. All of us have many different paths on life's journey. And many times, the most seemingly insignificant decision a person makes changes one's path in life sometimes with dramatic results. I'm a case in point."

Cal spoke up again. "But you said the *Donna Marie* has two fates."

"At this moment in time, yes. And they are based on what you will next decide to do."

"And that is?" Cal cautiously asked.

Johnny Mac looked into each of their faces before answering, settling on Donna. "They rest on whether you decide to let those who wear uniforms and badges chase what is not theirs and don't love. Or whether you let go of one love to chase what you both love."

Cal, sounding very confused, said, "Johnny, what the heck are you saying? Can you please dispense with the misty references and just talk so we can understand what you mean?"

Johnny Mac, still holding his stare in Donna's eyes, said, "Only one of you needed to understand, right, Mrs. Arnold? It was, after all, your original intent, was it not?"

A chill ran over Donna as she kept her eyes fixed in his. She knew exactly what he meant. "Yes, but not quite like this. This has real danger attached to it now."

Cal, feeling left out and a bit irritated at not being part of the whole conversation, blurted out, "Now just hold the mystery tour bus, you two. Just what the hell is going here? What are you two talking about?"

Johnny Mac cut his eyes to Cal then back to Donna. "Have you not told him of your original plan?"

Donna looked at Cal then to Johnny Mac. "Well, I...I was going to. But then you showed up, and I thought maybe you might make all of this go away somehow."

Johnny Mac smirked, shaking his head a little. "I see. And you thought I might work some kind of magical spell to fix this," he said, making spooky fingers. "Look, Mrs. Arnold, I know you distrust where my *abilities* come from. I don't even know that myself. But didn't I just bring some good news to you both?" She gave a small nod. "And isn't it said that a bad tree cannot produce good fruit? And a good tree cannot produce bad fruit?"

Donna, of course, recognized the Bible reference. "Yes, that is true."

"Then which do you say that I am, dear lady?"

Donna stared intently into the depth of Johnny Mac's dark brown eyes. She then turned to face her very confused husband, abruptly saying, "Cal, you have to go and find the *Donna Marie* and bring her home safe."

Cal started to speak but was stopped by Johnny Mac standing quickly up and saying, "Well, it looks like you two have some things to talk over tonight. And," he looked at Donna then to Cal and continued, "it looks like Cal and I have to get ready to leave on a Caribbean tide tomorrow."

Chapter 13

It was a long night for both of them. Donna had finally told Cal her whole plan of faking the *Donna Marie*'s disappearance so that they could go off on an adventure through the Caribbean to find her and then spend some time sailing her back home, just the two of them.

Cal wanted to be angry with her but found he couldn't, especially after she further explained the reasons for planning all this. Cal had to marvel at how well thought out it all was right down to where and how they were to regain possession of the *Donna Marie*.

This all had begun when Juky, by chance, had shown up three weeks earlier at the Salty Anchor. Cal had left for a couple of hours to go see about buying some used beer coolers. Short-handed, Donna was helping wait on tables that day. Juky heard one of the other waitresses refer to her as Mrs. Arnold. He mentioned to his waitress that he knew of a man by that name that had lived up near Hialeah some years back, and she in turn told Donna.

Donna stopped by Juky's table to introduce herself and told him that her husband Cal had once lived in that area. She then asked him his name so she could mention it to Cal when he returned to see if they might have known each other back then. He politely told Donna his name was Julius Kerns Youssaint, which of course meant nothing to Donna, that is until he told her his nickname which was a sort of acronym of his whole name.

She practically had to pick her jaw up off the floor hearing the name Juky. Seeing this as some kind of sign, she gathered her wits and asked if they could talk, to which he agreed. She quickly found Juky to be a very pleasant and engaging man. He seemed to be nothing like the backstabbing monster her husband portrayed him to be all these years.

Laughter came easily to Juky, and hearing Donna tell how Cal had portrayed him made him laugh even more. He explained how the cops back then had gotten his information completely wrong and had in fact accidently stumbled on Cal's little operation. His intent was for them find the operation of a man who was making bad liquor which was finding its way to his small island home of Marie-Galante. He laughed out loud hearing the story Cal had used to get the cops drunk that day.

Cal had listened patiently to Donna tell Juky's version of what had happened back all those years ago. He was still dubious about that version, to say the least. This was rooted in the distance of Juky's home island being South of Guadeloupe, Marie-Galante, was a long way from Hialeah, Florida. But he also knew that back then anything was possible.

The more serious subject of Cal's going off to find the *Donna Marie* is what had kept them up most of the night. Cal, even in his late fifties, was in good physical shape and still had his clever wit and quickness of thought. Even so, Donna was having second thoughts about his going.

Her concerns lay in who had likely taken the *Donna Marie*. She, like Cal, knew that the waters throughout the Caribbean held places of utter lawlessness, where you couldn't even trust the authorities, especially where it concerned anything of great value. And a sailboat the likes of the *Donna Marie* always drew attention, which up until now was only of admiration. There was little difference between the pirates of old and the ones who marauded through the Caribbean of the 1980s. They still took what they wanted when they wanted it. And like the pirates of old, they had no problem with killing to get what they were after.

It was after 2:00 a.m. and much discussion when they finally drifted off to sleep. Cal had convinced Donna that he would make only a cursory attempt at finding the *Donna Marie*. He and Johnny Mac would go to where they believed Juky was taking the thieves, get there ahead of them, engage the local authorities to help with regaining possession, and return home, hopefully all without incident.

Sunrise came far too quickly. With only a scant three hours of sleep, Donna awoke and peered through puffy eyelids to see Cal's side of the bed was empty. Quickly rising up on her elbows, she gazed around the bedroom. The amber morning light that peeked through a slit in the curtains revealed no sign of Cal. Pushing herself upright, she stretched and yawned then slid her legs over the side of the bed to stand. That's when a piece of notebook paper drifted to the dark wood floor. Picking it up, her heart sank seeing his handwriting.

> *Good morning, sweetheart, hopefully by the time you read this, Johnny Mac and me will be winging our way to…to, well, I'm not exactly sure. Probably Rum Cay since that's where you and Juky had planned to have the DM found. Anyway, I didn't want to wake you, so I gave you kisses on your forehead while you slept. I know you are worried, but it will all be okay. Not going to let anything happen to the DM…or me. Not going to let you get rid of me that easy.*
> *I love you, Donna Marie Arnold.*
> *Cal*

Tears dripped slowly on the page. "Darn you, Cal, you knew I was going to try and talk you out of going didn't you?" Donna gently placed the note on the bed beside her and looked up at the ceiling. "God, what have I done?"

Lowering her head, she turned from her seat on the edge of the bed, knelt beside it, and prayed like she never ever had before.

*****

In the air for about an hour, sitting in the copilot's seat once again, Cal stared out the window of the Water Lily for the second time in two days. Johnny Mac was asleep in a seat at the bulkhead behind the cockpit, and other than the drone of the engines and the occasional radio chatter, it was quiet. With the Water Lily's nose pointing directly into the sun, it was out of the question to try and look for the *Donna Marie* on the waters below. Rum Cay was their destination based on what Donna had told Cal and the hope that Juky would stick with that original plan. This seemed to be reinforced by what Johnny Mac had said last evening about Juky somehow being in control of where they were headed.

It was a crazy long shot, Cal thought, as he watched a bank of clouds drift in front of the sun, resulting in a brilliant show of orange, yellow, and white spires of light that fanned out around the edges of the cloud in front of them. Cal, to Donna's great dismay, would often call such spectacles "Jesus clouds" because they looked like the clouds often depicted in the paintings he saw in the church he attended as boy.

Continuing to gaze at the nephologic display before him, Cal embraced that moment to murmur a small prayer asking for everyone's safe return home and not simply to just find the *Donna Marie*. He did so, figuring they could use all the help they could get on this little endeavor. Tired from the lack of sleep, he began nodding off until sleep finally overcame him. Jim made a gentle course correction pointing the Water Lily in a more southerly direction for Rum Cay. The Water Lily slipped through the clear morning air with ease. The sun rose higher, and the morning's light was quickly changing the sky to a bright blue.

Small puffs of cottony clouds, the seeds of what would later become afternoon thunderstorms, dotted the sky. With another hour of flying time to go, there was little worry of having to fly around thunderheads this early in the day; the flight back would likely be another story. Reaching up, Jim adjusted the fuel mixture of the starboard engine for maximum economy, then scanned the instrument panel's bank of gauges, satisfied that the Water Lily was cruising tight and right. He settled in for the last leg of what was looking to be an uneventful trip.

They had flown comfortably along for about a half hour when Johnny Mac's eyes abruptly flashed open in a wild stare. He immediately began shouting out to no one in particular, scaring the hell out of both Cal and Jim. "Wait! No! No! We are going the wrong way! You must change course Now!"

Cal pawed the sleep from his face while trying to grasp what Johnny Mac was shouting about. "Jesus, Mary, and Joseph! Johnny Mac, you scared the shit out me, damn it! What the hell are you yelling about? We are going where I thought you said the *Donna Marie* was headed."

Johnny Mac ceased his shouting but still spoke excitedly at a high volume while leaning so far forward toward Cal that he practically left his seat. Still sounding panicked, he said, "*No!* No! I never said where. Remember? What I said was, 'When the namesake arrives not in the place of intent, the scoundrels anger they will vent.' That is what I said."

Clearly irritated, Cal said, "I thought that was Rum Cay?"

"No, *you* thought that. No, we must find the island that appears as the warrior's dao."

Cal's frustration with Johnny Mac was plastered all over his face and in his voice when he asked, "What the hell are you talking about, Johnny? I don't have the time or patience for this mumbo-jumbo stuff. Just spit it out, will ya?"

Johnny Mac wrinkled his brow feeling a bit incensed at Cal's mumbo-jumbo reference and simply said, "I did, dammit."

Cal questioned, "We have to find an island that looks like a dao? I don't have the slightest damn clue what a dao *is*, J-Mac. You've got to give me more than that to go on."

Johnny Mac was about to reply when Jim spoke up. "It's a type of sword some pirates used to carry. Dao is the Chinese name for a broadsword."

Johnny Mac smiled at Cal. "Yeah, what he said. You know, Cal, you don't have to be so angry. I'm just trying to help, ya know."

Still feeling frustrated, Cal said, "What the hell, why didn't you just say that? Jesus, you wake me up screaming and yelling that we are going the wrong way. Then tell us we have to find a damn Chinese sword-shaped island—how am I supposed to not get pissed off?"

"Look, I'm sorry. I can't help how this stuff comes to me. Sometimes the images are so strong it affects me that way. Why did you have to call it mumbo jumbo? That bothers me, ya know."

Cal felt bad about letting his emotions get away from him. "Look, I'm uh, I'm sorry I said that. You know I don't mean anything by what I said. I guess I'm just tired. I haven't slept much since this all started, okay?"

Johnny Mac rolled his eyes with a slight head nod. "Well, it's okay, I guess. But you know you do have some anger issues you need to deal with."

"Anger issues? What the heck are you talking about now?" Cal blared.

Johnny Mac gave Cal a funny look then smiled and told him with wave of his hand, "Ah, don't sweat it. It'll be ten or twelve years before that term becomes popular with people."

Cal was about to say something else when Jim interrupted. "Hey, I hate to break up you two's make-up session, but I still have the nose of this bird pointed for Rum Cay. If we are flying anywhere other than that, I need to know soon. One of you ought to start looking at some maps for an island that looks like a sword and quick. This bird doesn't run on my good looks," he warned, tapping the fuel gauge.

Cal looked at Jim then to Johnny Mac. Cal left his seat to retrieve his duffel bag and the maps he had packed. His concern was that with so many islands throughout the Caribbean all of varying sizes and shapes, there was a good chance that the one they needed to find might not be shown or in enough detail.

Clutching a fist full of maps, Cal pressed Johnny Mac for more details. He didn't have much more to go on except to say that "along the top of the blade is where the rich come to play." Cal was able to determine that he was referencing a resort of some kind. But again, those kinds of places were scattered all through the islands.

Cal sat down at the bulkhead behind the cockpit and unlatched a small fold-out desk. He then retrieved a small magnifying glass from his shirt pocket and unfolded a map. Holding the magnifying glass a couple of inches from the map, he began a methodical search.

Johnny Mac peered over his shoulder randomly pointing to different spots on the map. Cal mostly ignored him trying to remain focused and methodical.

Finally, annoyed, Cal barked, "Stop pointing at places for me to look! I'll never find a damn sword-shaped island hopping all over the place like a damn Mexican jumping bean."

Johnny Mac curtly replied, "You're going too slow. We'll be out of fuel before you get done."

Cal threw hard glare over his shoulder. "I suppose you could do it faster."

"Maybe, and maybe I'd try looking in the right place first."

"Is that so? Well, why don't you just show me that *right* place," Cal said, leaning to one side.

Johnny Mac bent over the map. "Well, I'd look right here," he smugly replied while haphazardly stabbing a finger in the middle of the map.

Cal looked down to see Johnny Mac's gnarled finger pointing to a small strip of land. He then placed the magnifying glass over it moving it up and down to focus in on it. Cal let out a huff as a sword-shaped island came into focus. He then quickly scanned over other points on the map to check other islands in the vicinity, then focused back on the one Johnny Mac had pointed to as if to verify what he was seeing. Sure enough, there it was—an island that resembled a broadsword.

With righteous indignation, Johnny Mac blurted out, "Well, you gonna keep staring at it or give the pilot the coordinates?"

"Okay, okay, smart guy! Just hope it's the right island."

Cal leaned into the cockpit giving Jim the new coordinates. With a quick nod of acknowledgment, Jim began banking the Water Lily in a northerly direction and set the transponder for the Exuma International Airport. Cal stepped back into the copilot's seat and plopped down. He was exhausted. They had maybe forty-five minutes of flying time before they landed. He wanted to keep scanning the ocean below for a glimpse of the *Donna Marie* but quickly figured that if she *was* heading there, they likely had already overflown her by now.

Not knowing what to expect once they landed, he decided it was best to catch a few winks of sleep. Cal turned back to suggest that Johnny Mac do the same only to find him with his head against the plane's fuselage already sawing logs. Cal shook his head and eased back in his seat, scrunched down, and pulled the bill of his ball cap down low.

His eyes heavy with sleep, he tried to think on just how to get the *Donna Marie* back. The low drone of the engines made the pull of sleep come on strong. He hoped this would be over soon. He was missing Donna. His eyes slowly blinked as her name drifted across his lips and sleep took him away.

The Water Lily flew on; below them a sapphire blue ocean scrolled slowly by. Time would reveal future events, events that Johnny Mac knew some of but didn't feel he could reveal yet. Outcomes do change, he thought. While the things he saw were not set in stone, he did, however, feel that they might be heading into great danger, and to get through it, he knew Cal was going to have to rely on his old self once again, a part of him he had buried long, long ago.

Chapter 14

Overnight the *Donna Marie*, with her sails stowed, sat anchored over the Great Bahama Bank. Juky, during a heated confrontation, had convinced his captors of the insanity of continuing to sail in unfamiliar waters at night. Nature stepped in to help to settle the disagreement; the wind, as it sometimes does at night, fell slack—something Juky had tried to tell them might happen. At first, they wanted to keep going on, relying on the diesel engine. But this was quickly dismissed because of fuel concerns.

Underway now since sunrise, Juky's captors had become less concerned about being right on top of him. He was free to move about the boat, not without question entirely though. Right now, he was below deck reviewing his route. According to his calculations, they should reach Rokers Point by around noon.

Over the last couple of hours, Juky had picked up the fact that they had never been to Pirates Well. This fact was what he hoped would allow him to sail the *Donna Marie* right into the yacht basin on the east side of Rokers Point. This was a far better plan, he thought, than simply jumping in the water at an opportune moment to try and escape. The one flaw in his current plan was how much his captors might know about Pirates Well. If they knew that there was no yacht basin like the one at Rokers Point, then jumping in the water and swimming for it might again become his only option.

*****

Kevin and Tammy were in the office early as usual and going over employee schedules and inventory lists, the usual mundane daily tasks that have to be done to keep an enterprise like the Salty Anchor running smoothly. However, the events of the last forty-eight hours made it seem more difficult.

The *Donna Marie*'s disappearance was on all the employee's minds and lips. Both Kevin and Tammy had worked to try and minimize the issue. But Cal being MIA and Kevin and Tammy's being so tight-lipped about why only served to power up the rumor mill even more.

An employee meeting had been called for this morning. Kevin and Tammy's hope was to quell any rumors about what was going on and why Cal was gone. The murmur of the gathering employees drifted into the open door of the office. Kevin glanced up at the brass ship's wheel clock over his head. Time to get the party started, he thought.

Tammy dropped what she was doing joining Kevin in the main dining room. Both stood side by side a few feet in front of a small group of twenty-five employees. After some morning greetings and a little joking, Kevin cleared his throat and began.

"Good morning, everyone. I know it's early, so I'll try and be quick with this. First, I know you all are wondering about Dad and the *Donna Marie*, and—" Suddenly, before another word left his lips, Donna burst through the office door excitedly talking at a high volume.

"Kids, kids, I'm leaving this morn—," she stopped mid-sentence seeing everyone gathered in the dining room. She looked quickly to Tammy and Kevin, then back at the silent group of bewildered employees.

"Oh, uh, good morning, everyone. I'm sorry, I didn't know you were having a meeting. I'll just wait in the office until you two are finished. I have something I need to tell you both."

Kevin drew a deep breath wondering what the heck was coming now. However, he seized the opportunity to include his mother in what he had to say. "No, Mom, stay here. You can perhaps help to explain what's going on with Dad and the *Donna Marie*, and settle everyone's mind." Donna politely nodded and stood where she had stopped a few feet behind them, placing two small suitcases on the floor bedside her. Tammy and Kevin both took note of it but didn't ask about it.

Donna went into a brief version of the recent events adding as much candy coating as she thought was reasonably believable. Everyone seemed to be placated to a fair degree, especially after Kevin surmised that both Cal and the *Donna Marie* would be back safe and sound in a couple of days.

That split second of relief was shattered when his mother, sounding like General Douglas McArthur, added to his closing comment by confidently announcing with a grand sweep of her arms out wide, "That's right, Kevin, and that is why I've decided to fly to Rum Cay this morning to help your father bring what belongs to the Salty Anchor *back* to the Salty Anchor!"

Chapter 15

Having landed around midmorning, Cal and Johnny Mac had spent most of the day getting familiar with the Rokers Point yacht basin as well as some inlets they had been told a boat the size of the *Donna Marie* could anchor in.

Staying at an older motel, called the Paradise, Johnny Mac wound up being the only one who got any real rest; Cal didn't. He suspected as much about Donna; neither of them rested well whenever they were apart, and the current situation only amplified that. Cal had intended to call Donna and let her know he was all right but had gotten caught up in trying to devise a plan to retake the *Donna Marie*—a plan which largely depended on the pirates who took the *Donna Marie* not knowing who he was or what he looked like.

Johnny Mac had headed out to the beach for an early morning stroll. Cal sat on the patio outside the room for a few minutes anxiously looking from his wristwatch to the beautiful blue bay the motel was nestled next to trying to decide the best time to call her. Finally bolting up from the wicker plantation chair, he decided to call her, figuring she would want to know what was going on no matter what.

Cal called out to Johnny Mac who was down near the water sitting cross-legged on the beach facing the open waters of the Atlantic. Cal couldn't tell if he heard him say he was going to the lobby to use the phone or not and didn't really care. He needed to talk to Donna. Walking the sandy brick path to the motel office, he went over what and how much he was going to tell her. He knew he wasn't the best at sugarcoating things, and worse, he was horrible at keeping secrets from her.

He scrolled through their plan of pretending that Johnny Mac was the *Donna Marie*'s owner and he being some phony made-up government agent. They were going to accuse Juky of being the one who had stolen the *Donna Marie*.

It was hoped that the real pirates would seize the opportunity to blame Juky and proclaim their own innocence in the whole thing in order to keep from being arrested. To add to the believability of their ruse, Cal hoped to convince Jim to do a low fast pass with the Water Lily directly over the *Donna Marie*.

That's when Cal would inform all aboard that the seaplane was full of armed agents sent to arrest Juky. It seemed foolproof. All they needed now was the *Donna Marie* to show up.

*****

Kevin had plopped down at the desk in the office shaking his head and staring at the back door his mother had just exited on her way to Rum Cay, allegedly to find Dad and return triumphantly with him and the *Donna Marie*. Kevin jumped in his seat when the phone suddenly rang loudly behind him.

Spinning around in the office chair, he grabbed the phone quickly before it could ring again. "The Salty Anchor, Kevin speaking." The voice on the other end came through a little scratchy and distant sounding.

"Kevin, is that you?"

"Dad?"

"Yes."

"I can hardly hear you, Dad, where are you?"

"I'm in Rokers Point. The phone connections from the islands aren't very good sometimes."

"What, wait. Did you say Rokers Point? You didn't go to Rum Cay like you said?"

"No, halfway there Johnny Mac had one of his premonitions that we needed to come here. Well, not exactly. He said we had to find an island that looked like a dao, a Chinese sword."

"What? Dad, I can barely hear. You're making no sense. Did you say you had to find a Chinese sword?"

Talking loudly, Cal exclaimed. "No, listen. I don't have time to explain—is Mom there? I want to tell her what's going on. I called the house but got no answer."

Kevin sat dumbfounded trying to make sense of all this. Cal asked again for Donna.

Kevin stretched his eyes wide open trying to absorb the last twenty minutes of his life.

"Dad, can you hear me okay? I've got something to tell you that you're not going to like."

*****

With his thoughts racing, Cal practically ran back to the motel room. His first concern was for his wife. He didn't like the idea of Donna being alone on an island he knew nothing about. These islands were full of every kind of rabble he could name and some he couldn't. And while she could handle herself pretty good in most situations, she had a naivety about her that let her trust some people too quickly, even if they had crossed gun belts over their chest.

Reaching for the doorknob to the room, he stopped. A thought came quickly to him. Twisting the handle, he shoved the door open, saying, "Yes, yes, that might work. I could still retake the *Donna Marie* and then go and get Donna. Instead of a horse, the hero, me, *sails* in like Gardner McKay on the *Kon-Tiki* to save the damsel in distress. What could go wrong that?"

With the safety of his wife on his mind and before he thought about it too much, he headed back to the motel office to inquire about Rum Cay along with the lower islands and how to get a message to the local authorities. After all, they needed to know that the wife of a United States senator was on her way and may be staying with them. And therefore, she needed special protection and treatment when she arrived.

He wasn't able to get a direct connection to Rum Cay but *was* able to get his message out via a combination of phone and shortwave radio to the lower islands. He felt assured though that Rum Cay would receive the message. It was a while before Cal returned to the motel room. Opening the door, he was met by a very excited Johnny Mac. Talking rapidly, he pulled Cal to the sliding glass doors of their room and pointed out to the bay.

Cal froze. Unable to speak for a moment, he just stared out at the bay. There she was! The *Donna Marie*, looking dreamlike and beautiful as ever. Maybe more so because of the idyllic setting. As he stood staring for a long moment, he thought to himself, *This is where it gets real though.*

Cal glanced over at his image in the dresser mirror, then turned to face it. The first thing he had to do was to come up with some kind of official-looking uniform because the khaki shorts, Hawaiian shirt, and deck shoes he was wearing wasn't going to convince anyone that he was a U.S. federal drug agent.

Cal took a look at Johnny Mac. The way he was dressed was fine for him to be the eccentric owner of a sailing yacht. Cal began to pace, his mind whirling. Back in the day he could pull something like this off without much thought. He stopped in front of the mirror again. It was almost like being a magician. Some misdirection, a little sleight of hand and buckets of bull shit, and you can make anybody believe anything...for a little while anyway.

But just like a magician, he needed a few props. He had to try to come up with a uniform of some type. His silent pacing became quicker. Cal knew that there were three main law enforcement agencies operating throughout the Bahamas. Since almost all of the RBPF were black islanders, no amount of misdirection or BS was going to pass him off as an officer of the Royal Bahamas Police Force.

The only disguise he could hope to pull off was that of an officer with Interpol. They also worked in the islands to help deal with drug trafficking, piracy, kidnapping, and such. He saw some of their officers arresting someone at the Exuma airport when they had arrived earlier.

A dark blue ball cap, light blue button-up shirt, and dark blue slacks. That should be no problem to come by here. What he was going to need, though, was a badge and a brass name tag along with some small epaulets or shoulder boards. Those might be a bit harder to find.

Cal was still staring at his image in the mirror when Johnny Mac stepped into view beside him, saying, "You know, Cal, if I'm going to pull off being an eccentric rich guy, I think I need to get some of the wrinkles ironed out my shirt, don't you think?"

Still facing the mirror, Cal cut his eyes to look at Johnny Mac's reflected image. "No, you're fine. Rich guys can be slobs too."

Johnny Mac furrowed his brow. Still looking in the mirror, he said, "No, no, I think I need to be a bit more refined looking. You know, like I just left the boardroom a couple of months ago and I'm not quite comfortable with not looking a bit pressed and neat."

Cal rolled his eyes and turned to face Johnny Mac. "Look, don't overthink this. What you're wearing is perfect. Muslin material wrinkles easy anyway. Besides, pirates are not fashion-conscious people. The closest they get to worrying about fashion is where in their clothes to hide all the guns they carry."

Johnny Mac never took his eyes off his reflection and kept pulling at his shirt in different places and tilting his head back looking down his nose at his image making adjustments to his clothing, as if he never heard a word Cal had said. Suddenly stopping his simian-like preening, he announced, "Yup, these wrinkles have to go!" Snapping his fingers, he continued, "I believe I saw a small laundry a little way up the road from here. They can steam these wrinkles out in no time at all."

Johnny Mac spun to his left and headed for the door. Cal took a step after him and grabbed him by his upper arm. "Hold on! We don't have time for that. Jim is on his way over here to run through the plan so we are all on the same sheet of music."

"You don't need me for that. You're going to be doing all the talking. I'm just the wrinkled-up rich eccentric guy who wants his boat back. Right?"

"Yes, but you need to understand the timing, and we need to practice this a little. Look, it's been a long time since I've tried to run a sting on someone. These guys could be heavily armed. This is going to have to happen fast, and we have to convince them to not even think about picking up a gun."

Johnny Mac turned to face Cal. "Look, I get it. But let me do this one thing, okay? I'm a little nervous. The last time I was around people with guns trying kill me was in Nam—we both know how that turned out for me."

Cal let go of his arm. He hadn't thought about what this might be like for him. His expression softened. "Okay, J-Mac, but listen, don't be too long. This is very important to me."

A bent smile came to Johnny Mac's face as he said, "I know, Cal, and it is to me too. Just want to get a few wrinkles out. It won't take long, I promise."

Cal gave a short nod. Just before Johnny Mac left, he gave Cal a devilish wink as he turned to leave, saying, "Now to get some of the wrinkles out of things."

Cal stood there staring at the room door as it clicked closed. Something about the way Johnny Mac had said that had him wondering if he was really talking about the wrinkles in his shirt. Shaking his head and shrugging his shoulders, he turned to face the mirror. He began studying his image again taking note of the little things he needed to do, like shaving and trimming his hair off his ears and such. Suddenly, a sharp knock at the door startled him out of his self-assessment.

"Who is it?

"It's me, Jim."

"It's open, come on in."

The two men nodded their greetings. Jim then said, "Hey, where the heck is J-Mac going in such a hurry?"

Cal huffed and said, "He said he was going to a laundormat to get some wrinkles out of his shirt."

"Really? Well, when I saw him, he was heading north, not south toward the laundormat."

Puzzled, Cal simply scratched his head and said, "Amazing how a guy can tell you all about your life but can't tell directions. Whatever, long as he's back soon."

"Why soon?"

Cal strode to the sliding glass door and pointed, standing still for a moment staring out at the waters of the bay. Jim said nothing but eased his way to stand beside Cal, his eyes widened though seeing what Cal was pointing to. "Boy, Cal, when you said she was the prettiest sailboat in all the islands, you weren't kidding were you? She's beautiful. I can see why you want her back so bad."

A big smile spread across Cal's face hearing that. Still holding his gaze on the *Donna Marie*, he said, "Yes, she is, Jim. But I have two Donna Maries to save now."

Jim threw a puzzled look at Cal. "What do you mean two Donna Maries?"

Cal turned away from looking at the *Donna Marie* and spoke as he walked to the center of the room. "Well, we have to get the one that's anchored in the bay out there first. Then I have to save one that's..." He stopped and looked at his watch. "One that should be in Rum Cay."

"What? You have two boats?"

"Nope. Only one boat, *and* only one wife."

It took a few seconds for that to sink in. "You mean your wife is in Rum Cay?"

"According to my son, she is."

Jim immediately understood Cal's concern. "Listen, I can fly there right now and bring her back here."

Cal smiled. Placing a hand on Jim's shoulder and without any elaboration, he calmly said, "Thanks, buddy, but I think I've taken care of things for now."

Jim gave Cal a serious look. "Okay, but we need a backup plan should things not go as planned."

Cal pulled out a chair from the small table in the corner of the room. "Well, there's no time like the present." Cal looked apprehensively at Jim, then out at the *Donna Marie* peacefully anchored in the bay. "If I mess this up, those guys will likely haul ass with me, Johnny Mac, and Juky, then scuttle the *Donna Marie* and all of us with an appropriate amount of bullet holes."

Jim grimly nodded his understanding of the gravity of the situation then said, "Well then, let's make sure that none of that happens."

Cal straightened a notepad in front him. "Have a seat, Jim. Here's how I think this should go down. You and the Water Lily are going to play a key role in helping me convince those bozos that they are outnumbered."

A somber look began to spread across Jim's face. Suddenly, he felt a tense anticipation wash over him like he hadn't in more than forty years—the same feeling he had in the briefing room in England. Taking a seat, he glanced down at the notepad on which Cal had jotted down notes. Again, his thoughts trailed back to 1943 and the briefing rooms he had stood in as a twenty-two-year-old. He remembered how the fates of men's lives were often changed by the flight ops officer with nothing more than a piece of rubber on the end of a pencil. He silently hoped that wasn't going to be the case here. Cal sat down and spun the notepad around to face him. Cal noticed the odd expression on his face.

"Jim, you okay? Got something you wanna say?"

Unaware of his thoughts showing, he hurriedly brushed them aside. "No, no. I was just remembering something from back in the day. I'm okay."

Cal shot him a curious look then said, "Well, we need to focus on today. We can reminisce about days gone by over beers later."

Jim gave a somber smile. "Spoken like a true flight ops officer, Cal. Let's have a look at that mission plan."

Cal stared at him for a second or two. In that moment, he realized then that even after more than forty years, the things Jim had seen and done during the war were still with him; most of it was buried deep, some not so much. All of it, good and bad, shaped who you became for the rest of your life.

Cal took a deep breath and began to run through his plan point by point, carefully noting each of their roles for this to work. One key thing that was not as yet resolved was coming up with a believable uniform for him to wear. Jim listened intently and frankly was impressed with Cal's plan, save for the uniform part.

"Cal, that sounds like it might just work," he began. "And you're right about the timing. We have to be spot-on. But it looks like none of this is going to work without a believable uniform. And the last time I looked, they don't sell those in the gift shops around here."

Cal's head dropped a little as he replied. "Yeah, I know, thought about trying to pull off being an undercover agent. But if these guys are the least bit trigger happy, they might be inclined to shoot a guy in deck shoes and polo shirt coming at them on the bow of the boat."

Jim nodded his agreement. "Yeah, a good uniform would make them at least wait to see what the problem might be."

Both men tossed some more ideas around but found themselves coming back to the uniform idea. Exasperated, Cal abruptly stood and began pacing. "Dammit! I used to be able to figure this stuff out in my sleep."

"Look, Cal, we aren't twenty years old anymore."

Cal swiped his palm down his face and groused, "Yeah, yeah, don't remind me."

Suddenly a loud knock came at the door. Irritated at the interruption, he stormed over and yanked it open. Glaring out expecting to see an adult, he then dropped his eyes down to see the startled face of a young black boy about age twelve holding two paper sacks.

With a heavy island accent, the boy stuttered out, "De...de maun with de beard told me to, to give dis to you."

Cal reached out to take the paper sacks, asking, "A man with a beard? What man with a beard?"

Just then Johnny Mac called out, appearing from around a large bougainvillea that shrouded the brick walkway.

"Uh, that would be this bearded man. Jeez, that kid can run fast. I told him to hurry, but I didn't think he was going to go breaking any sound barriers. Oh, by the way, you owe him twenty bucks."

"Twenty bucks! What the hell for?" Cal fumed, shoving the bags back at the boy.

Johnny Mac talked as he shuffled his way up to Cal. "No, no, take the bags—you're going to want what's inside them. Now pay this fine young man. He is going to be an important man here someday."

Cal grimaced reaching for his wallet. "This better not be some kind of joke, J-Mac. I'm not in the mood." Cal had barely finished counting out the money in the boy's hand when he snapped it closed, then darted away leaving puffs of dust from each racing footfall.

Leaving Johnny Mac standing at the open door, Cal grumbled his way over to the table tossing the paper sacks on the table right in front of Jim.

Johnny Mac excitedly said, "Well, open them up, dammit. Look inside."

Cal grabbed one and started unrolling the crinkled brown paper. "Better not be anything that's going to jump out at me." Johnny Mac bounced up and down on the balls of his feet like a kid watching a parent open a gift.

Peering down into the bag, Cal's eyes widened in disbelief. "Well, I'll be damned. How'd you pull this off, J-Mac?"

Chapter 16

The twin-engine Beechcraft circled the small Rum Cay airport. It was an airport only in the loosest of terms, consisting of a landing strip made of sand and crushed shell. In fact, the pilot took another trip around the entire island. At thirty square miles, that didn't take long to do.

Donna stared apprehensively out the window of the plane at the nearly uninhabited island. Port Nelson was the only settlement on the whole island, and it consisted mostly of single-story wooden structures in varying degrees of decay. The few concrete structures were near the coastline and were obviously built by people with money who used the remote seclusion as a getaway. Judging by the well-built docks and scattering of large boats moored there, fishing was the primary escape.

The pilot leaned toward Donna, saying, "Don't look like much, does it? Do you see your sailboat down there?"

Donna quickly scanned the waters below. The only thing she saw was a couple of deep-sea fishing yachts at what passed for a marina—no sign of the beautiful navy-blue hull and the majestic twin masts of the *Donna Marie*. Nor was there any sign of the Water Lily on land or in the waters around the island.

Donna looked at the pilot shaking her head. "No, I don't see her anywhere. My husband might still be en route here."

"Do you still want me to land and drop you off? Do you have friends here on the island?"

It was easy to see the apprehension in her face as she nodded yes. As if to reassure herself more than the pilot, she said, "Yes, it'll be okay. Cal will be along soon, I'm sure. He's never let me down yet."

The pilot, pressing lips tight, gave a shrug and a nod. Since there was no tower, he spoke into his headset to any planes in the area, "Ahh, this is Navajo one one niner. Alan Parker making a final approach from the southwest to Rum Cay airport."

The pilot's skill at landing on a dirt airstrip was evident as they touched down with hardly a bump. He quickly brought them to a safe but dusty stop right in front of what passed as the Rum Cay terminal, which was nothing more than a tin roof over four wooden posts and a couple of benches. The pilot and the one lone male passenger helped Donna out of the plane with her two small suitcases.

The pilot gave her a concerned look and said as he climbed back in the pilot's seat, "I have to pick up a passenger at the Colonel Hill Airport on Crooked Island south of here. On my way back, I'll make a couple of low passes right over this shed. If you want to leave, be back here and give me a wave and I'll pick you up, okay?"

Donna thanked him with a quick nod telling him she thought she'd be fine. She stepped back from the plane to stand under the roof of the shed. The plane's prop wash blew dust all around her as it taxied to the end of the airstrip. Donna waited there and watched the plane race down the airstrip and lift off into a perfect blue sky. She kept her gaze on the red-and-white plane until it disappeared from view. A cool ocean breeze swept the dust of the plane's departure rapidly away.

Suddenly she became aware of how quiet it was. Turning slowly around from where she stood, she realized she was utterly alone. No people, no trees or bushes, just some scruffy-looking grass growing in patches was all that could be seen. The houses and the few random buildings that she saw from the air couldn't be seen from the airstrip.

In fact, if she hadn't just flown over the nearly treeless island, she would have thought it to be completely deserted. Standing for a moment more, she got her bearings on the direction of the homes and cottages she'd seen from the air. Spying a narrow, worn path through the weeds and prickly pear cactus, she confidently stooped, picked up her bags, and started down the path speaking out as she went. Her voice sounded small in the wind-swept silence. "Cal, sweetheart, I really hope you're on your way."

She hadn't gone far when she spotted a trail of dust being led by what looked to be a Mini Moke. She slowed her pace a bit and kept a keen eye on it as it continued making its way toward her. Nearing her, she could make out the lone occupant and driver who was a black man dressed in khaki shorts and shirt. With the Mini Moke only a hundred yards away now, she stopped on the trail, set her bags down, and waited. A wave of relief came over her as she began to make out the huge smile on the man's face. Twenty yards away he was already talking to her as he made his dusty stop a few feet from where she stood.

His strong island accent poured through a broad smile. "Please, please, lit me 'elp you. We 'ave bean expecting you, ma'am. Actually, 'oping you'd pick our little island to visit."

Perplexed, Donna naturally asked, "You have?"

"Yes, yes. Word has been sent tru de lower islands dat a very important American senator's wife is touring des islands."

Donna had to laugh. She knew right then what that rascal husband of hers had somehow done. He must have called home; Kevin must have told him where she was headed. This was his way of protecting her until he could arrive. Feeling a great deal of relief, she asked, "And who might you be, my friend?"

Realizing he had not introduced himself, the broad smile slipped momentarily away from the big man's face but quickly returned. "Oh, I em so sorry. My name is Thomas Dumont. I em de caretaker of three of the homes just over der on the south shore. It is why I was late arriving. I called Mista Stratton to tell him of yo arrival."

"It is very nice to meet you, Mr. Dumont. Tell me, is Mr. Stratton here on the island?"

"Oh goodness, no, ma'am. Mista Stratton, 'e's a vury busy man dis time of year. But he told me to make sure you are well taken care of. He said to tell you dat he's home is yo-ahs fo as long as you like."

Although she had a strong dislike for lying, she quickly got onboard with the reasons why Cal had created this ruse. She had to marvel at his ability to convince people of things with little to no proof whatsoever. So if she was to be a senator's wife, well then by golly, she would be the best senator's wife Rum Cay ever saw.

"Mr. Dumont, if you would be so kind as to take me to Mr. Stratton's home, I'd like to freshen up before my husband arrives."

"Yes, yes, of course, straight away, ma'am. But please call me Thomas."

"Of course, Thomas it is then."

Starting the little Mini Moke's engine, Thomas spoke up. "Hold on, de road es a little bumpy." Soon Thomas had them bouncing along as Donna politely listened to Thomas tell her all about his island both past and present. She learned that it wasn't always called Rum Cay. He proudly stated that this was the second island that Columbus had visited in 1492 and that it was he who named it Santa Maria de la Concepcion.

Prior to that it was called Mamana by the island's native Lucayan people. Curious, Donna asked how it got its present name. Thomas was of course hoping she would ask. "Ah, dat is where de history gets a bit fuzzy. You see, some say et was from a shipwreck dat happened on de reefs and its cargo of rum that washed ashore. But others say dat it was de Spanish explorers who returned here and found a lone keg of rum washed up on shore. Who really knows, but 'owever et got de name, et has stuck."

"Well, I like the name. It sounds dangerous and exotic, like you're in a Humphrey Bogart movie."

Thomas laughed out loud. "You are right. I 'ave never thought of it like dat. Our little island might be exotic, but dangerous, no. Unless you count de reefs. Now dose can be vury dangerous. Many a good ship has been lost on de islands reefs."

Hearing that, Donna immediately thought of Cal. He was a good sailor, but she wasn't sure how skilled he was at sailing into a place like Rum Cay. After all, Thomas did say that many a good ship had been lost trying to sail into the island. Now she was worried again. But what could she do? she thought. There had to be a way to find out what was going on. Then just as Thomas brought them to a stop in front of a beautiful white two-story home, it came to her.

Turning to Thomas, she asked, "Thomas, how did you get word of my coming here? Do you have phones on the island?"

"Oh goodness, no. We 'ave no phones. Our only communication is by marine radio."

"So where did word of my touring the islands originate from? Do you know?"

Perplexed a bit at her questioning, Thomas worried he might be doing something wrong because the message he had received emphasized a certain degree of secrecy be maintained for security reasons.

"Yes, I do know. But de message insisted dat your exact location not be revealed on de radio for security reasons. Des islands can be vury dangerous and not from just de reefs. Der is worry of kidnapping."

"I understand. However, I need to know from where the message was sent so that I can contact my husband's staff to let them know I have arrived safely. Otherwise, I could trigger some kind of international incident. You understand of course, don't you?"

Thomas furrowed his brow in consideration of what Donna had said, then burst out laughing. "But of course. I should have thought of dat myself. If deh don't know where you are, den deh worry more. You can freshen up first. Or we can go to de communication office just over der," he said, pointing to a small flat-roofed concrete building a couple hundred yards away.

Donna glanced up at the home. She was tired and hungry and desperately wanted just to go in the house. But her need to know where her husband might be far outweighed her present longings.

Donna confidently pointed toward the small battered-looking structure. "No, I need to check in first. It's been a while since they have heard from me."

"Vury well den. I think dat best to do as well, Mrs...." Thomas stopped talking when he realized he didn't know her name. Please fo give me, but I do not know yo name, ma'am."

Donna was digging in her purse for a pen and paper and stopped upon hearing his question. She was thrown back a bit as to what to say. Should she make up a name? Did Cal identify which senator's wife she was supposed to be? Dammit, Cal, she thought. This why I don't like lying.

So she went with what she was comfortable with, the truth…well, partly anyway. "Oh, I'm sorry, Thomas. It was very rude of me not to introduce myself. My name is Donna Arnold. My husband is Senator Arnold."

She inwardly prayed that he wouldn't ask from which state. She figured with a name as common as Arnold, there was bound to be someone named Arnold who either served now or in the past…hopefully not too far in the past.

Fortunately, Thomas smiled and nodded then started them toward the dubiously named communication office. Reaching to hold on, Donna exhaled a sigh of relief. She only had a minute or two to figure out what she was going to do next. Staring out at the startlingly beautiful blue water, she thought about Cal and his quick mind. *How in the heck does he do this with such ease?* It was then that she decided that since being truthful was far more comfortable for her, that's exactly how she was going to be…at least as much the situation might allow.

Soon Thomas brought the Mini Moke to a smooth stop right in front of the faded red door to the communication office. There were no windows in the eight-by eight-foot concrete structure. Only two louvered openings were in the four solid concrete walls—walls that she was sure hadn't been painted since it was built.

But the bleached condition of the exposed concrete from a distance blended well with the little bit of white paint that still clung to its walls. Thomas quickly stepped out of the open-sided Moke and lifted the thick, wooden stockade latch from across the door. The ancient wrought-iron hinges groaned in protest as he shoved open the heavy wood door. Looking back at Donna, he motioned for her to stay put. Donna lost sight of him for a moment when he stepped inside.

Bending and leaning around trying to see what he might be doing, she scooted across the Mini Moke's seat to get closer to the open door. Suddenly he popped back out startling her, and she let go a little yelp. "Oh, I em so sorry. I did not mean to scare you, Mrs. Arnold. But I wanted to check and make sure der were no unwanted guest in here before you came in."

"You mean people?"

Laughing, he replied, "Well, dat happens sometimes. But mostly little six- and eight-legged visitors get under de door."

"Six and eight legs—"

"Yes, de spiders come in for de bugs, and de small crabs come in for de spiders."

Thomas laughed seeing Donna shudder. "Sounds like you have quite the pest control service."

"I make it sound worse den it is. Please come in and 'ave a seat. I need to turn on de radio and transmitter so deh can warm up before we can call Rokers Point."

Donna shot him a confused look. "Rokers Point?"

"Yes, yes, dat es where de message originated from. Why? Is der a problem?"

Donna shook her head no but thought they must have diverted to Rokers Point. But why? What could have happened? Maybe they spotted the *Donna Marie* from the air, she thought. Cal should have been here well ahead of her—so should the *Donna Marie*. Now to find out that he had sent a message from a place called Rokers Point.

"Ah, Thomas, where exactly is Rokers Point from here?" she questioned.

Thomas answered as he worked to get the antiquated marine radio up and running, the secret of which entailed a series of sharp raps to the radio's sides. Without looking, he pointed in the general direction while he continued smacking the sides of the radio. "Oh, it es dat a way about a hundred and thirty kilometers."

Donna began calculating the flying time in her head when suddenly Thomas shouted out as small red indicator light blinked on. "Yes, der she goes. Now we can call Rokers Point station." She had no sooner decided to have Thomas drive her back to the airstrip so she could flag down the pilot that had dropped her off when she heard the sound of the twin-engine plane flash by overhead.

Leaping to her feet, she shot outside in time to see the glint of the red-and-white Beechcraft bank out over the ocean to make another pass over the wooden shed. She ran out into a clearing in front of the communication shack waving her arms frantically and instinctively yelling. Her shouting, jumping, and waving ceased as she watched the pilot come back over the wooden shed at ninety degrees to his first pass. It was the logical thing for him to do. But it meant that he would not be passing over her location again. And being almost a half mile away, there was no way he could see her.

Donna's shoulders slumped, seeing the plane pull up sharply and bank back in a westerly direction; he was heading back to Marathon and home. Right then she felt she had made yet another big mistake.

Watching her from behind, it was easy for Thomas to see that she had changed her mind about wanting to stay on their little island. He too felt a little sad but for a much different reason. Neither he nor the island had ever had such a special visitor before, and likely never would again. He worried too that his boss, Mr. Stratton, would think that he had not made her feel welcome.

Donna turned slowly around to see Thomas. His seemingly permanent smile no longer graced his face. Just then radio squelched on. "This is Rokers Point station, over."

"What should I say, ma'am?" Thomas's tone was subdued. His smiling bright eyes had diminished.

Thomas's look tore her heart. She then took a quick look to her left and right at her surroundings then smiled brightly at Thomas, saying, "You tell them that the senator's wife has arrived safely and will be spending the night in anticipation of her husband's arrival."

In a flash, Thomas's whole demeanor changed. An exuberant smile spread rapidly across his face as he quickly replied, "Yes, ma'am."

Chapter 17

Cal stood in front of the dresser mirror. "Yes, yes, this will do just fine. So that boy's brother is with Interpol."

"Yes, he is," Johnny Mac said, still smiling broadly.

"Isn't he going to miss his uniform?"

"Well, not for at least twenty-four hours anyway."

"Only one day!" Cal barked. "That means we are going to have to pull off getting the *Donna Marie* either this afternoon or first thing in the morning."

Jim quickly added, "This afternoon? We haven't even come up with a contingency plan yet, Cal. If those guys don't buy what we're selling, then it's going to get ugly quick. Don't forget they have all the guns, and all we have right now is a fake Interpol officer."

"Uh, uh, uh. Not so quick, gentlemen," Johnny Mac said, wagging a finger at them. "Cal, you got so excited about the uniform you didn't even open the other bag."

Cal glanced over at the crinkled up brown paper sack, then at Johnny Mac. "You got a gun?"

Johnny Mac grabbed the bag from the table. Reaching in, he quickly produced not one but two guns. He began happily waving them around. "See? We have two guns. Watch out, bad guys, the cavalry is coming."

Both Cal and Jim recoiled, shouting at him, "Hey! Watch out. Those things could be loaded, dammit!"

Johnny Mac, looking puzzled at them, said, "Well, of course they're loaded. What good is a gun with no bullets?"

Jim emphatically added, "If you don't stop waving those damn things around like that, it will be a coroner coming, not the cavalry."

Johnny Mac's face contorted looking up at the guns he held over his head. "Oh. Yeah." Sheepishly, he placed the guns on the table. "Sorry. Guess I got carried away."

Cal and Jim threw looks of anxious relief at each other. Cal then went back to Jim's comment about a backup plan. "J-Mac, take a seat. We need to come up with a plan B if our plan A fails for whatever reason—one that I hope won't involve firing one of those guns." Cal then looked at Johnny Mac. "Wait, where in the hell did you get these guns?"

Johnny Mac started to reply, but Cal waved his hand at him. "Never mind, I don't think I want to know right now." Johnny Mac shrugged, plopping down in a chair and propping his elbows on the table. He rested his head on the knuckles of his hands staring at Cal.

Cal looked at Johnny Mac and wondered for a second if he was taking any of this seriously. "All right, listen up. First, I think we hit them about an hour after sunrise before too many people are moving around on the waters around here. Jim, what did you find for boat rentals? Anything that can pass for a boat used by Interpol?"

"Not from the local marina. I did talk to a guy that has a nice twenty-six-foot pilot houseboat. He does private tours and dive trips with it."

"That sounds perfect. But what do we do about him? I doubt he's going to want to get involved in this."

Jim pressed his lips and rubbed his chin in consideration of that fact.

Cal stood up and began to pace, combing his fingers through his hair. He spoke out loud. "Dammit, there's got to be something we can tell him," Cal said in frustration.

"What if we just say we are doing some kind of inspection...you know, for drugs or something like that?" Jim hopefully suggested.

Cal turned and looked at Jim while considering of his suggestion, then dejectedly said, "Nah, I don't think he would buy Interpol hiring his boat for that. They wouldn't risk a private citizen that way."

Jim nodded agreement, and Cal went back to pacing.

The sound of a steel-drum band drifted through the open patio door. No one spoke for a long minute. Johnny Mac looked at both men. Then as if he were reluctant to break Cal and Jim's quiet contemplation, he said, "Why don't we tell him we are making a training video. You know, like for new cops to watch."

Cal spun around to look at Johnny Mac. Jim likewise looked across the table at him.

A huge smile exploded on Cal's face. "Johnny Mac, you crazy coot! That's it. I think we can sell that. Somebody on this island has to have one of those new video cameras."

Jim reached over and patted Johnny Mac on the back. "Way to go, old man. But wait, do either of you know how to use one of those things? They look pretty complicated."

Their smiles and jocularity ceased as they considered that possibility. Video cameras had only been on the market for a few years. Though Cal had seen some of the tourists using them, he had never even held one.

Suddenly Cal snapped his fingers. "Guys, we are overthinking this."

"How so?" Jim asked.

"Yeah, how so?" Johnny Mac parroted.

Cal gracefully spread his arms out in front of him like Vanna White presenting the next puzzle. "Look, everything we are doing is fake, right? So we'll just fake like we are filming a training video."

Jim and Johnny Mac nodded in agreement. Then Johnny Mac abruptly spoke up. "Wait, wait. Who's going to be the cameraman? If I'm the eccentric owner of the *Donna Marie* and you're the fuzz, we need a cameraman."

Cal spun on his heels slapping his thigh in frustration. "Dammit. It wasn't this hard before. Man, I used to know people."

"What the hell are you talking about, Cal?"

Cal threw Jim a stiff glance. But Johnny Mac answered, "Cal here was like that Radar O'Reilly on the TV show."

Jim looked at Cal. "I thought you were a Navy man, Cal?"

Frustrated with this diversion, Cal was short and to the point. "I was. I was a purser on an aircraft carrier during the war. You learn how to get stuff in wartime, ya know. Horse trad'n', BS-in' people."

"Yeah, Cal here could sell an admiral his own epaulets. Right, Cal?"

Cal shot a whatever look at Johnny Mac. "Look, forget all that. Right now, we need to figure out who can be a cameraman. Or we'll have to figure out another angle to use on the boat captain."

Jim and Johnny Mac threw out a couple of ideas that immediately fell flat.

Cal turned to face the big glass doors. In the distance, he could see the *Donna Marie* serenely anchored in the bay. Seeing her like that and knowing someone else was aboard her made him fume. Pointing out at the bay, he said, "Look, guys, I don't care what we have to do, but I want my damn boat back. Think, dammit. We are running out of time. We have no idea how much longer they are going to keep sitting there."

Jim was about to say something when a knock came at the door. Frustrated at the interruption, Cal stomped to the door, snatching it open. The motel employee's eyes widened seeing Cal suddenly there. Not quite sure of what he had interrupted, he remained frozen for a second or two.

Cal didn't wait and barked, "What? What is it, man?"

In typical islander fashion, the man quickly gathered his wits. Mustering a tentative big, toothy smile, he held out a folded piece of paper, cautiously saying, "You asked to be notified of their arrival on Rum Cay."

Instantly Cal's whole demeanor changed. Nodding, Cal took the note and read it while the man waited. Seeing the big smile come to Cal's face, he too relaxed, pleased that he had apparently brought good news.

Cal read the note a couple of times over before he noticed the man still standing in front of him smiling broadly. He was about to ask why he was still there when Johnny Mac blurted out, "Tip the man, Cal, will ya? He hasn't got all day ya know."

Cal scrunched his face a little while reaching for his wallet. Flipping it open, he dug in it for a second or two looking for some smaller bills. Shrugging, he said, "Oh, what the heck. Thanks, man," and handed the man a twenty.

Holding the twenty out in front of his face, he exuberantly thanked Cal. "Oh, t'ank you, sir! Please let me know ef yo-ah need anything else."

"Yeah, ah, I'll, uh, I'll keep that in mind," Cal said while closing the door. The man repeated his final words again as Cal clicked the door closed.

Cal took a couple of steps back toward the table rubbing his chin in thought, then abruptly froze in his tracks. Snapping his fingers, he blurted, "That's it!" Spinning, he shot for the door. Yanking the door open, Cal bolted from the room as the door swung back hitting the wall. Looking left and right, he caught sight of the man rounding the curve in the walkway, disappearing behind a bougainvillea. Calling out to him, Cal trotted quickly to catch up as he called out to him.

Back in the room, Jim and Johnny Mac just looked at each other. Jim asked out loud, "Jeez, wonder what was in that note?"

Johnny Mac smirked. "Maybe Cal's just wanting change for that twenty he gave him."

Both men were still snickering when Cal appeared at the door with his arm around the smiling motel employee. "Gentleman, meet our new cameraman, Edmund."

Chapter 18

It didn't take long for his captors to see that where they were anchored was not Pirates Well. This caused them a great deal of angst, to say the least. Because of that, Juky now found himself lying sideways on the narrow couch, hands tied and duct tape over his mouth. All he could do at the moment was listen to the three men argue about what to do next. The two dull-witted minions wanted to tie some weights to his ankles and toss him overboard. However, the leader quickly put that to rest…at least for now.

Juky thought as he lay there motionless that the leader of the group was so, not because he was necessarily smarter than the other two, but rather, it was his size and attitude that did most of the work for him when it came to convincing people to listen.

While his assessment of his captors might be spot-on, his being tied up was preventing any attempt at escape. One thing was certain. His time was running out. The one good thing was they still had not discovered the magnet he had placed underneath the ship's compass. So as far as they were concerned, they were still unable to sail to their original destination, which was the immediate topic at the moment.

"What do we do now, Michael?" one of the accomplices barked. It was the first time Juky had heard one of them called by name. This brought a quick and angry retort.

"Dammit, you idiot! Didn't I say *not* to use our names around this bloke?"

"Oh, ta hell with that. 'E ain't gonna live to repeat any of what 'e' ears us say."

"Look, just shut yer trap, mate. And let me think, all right?"

The one named Michael looked over at Juky. His expression clearly showed his extreme annoyance that Juky had misdirected them here to Rokers Point. However, in the back of his mind, he had a suspicion they just might still have a use for him.

Michael paced in a tight circle, rubbing his hands repeatedly up his forehead and back over his head, combing back his sandy-blond hair. Turning back to face them all, he took a deep breath and spoke with confidence. "Look, 'ears what we're gonna do. I'm tak'n' the dingy and go'n' ashore and make a call to our contact. I'll tell 'em we've had some boat trouble and we'll be a bit later git'n' ta Pirates Well. That should buy us a bit a time. While on shore, I'll find some-one who can come 'ave a look-see at that frigg'n' compass. Then we won't need 'em anymore," he said, with a nod toward Juky. "Now come topside 'n' 'elp me with git'n' the dingy in the water."

"What about 'em?" one of the cronies asked.

Michael let out a haughty snort. "Don't worry about 'em. Trussed-up like a Christmas pig, 'e won't be going anywhere. Now come on. We're wast'n' time 'ere."

All three began laughing. One of the cronies oinked as he walked by, kicking the edge of the couch right by Juky's head as if to punctuate his predicament.

Soon Juky could hear the sound of the boat davit's electric motor lowering the dingy in the water. He then heard the small outboard motor fire up and fade into the distance. Were it not for his present situation, the sounds of gulls overhead and the water lapping against the boat's hull could have lulled him quickly to sleep.

However, sleep was the last thing on his mind. His predicament was dire. He needed to find a way to cut the ropes he was bound with. It was difficult for him to scan the cabin lying on his side, so he rolled onto his stomach and let his legs drop off the side of the couch. He then brought his knees up tight to the side of the couch and used his lower body to leverage himself up to a kneeling position. Then he thrust his upper body up while bringing his legs underneath in a rapid squatting position and quickly stood up, staggering a bit as he did so.

Not knowing when the either of his two captors were coming back down, he hurried to find something to perhaps saw the ropes against to free his hands, but nothing caught his eye right away. He briefly considered just trying a movie stunt and try to make a run for it and jump overboard and hope he could pull off some Houdini-like trick to get out of the ropes before he drowned. But since this wasn't a movie and he wasn't even close to being Houdini, he was back to trying to cut the ropes. Problem was he was surrounded by a lot of highly polished mahogany and brass. And while he knew the galley had knives, he doubted he had the dexterity to use a knife with just his fingertips.

However, with nothing else around, he headed to the galley to retrieve a knife—hopefully a serrated one. Before opening the drawer, he stood stock still and listened. He needed to see if he could get a fix on just where his captors were at the moment. Standing perfectly still, he strained to listen, trying to filter out all other sounds. It took a moment or two, but soon he picked out the murmur of conversation. It sounded as though they were up near the bow. He had to be sure, so he made his way to the steps leading up to the deck.

Poking his head slowly above the hatchway, he got a fix on the two of them as they sat smoking and muttering complaints about their predicament. He knew he didn't have much time to get out of the ropes and free himself. With his hands being tied, trying to manipulate the cabinet doors and drawer latches used on boats was not so easy, and it took precious time. He struggled to remain calm, but his frustrations were building with his continued empty results.

Pulling open the final drawer and last hope of cutting the ropes, the thought of just throwing himself overboard drifted through his mind again. The hopeless thought of how that likely would turn out with him being shot or drowning kept him from seeing it at first. But then his eyes focused on a most beautiful thing—an electric carving knife!

Juky spoke low to himself. "Cal, I can't imagine why you'd 'ave an electric carving knife on a sailboat. But right now, I don't care."

Working the knife out of the drawer was no easy task. He flipped it up on the counter. Turning around, he stared at it for a moment not quite sure how he was going to manipulate it to cut the ropes on hands that were swelling by the minute.

He quickly scanned the galley, needing some way to the steady the knife while he held his wrist over the moving blades. "Think, man," he whispered, his frustration creeping back on him. He then had an idea.

Finally he hit upon wedging the knife between a gap by the refrigerator and the cabinet countertop. After some struggle with trying to work with his hands tied, he succeeded in getting it wedged in tight enough, he hoped, to cut the ropes.

Smiling at what he had accomplished, he had just one thing left to do, plug it in. His hopes faded when he saw the outlet was too far away. Besides, he thought, the two cronies would surely hear it running.

So he did the only thing he could do and positioned his wrists over the upturned blade and began sawing his wrist back and forth. He just needed one cut rope and he was out. It was then that he noticed that the cronies had stopped talking. Worse, he heard footsteps on the deck above coming his way. Frantically, he sawed even faster as the footsteps drew nearer. Through gritted teeth, Juky quietly begged, "Come on, cut. Come on."

Chapter 19

Donna strolled through the rather large, well-appointed home. Thomas had dropped her off an hour ago with a promise to be back to cook a wonderful meal for her, although she assured him it wasn't necessary. However, he insisted and she relented. Actually, she was glad he was returning. Her footsteps echoed against the white plaster walls which only served to remind her that she was all alone. It would be nice to have someone to talk to over dinner.

It was quite apparent from the artwork and decorating appointments throughout the home that whoever owned this was very well-off. She resolved to find out who he was so as to be sure and extend a proper thank-you for his generosity. In the meantime, after having showered and changed clothes, she sat on the balcony just off the bedroom. The view of the ocean was stunning. She wondered what it must be like to have this kind of wealth. She thought again of the offer the northeast investors had made to buy the Salty Anchor.

It was a lot of money—well into seven figures; however, she found she still didn't want to sell. Doing so though would mean that she and Cal could retire and just enjoy life, maybe do some traveling. She then laughed to herself, saying out loud, "Yeah, travel, right? Trying to get that old coot to travel is like trying to get a tick out of a hound's ear."

Just then over the sounds of the waves crashing on the beach in the distance, she heard Thomas's voice calling out to her from the first floor. She then heard other voices from below as well—a woman's voice, maybe two, she thought. It was hard to tell with the sounds of the ocean and the echo. Rising up from the plush comfort of the chaise lounge, a place where she could easily see herself sleeping the whole night through, she headed downstairs to greet the laughing and excited voices, the sound of which filled the air like crystal glass wind chimes.

Exiting the bedroom door, she looked down, and to her complete surprise, there stood not only Thomas, smiling broadly as usual, but he was joined by a woman and three children all huddled around him, each one bursting with gleeful exuberance. A broad smile came to her face realizing he had brought his family too. Now her own joy burst forth.

"Mrs. Arnold, I 'ope you do not mind mah family coming to meet you and to per'aps have dinner with you so you do not eat alone."

Donna practically trotted down the last few steps going immediately to whom she presumed to be his wife, which he quickly confirmed. "'Dis es my wife Leeanna."

Donna took her small outstretched hand and gave her a short shake but then leaned in to give her a hug and kiss as well. "And who might these beautiful little ones be, Thomas?" she enthusiastically asked.

Donna saw Thomas's chest swell with pride as he introduced each child. "Dis es my oldest daughter, Clarisse. She is twelve. Aund my son Robert, who es nine, and finally the little one is Alvita. She is three."

Donna beamed at Thomas and Leeanna, saying, "What a beautiful family you both have."

Both Leeanna and Thomas gushed with pride. "T'ank you, Mrs. Arnold, we are vury proud of dem as well." He looked down at the two oldest ones, telling them, "Robert, go and bring in de food so that we can prepare a meal. Et es getting late."

Without a word, the children quickly departed. Leeanna, who was still quite shy, turned to look up at her much taller husband. "I must go to de kitchin to start de water boiling for de lobsters Thomas."

"Yes, yes of course. Be sure to 'ave Clarisse help you," Thomas said.

Leeanna looked quickly to Donna. "Et was vury nice to meet you, ma'am."

Donna nodded and smiled. "Please, please both of you please call me Donna. I don't like all this stiff formality."

Both nodded. Then Leeanna said before leaving, "Thomas, keep an eye on de little one in dis 'ouse. I don't want 'er to break something."

Before Thomas could reply, Donna quickly spoke. "Leeanna, don't you worry about this sweet baby—I can take care of her just fine. I have three of my own, plus I have a grandbaby on the way now."

Leeanna stopped, her surprised look was genuine as she said, "Why, Mrs. Arnold, I mean Donna, you look too young and beautiful to 'ave a grandchild."

"Well, I don't know about that. I'm not a grandma yet, just found out about it right before coming here. I have a few months yet to age and ugly up before the big event."

Leeanna put her fingers to her mouth trying to hold back a giggle before disappearing through the kitchen door.

Thomas had picked up Alvita. "'Ave you 'ad a chance to look around the home?"

"No, not really. I was really ready for a shower when I came in. Then I saw the view from the balcony and couldn't resist just sitting and watching the waves crash against the rocks in the distance."

"Ah, yes, I must admit I 'ave done dat myself a time or two. It is a great spot to sit and dream, I think."

Donna saw a faraway look in his eyes when he said that. Whether it was woman's intuition or the way he said it, she knew there was more hiding in those words than was being said. Looking past him, she saw a rather large wine cabinet.

"Thomas, do you think the owner would mind if we pulled the cork on one of those bottles of wine?" she asked, pointing past him.

Thomas quickly glanced back over his shoulder then back at Donna. "Oh goodness no, of course you can. He said to make yourself comfortable aund to take care of yo-ah needs. What would you prefer?"

"Since we're having seafood, then let's start with a white, shall we?"

"Of course. Any preference?"

"No, I'll let you choose one."

Thomas put Alvita down, who quickly protested this action. To which he spoke lovingly but firmly for her to sit down and be quiet. She complied in typical three-year-old fashion by crossing her arms and plopping down on her bottom.

Thomas just laughed. "She takes after 'er mother when et comes to being told what to do."

"Well, she's not doing anything I haven't seen from one that age before. She needs to hold onto that feistiness. It can serve her well when she is older."

Thomas turned to face Donna with two glasses of wine. As he walked past his daughter still sitting in the same spot, she called up to him, holding her arms up.

Thomas smiled down at her. "Just wait, baby, let me give the lady her wine, okay?" Thomas handed Donna the glass then turned and motioned to Alvita to come to him. She shot to her feet and ran the short distance into his outstretched arms.

Thomas steadied himself trying to keep from spilling any of the wine he held. "Easy, little one, or you will knock yo-ah father ov-ah."

"Oh, what's a little spilt wine, Thomas?" Donna said with a chuckle.

Thomas stood after scooping Alvita into his big arms bringing her close for a kiss on the cheek. "Ordinarily I would agree with you, Miss Donna. However, spilling this glass of wine would be expensive indeed."

Donna gave a wide-eyed look at Thomas then held her glass out in front of her. Tentatively she asked, "Just *how* expensive?"

"Well, in Freeport, a glass of this goes for about thirty dollars U.S. But I'm sure you being a senator's wife, you are used to such wines."

Donna pressed her lips hard together, thinking. There's that damn lie again. She was becoming more uncomfortable with this charade. "Well, one would think so. But not in my case, I'm afraid."

Thomas laughed. "Come now, Miss Donna. I read the papers from the States. Yo-ah politicians live quite well."

Growing more uncomfortable with the direction the conversation was going, she diverted it back to the view from the balcony and the look in Thomas's eyes.

"Yes, well, be that as it may, Thomas, a moment ago you mentioned sitting on the upstairs balcony. I noticed a faraway look in those eyes of yours. What sort of dreams do those crashing waves conjure up?"

"Oh, Miss Donna, I'm sure de dreams of a man such as me would be of no interest to you."

"Well now, I have made a living out of listening to people's dreams. So let's have a seat and you can tell me yours."

Not quite sure what she meant by that, he motioned for her to have a seat on the sofa. Happy that she had redirected the conversation from herself, she reiterated her question as Thomas sat down. Donna smiled as Alvita naturally tucked in close to her father.

"Miss Donna, I'm not sure how to answer yo-ah question really. Deh are de same I suppose many men such as me have. You always want better for yo-ah family. Deh are de dreams of living in such a place as this," he said, gesturing with his glass at their surroundings.

Donna gave a brief look around the room. "I get the feeling the owner doesn't come here often."

"Yes, that is true, about three or four times a year. However, he lets friends or clients stay here. So it keeps me busy."

"What exactly does he do?"

"Well, it is hard to pinpoint just one thing. I understand he has his hands in many things. For instance, many of de lawns in the de states, de grass is cut by mowers dat have his motors on them."

Donna's eyes widened. "Really? He's the Stratton of Briggs and Stratton?"

Thomas smiled broadly. "Yes, dat es correct. He es de third generation. Fredrick is a vury nice man."

"That explains the wine then." Taking another sip, Donna felt a little less guilty for drinking such an expensive wine.

Thomas then said, "Now, Miss Donna, it is yo-ah turn to tell me what et es you could be dreaming about on that balcony."

Donna looked wistfully into the glass of wine she embraced with both hands. "Well, for me I wasn't daydreaming—not at first anyway. No, I was ruminating on the problems of life and what to do about them."

"Miss Donna, I hope des problems are not too serious for you."

Looking up from her glass, a half smile pressed into her cheek. "They certainly could turn out to be. And worse yet, it is one I helped cause."

Refreshing her glass, he asked, "Can you tell me? Sometimes it is good to tell a friend yo-ah troubles."

Donna took a long sip of wine then looked right at Thomas, his face straight with concern. She did not like lying, especially to such trusting and kind people. Besides, she thought, maybe there was something Thomas could do to help the situation.

Taking another sip, she moved forward on the sofa and said, "Thomas, that balcony *is* a great place to sit and dream. But it is also a great place to confess your sins."

Perplexed, Thomas queried, "Miss Donna, de Lord knows we all sin. Dis es true. But I can't imagine yo-ahs to be so great as to make you so sad now."

Donna took a deep breath, then before she could think about it more, she blurted out, "For starters, I'm not who you think I am, Thomas."

She saw Thomas stiffen; the countenance of his face went blank. When he spoke, his voice firm yet tinged with disappointment. "So yo-ah not Mrs. Donna Arnold, de senator's wife?"

"Thomas, that is half right. Look, please let me explain. Then hopefully you can forgive me."

Thomas simply nodded.

Donna was petrified, worried now that she was about to be kicked out of this house and maybe off the whole island. *Too late to turn back now*, she thought.

With no idea how this was going to end up, she slugged down the last of the wine, took a deep breath, and plunged ahead. "First, let me say that I *am* Mrs. Donna Arnold, but I am not a senator's wife."

"Miss Donna, how could you lie to me aund my family like dis? It hurts me in my heart. You seemed so sweet and genuine."

"Please, Thomas, let me explain. Maybe once you hear what I have to say, you will understand."

"I hope so, Miss Donna. Mr. Stratton will be most upset dat you are here under a false pretense. He is a vury generous man, but he is also strict."

Donna acknowledged this fact. Right then she was wishing she had Cal's glib tongue, then remembered it was his glib tongue that helped put her in this position. Nevertheless, she had to tell him everything right from the beginning. Hopefully a full disclosure would at least keep a roof over her head for one night.

The sumptuous aromas coming from the kitchen and her words melded together filling the entire room and ascended into the heavy wooden rafters, high overhead. Words never meant so much to her. Words could keep her here. Or they could spoil everything.

There was an odd juxtaposition of culinary pleasure and the courtroom-like echo of Donna's testimony. The cooking would no doubt be judged quite favorably. Her story too would be judged— what the verdict would be, she had no idea.

Taking a deep breath, she plunged ahead. At the conclusion of her story, the room fell silent. Donna sat quietly trying to read Thomas's face but found she couldn't. Then one of Cal's salty sayings came unexpectedly to mind: "Time and hookers will tell," he would often say. She never really understood it.

Though no hookers were involved, time was. Donna watched as Thomas took a deep breath to speak. Her time, she thought, may have just run out.

Chapter 20

Juky had barely made it back to the couch after tossing the rope and knife behind the refrigerator. Taking the same position on the couch as before, Juky caught his captors completely off guard when he sprung up from the couch. The scuffle was brief but intense. Juky managed to snatch a gun from the tall lanky one, then at gunpoint force them into a small storage area at the bow.

With them now safely locked away, he watched and waited for their ring leader Michael to return. He had been gone a long while now. The sun crept ever lower to the horizon. Lights along the shore began to twinkle on, shimmering like diamonds on the water, while another light show played out in a distant thunderstorm. The mesmerizing effect of the thunderstorm had Juky thinking of the many times as a boy he would sit on the shore watching the nightly fireworks of such thunderstorms in the summertime.

Glancing at the clock over the sink in the galley—6:00 p.m.— he couldn't imagine why Michael had not returned yet. *Something must be up,* he thought. There was no way he would leave these two criminals masterminds alone for this long. Briefly he considered weighing anchor and sailing the *Donna Marie* right into the marina but thought better of it. After all, it was he who had two people tied up below deck. And it was he that couldn't establish why he would be on a boat that he didn't own. Further, it would get the local authorities involved, which was exactly what the Arnolds didn't want. He finally decided to sit out of sight near the dingy davits. This way he could get some much-needed sleep and yet still hear Michael's approach.

Juky kept the gun he had taken and wedged it in his waist-band. With the davits directly behind the ship's helm, he chose to lie down on the seat behind the ship's wheel. Exhaling a tired, ragged breath, he let his eyes drift closed, welcoming the sleep he needed. How much he would get he didn't know; what he was going to do when Michael returned, he didn't know either. But a little sleep and a clearer mind could only help. The sound of distant thunder tumbled and rolled across a gently rising and falling sea. And like a child in a cradle, the *Donna Marie* and the sea rocked him gently to sleep.

*****

Cal sat alone on the patio outside of the motel room. They had gone over in great detail what they were going to do. Johnny Mac was already asleep, and Jim had gone to his room to presumably do the same. Cal was anything but sleepy at the moment. A full moon had just crested a cloudless horizon. And as if to drive home the point of why he was here, the moonlight cast a perfect silhouette of the *Donna Maria* sitting a quarter mile off shore.

It was stunningly beautiful, and yet torturous at the same time. Wistfully he spoke, "I'm coming for you, *Donna Marie.*"

The second he heard his own words, the last image of his wife sleeping in bed when he left came sharply to mind. He remembered so badly wanting to kiss her before he left but was afraid to wake her. He wished now he had.

He hoped his ploy to help keep her safe was having the effect he intended. Further, he hoped his play-by-the rules wife could, just once, go along with it for her sake and his. It was killing him not knowing exactly where she was or if she was safe. His need to know she was safe was deeply rooted in his past. At fourteen years of age, being the oldest of four kids, he became the stand-in man of the house. His father had left for work one morning and was never seen again.

His car was found days later deep in the woods outside of town, the keys still in it and the driver's door open. The police suspected foul play. But with no sign of a struggle, it seemed like he had just vanished off the earth.

After that life-changing event, Cal became acutely aware of making sure his mother and his two sisters and baby brother were safe. On many occasions over the next months, he went to the exact spot where his father had vanished. The first few times were to try and find something the police had missed and perhaps solve the agonizing mystery.

Then, as time dragged on, he would simply go try to do what his mother did every day for the remainder of her life—pray for the safe return of the only man she had or ever would love. It was a very difficult time in his young life, and it had a profound effect on him. While his mother never gave up praying, Cal did. Not that he stopped believing entirely, he just stopped believing so much.

His youth and the self-imposed weight of looking after the family caused him to engage in some less than honorable ways to try and earn money to help support the family—nothing like stealing, though. He did, however, get quite good at poker and playing billiards, spending many hours doing both. His mother was suspicious of how at his young age he could earn some of the large sums of money he would give her. He became very good at making up very plausible stories to satisfy her curiosity. He was thankful when the questions became less frequent.

He was eighteen when Japan bombed Pearl Harbor. He joined the Navy that week, reasoning that he could send his pay home to help the family and save the world at the same time. His financial contributions did help the family, and he felt good about that. However, his contribution to the war effort fell short in his eyes.

Being a purser on a ship didn't do much to satisfy his young male bravado about going after the bad guys like being on a battleship, but he was on aircraft carrier. For him it still held the same helpless feeling he had about his father's disappearance. In letters between him and his mother, she would always tell him that what he was doing was just as important as being in battle. But in his young mind, the unseen Japanese enemy was no different than the unseen reason for why his father was gone.

All of that was a long time ago, and while time and life had veneered over that period of his life, it was moments like these that brought them back into clear focus. He held his gaze for a long moment at the serene image of the *Donna Marie*.

"Tomorrow we go and get your namesake." Turning around, he glanced at the bed in the room then at the thick-cushioned chaise lounge that faced the bay. He opted for the latter so the *Donna Marie* would be the last thing he saw when sleep at last overtook him.

The music of a steel-drum band in the distance was carried on a gentle salt-laced breeze that floated over Cal settling on him like a woman's gentle caress. This elixir of sound, smell, and touch soothed his mind and body. His last attempt to hold his eyes open failed. His sleep was deep and dream-filled. He found himself in a most pleasant dream of him and Donna swimming in some tropical flower-laden lagoon with the *Donna Marie* anchored majestically in the background. The two of them swam and laughed like school kids. But children they were not, for he could just make out her naked, womanly body in the clear water. It felt like heaven on earth.

Suddenly, indecipherable screaming and yelling ripped its way into the peaceful serenity of his dream. His mind and eyes heavy with sleep, he struggled to keep them open, while trying to make sense of what was being yelled at him. Abruptly a blurry face rimmed by bright sunlight flashed in front of his tortured his eyes. A hand gripped his arm shaking him violently.

"Cal, wake up, dammit! We're late! C'mon, wake up. She's gone!"

Chapter 21

The sound of waves folding and lapping the shore punctuated by the call of seagulls pirouetting in the early morning sky stirred Donna gently awake. A cool sea breeze puffed and rolled the gauzy curtains pulled across the open doors to the balcony. She moaned with the satisfaction of the best night's sleep she thought she had ever had. Her sense of satisfaction was amplified by Thomas's continued kindness and understanding of her situation. They had finished the evening as happy, if not happier, than it had started.

The food was sumptuous, the conversation delightful, and if that wasn't enough, Donna had been entertained by both Thomas and his daughter playing on the piano and singing. Seeing his family and the fun they had together did make her miss her own. The evening ended with a promise to be back in the morning to check on her even though she said it wasn't necessary. Thomas and his wife both wouldn't hear of it.

Sitting up in bed now, she got snapshot-like views of the ocean as the curtains rolled and bellowed open in the fresh morning air. Easing her way off the bed and over to the balcony, she stepped barefooted onto the warm Mexican tile.

Standing next to the coquina stone baluster and rail, she placed her hands on the rail closing her eyes. Tilting her head back, she leaned into the soft cool breeze inhaling a deep, cleansing breath. Opening her eyes, she scanned the horizon. Though her surroundings couldn't be more blissful, she longed to see the twin masts of the *Donna Marie* on the beautiful yet empty horizon.

Her hopeful search served to remind her of her current reality. She didn't know where Cal was or whether he had regained their beloved sailboat. Her next thought sent a shiver down her spine—whether he was safe and unharmed. She shook her head at the reality of what they had decided to do, even the stupidity of it. After all, it was insured. Another sailboat could be bought; another Cal could not. With that thought, her resolve to do something about the situation came storming back.

Leaving the balcony, she began pacing in front of the bed contemplating what she should do next. The first thing she needed to do, she thought, was find Thomas. She was about to head for the shower when she heard the lilt of Leeanna's small voice calling to her from the foyer below. Donna went to the landing at the top of the stairs to see her standing just inside the doorway.

"Good morning, Miss Donna, I 'ave brought some fresh fruit to go with yo-ah breakfast I will to make for you."

Donna started to tell her it wasn't necessary but stopped, knowing that she would do it anyway. Instead, she said, "Thank you, Leeanna. I want to take a quick shower and dress. Then I'll be down to help you. Is Thomas coming? I need to ask him some questions."

"Okay, I will start cutting de fruit. Yes, Thomas es coming, but he went to de communication building. He will be along soon, I think."

"Very good, I'll be quick, Leeanna." Just as Donna started to turn from the stair railing, she heard Thomas excitedly calling her name beyond the front door.

"Miss Donna, Miss Donna!" Leanna stepped aside just as Thomas swung the front door wide open. The brilliant sunlight that washed in with him made it appear as though Scotty had just beamed him there. He repeated her name again, this time adding, "I 'ave some good news, maybe. At least I hope et es."

"Calm down, Thomas, and tell me."

Thomas took a couple of gulping breaths, for he had run the distance to the house. "I sent a message out on the marine radio describing yo-ah boat.

"You did? Has someone seen it? Did my husband reply?"

Gulping again but calming down, he answered, "Yes, someone did see it, a maun replied, but it was not yo-ah husband. A local fisherman replied."

"So this fisherman, he saw the *Donna Marie*? Where did he see her?" Donna had begun descending the stairs as she spoke.

"It was vury early—de sun was just coming up. His description fit de photo you showed me last evening. But 'e never got a look at de stern for a name."

Almost pleading, Donna asked, "Thomas, where did he see it?"

Closing the door behind him, Thomas gave her a solemn look, and then said, "At Rokers Point."

"Rokers Point? Where exactly is Rokers Point?"

"Rokers Point, et es in de Exumas. Et es a settlement on de island. Et es northwest of he-ah."

Donna struggled to suppress her excitement. "Was the boat the fisherman saw anchored or underway?"

"He said most definitely underway. In fact, he commented on how beautiful she looked even in de dim light of dawn."

"Yes, she is all of that and more. Did he say what direction she was headed?"

"Yes, south, southeast toward the Turks and Caicos Islands."

Donna was having a difficult time trying to orient herself with all these different directions. Thomas saw this and stepped over to a credenza and retrieved a notepad and pencil from the drawer. Standing hunched over the credenza, he sketched a crude map and handed it to Donna.

Donna stared at the map. Her face fell as the realization sank in that the *Donna Marie* would likely not be coming to Rum Cay. To do so would require a northerly heading to go around the tip of an island that ran parallel to Exuma.

If it was the *Donna Marie* the fisherman saw, and it likely was given his description, then either Cal had not found her yet or, worse, failed to gain her back. That thought gave her a sick feeling in the pit of her stomach.

She needed to stay focused and not let herself get emotional. She asked Thomas, "What are some likely places one might go in the Turks?"

"Oh, Miss Donna, der are many places one could go, many islands, big and small. Hold on though, der are some good maps of all des islands in de book case. I will get them."

Leeanna popped through the door to the kitchen announcing that breakfast was ready.

Donna replied, "Leeanna, I'm sorry, honey. I don't know if I can eat anything just now. I'm too worried and upset."

"Don't you worry about dat—you need to eat. I will make you a tea that will help with yo-ah nerves so you can eat. You cannot help yo-ah man if yo-ah sick."

Donna looked at Thomas who smiled and said, "You 'ad better do as she says. You will not win de argument with her, dis I know."

Donna looked back to see that Leeanna had already returned to the kitchen. Thomas said, "See, I told you. She es a vury strong woman, dat one. Go ahead and have a seat at de table. I will bring de maps over so deh can be spread out."

Donna sat down at the large dining table. Taking a seat, she watched as Thomas made his way to the table with several maps. Setting them down and selecting one, he unfolded it in front of Donna.

"Des are nautical charts. Deh show many of de islands."

Donna nodded and added, "Yes, I'm very familiar with these types of maps. They show latitudes and longitudes as well as water depths and such."

"Dat es correct, so as you can see, der are many islands where someone could take a boat such as yours."

"Is there a magnifying glass? I'm in my fifties now, so these peepers of mine need some help seeing the small stuff."

"I don't know, but I'll check de drawer."

Thomas had no sooner begun rummaging through the drawers of a credenza when Leeanna returned with a steaming cup of tea. Handing the tea to Donna, she announced that she would be right back with breakfast.

"Ah-ha!" Thomas exclaimed. "I have found a magnifying glass." Slipping the drawer closed, he hurried to the table. Taking it from him, Donna began scouring the map. She had no idea of what she was hoping to find. What she hoped was that something would jump out at her. She quickly found Rokers Point. Hovering the magnifying glass over the odd-shaped island, she wondered why boat pirates would go to such a public place with a stolen sailboat, especially one like the *Donna Marie*.

Donna's concentration was so intent she didn't notice her breakfast had been placed next to her, that is until the delicious aromas captured her nose. She apologized to Leeanna for being rude.

Leeanna dismissed it, saying, "Yo-ah have vury important matters on yo-ah mind, I understand. But you must eat now. De maps are going nowhere."

Donna smiled, took a sip of her tea, and put the magnifying glass down. She took note of the marvelous plate of food. "My goodness, Leeanna, you have gone to way too much trouble for me."

Thomas laughed out loud then said, "I need to keep you around, Miss Donna. My wife makes you a better breakfast than for me."

Leanna shot Thomas a stern look. "Don't you believe hem. I feed hem plenty good, de children too."

Donna smiled and patted the back of Leeanna's hand. "Don't worry, I know how these men are. I have one just like him. They like to complain. But the moment you're gone, they are like lost puppies."

"Yes, yes, dat es how dat one es. A big lost puppy when Momma is not around. But you must eat now while the grits and corned beef are hot."

Thomas agreed, adding, "She is right. Be sure to take a bite of de johnnycake with de fried plantains and guava. It will melt in yo-ah mouth. My woman is de best cook on de whole island."

Leanna shot him a dismissive look. With a snort, she said, "Oh, a lot 'e knows. Dat is no big deal. Der are only a handful of women on dis island inna way."

Donna had taken a couple of bites then looked at Leanna. "My goodness, this is delicious, Leanna. You are far too humble. The dinner you made last evening and now *this*. You deserve every bit of praise your man gives you and more."

"Yo-ah are too kind, Miss Donna. Now I must go. I have de little ones to deal with yet dis morn'n'. I will see you later? Yes?"

"Sweetheart, there is no way I'll leave without coming to see you." Leanna smiled broadly and excused herself to leave.

While Thomas and Donna finished their breakfast, he kept her talking about life in the States. He had never been there but had always dreamed of going someday. Donna was happy to answer his questions and tell him of her life on Ramrod Key. For her it was just her daily existence. But to Thomas, it sounded like the creation of a novelist, exciting and adventurous. Not mundane and predictable like life on Rum Cay, he thought.

Thomas cleaned up the dishes and the kitchen, and Donna went back to pouring over the map. It was easy enough to see the island next to the one Rokers Point was on. She then saw just how close Rum Cay was to Rokers Point.

Donna shouted out to Thomas, asking how long a plane flight it was to Exuma airport. "About an hour, depending on the plane."

Donna sat thinking about what she should do next. She then trailed the magnifying glass down the west side of Long Island which lay between Rum Cay and Exuma, then on down the chain of islands. Suddenly, she stopped, hovering over one odd-shaped island. Her eyes widened in disbelief when she read the name of a settlement on the north side of the island. There it was—the name Juky had scrawled on the *Donna Marie*'s life ring—Pirates Well!

Her hand shook as she laid the magnifying glass down, realizing that Cal likely had not regained possession of the Donna Marie. Her mind reeled, trying to assemble the facts as she knew them. She went through them point by point. She and Cal didn't know what "Pirates Well" meant at first. But they reasoned that it had to be a place somewhere in the Caribbean islands. However, before they had time to research that, they ran into Johnny Mac who made it sound as if Juky was the one in control of where the *Donna Marie* was heading.

They all had assumed Juky would take her to Rum Cay. It was, after all, where she and Juky had originally planned for her and Cal to find the *Donna Marie*. She and Cal were then to take some time and sail her around the islands before heading back to Ramrod Key. Donna smirked at the last part mostly because she had no idea how she was going to convince Cal to do that and not simply sail straight back for home.

All of this tumbled rapidly through her mind. She was not sure what her next move should be. However, she was sure she wasn't going to just sit here or, worse—fly back home. No, she needed to find Cal and soon. That one thought though suddenly paved her course of action. Ceasing her doubt-tinged ruminations, she abruptly stood and shouted to Thomas while making her way to the kitchen, "Thomas, I need to get a plane to Rokers Point right away!"

Chapter 22

Michael had roused Juky from sleep by jerking the gun from his waistband and whispering in his ear while the mechanic went below deck to check out the compass.

"I'll take this. I don't know what you done to get free. But as soon as this bloke repairs that compass, it's going to get very bad for you, and don't even think about warning him either. I'll put a hole in 'em same as you, got that?"

Juky somberly nodded. He couldn't believe he had missed the sound of both Michael and the mechanic's boats coming alongside. He had to think of something quick. As soon as the mechanic repaired the compass and left, Michael would surely free his two cohorts tied up below deck.

As Juky suspected, it didn't take the mechanic long to discover what Juky had done to disable the compass. Coming back topside, the unwitting mechanic explained to Michael that you can't store things that have big magnets like a stereo speaker on a shelf that is that close to a compass. Although Michael nodded and made out like he was appreciative of the information, he kept giving Juky quick side glances that told him it was about to get very ugly for him.

The joviality and appreciation Michael was lauding on the mechanic was a veiled attempt to not draw any suspicions from the mechanic. He then paid the man very well for his time and trouble while thanking him profusely. The mechanic thanked Michael several more times while climbing down into his boat to leave. Michael waved and gave stiff laughs and nods but said no more. He wanted this guy gone. Juky had only seconds to decide what to do.

Staring down at the water, then to Michael at the stern, his only choice, he thought, was to jump in the water. He had no desire to be tied up again or to get the beating he felt was coming with it. Juky was forced to wait though until the mechanic was far enough away so that *he* was safe, but not so far that Michael would risk the mechanic hearing him and shoot at Juky in the water.

Michael continued to watch the mechanic's progress toward shore. He too was timing his next actions. He watched a long minute more. With the sound of the boat's motor growing fainter, Michael gave Juky a sullen stare.

Slipping his gun from under his shirttails, he pointed it right at Juky. "I'm going to give 'em a minute or two more to be sure es outta earshot. Then I think I'm going to shoot you right where you stand. Your little stunt here may have caused me to miss my contact in Pirates Well and lose a *lot* of money. I don't like that, and I really don't like you."

Michael started walking toward Juky. With the gun pointed straight at Juky's head, he angrily asked, "Now what did you do with those two dumbasses I left to guard you?"

Juky nodded and cut his eyes toward the hatchway. "Dey are locked in de storage locker below."

Michael shook his head in disgust. "Morons, I should shoot 'em too. Get moving," he said with a wave of the gun. "*You* are going to let them out whilst I keep this gun pointed straight at that 'ead of yours."

Juky hesitated a split second. Michael shouted his command again.

"I said, get moving!"

Juky glanced toward the shore and the mechanic's boat. This was it. It was now or never. Taking a few steps forward past Michael, he took a deep breath. Two more steps, Michael was right behind him. Juky froze a split second, then suddenly threw his right elbow back into Michael's rib cage, hammering it in with his left hand.

Recoiling, Michael stumbled backward in intense pain wrapping his gun arm around his midsection. Fruitlessly he lunged to try and grab Juky by the arm, managing only to tear off his shirt sleeve, then watched as Juky threw himself sideways into the water. A primal scream of rage flew from Michael's mouth.

Struggling to regain his footing, he screamed a string of curse words at the froth and bubbles left by Juky's rapid dive into the water. Michael pulled his arm from around his ribs just long enough to fire three haphazard shots into the stream of rising bubbles.

Two more rounds exploded into the water. "You lousy bastard! I'll fill this ocean full of lead to kill you, you son-of-a-bitch!" he screamed.

Taking a couple of painful steps toward the bow, he tried to follow the diminishing trail of bubbles but doubled over in pain again. With his arm around wrapped his midsection, he groaned out loud. Glancing up every few seconds, he desperately wanted to see blood in the water or, better yet, a body floating to the surface. He saw neither. Beads of sweat ran from his forehead into his eyes.

"Come on you, bastard, where are you? You can't 'old your breath forever."

Michael straightened as much as the pain would allow; adrenaline and rage helped to mute some of his pain as he began making staggered steps around the ship's perimeter. He kept cursing Juky, calling him everything but a son of God. He continued scanning the water immediately around the hull. With every painful footfall, his labored steps resounded like a drumbeat on the *Donna Marie's* teakwood deck.

Reaching the bow, he bent over trying to peer down around the bow spar to where the bow met the waterline. However, because of the sharp angle of the bow and his present condition, he was unable to hold onto the rail to see under the overhang of the bow.

His frustrations grew the more he searched for Juky. Five minutes had passed since he had jumped in the water. Straining to straighten up again, he heard muffled sounds and thumping coming from right below him. It was then that he remembered his two cohorts. Rolling his eyes, he scoffed, "Can't believe that bastard got them both locked up below." Taking another frustrated look around at the waters surrounding the *Donna Marie*, he began to gimp his way to the hatchway to go below and free his hapless shipmates.

Along the way he decided they needed to set sail and quick, for two very good reasons. One, the mechanic might just have heard the gunshots. The second and the more pressing reason was his contact made it very clear that if this boat was not in Pirates Well at the appointed time, not only was *this* deal off, but there would be no future deals.

After freeing his shipmates, he returned to the deck. He took another look around fruitlessly hoping to catch a glimpse of Juky in the water. He called out loudly, "I know yer out there, mate. You 'ad better be a good swimmer, 'cause I'm about to set sail. Oh, and I 'ere the sharks in these waters are quite unforgiving."

His quick laugh turned to a grunt of pain as he stepped to the helm, grabbing the ships wheel. All he could think of now was getting underway and quick.

Hanging on to the anchor rope, Juky had been able to maneuver himself back and forth under the bow of the boat to stay out of sight. It took a few seconds for him to realize the sound of Michael's footsteps had ceased. Perhaps he was no longer topside, he thought. He had to get to the stern where the dinghy had been left tied off and quick.

Diving underwater, he swam toward the *Donna Marie's* stern. He chose to swim the length of the ship's beam so that any bubble trail he made would show on both sides of the hull just in case Michael was still topside waiting him out. He was about halfway along when the low drone of the diesel engine reverberated in the water. Juky quickly dispensed with any efforts of stealth and instead launched into a full-scale Olympic charge for the stern. Pumping and clawing through the water, he could see the bottom of the dinghy bobbing in the water just ahead. A few more kicks and he could just reach the dinghy's bow rope that dabbed up and down in the water.

As he was kicking his way past the propeller, the prop suddenly spun to life.

Tumbling, rolling, and banging against the bottom of the hull, he caught split-second glimpses of a rope, then the bottom rung of the stern ladder, even the skeg on dinghy's outboard motor. He tried grabbing for each, but all flew past in a twist of boiling water and bubbles. In the ensuing violence of tumbling water and froth, his left thigh was grazed by the spinning prop. He never felt the slice of the prop's blade. Driven now by adrenaline and an even greater need for air, he clawed at the water not knowing which way was up or down.

He was twenty yards behind the *Donna Marie* by the time he popped to the surface. Gulping in air and treading water, it took a moment for him to get his bearings. Turning a slow circle in the water, he stopped. Blinking repeatedly, he watched through salt-water-stung eyes as the arched gold-leaf lettered name of the *Donna Marie* shrank away into the growing distance.

The sound of Michael barking orders and cursing at his two shipmates echoed across the water. It was then he felt a sharp stinging pain in his left thigh. He saw too the small crimson trail of blood he was leaving in the water. He looked to the shore a quarter mile away. His situation wasn't looking good, but he had no choice but to try and make it to shore. He had always been a good swimmer…in his younger days. But those days were long gone. But he had to try, or he was a goner for sure. Treading water would only make it easier for those unforgiving sharks Michael had laughingly warned him about.

Juky looked up into the bright blue morning sky. "Lord, you know I want to go to heaven. Just not today." With that, he started a slow methodical swim for shore. It was quiet with only the intermittent sound of a half dozen seagulls circling overhead following his progress in the water. He hoped they would remain the only thing following his swim to shore. He thought of how many times in history birds had been seen as signs of miracles. Tired and bleeding, he knew it was going to take a miracle to save him now.

Just then something long and gray flashed past him in the crystal-clear water twenty feet or more below him. Juky cried out, "No, no—not already…please!"

*****

Cal leapt up from the chaise lounge, turning the air blue with a string of curse words. Shoving his way past Johnny Mac, he ran into the room to check the time. Just then the door to their room swung wide open revealing a very irritated Jim.

"What the hell is going on? I was supposed to be in the air an hour ago. What are you two still doing in the room? We were to meet at sunrise down at the dock!"

"Don't you think I know that?" Cal blared. He then asked, "Have you seen the boat captain and our camera man?"

"Yes, they're at the dock wondering what's going on."

"No time to explain, Jim. You and J-Mac get back down to the dock fast, and keep those guys there while I change. I think we can still pull this off."

Johnny Mac started to ask a question, but Cal cut him off, hustling him to the door next to Jim. "Go, go! The *Donna Marie* has set sail. We might still be able to find her if we hustle."

Cal flipped the door closed and raced to get in his uniform. The whole time he dressed he mumbled to himself, at first bitching that he had overslept. He then began talking out loud as to where she could be sailing. There were hundreds of islands they could be heading for, but which one, and why had they stopped here? As far as he knew, they never came ashore. They had kept an eye on the *Donna Marie*; however, it wasn't like a nonstop surveillance either. Someone could have come ashore.

Heck, Rokers Point may have been the hand-off point to whoever had paid the pirates to steal the *Donna Marie* in the first place. If that was the case, it would likely be heading straight out into the Atlantic Ocean bound for who knows where.

Grabbing the guns Johnny Mac had acquired, he stuffed one behind his back. The smaller one he put in the top of his sock securing it with a rubber band just in case any running became necessary. He smirked, pulling his pant leg down over the gun. "Won't be much running if things go south—more like diving in the drink to keep from getting shot."

Standing up, he glanced around the room to make sure he wasn't forgetting anything. Checking himself out in the mirror, he gave his shirt a tug here and there and smoothed back his hair. Taking a deep breath, he stepped to the door. "Time to see if we get honey or just get stung."

Chapter 23

Cal and Jim did radio checks. Everybody was in place. The captain had been briefed on the general theme of the training film, with a slight twist. They had to now find the boat that was to be the subject of the video.

The boat captain, thinking this was all planned out by Interpol, asked one simple question that Cal had no simple answer for. What heading was he to take to find the boat? Cal, of course, had no idea what direction the *Donna Marie* was heading.

Johnny Mac stood just behind Cal and heard him stumbling around for an answer. Just as Cal's delay was getting uncomfortable, Johnny Mac spoke up.

"Hold on, Cal, don't give him the old coordinates. Remember, we changed them. They are heading for Galliot Cay. We had better pick our speed up if we are to catch them."

With a look of consternation, Cal turned to face Johnny Mac. "Are you sure that was the direction?" Scowling at Johnny Mac, he added, "We can't be wasting this man's time and the government's money."

"Oh yes, I'm quite sure—it came to me a moment ago…I mean I remembered it a moment ago."

Still facing Johnny Mac, Cal said, "Yes that's right—I, uh, I remember now. Yes, it was Galliot Cay." Cal silently mouthed, "Hope you are right."

Cal keyed his radio. "Come in, Water Lily, take a heading west, southwest toward Galliot Cay. We'll intercept them there, over."

A long pause followed. "Do you copy that, Water Lily?"

"I copy, changing course now. I'll radio when sighted and relay their coordinates, over."

The boat captain made a long sweeping turn, throttled up, and took a heading for Galliot Cay. Cal and Johnny Mac relaxed a little. Cal took a seat across from their continually smiling cameraman and pulled a chart from his shirt pocket. Unfolding it, he studied it for a moment, then looked over at Johnny Mac who had sat down next to the smiling cameraman. Cal said, "Good call, J-Mac. That would be the logical thing to do. Sail around the tip of Long Island then sail the outside of the islands to Pirates Well."

Cal felt good at how well things were going in spite of his getting up late, causing them to miss a chance to board the *Donna Marie* while anchored in the bay. The charter boat was going almost three times the top speed of the *Donna Marie*.

And with his eye in the sky, Cal was certain that they would catch up to her in short order. Leaning his head back against the cabin wall, he needed to run through options in case things didn't go as planned. Just for a brief moment, he let himself dwell on actually getting his feet on the deck of the *Donna Marie* again. With the sweetness of that thought still lingering, he closed his eyes and thought, *Nothing is going to stop me now.*

Abruptly, the engines throttled down, and the boat pitched wildly turning hard right, throwing everyone forward. The captain began shouting about a man in the water to the starboard side. Cal stumbled to his feet still trying deal with the rapid deceleration and course change.

The captain yelled for someone to get the stern rope. Cal raced onto the aft deck, searching the waters, still not seeing anyone. Coiling several feet of rope in his hand, he kept his vigil along the starboard side.

The captain's shouts came over a speaker. "Hold on, I've got him coming alongside twenty yards out. Get ready with that rope. He looks pretty tired. Shit! he's got friends circling him too. Don't miss with that rope."

Just then as the boat squared up with the man's position, Cal saw him for the first time. The captain slowed the boat as the man passed the bow making his way toward Cal's position at the stern. Gripping the rope firmly, he waited for just the right moment. The crystal-clear water made it easy to see the three or four sharks that were swimming in ever-tightening circles. The sound of the engines and shadow of the boat chased the sharks down deeper.

This was good and bad at the same time. Sharks tend come up from below their pray. Cal shouted for Johnny Mac to come help pull. They were going to have to race him to the boat then try and pull him onboard before a shark could make a last second lunge for his legs.

Johnny Mac shouted, "Hurry! Throw the rope, Cal. The sharks are coming back!"

Chapter 24

Sitting in the Mini Moke, Donna stared down at her lap nervous and anxious about her decision to fly to Rokers Point. By chance the pilot who had flown her in the day before made regular stops to the island, bringing small supplies like medicine, magazines, or repair parts.

She and Thomas watched as the pilot stopped the twin-engine Beechcraft a short distance from them. Thomas exited the Mini Moke shouting out greetings as he went. "Roger, ma friend, good to see you! What have you brought us today? Do you 'ave ma *Popular Mechanics* and those pipe fittings I needed?"

"I sure do, and I brought Leeanna and the kids a few things they had asked me get last time I was here."

"Dat is great. She will vury happy."

The pilot then looked at Donna. "Leaving so soon, ma'am?"

"Unfortunately, yes. I need to get to Rokers Point."

"Rokers Point?"

"Yes, can you fly me there right now?"

Glancing down and rubbing his chin, he said hesitantly, "Well, I *can,* but not exactly right now. See, I'm on my way to Colonial Hill Airport which is south of here first."

"How long will that take? I need to get to Rokers Point as fast as I can."

Rubbing his chin again, he glanced up at the sky then to Donna. "Well, ma'am, by the time I finish here, fly there, and back here, it'll be the better than an hour. I'm picking up a couple of fishermen. I'll be loaded pretty good too, so my top speed will be slower."

Thomas saw Donna's look of dejection; he knew how important this was to her. He walked a few feet from the plane and stopped.

"Roger," Thomas said, motioning him over. Roger edged his way to Thomas. Donna remained seated watching the two men talk. She had no idea what Thomas was saying but knew he was going to bat for her. Suddenly their conversation ceased. The pilot then turned partway around looking over his shoulder at Donna.

"What the hell. Those fishermen can wait. I had plane trouble, right, Thomas?" he said, slapping him on the back and laughing. "Sure, I can take you to Rokers Point. Let's get you loaded and in the air."

Donna jumped to her feet and ran to Thomas and the pilot giving them hugs and thanking them profusely.

"It's no problem. Glad to do it if it helps to get your sailboat back. Besides, it's been a bit dull lately what with flying half-drunk fishermen all over these islands. I could use a little adventure. Hadn't had any since last year when some local cops shot at me because they thought I was a drug plane."

Loading her suitcases into the plane, she asked, "How quick can you get to Rokers Point?'

Placing a hand on her shoulder, he said, "You hop in and hold on, 'cause we are going to be throttles to the firewall all the way there. This baby can really move when I want her to. Don't worry about that."

Donna went to where Thomas stood next to the Mini Moke. "How can I repay you and Leeanna's kindness? Oh my gosh, I didn't even leave a note of thanks for Mr. Stratton—he will think I'm some kind of leech."

"Nonsense, 'e will think no such thing. I will explain all of dis to hem. I'm quite sure 'e will approve. And remember dis, Miss Donna: A kindness is best repaid by passing et along."

Donna gave him a big hug with instructions to pass *that* along to his wife and children. Wiping tears from her eyes, she turned back toward the plane. Standing the on the plane's wing and looking over the cockpit, the pilot shouted to Donna, "Come on, Miss. If you're in a hurry, we gotta get airborne." Donna acknowledged it with a quick nod and trotted the short distance to the plane. Stepping up onto the wing, she opened the cockpit door. She stared back at Thomas and the surroundings—she wanted to never forget the last twenty-four hours. Fighting back tears again, she blew him a kiss and mouthed him a thank-you.

Thomas raised his big hand; smiling broadly, he waved to her shouting out as the engines burst to life, "Come back when you have her!"

"I will. You can bet on it!"

Roger shouted out, "Let's hit it, ma'am. Time's a wasting."

Donna gave one last wave then disappeared behind the closing cockpit door. Thomas stepped back all the way to the little shed next to the Mini Moke. The engines revved up blowing huge clouds of dust behind the plane. It had only moved a few feet forward when it spun around. Roger glanced over at Donna who was barely breathing and said, "Hold on, ma'am. Rokers Point, here we come."

With that he pushed both throttles forward. The engines roared louder; dust blew in violent streams below the wings. Looking straight up the shell runway, the pilot braked the plane for a second or two more then released them, while shoving the throttles forward.

Donna was instantly forced deep into her seat by the rapid acceleration. The landscape began racing past, the end of the runway loomed closer and closer until it appeared they would crash off the end, then abruptly they lifted sharply upward.

Donna's stomach instantly sank to her feet. The view of the ocean disappeared below her. It felt as if they were heading straight up. G-forces kicked in as the plane rolled hard around to take a heading toward Rokers Point. Roger caught a quick glance at Donna's ghost-white face.

"You gonna be okay? Don't have no air sickness bags, ma'am."

Donna only nodded. Relief soon came as they leveled off, and the engines were throttled back. She began to feel the blood to return to her face. The sense of heaviness in the pit of her stomach also began to subside. The whole plane seemed to relax and fall into a smooth and steady rhythm.

Roger pointed to the headset still hanging on the window post. Donna nodded and slipped it on. This gave her relief from the engine noise. Roger asked again if she was okay. She nodded, and replied rather loudly at first, "Yes, I think so. Wow, that was some takeoff!"

Roger smiled. "You don't have to shout now. I can hear you fine. Yeah, my little Bonanza might be a '62, but she can still get mov'n' when she's asked to."

"I'll say! How long do you think it will take to get there?"

"Gertie here," he said, patting the dash, "can cruise at about 185 knots, and with this tail wind, we should get there in about thirty minutes."

Hearing that, Donna felt a huge sense of relief. That was much quicker than Thomas thought. But he did say it depended on the plane. "That's fantastic, Roger. I just hope my husband will still be there when we arrive."

"Well, let's hope so. Say, if you don't mind me asking, what's the deal with this boat you're looking for—what is so special about it?"

Donna smiled and said, "I'm not quite sure how to answer that."

Roger glanced at his watch and then to Donna. "Well, we've got about thirty minutes—give it your best shot."

Donna thought for a moment then said, "Okay, I suppose the best place to start is at the beginning. For starters, my husband Cal won her in a card game."

"A card game? What kind of guy risks a sailboat on a bet?"

Donna gave him a smirk. "A guy who had more money than sense, I suppose."

"So was it a little bay slapper he put up?"

"A bay slapper? What is that?"

"You know, one of those twenty-foot single-mast sailboats that all the yuppies are buying these days."

Donna nodded and smiled. "Oh yes, we rent those at our marina back on Ramrod Key." She then dug in her purse and fished out a 5×7 photo of the *Donna Marie* holding it up for Roger to see.

"This is our boat, the *Donna Marie*," she proudly stated.

Rogers eyes widened. The picture was taken when she was in full sail with a setting sun back lighting her. It was a spectacular shot. A much larger print of this same picture hung in the restaurant above the bar.

"Holy cow! That's no bay slapper. No wonder you want her back. And you say your husband won that in a card game? He must be one hell of a poker player."

Donna gave him a crooked smile, and then said, "He is, but I insisted that he pay the man for it."

"What? Why? He won it fair and square, didn't he?"

"Well, I assumed so. But in either case, I would have insisted he pay for it."

"But why, if he didn't cheat the guy?"

"It was gotten by gambling, and I'll have no part of that. Nor would I have my name on such a thing. So it was pay the man, get rid of it, or take my name off it." Donna smiled looking at the photo, adding, "I remember I told him that I would never set foot on it if he didn't do as I asked."

"Wow, that's tough, Mrs. Arnold."

"Not half as tough as seeing what my sister went through with her husband, who managed to gamble away everything they ever had."

With pressed lips, Roger nodded his understanding, then asked, "Okay, so how did all of this come about?"

Retuning the photo to her purse, she said, "Oh, I don't think you want me to bore you with all of this."

"Are you kidding me? So far what you've said is anything but boring."

A warm smile graced Donna's face as she said, "Okay, but let me know if you start to nod off. I don't want you to crash into the ocean."

"If the rest of this story is anything like what I've heard so far, we'll be fine." Laughing, he added, "Besides, this might make a great book someday."

Donna giggled and said, "If you think this would make a great story, you should come hang out at the Salty Anchor. Now there are some real characters hanging out there at times." She thought for a second then added, "One of which is traveling with Cal right now. He's known as the Key West prophet."

"Really? I think I've heard of him. Isn't he that crazy guy I see people crowded around down on Caroline Street every now and then?"

"Yeah, he's crazy like a fox."

"So he's a fake, just ripping people off?"

Before she answered, she thought of how he knew Tammy was pregnant before any of them did, including Tammy. And that he knew something was up with the *Donna Marie* before either she or Cal had said a word to him.

She gazed wistfully out her window and said, "No, he's not a fake, at least as far as I can tell. If he is, then he's the best I've ever seen. He told us things that he had no way of knowing."

Roger laughed again. "Mrs. Arnold, this is one heck of a story you got going here."

She looked to Roger holding his gaze a moment. "Yeah, I suppose it is. I just hope it has a happy ending."

"I have no doubt it will. Looks like the gods of chance are with you on this one."

Smirking, she said, "I just hope their boss is the one calling the shots."

He stared back at her for a second, not understanding the comment. Seeing his look of confusion, she simply pointed up toward the sky while rolling her eyes upward.

Furrowing his brow, he glanced up. "Oh, yeah, I'm sure the big guy is looking over their shoulder on this one."

Donna, sensing his lack of comfort with the direction the conversation was taking, redirected it back to how she wound up on a wild goose chase through the Caribbean in search of a husband and sailboat.

"So you want know how all of this started, huh? Well, to begin with, the road to hell is paved with good intentions, as they say, which is what I had. While my intentions were good. My plan to put some spunk back into my husband's life hit a big kink from the beginning."

Roger made a course and altitude change. Adjusting the air speed, he settled them into a smooth but brisk trek toward Rokers

Point. Donna, likewise, fell smoothly into her story. The morning sun rose higher. The Atlantic waters shimmered in the new day's light. Up ahead awaited the next chapter in the story she told, unknown and unwritten. But ready to be lived.

Chapter 25

A rope splashed in the water just ahead of Juky. Thrusting an arm forward to grab ahold of it, he missed on his first two attempts. kicking hard, he lunged forward. With his third attempt, he found the end of the rope and latched on. Suddenly, a bump came at his midsection as a small four-footer checked him out. He had to get out of the water now!

Panic shot through him as he quickly spun the rope around his forearm. The second Cal and Johnny Mac saw this, they began pulling hard on the rope. Juky began moving rapidly through the water, taking him from a curiosity to appearing like a huge game fish. Juky knew well what the violence of a large hammerhead strike could do.

Disappearing in the froth of the churning water, all he could do was hang on as he sped toward the boat. Cal yelled out for the captain to come and help; he was about to yell out again when suddenly a rifle shot rang out exploding into the water. The bullet drilled into the churning water inches from Juky's belly. The circling cloud of razor-toothed predators shot away, leaving a ten-foot lemon shark, spiraling downward streaming blood, deep into the darkening water below.

Tossing the rifle down, the captain raced to help pull. All knew that when the sharks returned, it would be to feed. Juky heard all the yelling and commotion but could see nothing as he sliced through the water.

Suddenly something clamped down hard on Juky's arm, a blood-curdling scream erupted from him, "Noooo!" The water exploded. He was sure a large shark had tail-whipped him into the air. He knew what was next. *This is it,* he thought. "Jesus, help me!" he screamed.

Arching through the air, a hard hit came at his side before landing on the boat deck amid torrents of water and coils of rope.

Cal, Johnny Mac, and the captain all fell backward on the deck with him. Coughing and gasping for air, they all lay there moaning and trying to catch their breath and gather their wits. Lying on his back, Cal pawed the salt water from his face and eyes. Choking and coughing, Cal spoke out loudly. "Well…Jesus couldn't…make it…so…he, he sent us." Sputtering, breathless coughs and laughter erupted from all.

Pawing water from their eyes, all remained where they had fallen. Soon they became aware of someone standing next them. Slowly they focused on the broadly smiling face of Edmund, their pseudo cameraman, still with the large video camera poised on his shoulder.

Cal lifted his head for a better look. When their eyes met, Edmund happily stated, "I got all de action for you, Mista Cal. You all make et look so real."

Cal's head fell back to the deck. He said, "That's…good…real…good, Edmund."

Cal then pushed himself up to sit cross-legged on the deck. Looking over to Juky who lay on his back, slowly untangling himself from the rope, he sarcastically stated, "Well, of all the sorry-ass fish I could've hauled outta the ocean, it had to be you. You going to make it, old man?"

Giving himself a quick once-over, Juky said, "Yes, yes, maybe, but mah ribs really hurt."

"Good! Now what the hell were you doing in the water? And where the hell is my damn sailboat?"

The captain shot Cal a weird look. "Wait, hold on. You *know* this guy?"

"Yeah, you could say that. He was who we were coming to rescue from the *Donna Marie*." Looking hard at Juky, Cal then added, "So where is the *Donna Marie*?"

Juky brought himself to a sitting position, but before he could answer, a thunderous roar and blast of air hit them as the Water Lily streaked low overhead, banking hard around a few hundred yards out.

Cal cursed out loud. "Shit, I forgot all about him."

The boat captain jumped to his feet yelling up at the sky and shaking his fist. "What the hell are you doing, you crazy bastard!" He suddenly stopped in mid-rant. The captain looked back at Cal. "Wait, just what the hell is going here?"

"That's our air support. He was supposed to circle us when we came up on our target vessel—my sailboat! Which is nowhere in sight!" Cal yelled, glaring back at Juky.

Annoyed, the boat captain tossed a hand up in front of Cal's face. "Okay, that's it. I'm going back to port. I don't need or want to be involved this BS."

Struggling to stand, Juky winced in pain, cradling and rubbing his ribs. "Ahh. De shark dat tail-whipped me must 'ave been a big one. My ribs, de hurt so much."

Sullenly Cal retorted, "That was no shark. You hit the boat transom when we hauled your sorry ship-losing ass out of the water, which was about a half second before you became breakfast. You owe me big time. You've managed to lose my sailboat, and on top of that, I've had to save your worthless ass from being human sushi."

Rubbing his side, Juky held up his free hand. "Hold on, Cal. Calm down. I know where dey are going."

Cal abruptly ceased his rant. Glaring at Juky, he cautiously questioned, "Wait. You know where they are going? Well, spit it out man!"

Wincing in pain again, Juky held his breath for a second. Straining to talk, he croaked out, "De...life ring."

Cal's expression went from hopeful anticipation to one of total confusion.

"The life ring, what the hell are you talking about?"

"De...message I..." Juky doubled over in pain before he could finish.

"Message? What message?" Cal threw up his hands. Turning away from Juky, he let go a stream of curse words. Spinning back around, he took a step toward Juky, angrily pointing with his finger at him. "Enough bullshit. Tell me where she is headed or so help me, you'll have more than a few sore ribs!"

The captain shouted at Cal to calm down. Juky's moans of pain became louder. Cal kept yelling at Juky. Amidst all of this commotion, the cameraman kept raising his voice trying to be heard. "Mesta Cal, Mesta Cal, should I keep filming? Is dis a fight scene?"

Suddenly the ship's horn blared; the ear-piercing blast caused them all to bend low, covering their ears. It was a moment before they lifted their heads looking toward the wheelhouse. Easing their hands from their ears, they saw Johnny Mac smiling back at them.

"Now that I have all of your attention," he calmly began. "If you will stop yelling and cussing for a second and listen, Cal, Juky just told you where the *Donna Marie* is going."

Incredulous, Cal vociferously exclaimed, "He did no such thing. He's yapping about a stupid life ring, a message or whatever."

"Exactly! Shut up and think, man. What message did he leave on the *Donna Marie*'s life ring?"

Cal looked over at Juky clutching his ribs and gimping his way to a seat by the starboard rail. Glaring at Juky's back, he suddenly remembered the message he had scrawled on the *Donna Marie*'s life ring.

Practically shouting it at Juky, he sharply said, "Pirates Well! They're going to Pirates Well?"

Juky only nodded, while turning to ease his way down on the seat cushion.

The boat captain said, "Look, I don't know what's going here, but your friend there took a pretty hard shot to his ribs, plus he has a good cut on his leg. He needs to see a doctor."

Cal gave a sideways glance at the captain, then at Juky. "I said I know him. It doesn't mean we are friends."

"Well, whatever he is, he needs medical attention. So I'm ending this…this, whatever the hell it is right now."

The ship's radio suddenly crackled to life. "Hey, what's going on down there? I'm burning a lot of fuel up here just flying in circles."

Cal rolled his eyes. Sarcasm dripped from his mumbled words as he started for the wheelhouse. "This all certainly went well. I've spent a butt load of money, and I'm no closer to finding her." The instant he said it, his mind flashed to his wife and whether his ruse to protect her was working. He wanted desperately to find the *Donna Marie*. However, finding his wife was far more important. Without her, none of this mattered.

Entering the wheelhouse, Cal hesitated a second, then keyed the mike. "Ah, Water Lily, the mission is off. Head back to the airport. We'll meet at the hotel room at Rokers Point, over."

A few seconds of silence ensued. Cal was about to repeat the message when a flat "10-4" was Jim's only reply. Through the wheelhouse windows, Cal watched the Water Lily bank slowly away, heading for the Exuma airport.

Johnny Mac stood in the doorway of the wheelhouse and asked, "What now?"

Cal palmed a hand down his face. "I was hoping you'd know that. I'm fresh out of answers. All of this is my fault." Slapping his thigh, he added, "Can't believe I screwed this up by oversleeping."

"Don't take it so hard, Cal. I think perhaps she's coming to you," Johnny Mac said.

Cal watched Johnny Mac turn from the doorway and head toward Juky who sat rubbing his side still pondering what almost happened to him. Johnny Mac stopped in front of Juky. "Can I have a look-see at those ribs, my friend?"

Juky looked up to Johnny Mac a moment then simply nodded. Juky had no idea who the odd-looking man was, but for some reason—maybe it was the look in his eyes—he sensed he might actually be able to help. Juky winced in pain while lifting his T-shirt. Johnny Mac stooped a little and moved Juky's hand aside. He then placed his own hand on Juky's side. Johnny Mac began to feel and press gently on different areas along his left side. Juky pulled back a couple of times when Johnny Mac hit a particularly tender spot. Cal stepped up behind Johnny Mac as he straightened from his examination.

"J-Mac, what the heck *are* you talking about? You just said the *Donna Marie* is going to Pirates Well, right?"

"No, I believe you said that, and rather loudly too, I might add."

141

"Okay, okay, whatever. How can the *Donna Marie* be coming to me and going to Pirates Well at the same time?"

Johnny Mac looked down at Juky. "My friend, I don't feel any broken ribs. Some torn cartilage maybe in a place or two—you're pretty bruised up too."

Juky gave him a perplexed look while asking, "Are you a doctor?"

Johnny Mac let go a short laugh then said, "I have been pronounced to be a great many things in my life, including my being dead. But a doctor, I'm afraid, isn't one."

Cal grew frustrated with Johnny Mac's seeming indifference to his questioning. Putting his hand on Johnny Mac's shoulder, he pulled him around. "Didn't you hear me? How can the *Donna Marie* be going two places at one time, dammit?"

Unfazed by Cal's intense manner, Johnny Mac turned all the way around to look Cal in the eye. "Think, man! Don't you have *two* ladies by that name?"

Cal's mouth dropped open. His hand fell away from Johnny Mac's shoulder.

"Yeah, that's right!" Johnny Mac exclaimed. "You know, if you spent a little more time thinking instead of losing your temper, you might already have both of them back by now."

Cal's face softened looking at his friend. "I'm sorry, J-Mac. Its… its, well, *I am* very worried about her. I guess I've been taking this out on all of you. I know you are just trying to help."

Johnny Mac smiled, then did something strange. Looking Cal right in the eyes, he made a fist then raised his arm. Juky thought he was going to hit Cal, but just as he was about say something, Johnny Mac simply extended his index finger pointing it straight up at the sky.

Cal, along with everyone else, trailed their gaze upward, following Jonny Mac's extended finger. Craning their heads skyward, they stared into a blue cloud-dotted sky, wondering what the heck he was pointing at. It took a second or two, but just then the faint, smooth drone of a plane's engine could be heard.

Cal squinted trying to zero in on where in the sky the plane was and what direction it was headed. Abruptly, Juky yelled out, "There! Twelve o'clock, about two thousand feet."

Cal strained to find it. "I don't see it. My darn eyes aren't what they use to be, dammit."

"Right there, it's about to go behind that big cloud right over us."

Cal adjusted his stance a bit. Shading his eyes with his hands, he suddenly saw it—a twin-engine plane in quick descent, and heading for the Exuma airport.

Suddenly Cal stopped looking up. He reached over and placed a hand on Johnny Mac's shoulder. Looking at the boat captain, Cal earnestly stated, "I need to get back to the island, quick."

The captain gave Cal a surprised look, responding, "Yeah, sure. I'll run her as fast as I can, but what about your friend? He should see a doctor. We are twenty minutes away from my dock at Rokers Point."

"No, no. Don't go to Rokers. Take me to where the airport is."

The captain looked a bit perplexed. "That will take longer, and there's no place for me to dock this thing."

"Then get me as close as you can. if I have to, I'll swim the rest of the way to shore. Then you can run to Rokers Point."

The captain gave Cal a look of exasperation, then said, "Here's how this is going to go. I am going to run your butt as close to the shore as I can." Pointing at Juky, he added, "Then I'm going to run down to Hoppers Bay. There is a clinic there so this man can get the medical attention he needs."

"Fine, whatever. How long to get to the shoreline by the airport?"

"Forty minutes maybe."

"Forty minutes? You've got to get me there faster."

The captain stopped in the doorway of the wheelhouse. "Hey, look, this is a forty-foot charter boat, not one of those Scarab drug boats. On her best day she can do about twenty-two knots, and that's with the wind at my stern."

Hearing this, Cal looked up at the plane emerging from behind the cloud. Frustrated, he walked briskly away in silence.

The captain looked at Johnny Mac. "What gives with your friend there?"

"Oh, him? He's just in love…again."

A smirk pulled at the corner of the captain's mouth. "She must be one helluva woman to be with him." With a wink, he added, "Or just as crazy as he is."

Johnny Mac looked up, watching the plane disappear into the distance, and replied, "If you ask me, I'd say she's bit of both."

Cal went and stood at the stern continuing to watch the plane slip from view. Without warning, the boat's powerful diesel engine went from a low rumbling idle to near full throttle, causing Cal to nearly lose his balance. Cursing to himself, he looked toward the wheelhouse.

Over the roar of the diesel engine, the captain's voice bellowed from the wheelhouse, "Exuma Airport, here we come!" He then blew the ship's horn loud and long.

Chapter 26

Donna had a white-knuckle grip on the instrument cowling during their rapid descent. Her stomach felt as though it were floating in her throat. The pilot dropped down to five hundred feet and made a general radio call to any aircraft in the area of his intent to land, then gave his position. He then radioed Exuma control for clearance to land.

Given the all clear, he turned onto his base leg, then turned once again to make his final approach to land. Donna was very happy to see the runway come fully into view, *and* that it was paved this time. She noticed a bright yellow building that appeared to be a small terminal along with the typical things one might see at a rural airport back home.

Donna commented on how quaint it looked. Roger laughed while concentrating on his landing. "Yeah, well, they don't call it Exuma International for nothing." He then fixed his attention on the end of the runway. In another moment, the plane's nose went slightly up. The engines went almost silent. A gentle bump was felt as they touched down.

"Ahh. There you go. Like kissing your mother's cheek, that was," Roger said with obvious pride.

Donna felt a rush of relief and excitement. Relief that they had landed safely and excitement that she would soon be reunited with Cal. She had no sooner thought that when she realized that even though she had made it to the same island, she still didn't know exactly where he was, or if he was still even on the island.

Taxiing to where they were being directed, her excitement cooled a bit looking around at her new surroundings. There certainly were a lot more people here. Most were tourists that paid no mind to their arrival, caught up in their own fascination of where they were.

Maneuvering the plane to an easy stop, Roger brought the engines to an idle for a moment, then shut them down. Blissful silence filled the cockpit. Roger hopped out first and trotted around the nose of the plane to assist Donna out of the cockpit and off the wing. He then helped her with her bags and waved for a skycap to come and take them up to the terminal.

Turning to Donna, he said, "Well, Mrs. Arnold, you should be able to go inside and get directions to Rokers Point and the name of some of the resorts and hotels there. We Yanks stick out like sore thumbs in the islands, as you might imagine."

He then added, "One thing about these islanders—they really like to help folks. Well, most do. You gotta watch out for any who want to help you a bit too much, if you know what I mean, and that holds true for *anyone* you run into here." Roger's drifted eyes around looking at the surroundings then said, "Mrs. Arnold, you sure you're gonna be okay? I mean all by yourself."

Donna gave a quick survey around at the families and couples all going about their business, laughing and talking. It reminded her of home and the Salty Anchor. People from all walks of life, from all over the world were here to relax and have fun.

"Thanks, Roger, for your concern *and* all that you've done for me. But I'll be just fine. This place reminds me of my home on Ramrod Key. I know how to handle myself."

Roger looked at his watch, then back at Donna. "Look, I've got to get going. Those fishermen oughta be really drunk by the time I get there now. Look, you have my number. If you need something, give me a shout and I'll see what I can do. Hope you find your man. *And* make sure you get that gorgeous sailboat back."

Donna gave him a quick hug and thanked him. "I'll be fine, I'm sure. If I can't locate my husband, then I'll likely head back to Ramrod Key."

"I think that is an excellent idea. These islands are no place for a woman to be traveling by herself. True, there are a lot of good people here, but there are also some real nasties too."

Donna smiled and said, "Well, so far I've only encountered the nice ones."

"Well, let's hope it stays that way. Remember, watch out for the overly helpful ones." Turning to walk away, he added, "Snakes in the grass they are."

"Roger, just a moment. What do I owe you for the flight?"

Roger gave her a warm smile. "Not a thing. I'll, uh, I'll take it out in trade next time I'm on Ramrod Key. You take care now, ya hear?"

Donna smiled back at him, saying, "You be sure to stop by. Cal and I will make sure you have a great time at the Salty Anchor."

Donna stood for a moment watching him walk back to his plane. Just then, a man's voice came from just behind, startling her. Turning quickly around, she was relieved to see the skycap Roger had waved over standing right behind her.

"Oh, I em sorry. I did not mean to scare you, madam. Where do you want yo-ah bags to go?"

"Oh goodness, yes, my bags. Ah, to the terminal, I suppose. I need to rent a car. Is there a car rental here?"

"Certainly, der es. We have two. So you should have no problem with dat. Where es it dat you wish to go?"

"Rokers Point."

The skycap grabbed her bags and began walking to what passed for a terminal, talking as they walked. "Ah, dat is a vury nice place. Et es straight up Queens Highway. It can't be missed."

Reaching the door to the terminal, Donna held the door open for him. "Yes, when you leave he-ah, turn right onto Queens Highway."

The skycap guided them through the crisscross of people in the terminal lobby to a small car rental counter.

"He-ah you are. Dis young lady will help you with getting yo-ah car. Enjoy yo-ah stay with us."

Donna smiled and thought as she tipped the pleasant man, *Boy, we could sure use a dose of him back in the States.*

The young woman behind the rental car counter spoke to her just as pleasantly as the skycap. "'Ow can I help you today?"

147

Donna smiled and made her request for a rental car. The young woman went efficiently about the process of getting her information for two days rental, then called for a car to be brought to terminal entrance. A short a few minutes had passed when a dark blue '81 Datsun 210 hatchback pulled to a stop in front of the terminal doors.

A tall, slender black man who looked to be in his late teens unfolded himself from the diminutive economy car. Walking briskly through the doors, he approached her, holding out the keys. "He-ah are de keys, ma'am. Are these yo-ah bags?" he asked, pointing to her luggage.

Taking the keys, Donna acknowledged that the bags were indeed hers. In a flash, he gathered her bags under the stretch of his lanky arms. "Vury good, ma'am, please follow me."

The young man soon had her loaded and in the car. He cheerfully then explained some of the nuisances of operating the car that were a result of its age and use as rental car. And sure enough, just as he explained, with three quick pumps of the gas pedal and a little jiggle of the key while starting, the well-worn Datsun sprang to life.

Soon Donna was on her way. With no working air-conditioning in the car, she drove with all the windows down. Even though it was hot, it was not unbearable, as long as you stayed moving anyway. It was only a quarter mile or so to the intersection of the airport road and Queens Highway. At the intersection, she looked left then to her right. The traffic was intermittent with all manner of transportation drifting past, some of it appearing to be one breakdown away from the junkyard.

She sat a few seconds pondering on just what she was going to do once she arrived in Rokers Point. Her thoughts, however, were suddenly cut short by the honk of a truck horn behind her. Momentarily frazzled, she glanced in the rearview mirror to see a man waving for her to go. Hurriedly, she ground the transmission into gear. Quickly checking the traffic, she let out on the clutch. The little Datsun lurched out onto the two-lane highway. A couple of jerky shifts later she slipped it into high gear. It had been a long while since she had driven a manual shift, but in short order, she was moving briskly along.

The Datsun reminded her of the car she drove when she and Cal had first gotten married. That old '35 Chevy, though much bigger, had some of the same nuances of operation as this Datsun. A warm smile came to her remembering what her father said when he saw her driving that old Chevy for the first time, growling that he had seen better cars in a demolition derby. He offered to buy her a newer car. She refused, saying that Cal would get her one in due time. Donna snickered out loud recalling his answer, that the second coming of Christ would occur before that ever happened.

Donna drove along lost in her thoughts about her father and all the years that had passed since that first year she and Cal were married. Occasionally, she looked around at the passing scenery. Much of the landscape was nearly treeless with tall patches of a reedy-looking grass growing on sandy, flat land.

Intermittently along the way there were small businesses of various types interspersed with houses. Planned zoning apparently had not yet come to this part of the world yet. She took note of the name of a fruit stand sitting next to a small wood frame house with children playing out front. She read the name of it out loud as she passed by, "Lilly's Fruits by the Sea."

Something familiar struck her about that name, but she didn't know what or why. But it kept replaying in her thoughts, until just two words froze in her mind: Lilly and Sea. Suddenly she braked hard and drove off the side of the road skidding to a dusty stop and stalling the engine. A horn blared from the same truck that had honked at her earlier—this time with a fist being shook at her. She waved her hand, calling out an apology even though the truck driver couldn't hear it.

She sat there a moment trying to gather her thoughts. She repeated the words out loud. "Lilly...Sea." She said it two more times, stopping midway the third time. Snapping her fingers, she looked back over her shoulder in the direction of the airport.

"That's it!" she exclaimed out loud. "The Water Lily—the plane he left Ramrod Key on. I saw it at the airport. She proclaimed to herself. "I've got to get back there and quick."

Reaching for the ignition key, she twisted it to start the car. Nothing, not a sound. Growing more frustrated by the second, she did it again. Still nothing. "That's right, I've got to jiggle the damn key!"

A wave of relief washed rapidly over her as the engine started. Jamming the Datsun into gear, she gave a quick check of the road before pulling out. Revving the engine, she let out on the clutch. The Datsun lurched and shuddered, and the engine raced, but she didn't move. A cloud of dust lazily drifted back over the car from the sand and gravel being tossed by the rear tire.

"Dammit!" she yelled. "I'm stuck!"

She sat for a minute trying to figure out what to do when she remembered she and Cal getting stuck in some sugar sand when they were dating. He had pulled off the main road onto what was nothing more than a couple of sandy ruts trailing off through the palmettos and pine trees to a favorite make-out spot.

She remembered how he got them moving when they got stuck once by inching the car forward a little, then reversing going backward a bit and repeating the process each time going a little farther forward until they freed themselves.

So she did the same thing, and on her third attempt, she felt the little Datsun getting better traction, enough to make it out and onto the pavement again. Quickly she made a quick U-turn. Smiling to herself, she shifted into second gear and floored it. She had to get back to the airport fast to find that pilot.

Chapter 27

Under full sail for an hour, Michael still seethed each time he glanced down at the compass. And every time he did, he thought of all the trouble Juky had caused.

Watching the two buffoons he had as a crew trying to properly tie off the foresail only made things worse. "*No,* you idiots!" he yelled. "Let the damn sail 'ave a bit of slack. It needs to grab as much wind as possible."

Muttering to himself, he said, "I should 'ave known better than to pick these two damp squibs for this job. It'll be a bleed'n' miracle if I can still make the deal." Glancing at his watch, he continued, "Twenty-four hours and I can be outta this scrum."

Something else though had caught his attention, and it was beginning to be more of a concern to him. He had noticed a large sleek, dark blue-and-gray yacht that had been running parallel to them a half mile off their portside. It had shown up about thirty minutes ago after passing a small key. Michael kept a wary eye on it. Being on the open water with no fixed reference points, he knew it can play tricks on one's perceptions of distance and speed. It would take a bit longer before he could be sure if the yacht was indeed shadowing them.

For now, he chose not to say anything to his shipmates. He wanted them to appear to be going about things like normal. If whoever was on the yacht was up to no good, he didn't want to prematurely trigger them into action. His suspicion was that if they *were* up to no good, then they likely had a planned time and place to act on their intentions.

Michael gave quick cut of his eye to the yacht. He then shouted out for one of his cohorts to come take the wheel for a moment. The taller blond-haired one waved his hand and started for the stern. Arriving at the helm, Michael pointed to the compass and instructed him to keep them on the same heading while he went below to check the charts.

"Sure thing, Michael. I've got this, mate, no problem."

"Ya said the same thing, Terry, when I left you two buzz 'eads to watch after a guy what be tied up. I bloody saw 'ow that went."

"Aye, come on now—"

Michael cut him off. "Never mind all that. Just watch the bloody compass and keep us on that heading, got it?"

"Yeah, sure." As Michael stepped away, Terry asked, "Aye, did ya see that yacht, Michael? She's a beauty. Prolly some spawny nob wiff lotsa quid, aye?"

Michael glanced over at the yacht then at his smirking shipmate. "Well, let's 'ope that's who's on it, Terry."

Terry's broad smile slowly melted from his narrow face. Michael didn't wait for any response, just disappeared below deck.

Michael was almost certain they were being set up to be boarded by whoever was on the yacht. He had to get a look at the maps. He needed to try and figure out where they most likely would make their move and how soon that might be.

His original plan was to avoid as much attention as possible, something a sailboat of this type tended to get. To that end, he wanted to stay out of sight of land. However, after perusing the map, he decided it was a better risk to run close to Long Island rather than staying out of sight of land. Doing so should make them a less tempting target. Once nightfall came, that would be a different matter. He considered putting in at Crooked Island for the night and then heading out for Pirates Well early the next morning, but that would be cutting it really close on time.

Michael tapped the eraser end of a pencil on the map trying to come up with the best course of action. He then remembered a couple of things his father told him once: *Choose wisely the hills on which to do battle* and *If hiding, don't build a fire.*

Michael stood up from the desk at which he sat and took one more look at the map. "Well, Pop, ya didn't give me much when I was a li'l bugger, but I think I know exactly what to do now. I've just got to get those two knot heads up top to not screw this up."

Coming through the hatchway, Michael called for Martin to come back to the helm where he and Terry stood. Martin acknowledged him and started toward them. Terry proudly pointed to the compass exclaiming.

"'Ave a look, mate, right on the mark. Nary a waiver. Just like you wanted, Cap'n."

Michael only nodded and waited for Martin to make it to the helm before he said anything about the yacht.

Stepping to where Terry and Michael stood, Michael said, "As you two 'ave noticed, we 'ave a yacht off our starboard side."

"Yeah, she's a real beaut. If that was mine, I'd 'ave me a boatload o' chippies in bikinis lying all over 'er decks I would," Terry said, showing a big gap-toothed grin.

Martin guffawed, "Oh, 'oo are you kid'n'? They'd take one look at that mug-a yours and jump overboard."

"Ah, look 'oo's talking. I'm not the one 'oo's got a bleed'n' goiter grow'n' outta es neck the size of blooming brussel sprout."

"Look! Just shut up! The both of you!" Michael shouted. "We've many problems!"

Ceasing their quibbling with each other, they looked at Michael. "Problems? What kind of problems?" Terry queried.

"Yeah, what could be wrong? We 'ave the boat, and we'll be in Pirates Well by tomorrow," Martin added.

Michael looked each man in the eye then said, "It's that bloody yacht ya both 'ave been blathering about. It's been shadowing us for forty-five minutes."

Terry peeked over Michael's shoulder. "Yeah, so what? It's not the bleed'n' cops, not on a boat like that."

"Yeah, it's prolly some bloke 'oo's bank account is bigger than es wang," Martin added with a laugh.

"Maybe," Michael began, "but me gut is say'n' otherwise. Look, to be sure, I want to make like nothing is wrong. I want the both of yas to stay busy. And pay no attention to that bleed'n' yacht. Meanwhile, I'm going to start easing us within sight of land."

"But I thought you didn't want us to be seen?" Terry asked.

"I didn't. But right now, 'av'n' some bloody tourist or some locals see us sail by will be a 'ole lot better'n' getting boarded by who-ever is on that yacht."

Holding a slack-jawed expression, Terry asked, "So's ya want us to look busy-like, eh? Busy doing what, Michael?"

Michael's angry retort flew from him. "I don't care, Terry. Swab a deck, tie some damn knots—just make it look normal, which, I know, looking normal is a lot to ask of you two."

Terry scrunched his thick eyebrows, asking, "But why would a rich nob the likes of 'em want to board us?"

Michael rolled his eyes and started to explain, but Martin chimed in first. "'E may not be some fat rich bloke, ya numpty minger. 'E's saying they might be pirates."

"Eh, ya better watch what you be call'n' me, bloke. I 'ave aff a mind ta paste you right in the ivories."

"Oh yeah? Well, ya got one thing right! You've aff a bleed'n' mind, all right!"

"All right, all right! Enough! Shut up, the both of yas. Listen, if I'm right, they are going to stay right with us until nightfall."

"Then what?" Martin asked.

"That's when they will try to board us."

"What do they want? We don't 'ave noth'n'," Terry added.

"We know that, but they don't. Could be they want this bloody sailboat too."

Both men nodded agreement, then Martin asked, "So what's the plan, mate? We can't outrun 'em."

Michael gave a wry smile. "Not right now. But nighttime is coming. There is some open water once we clear the end of Long Island. That's when we'll make a run for it."

Both men considered what Michael had said. Martin then asked, "Michael, I don't see 'ow that's any better. We'll be running with our lights on. We'll be like bleed'n' beacons out on the open water."

"Not if we don't 'ave 'em on, mate. Look, there's a small key that is aff a mile off shore of Long Island. We'll pass between it and the mainland. That's when we go lights out. I want them to think we made for shore for the night on Long Island."

Terry and Martin both smiled and commented on the logic of what Michael was proposing.

"That'll put us way ahead when we start across the open water," Martin said.

Terry's gap-toothed smile showed prominently again as he said, "Yeah, by the time those blokes figure it out, we'll be long gone, won't we, Michael?"

"Look, this is a long shot. We 'ave about forty-five minutes after the sun sets, before the moon begins to rise. You two need to be ready for anything. It's a big enough risk to be sailing these waters at night and worse to be doing it lights out.

"Now go on, you two, we don't 'ave much time."

Terry went below to grab rags to clean the windows, while Martin went to the forward mast to make adjustments to the rigging.

Michael cut his eyes toward the yacht in the distance, then at the compass. Taking a heading, he began angling toward the coastline of Long Island. It would take a few minutes before he could be sure that the distance between them and the yacht was increasing. For now it appeared to be maintaining its heading, which could mean they were moving on, or they were biding their time until nightfall.

Michael glanced at his watch. It was getting late. The sun would set soon. Gazing the full length of the *Donna Marie* for the first time, he really took notice of just how majestic she was in full sail. She sliced through the water with the purpose and grace of an Olympic swimmer, her hull hardly disturbing the water. She was fast and graceful. It was no wonder the transporter he was to meet at Pirates Well was so willing to pay him such a large sum of money to get her out of U.S. waters.

Thinking of the money, he glanced up at the sails, searching them for any way to get more speed. He had to perfectly time their going behind the key just after sunset. This would only give them ten minutes or so to be completely out of sight of the yacht before they emerged on the other side of the key. For his plan to work, it had to be dark. With the running lights off, he'd make a hard course change and sail around the northern tip of Crooked Island to run south along its eastern shore and directly for Pirates Well.

If his plan worked, the yacht would have three choices; figure they had put in for the night at Gordons Settlement or sailed south down either the eastern or western shore of Crooked Island. The way Michael figured it, he had a two out of three shot of escaping scot-free. However, if they choose the eastern shore, then that yacht would run them down like a rabid dog.

With that thought in mind, he shouted out to Martin and Terry, "Hang on, mates—we be going lights out soon. Next stop, Pirates Well, or Davy Jones's bloody locker!"

Chapter 28

Donna had raced her way back the airport and parked straight in front of the Water Lily so it couldn't leave while she searched the terminal for the pilot. With no idea what he looked like or even what his name was, she had a page done over the PA system for the pilot of the Water Lily to come to the information desk. Donna nervously waited, even having a second page done.

A few moments later with her back to the small open concourse, making small talk with the young lady behind the counter, a man stepped up to the counter. "Hey, uh, I'm the pilot of the Water Lily. Is there some kind of problem?"

Donna immediately turned to him, thrusting out her hand. "Hi, I'm Donna Arnold, Cal's wife. I believe you flew him and another man here yesterday."

Looking a bit shocked, Jim cautiously shook her hand. "Hi, Mrs. Arnold, I'm Jim, Jim Abbot, and yeah, I flew him and some oddball guy here."

Donna, ending the brief handshake, let out a relieved breath, quickly asking, "Do you know where he is, Cal I mean?"

Looking bewildered, he said, "Well, the last thing he said to me over the radio was that we would meet back at the motel."

"Over the radio? I don't understand. What's going?"

"Heck if I know. I was just about to rent a car and head back there now. I can give you a lift."

"That won't be necessary. I have already rented a car, so it looks like I can give you a ride."

"Great, where are you parked? I need to grab a couple things out of the Lily's cockpit."

"As a matter of fact, Mr. Abbot, I'm parked right in front of the Lily's nosewheel."

Jim let out a chuckle. "You were making sure I wouldn't go anywhere, weren't you? Listen, can we drop the formalities? I'm Jim."

Turning to leave, she gave him a crooked smile. "Well, Jim, it seemed to be the smart thing to do."

Donna suggested Jim drive since he knew where they were going. On the way there, he filled her in on what he knew; none of it gave her any comfort. Jim helped secure a key to Cal's room then excused himself and went to his room to work on flight logs and make phone calls.

Donna had anxiously awaited Cal's return for the last couple of hours. Walking around the room, she could tell Cal had been there. A shirt of his was draped on the corner of the bedpost. A pair of trousers lay across the bed. His socks, of course, were on the floor. She smiled, thinking if this were home, she would be fussing at him about leaving all his stuff scattered all over the place.

Plucking the shirt from off the bedpost, she pressed it to her face inhaling deeply. Even though it had only been a little more than a day, she missed him greatly, and the smell of his shirt only deepened her sense of longing. Placing the shirt back on the bedpost, she went to the small table in the corner of the room and sat down. On the table she found a notepad. Scribbled on it were random notes about a cameraman, Interpol, and something about a uniform having to be back by 3:00 p.m. today.

Donna glanced at her watch and said, "Well, honey, you missed that by several hours."

Then she saw a note near the bottom of the page—a note that sent a chill through her.

It made mention of guns. She looked down at her watch again, then around the room. Jim had said it was about a twenty-minute trip back to Rokers Point from where he had last seen them. He should have been here hours ago.

Standing up, she decided to go to Jim's room. She didn't know what he could do, but she knew if she stayed here with no one to talk to, she would go crazy with worry.

Arriving at his room, she gently knocked. When the door didn't open right away, she knocked again, a little harder. A muffled voice called from the other side of the door. She soon heard the locks click just before the door drew open a few inches.

A sleepy-eyed Jim greeted her. "Oh, hey, Donna. What's up? Cal and that weird guy...uh, what's his name?"

"Johnny Mac," Donna said.

"Yeah. Did they get back all right?" he asked, pulling the door open and motioning her to come in.

Donna nervously stepped in only a couple of steps and said, "No, they haven't. I'm really worried now."

Jim raised his eyebrows at hearing this. "Okay, well, if I know that husband of yours, he is probably sitting somewhere concocting another plan. Listen, don't worry—give me a minute to wash my face and change. Then we'll make some phone calls."

"Phone calls? To who?"

"Well, to that charter boat captain, for starters."

Donna started to question him, but he stopped her and said, "Listen, why don't you go over to the pool bar and wait for me there. That'll give me enough time to freshen up and make a couple of calls, okay?"

The look of anguish on Donna's face was apparent as she nodded.

Jim placed his hand on her shoulder, and giving her a sympathetic look, he said, "He's fine. I'm sure of it. Cal is a very resourceful guy. I'm sure you know that."

Donna only nodded while swiping at a couple of escaping tears. Jim gently guided her out the door with a promise to not be long. As she walked away, he called to her to have a whiskey sour waiting for him.

She looked back over her shoulder, smiled, and said, "Okay, I'll see you there."

True to his word, Jim wasn't long. He found her sitting alone at the far corner of a serene tropical patio lounge area. A short distance in front of her table, two couples danced to the music of the steel-drum band. Making his way over to her, she smiled. He gave her a smile while pulling out a chair to sit.

"You're smiling, Jim. I hope that means you have some good news."

"Well, yes it does, at least *some* good news."

Worry returned to Donna's face along with rapid-fire questions. "He's not hurt, is he? Do you know where he is? How far from here is he?"

Jim held up a hand, telling her, "Whoa, whoa. Wait, let me get out what I do know. Then we'll go over what I don't know."

"I'm sorry. I just want to find him and go home and get our life back to the way it was."

"Okay, it took a few calls, but I finally got ahold of the charter boat captain who was helping us with our little plan to get your sailboat back. He told me that he dropped Cal on shore near the Exuma airport several hours ago.

"Well, not exactly on shore—he had to jump in and swim fifty yards or so to the beach. Seems there are no docks by the airport, and the boat's draft was too deep to get close to shore."

"Did he make it to shore all right?"

"Oh yeah, the boat captain said he stayed put until he saw him on the beach and heading for the airport."

"Did the boat captain know why he wanted to go to the airport?"

Jim got a big smile on his face as he looked Donna in the eyes. "Yeah, it seems he wanted to get to the Exuma airport to find you!"

"Me? But how could he know that I was coming there? I hadn't told anyone that."

"Well, here's where it gets screwy. According to the captain, that weird guy, Mac, seems he told Cal that you were going there."

A look of total bewilderment came over Donna's face for a moment. Her bewilderment quickly faded to astonishment as she realized that Johnny Mac must have had one of his visions and relayed that to Cal. How else could Cal know to go to the Exuma airport?

Donna, feeling very confused, asked, "But why isn't he here? The airport is not that far away."

"I asked the captain that, and here's where it gets even weirder. On the way to find the *Donna Marie* this morning, they came across a black man swimming all alone out in the water. They narrowly rescued him from being eaten by a school of sharks."

"All by himself? No other boats around? That *is* weird."

Jim laughed. "That's not the weirdest part."

"It's not?"

"No, the weirdest part was when they hauled that guy aboard, turns out Cal knew who he was. Called him by name. The captain said his name was uh...uh..." Jim snapped his fingers trying to remember. "It was...was, uh, something with a J, Jackie maybe."

Donna quickly interjected, "Juky. Was it Juky?"

"Yeah, that's it! Seems he was injured during the rescue, some broken ribs maybe."

Donna anxiously asked, "Where is the hospital? Maybe Cal went there when he couldn't find me at the airport."

"See, they don't have hospitals here. There are a few clinics scattered on the island. So the boat captain took the weird guy and the Juky fellow to Hoppers Bay. Guess they have a clinic there."

It was easy to see the worry on Donna's face. "Look, these clinics can be very busy places. It can take hours to be seen by a doctor. If Cal did wind up going to Hoppers Bay, then I think it's best to just stay put. If we start running all over the place trying find him, well, we'll be like a dog chasing his tail."

Donna sat considering what Jim had said. Jim smiled and added, "Actually, sitting at a tropical island lounge is better than traipsing all over this island. And sooner or later, Cal *will* have to come back here to at least square up with the resort."

Donna smiled and said, "Okay, I guess we wait, huh?"

"I could think of worse places to do that," he said, while looking at their surroundings.

Wanting to take her mind off things, he then commented on the good luck Donna had after she found herself stuck in the sand on the side of the road.

"It was a real stroke of good luck that you managed to get out of that sugar sand. How did you get stuck in the first place?"

Setting her glass of wine down, she smiled at Jim then said, "I don't think it was luck at all, Jim. It was the name of that fruit stand across the road from where I was stuck that made me stop alongside the road."

"What was so special about the name?"

"It was called Lilly's Fruit by the Sea. It made me remember the name of your plane, the Water Lily, *and* that I had remembered seeing it back at the airport. I was turning around to go back to make sure. I wanted to try and find you. If I couldn't, well, then I was going to camp by the plane until you showed up."

"I can see how you made the connection. But still it *was* a stroke of good luck."

Donna smiled but elected not to get into the divine inter-vention aspects of how she saw her recent good fortune. Instead, she looked around at her very pleasant surroundings. The melodic sounds of the steel-drum band floated on a cool ocean breeze; tall lanky palms swayed as if in time with the music. Frangipani trees ringed the whole area; their pink and white blossoms nudged from the trees by this same soft breeze pirouetted down like tiny ballerinas, swirling in the flickering amber light of tiki torches surrounding the cobble stone patio.

The romantic and peaceful surroundings enveloped her. She longed for Cal to be there. This was the sort of place she had envi-sioned when she planned this whole little scheme of hers. Glancing at her watch again, then at Jim, she worriedly questioned, "Where could he be, Jim? Shouldn't he have been here by now? It's been hours."

Jim looked at her, then something caught his eye. From out of the shadows, someone was walking toward them. Donna caught his odd look and was about to ask him what was wrong, when suddenly a pink flower blossom appeared in front of her face from behind, accompanied by a deep voice. "I believe you are supposed to wear this over your left ear if you are taken. Are you, milady?"

Donna spun quickly around looking up. Her startled expres-sion went to one of absolute delight. Letting out a little scream, she jumped to her feet. Throwing her arms around Cal's neck, she began kissing his cheeks and mouth, repeating his name over and over again.

"Cal, Cal, honey, where have you been? I've been worried out of my mind."

Cal smiled and pulled her deep into his arms and whispered in her ear, "You had me worried sick too, sweetheart."

Suddenly, right in midst of their happy reunion, Donna crinkled her nose while pulling away from Cal's chest. "Oh my goodness. Cal, you smell like something a dog left on the lawn. What in the world have you been into?"

She took a step back pinching her nose and fanning her face. Even though her brow was furrowed, her face still glowed with the joy of him standing right in front of her safe and sound.

Looking a bit sheepish, Cal said, "Sorry, honey, but for the last few hours or so, I have been drenched in sweat, salt water, and God only knows what was going on in that clinic.

"You went to the clinic in Hoppers Bay. Is that why you're so late getting back here?"

"Yeah, well, I didn't go there first," Cal began. "Like I said, part of my wondrous aroma is hours' old salt water and sweat. I first tried to find you at the airport for a good while. I even began asking people if they had seen you. But I obviously came up short. So figuring Jim was back here, I decided to take a cab to the clinic. I wanted to get some information out of Juky about who had the *Donna Marie* and where they were going. How did you know to come here anyway?"

"Well, Jim and I, with a little help, managed to cross paths at the airport."

Cal widened his eyes, saying, "A little help? What do mean, baby?"

Jim immediately chimed in. "Seems your lovely wife here thinks we had a little help from above," he said, pointing a finger straight up. "That and the name of a fruit stand."

Cal looked past Donna to Jim, saying, "A fruit stand? How could a—"

Donna rolled her eyes and held up her hand. "Stop, don't either of you say another word." She then looked Cal in the eyes and simply said, "Let's just say I was guided here and let it go at that."

Hearing that, Cal said, "Oh," making the face that goes with it, because knew exactly what she meant. "Well, however you got here, honey, I'm as happy as a whore in a Navy town that you're here."

Donna gave him a curt look then said, "I see our time apart hasn't taken any of the salt from your language, has it."

Cal placed his hands on her shoulders and said, "I'm sorry, honey. Let's not get upset with each other. Look, the good news is I did get some info out of Juky. I know where the *Donna Marie* is heading. She's heading for Pirates Well."

Donna gave a Cal tired look. "Pirates Well? Look, Cal, sweetheart, I'm tired—"

Cal interrupted her. "Of course, you are. Look, it's late. Let's go to the room, get some sleep, and then in the morning, we can—"

Donna interrupted him this time. "We can go home. I'm tired of this. We need to go back to Ramrod Key and run our business and live our lives and try to forget this whole mess."

Dejectedly, Cal said, "Wait, you're saying you want to just give up on the *Donna Marie*? To just let those thieves get away?"

Donna turned away from Cal and plopped back down in her chair. Jim, feeling more than a little uncomfortable at the moment, stood up from the table. "Look, I'm, ah, tired. I'm going to my room and get a little shut-eye. I, uh…guess you'll let me know what we're doing in the morning."

Both Cal and Donna simply nodded and waited until he left. Cal then sat down pulling his chair close to hers. Speaking softly, he said, "Donna, sweetheart, I didn't mean it the way it sounded. I know it's breaking your heart too."

Donna turned to face Cal; her face etched in pain. "Cal, it's more than just losing the *Donna Marie*. It's knowing that I had a hand in doing that. Plus, the fact that I put people's lives at risk all over some silly notion."

"Notion? What are you talking about? What silly notion?"

Donna explained what she meant. "I was scared, Cal, scared that if we sold the Salty Anchor, our family would drift off our separate ways. And you...well, I thought that without the business to run, well, you'd start to be like my dad. Just kind of waiting around to die. No sense of purpose."

"But sweetheart, how was faking the *Donna Marie* being stolen going to change any of that?"

Donna took a deep breath. She never liked trying to explain her logic. She placed her hand over Cal's on the table and looked him in the eyes.

"I thought that if you were gone from there for a while that when you got back, you might see the place the way I do. We named it the Salty *Anchor,* and...well, that's what it is to me. It anchors our family. It's our harbor in the world. Don't you see?"

Cal pressed his lips together before he spoke.

"I do. I guess the reason I was trying so hard to get the *Donna Marie* back was so that I would still have a connection to the business if we did sell it."

Donna squeezed his hand. She looked lovingly into his eyes and softly said, "Let's go home."

Cal looked down, then back into her eyes, nodded, and said, "Is that what you really want? The place won't be the same without her." Donna only gave a hesitant nod.

They both leaned back in the cane-back cabana chairs to let that decision rest in their minds. The rhythm of the steel-drum band and their tropical surroundings offered little to comfort in dealing with the idea of never seeing their beloved sailboat again.

Cal rolled his head to face Donna, somberly stating, "I'm sure gonna miss her. She looked so majestic last night sitting on the bay."

Donna had likewise turned to face Cal. "At least you got to see her one more time and in a way that I've always loved to see her."

Both let go a sigh. Cal looked at Donna and was about to suggest they go to the room and get some rest. The solemnity of the moment was abruptly shattered by a panicked voice coming from behind them.

"There you two are! I've been looking for you. We have to get to going. We need to go to Pirates Well! If we don't, the *Donna Marie* will be lost forever. But we need to go and soon!"

Chapter 29

In the next moment, Johnny Mac was on the opposite side of the table admonishing them to get moving.

"Hold on, J-Mac. It's already gone," Cal began. "We have decided to just go back home, report her stolen, and hope for the best."

"No, you don't understand. We still have a chance to get her, but we have to go now. She is being pursued. She is in a race for her life."

Donna scoffed. "Johnny Mac, you talk as if she is alive. It's just a sailboat." Her last words stung even her own ears. For she and Cal had many times talked of the *Donna Marie* like she was a living thing. Cal would often say that her sails were her lungs, and the sea breathed life into her every time she set sail.

Johnny Mac looked at them both. "Look, I know that neither of you believe that. But if you've decided to give up on her, then I guess there's nothing I can say that will change that. I just thought you might want to have one more shot to save her from the fate that awaits her."

"Johnny Mac, that's not fair," Donna began. "Of course, we would love to save her. But we're in way over our heads here."

"She's right. It's way too risky. You just said she is being pursued. By who? She's already in the hands of pirates."

This time it was Johnny Mac who scoffed. "Those bumpkins aren't pirates. They're just mules. They just deliver stolen boats to the real pirates. They're going to hand her off in Pirates Well tomorrow. That is, if they make it there."

"Wait, how do you know all of this?" Cal asked.

Johnny Mac shot a "well duh" look at him.

"What, you had some kind of vision? Wow, that is pretty detailed."

"No, dummy, I came across a teenage boy who works around the marina. He saw a guy come into the marina in the *Donna Marie's* dingy."

Cal and Donna's eyes widened. Each shot rapid-fire questions. "He did? What did he say? What was he doing in the marina? Was he getting supplies? Maybe he used a credit card. We can find out who this guy is maybe."

Suddenly, Cal held up a hand and halted Donna's next question, saying, "Hold it, hold it. Our minds are made up. We are not chasing after that guy, whoever he is, or the *Donna Marie*."

Johnny Mac reiterated again the need for leaving soon. However, both Donna and Cal still weren't convinced to go chasing after her.

"Okay, look, he did get a few supplies, but he also took a mechanic out to the *Donna Marie* to repair the compass."

"The compass? There was nothing wrong with the compass… at least there wasn't—"

Growing more impatient with Cal's interruptions, Johnny Mac snapped at him. "Stop it and just listen, will you! That's not what's important."

Cal rolled his eyes and waved a hand for Johnny Mac to continue.

"Okay, here's the deal. The kid has seen this guy a number of times before and always with a different kind of boat. That's how he figured out he was a runner."

"What the heck is a runner anyway?"

"It's someone who is paid to take boats out of U.S. territorial waters. They hand them off at predetermined places to a smuggling ring. They are paid very well to do so. A boat like yours, he said, could bring as much as five thousand bucks."

Cal was skeptical. "How does this teenage kid know so much about this stuff?"

"The kid gets paid to clean these boats. And not just the outside. He hears things. Sometimes he sees things."

"Then why doesn't he report them to the police?" Cal questioned.

Johnny Mac gave a look of incredulity. "Come on, Cal. He's a seventeen-year-old boy. It's not just one smuggler, it's several. There's a sort of cabal of them. If he reported any one of them, one of the others would turn him into fish bait, and not just him but maybe his whole family."

Cal rubbed his face. "Great, then that's even more of a reason to go home and let the authorities handle it. 'Cause I have no intention of getting Donna or me or even you turned into fish bait."

"Cal, Donna, listen. Here's the part where we can get her back. See, the runners and the international smugglers never actually meet for the handoff. There is a third party to verify that the boat has been delivered in good condition. The money is paid by the third party. And here's the beautiful part. While it is there, phony papers arrive showing a change of ownership. The name is changed, and it might even get repainted. Then when they're ready, she just slips out one day, and she is gone, heading across the Atlantic for the new owner who is unaware that the boat they just paid big bucks for is stolen."

Cal's mood went slowly from skepticism to piqued interest. "So how do we get her back from there? Won't people be guarding the boat?"

"No. That's the beautiful part. They let it sit for a few days just to make sure nobody is looking for it. From the time the boat arrives, things are done to make it appear completely normal. Kind of a 'nothing to see here' thing," Johnny Mac said while making air quotes.

Cal gave Donna a quick glance then back to Johnny Mac. "So let me get this straight. The *Donna Marie* is going to Pirates Well right now. And once she arrives, she'll be berthed for several days. What's the rush? I'll show up with my paperwork that shows I'm the owner and take her back home."

"No, you won't. While it sits a few days, phony paperwork showing a sale from you to a phony yacht sales company in Europe will be delivered, and is likely already there, so as soon as they feel it's safe to move it, she'll be gone, and quick."

Johnny Mac's tone became consoling. "Don't you see, you have a shot, *if* we get there by first thing in the morning. There's a chance that you might be able to just walk onto her and sail her right out of there. It's a move they won't be expecting. But we have to be there early."

Cal saw Donna's apprehensions suddenly vaporize. He thought he knew where she stood on the matter. But in the next instant, she pressed her lips tight. With a look of pure defiance on her face, she commanded, "Cal, let's go get our damn boat!"

Chapter 30

The strong breeze that propelled them when they first emerged from behind the small key grew weaker as the night wore on. In the distance, Michael watched their pursuers' searchlight methodically scan the waters. Michael was sure that if they could make it around the tip of Crooked Island undetected, then they would make it to Pirates Well. Conversely, if they were spotted, then all bets were off on what would happen next.

Whoever was on the yacht knew how to conduct a search on open water. But so far, the distance prevented them from casting any light on the sails or hull of the *Donna Marie*—something Michael was desperately hoping wouldn't happen. But the search pattern was moving ever closer to crossing the course he had plotted. Any deviation he made now from that course would mean arriving there too late. His contact was adamant about the arrival time.

Suddenly the low drone of the yacht's diesel engine went silent. The search light ceased its constant sweep of the surrounding ocean.

Curiously Michael watched. "What are you blokes up to now?" he murmured.

"Sure is quiet now," Terry whispered.

As soon as Terry had spoken, the proverbial light came on for Michael. He turned to Terry and Martin who were sitting immediately behind him. Putting his finger to his lips, he whispered ever so quietly.

"Shh. I know what they be doing, lads. They're listening."

Martin leaned well forward. "For what?" he breathed.

Michael turned and bent down on one knee, gesturing for them both to lean in close. He spoke very quietly. "Sound carries a

171

long way on open water. They are listening for any sound that will give away our position. Now, no more talking out loud. Don't move unless I tell you to. And take your shoes off just in case you have to work the sails."

As if on cue, two of the foresails snapped in the faltering breeze. In the next instant, the yacht's searchlight swept up and began sweeping twenty-feet off the water in their general direction.

Michael glanced quickly up then back to his shipmates. His panicked whisper came fast. "Get the shoes off and go tighten the rigging—all of it. Work together, but be quiet about it."

Both men nodded while slipping off their shoes. They made quick soft steps to the forward mast. Michael watched them fade into the darkness shrouded bow.

"I need a bleed'n' miracle to get out of this one I do," Michael murmured.

Terry and Martin worked in silence carefully tightening the rigging. But they all knew there was no way to make it completely silent. For it wasn't just the sails; it was also what connected them to the masts. There is all manner of metal hardware in the form of clevises and brass rings all over the ship. It was only a matter of time before a wave or a gust of wind could make the rigging of the *Donna Marie* sound like a nautical wind chime.

Michael was racking his mind trying to come up with a way out of this mess. If the breezes stopped, then they would also stop. Firing up the *Donna Marie*'s small diesel would draw that search like a bee to honey, and making a run for it was hopeless. The only thing going for them at the moment was that the one sound the sails had made wasn't enough to zero in on them, but it did narrow their sweep, but they hadn't been able to pinpoint them, not yet.

The yacht's engine remained off, which meant they were drifting, hopefully farther away. Michael breathed a small sigh of relief at seeing the distance growing wider and wider between them. The breeze though was still slacking off for them.

Michael shook his head at the thought of their predicament, saying to himself, "I'm in some kind of ruddy game of chicken 'ear." Looking up at the star-filled sky, he continued, "Look, I know you don't care to 'ear from the likes of me, but I could really use that miracle about now. Maybe I don't deserve it. But those two blokes with me might 'ave one due 'em."

The distance continued to grow between the two vessels. Terry and Martin stayed at mid-ship keeping a careful eye on all the sails and rigging. A bit of relief began to settle on the three of them, but it was short-lived. For from out of the blackness, rolling fast and silent, a three-foot wave struck the *Donna Marie* diagonal to the hull. She pitched violently side to side and up and down causing all the rigging to explode in rattles, clacks, and bangs. The brass bell clanged wildly. Michael lunged to silence it. Terry and Martin grabbed for the cabin railing narrowly missing being tossed overboard.

In an instant, the yacht's searchlight swept back in their direction scouring the darkness. But a moment later, the same wave began rolling the yacht wildly up and down, briefly rendering the searchlight's efforts useless. Once the sea calmed, the searchlight would no doubt quickly find them. Terry and Martin rushed to where Michael stood. Martin quietly asked, "Where the hell did that come from?"

Michael kept his voice low, saying, "We're in the shipping lanes. Probably the wake of some oil tanker or container ship."

"But I didn't see no lights from ship, Michael," Terry exclaimed.

"Those waves can travel for miles out 'ear. You'd never see what made 'em."

Martin nervously said, "They still 'av'n't spotted us yet."

Martin's words had no sooner fell away into the cool night air when the yacht's searchlight caught the top of the *Donna Marie*'s main mast. It sat frozen for a moment. All three men stood motionless watching the searchlight. It moved like the finger of a psychotic killer stroking the face of their next victim, slowly moving down the mast until the center of the *Donna Marie* was awash in bright light.

The searchlight held its fix on the hull. With only a quarter mile's separation, the ominous sound of the yacht's powerful diesel engines powering up was easily heard bringing a wave of dread washing over all three men. Slowly, the sleek yacht, like a panther stalking its prey, began slowly moving toward them.

Michael's blood ran cold. *This is it*, he thought. It was all going to end right here, right now.

Terry looked pleadingly at Michael. "What are we gonna do? Michael!"

"Pray, mates, pray."

Chapter 31

Cal and Donna stood in the doorway to Jim's room. "C'mon, Jim," Cal beseeched. "Just fly us there. You can drop us off and fly home. You're our only hope to get to Pirates Well before sunrise."

"Do you have any idea how dangerous it is to try and make a water landing in the dark?"

"Look, I know it's tough, but we did them in the Navy."

"Tough! Cal, look, back then you did what you were told 'cause you were too young and stupid to know better. Well, I ain't young anymore. And I'm damn sure not that stupid anymore."

Cal turned away for a second combing his hand through his hair. Turning back to face Jim, he said, "Okay, how about getting us there right at sunrise. Will that do?"

Jim pressed his lips tight glaring at Cal. He then caught a glimpse of Donna just behind Cal. "Are you wanting to do this too?"

Donna nodded and said, "It looks like it's our last chance to get her back, Jim."

Pulling a hand down his face, he murmured, "I just don't know."

Before anyone could say another word, Johnny Mac tried squeezing between Cal and Donna. Perplexed, they moved aside enough to let him squeeze through. As if coming to plead a case before a judge, Johnny Mac first straightened his baggy shirt. With both hands, he then stroked his beard a couple of times.

Taking a short breath, he said, "It would be best if you took them to Pirates Well."

Jim narrowed his eyes. "Is that some kind of threat? 'Cause if it is, you're gonna need someone in better shape than you to follow through on it."

"A threat? From me? Oh, heaven's sake, no. But a threat there is." In an instant, Johnny Mac's expression became far off. His voice became smooth and soft. "Your path home is crossed. A split second's time will drop it from the element above, to one that rolls below."

Jim's eyes widened. He stared at Johnny Mac a moment. He then looked at Cal. "What the hell is this nut talking about, Cal?"

Cal and Donna stepped on into the room. Cal asked, "J-Mac, what the hell *are* you saying? We don't have time for this now. We need Jim to fly us to Pirates Well."

Johnny Mac started to explain, but from out in the hallway, a deep island-accented voice came from the open doorway.

"Et es clear to me what es telling you." Just then Juky stepped into the light that spilled from the room.

Donna immediately spun around to greet him. "Juky, where have you been? I have been worried sick about you." Donna poked Cal in the ribs. "All this one said is that you were in a clinic getting taped up."

"I was. But afterward I went to a friend's home to rest for a while. I meant to be here sooner, but…" Pointing to Johnny Mac, he added, "Your friend here stayed with me. And I must say he is quite extraordinary aund knows what he es talking about."

Jim began waving his hand in the air and talking over them all. "Okay, okay, hold on, hold on just a second. This guy"—he began pointing at Johnny Mac—"said something that's completely sense-less. And you," he continued, while pointing at Juky, "and you say he knows what he's talking about?"

"Dat es right. You *are* de owner and pilot of de seaplane called Water Lily, right?"

"Yeah, so?"

"Tell me what 'appens to aircraft whose paths cross at de same moment?"

Jim looked at Johnny Mac, then to Cal and Donna, then at Juky. "Well, they collide. Wait, so you're saying that me and another plane are going to collide if I fly for home instead of flying them to Pirates Well?"

Juky shook his head "no." "No, it es not I who say dis. It es he, he who can see de things others cannot."

Jim threw up his hands and turned away from them all. "Oh my god, there has got to be something in the water around here. You *all* are nuts."

Turning back to face them, Jim continued, "Look, I planned on taking off around nine this morning and head straight home to Marathon. I fly over these waters all the time. Mornings in the summer are almost always clear blue skies. I can spot a plane miles away. I'm not worried about bending wings with another plane, got it?"

Johnny Mac had remained quiet. Suddenly he spoke up. "Look, I only said that you crossed paths. I didn't say how."

Jim's retort was short and terse. "Just what is that supposed to mean?"

Johnny Mac jutted his jaw out a bit while making a downward circular motion with his index finger, saying. "It is not what is ahead that you must watch but rather the hands of the clock."

Jim stared at Johnny Mac still making the circular motion with his finger. His eyes widened realizing he meant. From above at twelve o'clock or maybe from his six below, either one was out of his line of sight.

Jim gazed around at all. "Okay, this is bullshit. But if you want me to fly you to Pirates Well this bad, I'll do it, but no landing at night. It's gonna be thirty minutes after sunrise and not a minute sooner, got it?"

A wave of relief washed over all. Cal glanced at his watch. "Hey, sunrise isn't that far off."

Jim spoke up, sounding like the commanding officer he used to be. "That's right. We don't have any time to waste. Its 2300 hours right now. We need to be in the air by 0500. Got it?"

Donna sarcastically blurted out, "Hey, General Eisenhower, what's that in normal people time?"

Before Jim could say anything, Cal interjected, "Don't worry about it, Donna, I know. We have a little time to catch a couple hours of shut-eye. So let's head back to the room. We need to be back by 4:00 a.m. Is that enough time, Jim?"

"Yeah, gives a little cushion, but not much, so don't be late...
again. If you fall behind, you get left behind. Understood?" Everyone
nodded. "Good. Now get out of here so I can get some shut-eye. I
got a feeling I'm going to need it."

Cal gave Jim an apologetic look. Stepping in close, he asked,
"Listen, uh, Jim, can, uh, can J-Mac and Juky bunk with you?"

Jim gave him an odd look, and then to Donna, who stood
talking quietly to Juky. Smiling, he said, "Sure, it'll be like the ole
days back at Bassingbourn when we'd sneak one of the local girls on
base."

Cal smirked. "No, it's not quite like that. I just need to be alone
with her. We've only been together for one night in the last few days."

Jim's naughty boy smile fell away. But before he could ask why,
Cal put a hand up halting him. "I'll explain later. But it is the reason
we are on this mission."

Jim nodded and simply said, "Okay, buddy."

Cal turned to face Donna and Juky. "Donna, let's go back to
my room. Juky, you and Johnny Mac are bunking with Jim the rest
of the night."

Juky stepped around Donna. "Look, I can return to ma friend's
home if dat es better."

Cal held up a hand. "No, no, look. I want everyone here. No
stragglers. We are all leaving together. Understood? We'll meet here
at 4:00 a.m."

All nodded agreement. "Good, let's all get some shut-eye.
C'mon, Donna, let's go." Grabbing her by the back of the arm, he
began to usher her out of the room.

"Who are you, Jessie Owens? What's the rush?" Donna
protested.

Subdued snickers ensued from Jim and Johnny Mac. Cal
stopped short and looked back at them. "What? Are you guys fourteen? C'mon already."

Donna giggled too, saying, "Well, Cal, I haven't seen you this
excited to get me in a motel room since our honeymoon."

Laughter then erupted from all but Cal. "Oh, knock it off, you
bunch of hyenas. It's not like that. Now come on, Donna, let's go."

Seeing Cal's irritation only made Donna laugh harder. Saluting, she chided him between laughs, "Aye, aye, Captain. Wait, no, no, this feels more like you should be dragging me by my hair down the hallway lake a caveman." She then doubled in laughter.

"Oh, come on now, you too. Fine—you all can stand around laughing like idiots. I'm going to the room to get some sleep," Cal fumed.

Cal was a few feet away when Donna called after him giggling, telling him to wait up. Catching up to him, she slipped her arm around his waist and leaned into him.

"Cal honey, don't be mad. We're all very tired and little punchy." With a chuckle in her voice, she continued, "C'mon, sweetheart. Look, we are on a beautiful island in the Bahamas. Can we just go back to the room and let all of this stuff go for a couple of hours?"

Cal put his arm around her shoulder giving her a sideways glance. "A couple of hours? Baby, I'm not in my twenties anymore, you know."

Donna stopped dead in her tracks. "Hold on a second there, Mister Arnold. What was all that 'Oh, this isn't about that' stuff?" Donna asked.

Cal stopped, turning to face her. A sly grin drew across his face as he said, "I lied. It's exactly about that."

Donna's face brightened into big smile. "Why, you old horndog you."

"Horndog? Donna sweetheart, it's going on two weeks for heaven's sake."

A mischievous look washed over her face. She then challenged, "Race you back to the room." Quickly slipping her flip-flops off, she stooped to grab them, and then shot off down the hallway giggling the whole way.

Cal stood for a second or two watching his wife trotting off taunting him like a teenage girl on prom night. Shaking his head, a big smile spread across his face. He then raced off after her. Glancing back over her shoulder, she squealed out a laugh, running even faster.

Seconds later she skidded to a stop, turning her back against the door. Cal stomped to a stop right in front of her. She breathlessly laughed while telling him, "You run pretty slow, old man. I beat you here."

"Moving in closer," he taunted. "Yeah, you did, but I have the room key," he said, holding it up by her face. He then leaned in giving her a kiss.

When he drew back, she cut her eyes up to the key dangling from his fingertips. "Not anymore." Instantly she swiped it from his fingertips putting it behind her back, clutching it tightly in her fists.

With a playful grin, she challenged him. "What are you going to do about it now, big boy, huh?"

Cal looked softly into her blue-green eyes. "Just this." Leaning in, he gently cupped her face with both hands then kissed her softly at first, then with increasing passion. Donna's whole body began to relax. She too began to match the intensity of the kiss.

The room key slowly slid from her hands, landing at her tiptoed feet. Wrapping her arms around his neck, she prolonged the deep passionate kiss. In the ensuing moments, nothing else mattered. Cal slowly slipped a hand behind Donna's waist and twisted the doorknob, letting it drift partly open.

Donna's eyes abruptly opened ending the kiss but remained close to his lips. Breathlessly she said, "How did you do that with no key?"

"Easy. I forgot to lock the door. Sometimes an old man's forgetfulness has its advantages."

Donna's eyes held a saucy look. "Well, this old man is about to see another advantage he has." With one foot, she eased the door open then guided Cal through. Without ever letting go of each other, he pushed the door closed with his heel.

The soft amber light of the patio lounge tiki torches flowed through a gap in the curtains, tracing a path across the bed. Donna settled to sit on the edge of the bed; Cal sat down beside her. With the tips of his fingers, he gently turned her face to him and kissed her again.

Still enveloped in their kiss, they slowly eased down into the soft coolness of the bed as their passions intensified. Soon the room was filled with the sounds of their love. Like revisiting a favorite book, the pages leafed rapidly back to the days of their youth, when their love was new and intense and all that mattered.

Tomorrow would add new chapters, perhaps fraught with danger or adventure with the hand of fate as its scribe. But for now, in this small moment of time, vows made decades ago were being wordlessly renewed in the fluid motions of two people still very much in love.

Chapter 32

With the yacht edging ever closer, Michael spoke quickly without looking at either man. "Martin, I want you to go below. Open a port window, take our rifle, and when I yell, shoot that damn searchlight out. Terry, the second 'e does that, you turn our searchlight on and put it right on their bloody hull at the waterline. Martin, you put some well-placed shots right along their waterline. Got it? Don't talk, just go now!"

Both men ran to do as told. Martin positioned himself at the open window ready to take the shot on the yacht's searchlight. Terry crouched down behind the roof of the cabin and pointed the *Donna Marie*'s light in the direction of the slowly approaching yacht.

Michael hunkered down in the seat well behind the ship's wheel. Drawing his 9mm pistol from his waistband, he took aim at the yacht. He waited for it to be close enough for Martin to have a good shot but not too close. Terry would have only seconds to zero in on the yacht's hull. Once he did, then he too would open fire.

Michael waited a moment more, then suddenly he yelled out, "Now, mates, now!" A single shot erupted from the port window. The yacht's searchlight exploded in a flash of fire and smoke. The *Donna Marie*'s searchlight flashed on, sweeping wildly at first, then coming to rest at the waterline of the yacht's gleaming hull.

The flash of gunfire erupted in both directions, but with the yacht's light shot out and the *Donna Marie*'s light in their faces, the return fire from the yacht was wild and inaccurate. Martin's shots were precise, five right along their waterline. Michael fired at the lit-up areas of the deck to keep the return fire at a minimum. Blindly fired shots from the yacht spattered into the *Donna Marie*'s deck, blasting chunks of teakwood into the night air. Another lucky shot shattered the port window next to Martin. Ducking down, he punched in another clip and took aim again.

Abruptly the gunfire ceased. The yacht stopped three hundred feet away. Panicked shouts could be heard. The engine went briefly to idle, then reengaged. It was moving again but not toward them. They had reversed course.

The *Donna Marie*'s spotlight illuminated the water pouring furiously from the yacht's bilge ports. Michael breathed a sigh of relief. The yacht was taking on water. How much, he couldn't know. Michael called to Terry telling him to kill the searchlight. Instantly the sea went dark. The only light came from the deck of the yacht. Shadowed figures could be seen scrambling back and forth shouting to one another. It took a few seconds to realize their shouts were not in English. Michael struggled to recognize the language, then it hit him, Russian. Though he couldn't understand what was being said, it was clear that they were in a panic to get things under control.

A few minutes had passed when all the shouting and commotion aboard the yacht abruptly ceased. Then a lone backlit figure stood boldly on the yacht's bow facing in the *Donna Marie*'s direction. A bullhorn crackled, and a deep Russian-accented voice blared through the blackness.

"You on za sailboat. You haff made a grave error. We vill have ze situation under control soon. You vill surrender ze vessel, or you vill go to za bottom of za ocean. I give you five minutes to decide."

Terry and Martin joined Michael in the seat well. Martin spoke up. "We don't 'ave much ammo left for the rifle. Maybe two clips' worth. And our pistols aren't much good at this distance."

It was again looking hopeless. Michael looked grimly at his partners in crime. Taking this sailboat was supposed to be easy. *Just nip the boat and deliver it to Pirates Well*, he thought.

He then looked at the dingy and said, "Look, why don't you two blokes drop the dingy over the side an 'ed for Long Island. It's close enough still. Meanwhile, I'll make off in a different direction."

Martin spoke up first. "And what do you plan on doing when they catch you?"

Shrugging his shoulders, he solemnly said, "I don't know, mate, 'ope for a bleed'n' miracle, I suppose."

"No, we ain't leaving. We come this far. We be staying with ya," Terry defiantly said.

Michael put a hand on Terry's shoulder. "Look, both of you, you 'ave someone to go home to. Martin, you got a wife, and Terry, you've got your mum and pop. Me, I've got no one. No one's going to miss me. Now get the dingy overboard and go. We're almost outta bloody time."

Martin looked Michael in the eye then to Terry. Reaching into his pants pockets, he pulled out a full clip of ammo which he jammed into the rifle. "I'm staying. Me old lady 'ates me guts anyway."

Terry gave a short laugh. "Yeah, me mum and pop, well, they're so old they barely know what day of the bloody week it is. They prolly forgot they even 'ave a son."

Michael placed a hand both their shoulders. "Looks like we've become the bloody three musketeers."

Suddenly the bullhorn crackled on again. "You time es almost up. Surrender za vessel."

Michael looked quickly to Terry and Martin then suddenly shouted out into the blackness. "Kiss me bloody British ass!"

The Russian's voice echoed back across the water. "Zat es a poor choice." The bullhorn snapped off.

Tension filled the air. Terry asked, "What should we do, Michael?"

Michael thought for a second or two. He then spoke to Martin. "You have two clips left. We'll use them to 'old 'em off for a bit. Terry, you get the dingy in the water. Put whatever pistol ammo we 'ave in it."

"Martin, when I tell ya, fire two rounds right in the bottom of this boat. Then make for the dingy. I'm 'op'n' they care more about sav'n' this boat than shoot'n' us."

A chill ran over them as the air began to turn off cool. The water was calm; all was quiet. A moment later, the ominous low rumble of the yacht's engines firing up vibrated the heavy night air. Once again Michael had that sick feeling in the pit of his stomach. Glancing up at the stars, he quietly mouthed to himself, "Just one bleed'n' miracle, that's all, just one."

He held his gaze on the star-filled sky, the clarity of which was stunning. Standing there quietly, he felt it could be the last time he ever saw stars, or anything else for that matter. At first unnoticed, the sky began to be obscured. A mist began folding and rolling in overhead. "Great, guess I'm not even gonna get to enjoy that."

Dropping his head down, he looked out toward the yacht. He couldn't believe what he was seeing. It was fog, thick fog! An intense feeling of relief suddenly washed over him. A huge bank of dense sea fog was rolling quickly over them. Michael's eyes widened. He then shouted to Terry, "Stop lowering the dingy over the side."

"Martin, get up 'ear quick, hurry! Terry, forget the dingy and start dropping sails. Get moving now!"

Martin exploded up onto the deck. "What's going on? What are you yellin' about?"

"Help Terry drop the mainsails down. I don't care how. Just drop 'em and fast.

Michael jumped behind the helm. In the dark he began looking over the control panel searching for the starter key or button to the diesel engine. Finding it, he shouted out, "Yes!" Pressing a small chrome button, nothing happened at first. "C'mon." Anxiously pressing it again, the small Perkins diesel engine came to life; you felt it more than heard it. The vibration could be felt directly below his feet. Flipping on the running lights, the console lights came on as well, checking the compass. He then engaged the prop. The *Donna Marie* surged forward but struggled against the resistance of the sails that had yet to be dropped. But as each one sagged down onto the deck, she gained more speed.

The sound of the yacht's engine speed increased. The bullhorn crackled on again.

"Zis fog will not help you. Our radar will locate you, so stop now and we will spare you."

Moving to the bow for the last sail, Martin grabbed the handle to the foresail's winch. Releasing the tension on the pawl, he drew it back, letting the sail free fall to the deck with an air rushed thump.

The *Donna Marie*'s masts were now naked of any canvas. Ropes and rigging hung and dangled all over the masts. Metal d-rings and spring clips clacked and clanged against the spares and yardarms. Terry and Martin worked feverishly to fold and pile the canvas as best they could on top of the cabin roof.

Terry spoke out loud, "'Ow long do you think we 'ave before they find us with that radar?"

Michael said as they folded the last sail, "'E's bluffing. I shot at it before you shut off our spotlight. If that bleed'n' radar was working, they'd be here already. That's why they be moving so slow, 'cause they can't see any better in this fog than we can."

"I just wish we could get a bit more speed outta that engine of ours."

Martin said, "I think I can 'elp with that. I use to work on those buggers with me father when I was a young lad." Martin quickly stood and headed for the cabin door. He motioned for Terry to come help move some of the sail canvas off the cabin door opening.

A moment or so had gone by when Michael saw the needle on the rpm gauge move to nearer the redline. The *Donna Marie* responded quickly with a bit more speed.

Michael spoke out loud. "That's good, mate, 'old 'er right there. We're making maybe thirteen or fourteen knots now."

It was a few minutes before they realized that the sound of the yacht's engine no longer accompanied them.

Michael shook his head. He thought about how they had twice cheated certain death. Looking down at the engine's rpm gauge, the indicator needle bounced menacingly close to its maximum rpm. Speaking quietly to himself, he said, "If that engine can 'old together and we don't get split into by a freighter, it will be another bleed'n' miracle."

Michael worried how the *Donna Marie* would look in the morning's light and how the damage would affect his being able to close the deal. Checking his heading, he made a small course adjustment. Taking a deep breath, he gazed upward into the heavy mist, saying, "One bleed'n' problem at a time, mate, one at a time."

He glanced down at his watch. "It will soon be over one way or the other." Letting out a huff, he added, "And this was supposed to be easy money."

Chapter 33

The pounding on the door startled them awake. Cal's eyes flashed open, grousing at first about the noise. He then saw the clock on the nightstand. "Oh my god. Donna, get up. We have to get moving now!" Cal bolted for the door, jerking it open to see Johnny Mac anxiously pacing in the hallway. "We're up, we're up, J-Mac. We'll see you at Jim's room in five minutes, and tell him if he leaves, I won't pay him for any of this trip."

Johnny Mac chuckled a bit, saying, "Okay, he knew you'd say that. So he said to tell you he doesn't care about getting paid."

"Okay, okay, we're coming."

Cal shut the door. Hitting the light switch, both lamps flashed on. "Donna, come on. Get outta bed, honey. We have to get moving now!"

Grumbling and squinting, barely awake, she pushed herself up on her elbows. "What the hell, Cal, where's the fire?"

"The fire is Jim is about to leave us here if we don't get moving. Now come on. Get up, girl, and get dressed."

Donna pushed herself up to a sitting position. The bedsheets slipped down around her waist. Groggy and still trying to gather her wits about her, she looked down to see she had nothing on. The memories of a few hours ago brought a warm smile. Cal was bent over sliding on his pants still admonishing her to get moving. Looking up while fastening his belt, he saw Donna just sitting there smiling.

He froze and smiled. "It *was* good last night, wasn't it?"

Donna's sleepy smile broadened. "Yes, yes it was."

They stared at each other for a second or two, both in consideration of a short encore performance.

Cal's face went suddenly straight. "No, no, we can't. Not that I wouldn't like to. But we are going to miss our chance of getting the *Donna Marie* back. Now come on, baby, *please* hurry and get dressed."

Her mind clearing of sleep, Donna reflexively pulled the bed-sheet up to cover herself. "Cal, I'm not getting dressed without taking a shower. That's disgusting."

Buttoning his shirt, Cal retorted, "Baby, we don't have time for that now. You can bathe when we have the *Donna Marie* back, okay?"

"I most certainly will do no such thing. Caleb Arnold. Now you just march down the hall and you tell Captain Impatient he can wait ten lousy minutes. I'll be right there."

"Donna, how am I supposed to do that? He is ready to go *now*."

"I don't know. Use that glib tongue of yours. It worked pretty good kissing me last night."

A wide grin showed as Cal said, "I doubt my kissing him is gonna work."

"Oh, stop that. You'll think of something to say, but it has to be something a little less personal than a kiss."

"I don't know. You saw how adamant he was last night."

"Oh, pshaw! He wants to do this as much as we do. Now go!"

Cal finished tying his shoes. Standing up, he buttoned his shirt and started for the door. "I'll give it my best shot. You need to hurry though."

"I will, I will. Now get going. I'll be there before you know it."

Cal went to the bedside and bent to give her a kiss. And like the school boy he was feeling like, he also tried to slip his hand under the bedsheet Donna had wrapped around her.

"Caleb Arnold! Stop that. Now get going. You've got to stop Jim from leaving without us."

"Okay, okay. But can't I have just one little—"

Donna cut him off before he finished what he was going to say. "*No!* Now go!"

Feigning disappointment, he straightened. "Boy you've gotten a lot stricter in your old age."

Donna scowled at him. "Oh, for heaven's sake. Give a guy an inch."

Donna saw the devilish look in Cal's eyes and knew he was going give her a naughty reply.

"Stop! Don't even go there, mister."

Pulling the door open a crack, he looked back at her. "Now how do you know what I was going to say?"

"Are you kidding me? After all these years, I know everything that goes on in that dirty little mind of yours."

Cal stood for a moment just staring at her. He then gave her a look of desire and said in a deep sultry tone, "Not everything you don't."

Cal then slipped out the door. Donna felt a shiver run over her. She thought, even after all these years, he could still do that to her.

Cal trotted his way to Jim's room. Arriving, he shoved the door open. The door banged back against the wall. Looking around, Cal only saw Johnny Mac sitting on the edge of the bed. Jim nor Juky were anywhere in sight.

Johnny Mac answered him before he even asked, "He left a couple of minutes ago."

"What? Why didn't you and Juky try and stop him?"

"We tried, but he insisted on going. Juky followed after him."

"C'mon, we've got to stop him!"

"How? He won't listen to anything we say."

"I don't know. I'll think of something—let's go! Hurry up, dammit!"

Cal turned and took off running for the parking lot.

"Hey, wait up! You know I can't run like that."

Not bothering to answer, Cal disappeared around a corner and was gone.

Cal had no idea if he would make it or what he was going to do to stop Jim from leaving. He'd worry about that if he caught him before he left. Bursting through a pair of double doors to the parking lot, he skidded to a stop scanning the parking lot, not seeing or hearing anyone. He trotted a little farther out from the building, scanning the small shell parking lot in every direction.

Nothing or no one could be seen. He was gone! Cal's head dropped. He had failed once again, he thought.

From out of the darkness, a deep voice spoke anxiously. It was Juky.

"Way-ah es everyone? We might still catch hem. He just pulled out."

"Why didn't you stop him before he left? He'll be in that plane and gone by the time we get there."

"I tried to, but he wouldn't listen."

"How is he getting there anyway?"

"He made arrangements to be picked up last night. Seems he did not trust yo-ah being on time."

Cal's eyes widened. "Really? Great, here's the keys to our rental. Go get it and meet us here—I'm going back for Donna." Cal spun around and blasted back through the double doors practically running over Johnny Mac.

"Look out, J-Mac! I gotta go get Donna. Wait outside for Juky—we might still have a chance to stop Jim at the airport."

Looking and feeling a bit befuddled, he shrugged and went on outside mumbling to himself as he went, "Cal really needs to learn to relax more."

Racing up the hallway, he saw Donna coming out of Jim's room. "Donna baby, come on. We have to hurry. Jim left. But we might still be able catch him at the airport."

Donna pulled the door closed and hurried to him. "Jim left us?"

"He sure did."

"Huh, I didn't think he would really do it."

"He's an old bomber pilot. Those guys hate waiting."

"Cal honey, if he has a head start, how are we going to catch him in time?"

Cal started them back toward the parking lot explaining as they trotted side by side.

"I'm betting he needs to fuel that bird up and do his preflight checks. That's not some single engine Cessna he's flying, so he can't just jump in and take off."

Donna, giving Cal a hopeful look, prayed they would catch him in time, because she really wanted this craziness to be over and to get back to Ramrod Key. At least *that* craziness she knew and could handle. This was another matter entirely. And the element of real danger didn't help either. One thing she was glad for was that she and Cal were together. And that's the way she wanted to face whatever was coming.

Trotting up to the double doors, Cal shoved them open. Juky and Johnny Mac were waiting there with the car. Cal and Donna quickly jumped into the back seat. Cal was shouting for Juky to take off before he had even closed the car door. Juky dumped the clutch, and the little Datsun lurched forward. Wheeling out of the parking lot, they found the roads to be practically empty. Juky pressed the little Datsun hard.

With only the occasional streetlight, the Datsun's poorly aimed headlights were all they had to light the dark road ahead. Zooming past ramshackle houses, chickens flew and scattered in all directions. No one spoke; all eyes were on the dimly lit road ahead. Speeding along in the darkness, their collective worry was about something bigger meandering across the road at the wrong time.

Finally, Cal shouted over the wind and engine noise, "Go faster. We gotta get there before he takes off."

With his eyes locked on the road ahead, Juky shouted back, "I 'ave to be careful. Ef we hit a cow or a horse, we could be killed."

Cal barked, "What the hell. Don't they have fences here?"

Juky shot Cal a quick annoyed look then back to the road just in time to let off the gas to weave and swerve his way through another feather swirled cloud of chickens roosting alongside the road.

Unfazed, he mashed the gas pedal to the floor. The little four-cylinder engine made a lot more noise but not much more speed. Approaching yet another small farmhouse, chickens flew past the car windows in a blur of feathers, cackles, and dust. Suddenly the car's headlights lit up something black, white, and large in the middle of the road.

A split second later they all shouted, "*Hog*!"

Chapter 34

Juky veered the car hard right, narrowly missing the sleeping hog. The hog was missed, but the ditch and the ruddy picket fence next to it weren't as lucky. The Datsun careened down into the shallow ditch getting airborne up the other side right through the multicolored fence. Hunks of baby blue, yellow, and pink fence pickets flew in every direction.

Landing front wheels first, everyone pitched forward then backward as the back wheels landed hard. Juky steered hard right avoiding a huge water trough sending the car skidding sideways up on two wheels, almost rolling over. Donna screamed while clawing to hold onto Cal who had a death grip on the passenger seat headrest. The little Datsun's engine stalled as it dropped back on all four tires.

A huge cloud of dust and sand rolled over them and through the open windows. Coughing and choking on the thick dry dust, a bare bulb porch light flicked on casting raw white light on a rough clapboard shanty just fifty feet from where they came to rest.

Cal began yelling for Juky to get going. "C'mon, start this damn thing and get going now!"

"But, Cal, we 'ave broken de maun's fence. We can't just drive off."

Cal cursed. "Dammit, just get this piece of crap started—I'll take care of this."

With that, Cal opened the car door, jumped out, and ran to meet the confused and upset old black man coming out his front door in nothing but his boxers and undershirt. In the stark light, the old man stared at the whirlwind of destruction he saw in front of his house.

Cal was already waving some cash at the man before he even hit the steps of the porch.

"Here, sir, very sorry. There was a pig in the road. Ah, we had to swerve to try and miss it."

Cal showed him the cash as he stepped up on the porch. Dim light shown from a pull-chain light that hung just inside the open front door. The man's eyes widened as he got a look at the hundred-dollar bill Cal was still frantically waving in the air.

The old man then looked out at the dark road. "Did ya hit ma pig too, maun?"

"Well, no, I think we missed it."

The old man's focus then narrowed on the hundred-dollar bill spilling out of Cal's clinched fist. "Den dis well do, maun. Now you must go. Before ma old lady wakes up and say she wants more."

Cal looked around at the small wooden dwelling and wondered how in the world she could still be asleep with all the racket they just made. But as he opened his hand, the old man quickly pinched the C-note from Cal's palm.

Suddenly, Cal heard the Datsun sputtering to life. Juky revved the engine a couple times as Donna leaned out and opened the rear door. "C'mon, Cal, let's go!" she yelled.

Cal nodded to the old man, spun around and bounded off the low porch, and raced for the car, hurling himself in the back seat as Juky dumped the clutch, throwing dust and gravel. The spinning tires screeched as they careened their way onto the pavement. Cal's wild entry landed him sideways in the middle of Donna's lap; the rear door still hung wildly open. Johnny Mac turned in his seat and put his hand out his window shoving the rear door closed.

Johnny Mac gave Donna a wink and smile. "Haven't done that since a bunch of us TP'd my high school math teacher's house."

Juky kept a wild-eyed death grip on the steering wheel as they sped down Queens Highway. A road sign flashed by. "Moss Town is up ahead. We are almost there," he shouted out to no one in particular.

After surviving their version of Disney's Mr. Toad's Wild Ride, they were too keyed up to respond. Another gut-knotted minute went by. Suddenly up ahead they all saw it: a simple black-and-white sign. Exuma Airport next left. Donna and Cal let out deep sighs of relief. They had made it to the airport. The question though, was Jim gone?

Juky turned on the road leading into the airport. About halfway up the quarter-mile long road, Cal spotted the blinking red and green of a plane's running lights out on the runway. He stared at it for a moment, trying to make out its size. Cal suddenly slapped the headrest in front of him, startling Johnny Mac.

"Shit! He's lined up on the runway getting ready to take off! Go, Juky. Dammit, go!"

"Go where?"

"Out on the runway right up to his nosewheel!"

"Yo-ah crazy, maun!"

"No, I'm a gambler. Now go!"

Juky shook his head, then gunned the Datsun forward once again. Nearing the terminal, a small night watchman's hut sat by an open gate that led out onto the tarmac. Cal shouted at Juky not to stop. Juky gritted his teeth as they blew past the shack sending bellows of dust and sand all around it. If the watchman *was* in there, he was not going to be happy with that maneuver. Clearing the gate, Juky made a wide arching turn toward the plane that sat running at the end of the runway. In the next instance, they heard what they feared, the sound of the turbo prop engines revving up.

Cal shouted even louder, "Don't stop! Hurry up! Go, dammit, before he starts moving!"

The big albatross's engines ramped up even faster. Juky pointed the little Datsun straight at the nosewheel of the plane. Two hundred feet away the plane's bright landing lights flashed on, searing the inside of the car in brilliant light. Juky tried to shield his eyes; no one could see. A second later the big plane began moving straight for them. Instinctively, Juky slammed on the brakes sending them sliding once again sideways directly at the nose of the plane.

Cal grabbed Donna shoving her down on the seat covering her with his body. Johnny Mac and Juky vainly leaned away from the approaching plane.

Fruitlessly, Cal yelled out, "Stop! You son-of-a-bitch!"

At the last second, the Datsun slid to a tire-smoking stop right in the path of the approaching plane.

The roar of the plane's engines changed. The high-pitched sound of the turbo props began spooling down; the landing lights blinked out. The inside of the Datsun went dark. No one moved or spoke for a second or two. Slowly Cal sat up. Donna rose up along with him. They all turned to look out the right side of the car. A wave of shocked disbelief washed over them at seeing how close they were to being hit by the plane.

Juky spoke first, "Yo-ah one crazy bastard, Cal."

"Maybe. But he stopped, didn't he?"

With his gaze still on the nosewheel of the plane sitting only feet from his door, Johnny Mac deadpanned, "Remind me in the future to never play cards with you, Cal."

With the plane's props slowly rotating to a stop, the side door of the plane opened. Cal shot out of the car storming his way to the plane's open door. Everyone quickly followed suit. Cal was stomping his way around the nosewheel just as Jim stepped onto the runway turning to face Cal. He called out, "Hey, it's about time you kno-theads got here. I've been sitting here idling for five minutes." He added with a haughty laugh, "What took you so long?"

Cal said nothing as he continued his purposeful march straight toward Jim with both fists balled up. Just as Cal was five feet from him, Juky shot past Cal to stand between them.

"Wait, wait, dis is not de time for dis. Yes, believe me, Cal, I want to punch em too. But we must get going if we are to save de sailboat."

Cal glared at Juky. "Okay, okay." And then back to Jim. "But buddy boy, you've got one coming. You damn near got us killed, damn it!"

Cal turned back to look at Donna and Johnny Mac. "C'mon, let's go," he said with a wave of his hand.

"Juky, go park the car over by the terminal and hurry back here."

Jim looked at Cal as he stalked past. "Why are you so steamed? I wasn't going to leave ya. Honest. Besides, if you had been on time, none of this would have happened."

Cal stopped and looked back at Jim. "Just get in the cockpit and fire this bucket of bolts up and let's get out of here before the gendarmes show up and haul us all off to jail."

Jim just shrugged and walked past Cal and up the ladder and through the door. Johnny Mac wordlessly followed suit.

Donna stopped and spoke to Cal before going up the ladder. Sporting a crooked smile on her face, she confidently stated, "See, I told you he wouldn't leave without us."

Smashing his mouth tight, he shook his head, saying, "All right, Edgar Cayce, just get in the plane."

Cal waited by the steps looking back toward the terminal building. Juky was fifty yards off. In the distance, Cal saw flashing blue lights moving fast along Queens Highway.

"Hurry up, Juky, we have company coming!" Cal shouted up to the open cockpit window. "Hey, get it fired up. The cops are coming!"

Juky shot around the nose of the plane and up the ladder. Cal followed right behind him as the right engine spun to life then the left engine. Jim shouted from the cockpit, "Get that side door closed and locked, and everyone sit down. I gotta make this fast."

Jim braked the plane as he revved the engines up still higher. The plane's fuselage vibrated from the turbulence of the prop wash. Looking out the cockpit window, Jim saw two cop cars turn on the airport entrance road a quarter mile away.

Cal kept shouting for him to take off. Jim revved the powerful engines up a bit more, then released the brake. Instantly the big plane moved forward rapidly gaining speed. Jim grimaced seeing the cop cars barrel through the gate right past the night watchman's shack.

"Dammit, I don't have much runway for this," he coolly said to himself.

Nearing takeoff speed. Jim tensed seeing the cops race right onto the runway right in front of them. Rolling his eyes, he said, "Not that shit again." He reached up and pushed the throttles all the way forward. The cops jumped out to stand by the cars but quickly abandoned that idea and ran when they saw that he wasn't stopping.

The engines roared. The plane shuddered and shook under the strain of its rapid acceleration. With teeth-gritted determination, he waited until the very last moment before impact then pulled back hard on the yoke. The view instantly changed; the flashing lights and the cop cars vanished beneath them. The Water Lily's landing gear cleared the cop cars' roofs by a scant few feet, but they made it. They were airborne!

Chapter 35

Michael gave a worried look to the fuel gauge; the needle was nearing the empty mark. That was a minor issue compared to what they had narrowly escaped in the last few hours. The sea fog that had shrouded and protected them from their pursuers drifted away about thirty minutes after they skirted around the tip of Crooked Island.

The sky was clear and star-filled once again. There was no sign of the yacht that had menaced them anymore. Michael surmised that either their pursuers had guessed wrong and had sailed down the western side of the island or had simply given up. Whatever the reason, the sun would be coming up soon, and it felt good, good to know that against all odds, they would make it to Pirates Well.

The big question now was the condition of this sailboat. Sails and rope were scattered all over her decks. And it wasn't clear how much gunfire she had taken either. Michael knew he was going to take a hit on the original agreed price because of the damage. He was okay with taking less money. What he didn't want to happen was for it to be a deal breaker. If that happened, he didn't know what he was going to do. It took all of his money just to get this far. He was broke.

Looking to his left, he could see the faintest hint of a new sunrise on the horizon. "Guess I shouldn't worry too much about the money. We was bleed'n' lucky to escape with our skin on this one."

Terry and Martin had lain down to sleep on top of the sails that lay draped over the cabin. It was an exhausting night, to say the least. Michael had let them sleep once he was sure they were out of immediate danger.

But with the sun about to rise and their destination only a half-hour away, he wanted them up when the sun came up. They had to do whatever they could to try and make the sailboat look more presentable.

"Aye, wake up you two. We made it. C'mon now. Let's get a move on."

Neither man stirred, so Michael reached for the rope on the ship's bell. With three hard yanks, the bell rang sharply in the cool predawn air. Instantly, both men's heads popped up.

"C'mon, get up, you two. We've got work to do before we make port."

Terry sat up on one elbow rubbing his eyes. "Jeez, did ya aff ta ring that bleed'n' bell?"

"Yeah, what's the deal, Michael?" Martin added.

"I'll tell ya what the bloody deal is. We need ta git this train wreck of a boat look'n' better if we hope ta get any bloody money. Now c'mon, mates, let's get crack'n'."

Terry and Martin rubbed their faces and stretched trying to pull their wits about them. Michael began instructing them on what he wanted done. "Don't worry with running the sails up, mates. Just get them stowed in their rightful places, got it?"

Wordlessly, both men nodded and began stepping over and around the ropes and sail canvas lying all over the deck. Starting with the last sail they dropped, they worked their way backward in the order that they found them.

Michael slowed their speed to help give them more time, but more to conserve the fuel they had left. He was tired and hungry and desperate for sleep, having not slept for thirty hours now. However, he had to shove all that aside for a little while longer.

Slipping through the morning stillness, the only sound came from Terry and Martin working to straighten up the mess of the sails. The sky brightened with the first peak of sun shooting spires of orange and yellow light into the retreating night sky.

The dark silhouette of the island of Mayaguana and the settlement of Pirates Well lay dead ahead. Michael called out to his shipmates. "'Ave a look, mates," he said, pointing straight ahead. "We made it. Now finish up and be quick about it. I've got to come up with a story to sell that bloke so's we don't lose everything we came to get."

Terry and Martin stopped their work on the last of the mainsails to have a look. Seeing the gray outline of the island straight ahead, they patted each other on the backs, each excitedly exclaiming, "We made it!" With renewed vigor, they sped up their work on stowing the sails.

In the gray light of dawn, Michael was able to make out the condition of the *Donna Marie*. He shook his head. She had taken a number of hits. The beautiful teakwood deck and cabin were splintered where several bullets had smashed into her. He saw the shattered port window too, but overall, not too bad, he thought. Standing there still assessing the value of the damage, Michael thought, why try and come up with some half-assed story to tell the contact? Just tell him the damn truth. They narrowly escaped being boarded by someone trying to steal the *Donna Marie* from them.

Soon the sun's full disk rose to sit on the horizon like a flaming cauldron. Color began flowing into everything that surrounded them, chasing away the black and gray of night. The shoreline too was no longer a one-dimensional silhouette. The harbor moved and stretched with life as people went about starting their day. All manner of boats rested comfortably at their moors, while fishermen went about preparing for their day on the water. It was an utterly beautiful yet normal day dawning once again in the small settlement of Pirates Well.

Michael began searching for a place to dock. He soon spotted a suitable spot near the end of a long pier. Slowing to just above an idle, he steered for the dock, which, to him, was the most beautiful dock he had ever seen. Bringing them alongside, a broad smile of relief spread across his face as they bumped to a stop. From a distance he was sure that the *Donna Marie* looked like nothing had happened. He laughed a bit wishing he could finish the deal from a distance too.

Terry and Martin grabbed the pilings and tied off. The moment they did, they were struck by the peacefulness of their surroundings. The sound of water rippling along the shore and the call of seagulls circling overhead mingled with the casual conversations of fishermen readying their boats for the day's work ahead. This serenity was suddenly overcome by the sound of a large plane's approach which rolled and rumbled over the water. Some of those on the docks turned, squinting into the distance for a look at what was coming; others didn't, for it wasn't that unusual for a plane to arrive here this early.

Terry and Martin turned their attention from the approaching plane, and like sailors who had spent months at sea, they bounded their way onto the dock. Feeling giddy and a little off balance at having something solid under their feet again, they began to laugh and jab at each other with glee, saying, "We made it, mate. We made it!"

Stepping onto the dock, Michael chided them, "All right, all right, you two rubber 'eds. When you're finished congratulating your bloody selves, you need to get this tub cleaned up whilst I go ashore and find our contact. Do you think you can do that?"

Terry's gap-toothed grin prominently showed as he happily replied, "Yeah, yeah, Michael. We got this, right, Martin? I mean what could 'appen now? We made it, mate." This set off another round of giddy punches and jabs between the two men.

Michael shook his head, then before starting his way up the dock, he added, "Look, just make sure that when I get back with our contact, you have her looking as best as you can. Got it?"

"Aye, aye, Captain," Terry said, snapping to attention and saluting while fighting to hold back another wave of giggles. Michael rolled his eyes and walked off down the dock. He understood their high spirits. He also knew they weren't out of the woods just yet.

Just then a deep rumble rolled through the harbor. Some ceased their activities to watch the large seaplane glide smoothly onto the calm waters just outside the harbor's entrance. Michael called back to Terry and Martin. "Aye, mates, we might need to get with the bloke what be flying that bird to give us a lift off-a this pile o' sand."

Walking along, Michael glanced back over his shoulder as the plane trundle into the harbor making note of its name. "The Water Lily, that's a right catchy name for seaplane."

Gradually, everyone in the harbor returned to their current labors. Terry and Martin watched the plane a bit longer. Terry asked, "I wonder 'oose on that plane?" Answering himself, he said, "Prolly some bloody rich Americans coming 'ear for a few days of fish'n', I'd say."

Martin rolled his eyes. "C'mon now, every bloke you see that has a couple pence to rub together is rich to you. C'mon, let's do as Michael said and be quick about it. We don't know 'ow long 'e's going ta be gone."

Terry frowned a little, but a smile quickly returned to his face. "Aye, Martin, do you know 'ow to tell a rich American from a poor one? The poor one washes 'is own Cadillac." Terry burst out laughing at his own joke.

Martin just smirked and kept folding a sail around its spar. "C'mon, ya bloom'n' hyena, let's get this finished before Michael gets back."

*****

Jim skillfully guided the Water Lily next to a long dock made just for seaplanes to tie off. A couple of local men trotted down the dock to help bring the large plane to a safe stop, swinging the left wingtip right over the dock. He shut both engines down when he saw that the men had grabbed a wing tank. With the wing tank in hand, both men held it there until Jim had opened the gangway door. A brief moment passed before out jumped Jim onto the dock speaking to the men as he did so. "Great job, gentlemen. I can see you've done this a time or two before."

Both men nodded, smiling broadly at Jim's complement, and went about tying the plane off to the pilings. Jim then called out to Cal.

"Hey, Cal, hop on out here—you've dock fees to pay, buddy."

Cal poked his head out the doorway looking around. Spying Jim standing between two older lanky barefoot islanders in cutoff shorts and undershirts, he barked, "What the heck are you talking about?"

Jim rolled both hands over, pointing with his thumbs to the two smiling men on either side of him. "These two gents. They helped us dock this bird. And listen, make it worth their while. I don't need the Water Lily accidently drifting away from this dock, if you catch my meaning."

Cal stepped out onto the dock fussing as he went. "Well, for Pete's sake, just how much are we talking about? Twenty bucks?"

Jim bent over laughing then said, "Twenty bucks? I need them to watch after it, not sell it for scrap, ya cheap ass. Now peal one of those Grants outta that squeaky-hinged wallet of yours and pay these two fellas."

"Fifty bucks!" Cal demanded.

"Shhh, dammit! You wanna draw a crowd? Look, that's how it works. You gotta make it worth their while so things don't turn up missing."

Reaching for his wallet, Cal grumbled, "Well, so far the only thing that's turned up missing on this trip is my cash."

"Oh, quit yer bitch'n', and let's go see if we can find something to eat. I'm starved."

Cal handed a couple of twenties and a ten to Jim who in turn stuck the ten in his pocket and pulled out two fives. He then counted out the money to each man. Cal grumbled again watching the men quickly fold the money into their pockets while profusely thanking Jim.

"Hey, why are they thanking you? I'm the one who coughed up the dough."

Jim laughed at Cal and said, "Maybe so. But in their eyes, I'm the one who negotiated the deal. So that makes me the big Bhawana."

"That may be, Kemosabe. But just remember I'm not a bottomless well here. You're buying breakfast."

Donna poked her head out of the plane's hatchway, exclaiming, "Are you two finished making bad movie references? We're all hungry."

Johnny Mac leaned into the open hatchway next to Donna. "Yeah, I'm so hungry my stomach thinks my throat's been cut."

Cal turned to help Donna out onto the dock, chiding all, "Might I remind everyone of why we are here? We came to look for the *Donna Marie*. We aren't on vacation."

Johnny Mac and Juky followed Donna out onto the dock. With them all gathered around, Cal added, "Look, we'll go and get a quick bite to eat and plan our next move once we have found the *Donna Marie*. Okay?"

Everyone nodded agreement. Johnny Mac, who had stepped away from the group a couple steps while Cal was talking, spoke up. "Hey, Cal. Everyone. You might want to start planning our next move a bit sooner. Look over there."

Everyone turned to see what Johnny Mac was pointing to. A collective wave of disbelief washed over them all. Fifty yards away quietly moored at another dock among several other boats sat the *Donna Marie*. She was partially hidden by a large yacht with only her bow poking out.

Cal said, "I'll be dammed. Let's go get her."

Chapter 36

Jim grabbed Cal's shoulder. "Hold on a minute, pilgrim. Check out who is coming up the dock toward her."

Annoyed, Cal swiped Jim's hand from his shoulder, saying, "I don't give a damn who's coming toward my boat. I'm going to get her back."

Juky stepped forward, telling them, "Cal, wait. I know of dis man. He es known as de Sawfish, and et's better to keep yo-ah distance from dis man."

Cal stopped to take a good look. What he saw was a medium-built black man dressed in white linen pants, mint green floral print button-down shirt. He walked slowly down the dock in woven leather flat shoes, all topped off by a tan Panama hat and sunglasses. A couple of steps behind him were two rather large muscular men dressed in khaki pants and untucked black button-down shirts and sunglasses. Walking beside the well-heeled black man was a disheveled man who appeared as though he were coming off a ten-day drunk.

"C'mon," Cal said with slight wave of his hand. "Let's all walk down the dock like nothing's wrong. I want to try and get a better look at them."

Juky spoke up. "Cal, you must wait. You see de white man, es name is Michael, aund de one who stole de *Donna Marie* from me."

Cal looked to Juky. "Wait! You're telling me that that poor excuse for a bum is who stole my boat from you? My god, man, I can't imagine what would have happened if a group of angry girl scouts had gone after her."

Juky rolled his eyes. "He had two accomplices, Cal, with guns. I did what I could to save her."

"Save her! Hell, man, you should have sunk her. At least she wouldn't be in the hands of...of..." Cal glanced back over his shoulder at the men now standing at the bow of the *Donna Marie*. "Of who knows what now."

Donna shoved herself between them. "Cal, stop it!" Donna growled through gritted teeth. "If you want to be angry at someone, be angry at me. Juky nearly died trying to stall these guys so we could at least have a chance at getting her back. I suggest you listen to him."

Donna continued her admonishment of Cal by saying, "You'd best listen to him—he knows these islands and a lot of what goes on here and who is doing it. Now pull your head out of your ass and listen."

Cal shot a quick look into Donna's searing stare. He then shifted his eyes to Juky. "Well, Juky, any time my little bride uses a cuss word, that's when I know she is deadly serious. So what would you suggest we do?"

Juky held his eyes on Cal. "First we need to figure out a way I can walk down the dock without being noticed. The white man with them definitely knows my face. Right now, he thinks I'm dead, so et's better that way."

"Hey, I know," Johnny Mac interjected, then disappeared back inside the plane. A moment later he popped back in the doorway holding a small Styrofoam cooler. Here, put this on your shoulder. That way they won't be able to see your face when you walk by."

Jim let out a laugh and reached for the cooler. "That's a great idea there, swami. Now let's go find something to eat."

Johnny Mac handed the cooler to Jim, saying, "I'm not a swami!"

Jim took the cooler, handing it to Juky. When Johnny Mac stepped out onto the dock, Jim asked, "Well, if you aren't a swami, what the heck are you?"

Straightening his oversized muslin shirt, he replied, "Well, I'm, uh...well, I'm a Johnny Mac, that's who. The one and only."

Cal rolled his eyes at hearing this. "Great. Now we *sound* like the circus act we look like. C'mon, let's go. I need to eat. My head is hurting from all of this."

Juky placed the cooler on his shoulder effectively hiding his face. The five of them then started off down the main dock. Soon they were parallel with the *Donna Marie*.

Slowly walking along, each of them stole glances at her and the men who were gathered on the dock next to her. At first all seemed normal. However, it was Donna who saw the damage first. She grabbed Cal by the back of the arm and whispered in his ear.

"Cal, the port window…it's shattered."

Cal took a quick look. "I see that. The wood around it is splintered too. The rigging isn't right either."

Johnny Mac overheard their conversation and moved up closer to them. "She looks like she was in a storm or something, Cal."

Jim quietly said, "Stop talking about the boat. Talk of fishing. We are starting to draw the attention of the fancy guy's muscle, if you know what I mean."

Cal nodded and spoke up louder. "Yeah, so when is our fishing guide showing up? I'm ready to hit the water."

Jim chimed right back, "We have to meet him at the settlement."

"Good, let's get something to eat before we head out," Cal added.

Cal took the lead and picked up their pace down the dock. Donna walked just behind them all. While she walked, she dug a small compact out of her purse and held it up pretending she was checking her makeup. In the little mirror, she saw the well-dressed black man pointing at the damage on the *Donna Marie* and shaking his head "no." The disheveled man made large sweeps with his hands in an effort to draw attention to the overall condition of the *Donna Marie*.

Once they were far enough away, Donna closed her compact and sped up to catch Cal.

"Cal, that ragged-looking man is trying to sell the *Donna Marie* to that black man. I'm sure of it."

Cal started to answer her, but Juky interrupted. "No, Miss Donna, he es not de buyer. He es de one who verifies dat de buyer es getting what es paying for."

Cal looked over to Juky. "So that guy is what? A front man?"

"Yes, he is just one link in what could be a very long chain, I'm afraid."

Nearing the one main road that ran parallel to the shore, Cal spotted a small café called the Conch Shell Café. "Let's go see what we can scare up to eat in there. Juky, I need you to tell us all you know about what is going on with our boat. This might be our one and only shot at getting her back."

Donna looked back over her shoulder toward the dock, then stopped and turned all the way around to face the docks. Cal stopped to hold open the door for everyone to enter. When Donna didn't walk past, he turned to see her standing alone looking back toward the docks. Letting go of the faded blue screen door, he stepped back to her.

"Donna? What's the matter? What are you looking at?"

Holding her stare toward the harbor, she somberly replied, "I'm looking at the horrible mess I've made of things." Cal saw her shoulders slump as she began to cry.

Seeing her cry always tore his heart out. Moving up beside her, he put his arm around her and pulled her in close. Donna rolled her face into his chest. "I'm so sorry, honey. I never meant for any of this to happen."

Cal struggled to think of what to say to comfort his wife. He knew she had nothing but the best of intentions with her plan. He thought for a moment longer. Instead of trying to come up with some flowery comment of how it was all going to be okay, he simply told her how he saw things—something he was far more comfortable with.

Talking softly to her, he said, "Right now there are two Donna Maries on this island." Nodding toward the docks, he continued, "The one out there I can replace. But this one, the one in my arms, I can't." Giving her shoulder a squeeze, he added, "And *this* Donna Marie is the only one that I really love and give a damn about."

"Cal, can you ever forgive me for this?"

Cal turned her to face him and lifted her chin to look her right in her tear-soaked eyes. "No." Donna's eyes widened. "There's nothing to forgive. You did this for all that you hold dear. I'm just glad I'm a part of that."

Donna retrieved a tissue from her purse and looked up into Cal's eyes while dabbing away her tears. "My daddy was *so* wrong about you." She then rose up on her tiptoes and gave him a quick kiss. Dropping back down, she reached for the screen door, its rusty hinges squeaking as she pulled it open.

Stepping inside, she waved for him to follow her. "C'mon, let's get something to eat."

Cal's eyes widened. "What? Wait a minute. What did you mean by that? Just what about me was your dad so wrong about?"

"Never mind that now. Let's go talk about getting the *Donna Marie* home safe where she belongs."

Cal stood watching the screen door slap closed behind his wife. Shaking his head, he murmured, "That girl can be a real roller coaster ride some days."

Cal looked back toward the docks. From this distance, the *Donna Marie* looked as beautiful as ever. For the first time since this all began, he was genuinely worried, worried that there was no way they could get her back, and a greater worry that something could go terribly wrong in the process. He was torn. Should they just leave and go home safe and sound? Or should he go inside and plan yet another attempt to get her back?

Turning his gaze up from the *Donna Marie*, he stared into a perfect blue, cloud-dotted sky. "I could use some help on this one, big guy." He gave a nod toward the sky, then pulled the screen door open. The squeak of it hinges punctuated his decision. They would try one more time.

Chapter 37

Smiling broadly, Michael watched the black man and his two body-guards stride their way slowly down the dock to shore. He waited as long as he could before turning to Terry and Martin who sat nervously waiting at the *Donna Marie*'s stern. Michael trotted his way toward them but remained on the dock. Nearing them, he enthusiastically blurted out, "We did it, mates—I made the bloody deal!"

Both men jumped to their feet hugging each other and jumping up and down, punching and back-slapping.

"We didn't get as much as we thought," Michael added.

Terry and Martin stopped their exuberant jostling of each other and stared up at a grim-faced Michael standing on the dock. Martin asked, "'Ow much *did* we get, mate?" Martin asked.

A smile suddenly burst across his face as he said, "We still got six thousand bucks, we did."

This ignited another round of congratulatory pokes, jabs, and laughter from Terry and Martin, which was as much about their having survived as it was about the money.

Terry then asked, "When do we see all that quid?"

Michael stepped onto the *Donna Marie*, telling them, "Soon, mates. I aff ta go and meet 'im in town in an hour. He wants us to get this tub cleaned up and get our stuff off it. And then his people will take over from 'ear on out."

Smiling from ear to ear, Terry asked, "Aye, whut are we gonna do now, Michael? With no boat, we are stuck 'ear."

Michael put a hand each on man's shoulder and said while nodding toward the Water Lily, "I betcha that bloke what be flying that rig will be 'appy ta fly us any bloody where we want."

Martin slapped Terry on the back, saying, "And we've got the quid ta pay the bloke with now, don't we, mates." This time all three of them broke out laughing and shoving each other.

*****

The Conch Shell Café's screen door announced the arrival of another patron. Cal and the others looked to see who was coming in, then quickly looked away. It was the black man from the dock along with his bodyguards.

Sitting at a round table, Cal's back was to the door. After seeing who had come in, he gestured with his hand for all to remain calm. Quietly he said, "Look, we are here for the fishing, so let's all talk normal-like about that. No nervous chatter. We need to see if we can pick up on anything he might say."

Donna poked Cal in the ribs and whispered in his ear, saying, "I know who he reminds me of now—the black guy in those 7UP ads. I wonder if he sounds like him too?" Then in as deep a voice as she could muster, she mimicked the ad's tag line, "7UP, no caffeine, never had it, never will. Ha-ha-ha."

Johnny Mac gave a little snicker. "Hey, that's pretty good, Donna."

Cal gave them both a look of annoyance. "Yes, yes, I know the commercial. You can't turn on the TV without seeing it." Cal turned halfway around and took a quick glance at him. "He does look a lot like him."

With a silly grin, Donna added, "I bet he sounds like him too," then let go another snicker, planting her face in Cal's shoulder.

Out of the corner of his mouth, Cal admonished her, "Donna, cool it! This is serious now. People with bodyguards don't play around."

"I know. I'm sorry. I just wanted to lighten the mood a little."

"Getting what we came here for will do that."

Cal looked at Jim and asked, "So when did you say those guides are getting here?"

"Oh, uh...soon. Uh, a couple of hours, I think." Jim's clunky reply annoyed Cal.

Cal then took over with the small talk. He was far more adept at making stuff up on the fly. He was in the middle of a fabricated fishing story when the Conch Shell's owner, Miss Ginger, a rotund middle-aged islander returned with their breakfast called Fire Engine, a mixture of corned beef, chopped onions, and bell peppers amid a seasoned tomato sauce and accompanied by bowls of rice and grits.

Placing the plates and flatware around the table, she cheerfully chatted telling them all about what they were about to enjoy. "Dis es ma breakfast version of Fire Engine. Der is no hot peppers in et." Suddenly, the mysterious man called out to them from across the small dining room. "You folks are in fo-ah real treat. Miss Ginger makes de best Fire Engine in all de islands. Aund her fish stew es to die fo-ah," he finished with a deep hearty laugh.

Donna nearly spit out her food at hearing his deep voice and laugh, elbowing Cal in the ribs. "See, I knew it," Donna said, working to hold back her laughter.

Cal turned to face him, saying, "I believe you. It looks and smells fantastic."

Miss Ginger chimed in, "Cesar, you tell everyone dat same thing."

"Ah, Miss Ginger, dat es because et es true."

She stepped back from the table placing her hands on her ample hips and said, "Yo-ah just saying dis because we are cousins. Yo-ah not fooling me."

She then looked around the table asking if everything was good. But seeing the smiles of pure satisfaction showing on their faces was better than anything they could say.

"Day'ah, you see, Miss Ginger, day are proving me correct, yes?" Cesar remarked as he stood and started for their table.

Juky's eyes widened seeing him coming toward them. Cal saw Juky's expression and was about to ask what was wrong when a hand suddenly appeared on his left shoulder giving it a couple of firm pats. Cal turned halfway around and looked up to see the man towering over him.

"I noticed you all out on the docks. Yo-ah all American, correct? Well, except fo-ah you," he said, pointing to Juky. "What brings you he-ah to our little island? A fishing excursion perhaps?"

Cal spoke up quickly and confidently. "Yes, that's right. We have talked of doing this for years. We finally stopped talking and decided to just do it."

"Ah, dat es good. Do you have guides?"

Of course they didn't. So Cal did what he used to do years ago— BS his way through tough situations. "Well, we were just discussing that. Our guides were supposed to meet us here when we arrived. But we haven't seen them yet."

Patting his shoulder firmly again, Cesar exclaimed, "Oh, then they are not locals. See, dat es de mistake you Americans always make. You should always hire de locals, for dey are right here on de island and dey know des waters better than anyone."

Cesar then looked straight at Juky. "I em surprised you did not tell yo-ah friends here about dis. You are after all an islander, yes?"

Juky, obviously uncomfortable with the attention on him, gave a slight nod and clipped answer, "Yes, but not from here."

Cesar let go a boisterous laugh. "Oh, of course not. I would know you if you were. I'm thinking more down island, yes?"

Miss Ginger spoke out from behind the counter where she was busy preparing Cesar's usual meal of corned beef and grits. "Ma cousin, es right about dat. 'E know everybody and everybody know hem."

Cesar questioned Juky further, "You 'ave a touch of de French accent. So I'm thinking French Guadeloupe, or maybe Marie Galante. I go down dat way from time to time. Am I correct?"

Juky nodded, saying, "Marie Galante."

Before Cesar could question Juky further, one of the bodyguards came over from his post by the door and whispered into his ear. His face went expressionless acknowledging what he was being told. The bodyguard went immediately back to his post by the door.

Looking over to Miss Ginger, he said, "Miss Ginger, I'm afraid I need you to 'old onto ma breakfast. I have some business to attend to on de other side of de island, an annoyance really. But et must be dealt with."

Miss Ginger glared at him from behind the counter. "I know, I know. Dis is not de first time yo-ah *business* has done dis. I'll keep it hot fo-ah you." Pushing open the swinging door to the kitchen, she added, "Et will be here we you come back, but don't you go complain'n' about it. You know it es best when served fresh."

Cesar looked back at Cal. "My cousin, she loves to fuss at me, and she es de only one I let get away with it too." Turning to leave, he let go another deep loud laugh. Snapping his fingers in the air and pointing to the door, both bodyguards exited and waited just outside the door.

Out of the corner of her eye, Donna watched through a large window the three of them stride their way down the street. It was then that all of them let out a huge sigh of relief. Donna spoke up to no one in particular, "Wow, talk about your imposing characters."

Johnny Mac added, "Yeah, no kidding. I felt like I weighed a thousand pounds the whole time he was here. He sounds pleasant enough, but I get the sense he's a lot more then he appears to be."

Juky looked at them all, quietly adding, "You are right about dat. He is known as de Sawfish because of how he deals with those who cross hem."

Donna looked at Juky. "You mean he—"

Juky interrupted her. "That's what they say. Oh, but he doesn't do it. But like he did just now with his bodyguards, all he has to do is snap his fingers and his problems are turned into crab bait."

"So he's like the Caribbean mobster," Jim said.

Donna cast a nervous look at Cal who sat quietly eating more of the Fire Engine he had poured over the fluffy white rice. "Cal, how can you eat when that guy just had his hand right on your shoulder like that, doesn't that creep you out?"

Taking another bite of food, he chewed through his answer. "Well…as long as…he isn't snapping his fingers about us…what's to worry?"

Juky looked at Cal in total surprise. "Cal, you do understand that he is the go-between for whoever et es that will take yo-ah boat across the Atlantic. They are big-time players with lots of cash and connections."

Raising his voice, Cal retorted, "So what are you saying, that I just give up and go home when *my* damn boat is sitting right out that door?"

"Shh, Cal honey, Miss Ginger will hear you."

Just then Miss Ginger came back through the door from the kitchen. She came straight over to the table asking if they wanted anything else. Cal asked for more coffee which garnered an immediate eye roll from Donna.

Stepping back from the table, Miss Ginger folded her hands backward on her hips. Tilting her head, she cast an assessing gaze around the table then said, "Now what 'as 'appened to ma happy table of people?

"If et's ma cousin, don't you worry about hem." She then looked straight at Cal, asking, "And which boat out der is yours?"

Donna elbowed him the ribs. "See, I told you she would hear you."

Cal held his eyes on her for a long moment then said, "The blue-and-white sailboat."

"Ahh yes, I saw dat one when I opened up this morning. Vury beautiful, dat one es. And you say it es yo-ah boat?"

Cal nodded. "It's the *Donna Marie*. It's named after my wife here," he said, pointing to Donna.

"Oh, dat is a beautiful name aund from a beautiful lady."

Reaching behind her, she pulled a chair around, pushed it close to the table, and sat down, looking to her left and right then back to Cal. "What es yo-ah name?"

"Cal," he simply said.

"Well, Mr. Cal. I'm going to do you and yo-ah beautiful wife a big favor."

Cal stopped chewing and took a sip of coffee and asked, "And that would be?"

Miss Ginger drifted her gaze over all of them, then fixed her big dark eyes squarely on Cal. "I take it de boat has been stolen from you." Cal nodded affirmatively. "I think I can 'elp you get yo-ah boat back."

Chapter 38

Caught off guard with her offer to help, Cal asked, "But how? Why?"

"Don't worry about dat, but as to why?" Cutting her eyes to Juky, she added, "Because of hem."

All turned to stare at Juky who sat straight-faced and wordless.

Cal looked back at Miss Ginger. "Because of Juky? I don't get it. We hardly know him. In fact, up until recently, I thought he was dead."

"Et does not matter. Et should only matter dat *I* know hem."

"Cal honey, quit with the third degree. If she says she can help us get the *Donna Marie* back, then let's hear what she has to say."

The screen door's squeak announced the arrival of three men who entered all talking loudly about their fishing adventures the day before, seating themselves at the same table where Cesar had been.

Miss Ginger immediately stood telling them the table was reserved and to please sit at one of the other tables. Amid a couple of snarky comments and jokes, they complied. While the men relocated to another table, she told them where to get rooms for the night.

Cal started to ask why they had to stay the night, but she stopped him, saying, "I will call you later. Now hurry and get a room before dey are all gone. Dey don't take reservations. Et es first come first served."

Standing to leave, each told her thanks for the great breakfast. Donna stopped next to her giving her a sweet look. She put a hand to her shoulder, saying, "Thank you, Miss Ginger."

Smiling, she let go a laugh, saying, "Oh, et es nothing. I cook all day fo-ah years. I better be good by now."

"Not just for the food, dear."

218

"Scoot now, go and get some rest. We will talk later."

Cal held the door open as everyone filtered out onto the street. Donna was the last out stopping by Cal. No one said a word. Jim was in the lead and was headed in the direction of the Baycaner Resort, a short walk away.

Juky was walking a step or two behind and to the right of Jim. His gaze was downcast and lost in thought. Johnny Mac was behind them both. Donna and Cal followed the trio walking arm in arm. Each of them with the exception of Juky took in the sights as they walked along.

The only traffic to speak of were a smattering of scooters and Mini Mokes that scrambled past. Johnny Mac, walking directly behind Juky, suddenly spoke up loud enough for all to hear. "Well, are you going to tell everyone why Miss Ginger is doing this or should I?"

Juky froze in his tracks, causing Johnny Mac to bump into him. Turning around, Juky glared at Johnny Mac. "No, I em not, aund neither are you. Do you understand?"

Donna and Cal stepped up to the two of them and stopped. Cal asked, "Yeah, Juky, Donna and I were just wondering that same thing. Just what could you have done that would make someone take a risk to help total strangers like us. Strangers, except apparently for you."

Uncomfortable with the subject of his past, he curtly replied, "Look, it happened a long time ago. Aund I don't want to talk about it. Just be happy dat she es helping."

Donna commented. "It sure must have been something really nice for her to be doing this just because of you."

"You bet it is," Johnny Mac added.

Jim had stopped five feet ahead of them but stood listening to what was going on. "Wait, how do you know what he did if he hasn't told anyone about it?" he asked, stepping in closer.

They all looked at Jim with "well duh" expressions, then at Johnny Mac. Jim shifted his gaze from Donna and Cal to Johnny Mac. Rolling his eyes and head, Jim said, "Oh, yeah, right, he's that swami guy. I keep forgetting that."

Irritated at Jim's off-handed swami reference again, Johnny Mac shot back, "Hey, look, I ain't no swami. I didn't ask to be this way. I can't help it if I know things about people, so give me a break."

Rolling his eyes again, Jim stepped up closer to them. "Okay, okay, I'll stop calling you swami. But come on, how can you know things about people? That's impossible."

Johnny Mac locked his eyes in Jim's. His face went straight. In a low even tone, he remarked, "You mean things like knowing that on your last mission over Regensburg, the belly gunner on the B-17 you were piloting was killed. You mean things like that? I can tell you his name if you like."

Jim's expression abruptly changed to one of confusion then to tortured remembrance, and just stared at Johnny Mac. Suddenly he spun on his heels and stormed off. Cal gave Johnny Mac a stern look. "Dammit, J-Mac, why'd you do that?"

"Look, I'm sorry, but he kept calling me a swami. I just wanted him to see how it feels to hurt over something you can't help, that's all. For years I've had people call me all sorts of things since this happened to me. It gets very tiring after a while."

Cal pushed his way past Johnny Mac to go and catch up with Jim. Johnny Mac looked at Donna, saying, "I'm sorry. I don't know what came over me. I guess I let my emotions get the better of me. I should go and apologize to him."

Donna moved up to Johnny Mac. Putting a hand on his shoulder, she said, "It's okay. We all have our weak moments. Let Cal talk to him. It was after all a time in their lives they both shared. Oddly enough, Cal can be pretty good at that sometimes."

Johnny Mac looked from Donna to Cal and Jim walking fifty feet ahead of them. "I still need to apologize to him. That cut him pretty deep. It's something he's carried with him ever since. That guy was only nineteen. He was the only casualty that ever happened on all the missions Jim flew."

Johnny Mac turned and walked off leaving Donna and Juky standing on the side of the road. Donna lamented, "That was an unexpected turn of events."

"Yes, et was. I suppose I should have just told everyone."

Donna said, "Well, Juky, if it's is a good thing, why would you not want to tell us?"

"Because, Miss Donna, et wasn't all good es why."

"Miss Ginger must not see it that way."

Juky drew a reluctant breath; a solemn look came to his face as he began. "Several years ago, I pulled her two young daughters from der burning house."

Donna's eyes widened. "Oh my, Juky, no wonder she feels the way she does about you. How could any of that not be good? I don't understand."

Juky looked at the ground then back into Donna's questioning face. "Because I could not save der grandmother from de fire too. I tried, but der was just too much fire and smoke."

Donna immediately felt a huge lump in her throat. Placing her hand on his shoulder, she said, "Juky, I'm so sorry. I'm sure you did all you could. But you saved her daughters. And she is obviously still very grateful."

"Yes, I know. Everyone told me da same ting after et happened. But sometimes when I lay down to sleep, I still hear her cries. Aund dat es why I don't want to talk of et. When I do, den day es reborn in my mind again."

Donna struggled to hold back her tears. She then did the only thing she knew to do. She pulled him in close, hugging him tightly. She quietly spoke, "God loves you for what you did, and so does those girl's grandmother."

Pulling back from him, Donna saw his own eyes rim with tears. Giving her a crooked smile, he said, "Now 'ow do you know dat, Miss Donna?"

Donna, blinking back her own tears, said, "You risked your life without thought for your own safety. And that, Juky, is the purest love of all. That's how I know."

Juky gave her a tight smile and nod. "Miss Donna, I'll try seeing it yo-ah way." He glanced up the street to where Jim, Cal, and Johnny Mac had stopped, then back to Donna. "You say dat Cal es good at smoothing out de wrinkles in one's life. I think I know who he gets et from."

Giving him a warm smile while dabbing her eyes with a tissue, she said, "Juky, if he does, that ole buzzard will never admit it, that's for sure." She had no sooner said that when Cal began shouting back to them.

"Come on! What are you two doing way back there? You look like you're planning a mutiny or something. Come on, catch up."

Donna rolled her eyes. Then snapping to attention, she stiffly saluted him. "Yes sir! Coming, sir!" She then began an exaggerated march straight for him. Juky hesitated a moment then fell in behind Donna.

Donna continued her march right up to Cal, then stopped. "Reporting for duty, sir."

Cal chided her, "Donna, will you stop that? Be serious, will ya?"

"I thought I was, sir."

"Cut it out I said."

"I will when you stop barking at me like a drill sergeant...sir," she said, flipping him another stiff salute.

Jim and the others stood there for a brief moment listening to them jab at each other when Jim, looking for any reason to get away from their quibbling, said, "Hey, look, I can see the sign for the motel up ahead. Let's get going." Not waiting for a response from anyone, he took off down the street. Johnny Mac and Juky quickly followed leaving Cal and Donna standing looking at each other for a beat or two.

Donna looked up at Cal and said, "Well, Colonel, are we just going to keep standing here looking stupid?"

Cal's face softened. "Donna, look, I'm sorry. I didn't mean to bark at you like that. It's just that I'm worried about what we are getting ourselves into. I mean we are talking about ripping off a guy that's known as the 'Sawfish,' for God's sake!"

Donna held her eyes in his for a moment then looked back at the Conch Shell Café. "I know that, but I got a feeling that Miss Ginger knows just how to handle him."

Cal added, "Let's hope so. I have no desire to be made into crab bait."

Donna turned back to face Cal. "You know, honey, you should try having some simple faith once in a while. You just might be surprised at what can happen."

"You sound like my mom now."

Donna gave him a look. "That is not a dig. It's a compliment."

Cal rolled his eyes. "Be that as it may, I'm having a hard time trusting a total stranger with our lives. How do we know she's not on the take right along with the Sawfish?"

"She isn't, Cal."

"How can you be so sure? And don't give me that 'woman's intuition' jazz. I need more than a whim to go on."

"I'm sure about her because of Juky."

Cal threw up his hands, turning halfway around then back to face Donna. "That's great! Now we've gone from whims to…to…I don't even know what now. Juky? Really? What could a half-assed boat thief have to do with any of this?"

Donna shot her fuming husband a look, a look that he knew all too well. "Walter Caleb Arnold! Juky has done nothing but try and help right from the beginning. He has even risked his life to try and help us get the *Donna Marie* back. I'm not going to stand here and have you talk about him like that. Do you understand me?"

Wagging her finger at him, she added, "And don't even think about saying that I sound like *my* mom, or, or you just might need dental work!"

Cal stood silent just looking at his wife while fighting the urge to say just that. Deciding that he didn't want to see if she really would smack him, he calmly replied, "Look, I'm sorry, Donna. You're right about Juky…well, mostly. But you're asking me to trust him again when you know what my history with him has been."

Donna drew in a long calming breath then said, "Cal, you are letting one event in a person's life paint the entirety of that life. Would you want to be judged by that same measure?"

"Of course not, but I just don't see why Miss Ginger is so willing to help us because of him."

Donna glanced at the ground then back up at Cal. "I probably shouldn't tell you this, but it's because he saved her two daughters from a house fire, that's why. And don't you dare say a word to him about it. Understand?"

Cal looked up the street at the three of them who were just going inside the lobby of the Baycaner Resort. He nodded his head then put his hand on Donna's shoulder and started them walking. "Donna, if Juky saved Miss Ginger's daughters, why'd he get so upset with Johnny Mac about it?"

Donna leaned into Cal putting her arm around his waist. "Because he wasn't able to save the little girls' grandmother from the fire. He tried, but the fire was just too intense. That's why he has those awful scars on his forearms and his chin."

Cal suddenly stopped, looking up at the sky then back down at Donna. "Dammit! Well, that's just great."

Donna scrunched her face, asking, "Huh? What's the matter with him now?"

"I'll tell you what's the matter. I gotta somehow go from not liking or trusting him to respecting him. You know I can't shift gears that fast."

Donna gave him an impish smile. "Oh, I don't know about that. You shifted gears pretty quick at the motel last night. In fact, I'd say you never missed a gear."

She then rose up on her tiptoes giving him a quick kiss. Cal's eyes widened bringing a broad smile recalling their passion-filled evening. "Yeah, I was on fire, wasn't I?" He then started them walking in a slow saunter, arm in arm, each watching their footsteps as they went.

"Yeah, you were. But don't forget, every fire has its spark, big boy," she said, pinching him in his ribs.

Cupping the hand she had pinched him with, he gave gentle squeeze, saying, "Yeah, you have been my spark for a long time now, an annoying one at times. But my spark just the same."

"What? Annoying? Well, it only seems that way because I have to pound on that hard head of yours so much to get something through it."

Cal let go a laugh. "That's just my way of keeping you physically fit and sexy," he replied, pinching *her* in the ribs this time. He then took off running toward the resort's portico fifty yards away.

Donna stood for a moment watching Cal run off laughing and looking back at her. She shouted at him, "What? Why, you old buzzard! I'll show you what physically fit looks like." Then as if a starter's pistol had been fired, Donna suddenly vaulted after him like an Olympic sprinter.

Cal glanced back over his shoulder again to see her coming at him like a missile. Her form was fluid and precise. Laughing, he began pushing even harder trying to beat her to the front doors. Quickly gaining on him and watching him run, she too began to laugh at her less than in shape husband.

Fifty feet away and closing in fast she began chiding him, "You look like a locomotive chugging through a mountain pass."

Catching up to him, side by side, they shot underneath the portico roof with arms outstretched reaching for the entry doors. Trying to time their stops perfectly, they both began sliding on the sandy concrete driveway. Suddenly Cal's feet shot out from under him landing him on his ass and skidding feet first in a cloud of dust straight for the double glass doors.

Donna stayed upright sliding in a crouched wobbly stance right up to the doors. Grabbing the door pull, she triumphantly shouted, "Ha! I beat you, old man!"

Choking and gasping for air, Cal coughed out, "I...I don't think so. Look!" he said, pointing to the tip of his canvas shoe just touching the bottom of the door.

Johnny Mac who had been standing just inside the doorway watching the whole scene unfold suddenly took an umpire's stance. Bending over low, he spread his arms out wide, yelling, "Safe!"

Donna yanked the door open. "What, are you crazy? There's no way he beat me!"

Cal rolled up on one butt cheek, laughing, coughing, and patting the dust off while taunting her. "What's the matter, don't like losing to a chugging locomotive? Ya can't argue with the ump, baby."

Donna looked back at Cal who was just getting back up on his feet still slapping and smacking the dust off his pants and shirt. "Well, Casey Jones, you look as if your boiler exploded. Me, I could race you again right now."

Johnny Mac busted out laughing. "Hey, he did look like an old locomotive coming at me. Now he looks like the wreck of the ole number 97. Donna, you, you looked like a gazelle."

"Why, thank you, Johnny Mac, I'll take a compliment over winning a race against an old coal burner any day."

Both of them snickered and snorted watching Cal check out his scraped-up elbow. "Well, at least I won," he said, switching his attention to his other elbow.

Annoyed at being the butt of their joke, Cal thrust up a hand. "How about giving me a hand up instead of standing there laughing like a couple of fifth graders?"

Johnny Mac grabbed his hand and gave a yank. Cal grunted as he stood up grousing about the entryway having so much sand on it. Donna put a hand up to hide her big smile. Looking at him through squinted eyes, she remembered a time when he could have outrun her by several yards. A little part of her wished he still could.

Jim and Juky came over from the front desk holding a couple of room keys. "Are the three of you finished horsing around?" Jim asked. "Look, we got two rooms. It's all they had left. But check this out. The rooms have been covered. There is no charge."

"Covered. By who and why?" Cal asked.

"Apparently by Miss Ginger." Jim cut a look at Juky, adding, "Juky ole boy, I don't know why that lady likes you so much, but I'm damn glad she does."

Cal rolled his eyes. "Let's not start that whole mess again. Two rooms you say. There are five of us. Donna and me will stay in one while you three take the other I guess."

Jim spoke up quickly. "Hold on, I'm not sleeping dog-pile style. I can sleep in the Water Lily. I've got a nice big hammock I can stretch out in her. And floating on the water like that, she'll rock me to sleep like a baby."

"Okay, have it your way. Right now, I just want to go get cleaned up and grab some shut-eye."

Donna suddenly interjected, "Cal, we need to get word to the kids. We need to let them know we're okay and where we are and what's going on."

Jim interrupted, "I already checked, and there's no phone service off the island."

Donna's face went straight when confronted again with that reality. She thought for a moment more, then snapping her fingers with a hopeful look, she said, "Wait, I think I know how. Jim, we can use your plane's radio, right?"

"Well, we can't call the Salty Anchor on it, if that's what you mean. It doesn't work that way."

"No, I know that, silly. We just need to be able to speak to another plane, that's all. We can do that, right?"

"Yeah, sure. But you can't just go yakking on it. It helps if you know the plane's call number and then it's got to be in range."

Donna glanced at her watch, then back at Jim. "I think we may just be in luck. C'mon, we have to hurry. If I'm right, there will be a red twin-engine plane flying right over us soon."

Cal looked at his wife in amazement. "Donna, how in the heck do you know that?"

Donna smiled, stepping back from him a bit. She swept her hands gracefully down both sides of her body while saying, "Hey, there's a brain riding on top of all of this gorgeousness, big boy."

Donna's calling attention to herself in front of the guys that way made Cal feel something he hadn't felt in years—a twinge of jealousy. "C'mon, Donna, stop being silly. You could just answer the question, ya know."

Donna knew that look and that tone. Having not seen it in a long while it made her feel good that she could still make him a little jealous. She briefly considered toying with it little more but figured she had already bruised his ego enough and thought better of it.

"Oh, all right. I know because the pilot that flew me to and from Rum Cay flies a regular route down to the Caicos Islands south of here. The time varies, but it's worth a try."

"Do you know the call number of the plane, Donna?" Jim asked.

"I remember part of it."

"Donna, part of a number may not be enough."

Looking thoughtful for a moment, Donna's face brightened. "I also know the pilot's name—it's Roger. The plane he's flying is a Beechcraft Bonanza. And he calls her Gertie. Does any of that help?"

Jim pursed his lips in thought, and then blurted out, "I guess that'll have to do. If he's flying over soon, we need to get to the Water Lily right now and start trying to raise him on the radio."

Donna looked at Cal. "C'mon, let's go, honey."

Cal gave himself an accessing once-over especially his scraped-up elbows. "Nah, you and Jim go ahead. I need to go wash some of this embarrassment off me."

Feeling a little sorry for him, she smiled warmly, leaned in, and gave him a soft kiss on the cheek. "I'll be right back, honey, hopefully with some good news."

Cal half smiled and nodded. But as Donna and Jim started out the lobby doors, he said, "Donna, listen, don't get too specific on what's going on. If Kevin thinks we are in trouble, he'll have half the U.S. Navy steaming straight for this island."

With the door pushed half open, Donna looked back at Cal. "Don't worry, honey, I know our son just like I know you." She pushed the door open and held it for Jim. As he passed, she gave Cal a little smile and wink then followed after Jim.

Cal stood watching her through the double glass doors and thought to himself, *That girl sure is a roller coaster ride, but I'm damn glad I bought a ticket to ride.* He then looked to Juky and Johnny Mac. Tossing the room key up and down in his hand, he said, "Well, boys, I'm off to shower and take a nap. I'll leave you two to your own devices. He then spun around and headed off to find his room.

Juky and Johnny Mac looked at each other. Juky said, "Well, I don't know about you, but I could use a beer."

Johnny Mac nodded agreement but said, "Well, I can't have a beer, but I'll get some kind of fruity kid's drink."

Juky chuckled. "Ah, so you are not a drinking man I take it."

Johnny Mac eyes widened. "Oh, no, I like a beer as much as the next guy."

"Den why will you not 'ave one with me?"

"Simple. When I drink, I tend to say the things that pop into my mind."

"Well, ma friend, even I do dat too when I drink too much."

Johnny Mac gave Juky furtive look. "Yeah, well, fortunately for you, you don't have the things I have pop into your mind that I do."

Juky's warm smile melted away seeing Johnny Mac's face.

Johnny Mac looked out the glass doors then back to Juky. "And right at the moment, I don't like the things rolling around in this head of mine."

"Ma friend, et es not a good thing to keep dose tings bottled up. Drink or not, we should go talk."

Johnny Mac rolled his eyes and head. "I'm not so sure you will want to know what might be about to happen on this little adventure do you?"

Juky gazed at Johnny Mac a long moment, then he smiled broadly and said with laugh, "Ma friend, I 'em not worried."

"You aren't? Why not?"

"Because, ma friend, you said 'might' be about to happen. Which means it doesn't have to. Now let's go aund have a beer aund see about changing de future, you aund me."

Chapter 39

After several attempts, Donna and Jim were able to make contact with Roger as he flew past. He promised that when he got back to Marathon, he would go straight to the Salty Anchor and relay Donna's update to Kevin and Tammy.

Jim had just signed off the radio when a stranger's voice echoed through the Water Lily's fuselage. "Helloooo, anybody in here, mates?"

Jim and Donna, sitting in the cockpit, shot brow-furrowed glances at each other. Jim immediately rose up from the pilot's seat. "Donna, you stay put. I'll go see who this is and what they want. Pointing to a small ammo box beside the pilot's seat, he said, "There's a gun in the box. Take it out, and anyone but me comes to this cockpit, drop 'em. They'll be after my plane. Got it?"

Donna eyes widened. "But I…I…I—"

Jim stopped her before she could finish. "It's probably nothing, but better safe than sorry, I say."

Donna felt her entire body flush with heat watching Jim head for the back of the plane. In seconds she went from feelings of relief at getting word back home to one of dread. Nervously she stared at the ammo box. Bending slowly down from the copilot's seat, she fumbled with the latch for a few frustrating seconds until she figured out how it opened. Popping the latch open, she raised the heavy metal lid to reveal a large shiny chrome pistol.

While hearing the echoed conversation between Jim and the stranger, Donna slowly reached into the ammo box and gingerly picked up the large gun as if it might go off just by touching it.

Holding it in her small hands made it appear even bigger, and she couldn't help but admire the pearl-handled beauty she was holding.

She ran a finger over the name stamped on the barrel, Smith and Wesson model 29. "Holy cow, this thing is a cannon," she quietly said to herself. She didn't know much about guns, but she had seen *Dirty Harry* with Cal at the movies. This only made her more nervous handling it.

Suddenly she was jarred from her transfixion of the gun by Jim's return to the cockpit door, letting out a shriek and nearly dropping it. "Whoa! Easy there, Annie Oakley. They work better if they stay in your hands."

"Oh my god, you scared the crap out of me, dammit!" Donna scolded.

"I see that. I'm sorry, Donna. I thought you heard me telling you it was okay and that I was coming forward."

Seeing how many of her fingers were shoved in the trigger guard, Jim cautiously reached for the gun. "Here, let me just slide that thing out of your hands there, Donna, before the Water Lily winds up with a couple of new vent holes in her."

Relaxing her hand, Donna felt as if a ton of bricks were being lifted from her as Jim deftly lifted the big gun from her hands. "Geez, Donna, I figured being married to a guy like Cal, you'd have handled a gun before."

Taking a calming breath, she said, "Well, I have. Cal has a .38 in the desk drawer back in Anchor's office, but that thing is covered in paper clips and pushpins. He keeps one in the *Donna Marie* too. Why, I don't know. Neither have been fired in years. Do you really have to worry about someone stealing the Water Lily?"

Palming the big gun before placing it back in the ammo box, he said, "Drug runners, pot and coke smugglers would kill to get their hands on a bird like the Water Lily. Hell, one time I was shot at by the Jamaican police while making a water landing near Morant Bay. Even *they* thought it was drug plane. Donna it would blow your mind to know how much of that stuff is being run through these islands. That's why if we do get your boat back, you and Cal need to sail her straight as arrow back for Ramrod Key."

Donna shook her head hearing what Jim had to say. She then looked past him out the cockpit window at the *Donna Marie* peacefully moored a short distance away. "I'm beginning to think we've made a huge mistake chasing after her," she said, nodding toward the window.

Stooping down, Jim peered out the same window then back to Donna. "Well, it's probably not the smartest thing you and Cal ever did." He then wistfully added, "But damn, she sure is beautiful. I'd hate to lose her too."

Donna smiled hearing that, but her smile was in contradiction to the worry in her eyes. "Well, let's just hope it doesn't turn into the worst thing we ever did."

Jim placed a hand on her shoulder. "Don't you worry about that. I've got a feeling that Lady Luck is on our side."

Donna smiled a little bigger and said, "Let's hope so 'cause if she's against us, we are in deep doo-doo this far from home."

Jim patted her shoulder. "C'mon, stop worrying yourself. Let's get back to the resort before that jealous husband of yours comes looking for us."

Donna let out a laugh. "Oh, you noticed that?"

"Oh hell yeah. You can read him like a book when it comes to how he feels about you, Donna, and I can't say as I blame him either."

"Oh, stop it. I'm a fifty-six-year-old woman. I'm like an old boot he's gotten used to wearing."

"Well, you sure don't look or act like one," he said with a laugh.

Donna, never comfortable with compliments from men other than Cal, quickly changed the subject by asking Jim, "You never said what that British-sounding guy wanted anyway."

Jim gave her a look of astonishment and a laugh, saying, "C'mon, let's head back to the resort. I'll tell you what's up on the way. You are not going to believe it. Cal and the others are going to love this too."

Jim helped Donna through the plane's hatchway door onto the dock which was much lower now due to the rising tide. Once down on the dock, Jim let go a short laugh again as he began to tell Donna who and what the stranger wanted.

"You'll never guess who that was," he said, sounding gleeful.

"Come on, Jim, I'm not in the mood to play Jeopardy with you, just spit it out."

"Okay, okay. It was that ruddy-looking guy that Juky said hijacked the *Donna Marie* from him. He wants me to fly him and his two cohorts up to Grand Bahama Island."

Donna stopped their brisk pace down the dock. Turning to face him, she asked, "What? You're kidding me?"

"No, I most certainly am not. And the best part is he's coughing up a thousand bucks to do it."

"You're not going to do it are you?"

"Well…Donna, I could sure use the money. This little endeavor is costing me a ton just in fuel. Not to mention the lost business."

Donna scrunched her face. "But you'll be helping these guys escape. We don't even know who they are."

"Relax, Donna. I'm not going to help these guys get away. I think I might just have a plan."

"A plan? What kind of plan?"

"C'mon, I want to stew on it while we walk then we can talk about it with Cal and see what he thinks."

Donna turned and resumed their trek down the dock. "Well, I can tell you what Cal would want to do—he'd let that creepy Sawfish guy have them."

"That *is* a tempting thought. But what I have in mind might be just as satisfying…and with a lot less blood involved."

Donna glanced over to the dock where the *Donna Marie* was moored. Grimacing, she said, "After all the trouble those guys have caused, even I wouldn't mind a seeing *little* blood."

Jim gave her a surprised sideways glance. "Rrrrr, this kitty's' got claws."

"Oh shut up, ya dork. Let's hurry up and get back. This has really put a twist on things."

Chapter 40

The low rumble of diesel engines caused everyone along the docks to stop and take notice of the large sleek yacht idling into the harbor. Almost to the end of the dock, Donna and Jim stopped to watch as the yacht slowed to a crawl right behind the *Donna Marie*. A lone man stood on the yacht's bow facing the *Donna Marie*. He was a large man, oddly dressed given that this was the tropics and it was summertime. The bald man wore a turtle neck pullover, slacks, and shoes, all of it black, his sunglasses black as well.

"Man, what's up with that?" Jim asked.

"I don't know, but he looks like a character straight out of a James Bond movie. And I sure don't care for the way he's eyeing our boat either," Donna moaned.

"Yeah, well, don't look now, but that fancy-ass yacht he's standing on looks as if it has some serious damage to it similar to your boat—like it was shot up."

Donna quickly surveyed the yacht, and sure enough, it had a good deal of damage from what appeared to be gunfire.

The mysterious man in black stared a moment more then turned sharply on his heels and marched down the gunwales to the stern disappearing inside the cabin. Donna shot a worried look at Jim. "This doesn't look good at all."

Jim nodded agreement then grabbed Donna by the elbow and started them on a brisk walk back to the resort. "Your old man sure isn't going to like this new development."

"No, he isn't, especially if we wake him up to hear it."

Jim let go an abbreviated laugh. "Well, I'll let you do the waking-up part."

"Gee, thanks, guess chivalry *is* dead."

"Not dead, but it has gotten a little smarter."

"Smarter or just chicken?"

Tucking his arms wing-like high up under his armpits, Jim made a silly face at Donna and began high stepping in a zigzag fashion clucking like a chicken.

Donna shook her head. "Yeah, I thought so. You dumb cluck, hurry up, let's go."

Donna looked back over her shoulder to see the big yacht being tied up to a dock a short distance away from the *Donna Marie*. Worriedly, she said, "I wonder what Miss Ginger will have to say about this new wrinkle. Sure hope she can still help us."

Jim ceased his chicken dance, returning to the seriousness of the moment. He said, "Hey, look, Donna, I think that Miss Ginger has got quite a few tricks up her sleeve, so I wouldn't worry too much about that yacht or any of the rest of this. Like I said, I think Lady Luck is on our side."

"Lady Luck is for gamblers. Frankly, I'm hoping that someone with a lot more rank than her is on our side."

"I don't know, Donna. Cal did win her in a card game, so maybe Lady Luck is exactly who we need."

"Let's not go there. I prefer to not remember how my husband initially acquired her."

Perplexed, he asked, "What do you mean by initially?"

Reluctantly, Donna said, "Yes, it's true that he won her in a card game. However, I made him pay the owner."

"What! Donna, boats like the *Donna Marie* cost a pretty penny—in fact, lots of pretty pennies."

Donna gave Jim an odd stare, and then looked toward the front doors of the resort that were now only a few feet away. In a strange faraway tone, she said, "Yes…yes they do."

Not sure of what was going on in her mind at the moment, he decided to steer her back on the two recent developments by asking, "Hey, uh, should we tell Cal about the guys who want me to fly them out of here first or about that shot-up yacht?"

Pushing the door open ahead of Jim, Donna tersely answered, "Before I tell him anything, I think I need to ask him something. And he better have the right answer or else you'll be flying all of us out of here…except for one."

Jim looked at Donna from behind, totally confused about what just happened, and wondered just what he had said to make her get upset so quickly. Whatever it was, he was glad he wasn't Cal at the moment. He wondered too if things were about to change and maybe change very quickly.

Chapter 41

Donna entered the room but kept the door partially open behind her. She stared at Cal asleep on the bed with his back to her. The curtains were drawn, and no lights were on; the room was dark except for the light she was letting in through the partially opened door. She stood for a moment hearing a soft snore coming from her peacefully sleeping husband.

For a moment her dark mood softened a bit seeing him this way. She then softly repeated to herself what Jim had said, "A pretty penny." She then slapped the door closed and flipped on the room lights, startling Cal awake.

Angrily Cal flipped over to face the door and whoever it was that had dared to wake him this way. Not expecting it to be Donna, he pulled back on his temper a bit but still gruffly barked, "Good grief, Donna, what the hell did you do that for? I was sleeping really well for a change."

"Can it, sleeping beauty. I need to know something, and I need to know it right now."

Pawing and rubbing his face trying to wake himself up, he rolled into a sitting position on the edge of the bed. "Donna, what the hell has gotten into you? What's the matter?"

Donna remained rigidly frozen by the door. "I'll tell you what's the matter. You never paid that man...that Mr. Edwards for the *Donna Marie*, did you?"

Cal stared at his wife for a long moment trying to figure out what had brought this up after fifteen years. "Well, did you, Cal?" Donna tersely repeated.

"Donna honey, why are you asking me this after all these years? I told you I did back then. What's this about?"

"I'll tell you what this is about. I don't remember seeing any large sums of money being withdrawn from any of our bank accounts back then. Did you have some secret stash hidden somewhere?"

Cal dropped his head staring at the floor. A lump built in Donna's throat. She had always known she could trust him no matter what. But right now, it looked like he had lied to her all those years ago. She wondered too what else he may have lied to her about.

Disappointment was thick in her voice as she somberly asked, "Cal, how could you lie to me like this? I believed you. I fell in love with that boat. The kids practically grew up on her. We've all had so much fun on her over the years, and now...now I don't know what to think except that there is no way I'm putting people at any more risk to get back a lie!"

Donna's words hit Cal like a thousand gut punches at once. Donna turned her back to him to face the door. He heard her soft sobs. He wasn't sure what to say. So he decided to tell her what really happened.

He had never, in all the years they had been together, seen her upset with him like this. Sure, she had been angry with him plenty of times over the years. But this was different; she was genuinely and deeply disappointed in him. Standing up, he slowly made his way to her stopping just inches behind her. He wanted desperately to touch her. He hated to see her cry, always did, but this was worse.

"Donna, listen to me please. I didn't lie to you. I did pay for the *Donna Marie*. Just not in the way you think." Except for her occasional sniffle, she remained silent and motionless. "Look, I tried to pay him, but he wouldn't accept any money. He said as a Texan, it would be a dishonor for him to take the money, saying he lost her fair and square. I explained to him what you had said and how you felt about me winning it in a card game, that you would never go aboard her if I didn't pay for it."

Donna turned around to face Cal, wiping the tears from her face. "So what *did* you do?"

"Will you promise not to get mad?"

"No, I won't. Cal, this hurt me. I have always trusted you no matter what you said or did. I never imagined you would lie to me and then keep it a secret from me all these years."

Cal, bothered by her insistence he lied to her, spoke curtly, "Donna, stop saying I lied to you. I didn't.

"Well, you have certainly kept something a secret from me, now, haven't you?"

"Look, will you just let me explain? I tried to work it out so everyone would be happy."

Donna gave him stern glare. "Everyone except for me, huh?"

"Stop it and please listen. If you still want to be mad at me, then we can leave the *Donna Marie* here and go home. And when we get back, I'll throw out all the photos of us and the kids and Roxy, our old golden retriever, on that damn sailboat. That way you never have to see or think about it again."

Donna glared at him for what seemed like a much longer time than it actually was, and then in an exceedingly calm tone, she said, "Okay, Mister Arnold, then please explain it, and it better be really good."

Cal briefly held his eyes in hers then spoke, choosing his words carefully. "All right, like I said, Edwards, he wouldn't take any money for it. So as you know, he comes once a year to stay at the Salty Anchor and take his buddies or business clients out fishing."

"Okay, so what has that got to do with not paying him for the sailboat?"

"Let me finish, Donna. Since he wouldn't take any money and since Edwards loves to be a wheeler dealer, he suggested we swap it out for cabin and boat rentals, meals, etcetera when he comes to stay at the Anchor. Each time he comes I deduct it from the balance. So you see, he *is* getting paid for the *Donna Marie*, just not in cash. In fact, next year will be the end of our deal."

Donna held her eyes in his for a moment before speaking. "Okay, okay, I get it. Actually, I'm all right with doing that. But why didn't you just tell me that back then?"

"Donna, you were just as mad at me then as you are now…well, maybe not this mad. I didn't know what else to do. And I wasn't sure how you would feel about my bartering for it either. Heck, I even offered to just forget the whole thing and told him he could just keep the boat. Well, he absolutely wouldn't hear of it.

"That's when he came up with the whole trade-off idea. I have no idea how that was really any different to him, but it was. It seemed to get us both off the hook, him with his Texas pride and me with… with you."

Donna's expression softened. The second Cal saw that, he reached for her. Cupping her upper arms in his hands, he said, "Donna, I love you. I would never do anything to hurt you. I didn't know how you would feel about my doing that. So I let you think I paid him."

Donna looked up into his eyes. "Walter Caleb Arnold, you are a roller coaster ride."

Cal let go a strained laugh. "Funny, I was thinking the same thing about you earlier."

"Me? I'm boring."

"Donna, you are a lot of things, but boring isn't one of them."

A soft knock came at the door interrupting their slow makeup session. Donna stepped away from the door. "Who is it?"

"It's me, Jim. Donna, did you tell him about those British guys?"

"What British guys? What's he talking about?" Cal asked as she opened the door.

Jim stepped partway into the room.

"No, I haven't. We have been discussing another matter. But you can tell him."

Sensing the lingering tension between them, he said, "Hey, look, it's no big deal. I, uh…I can come back later." He began to retreat back out the door when the phone on the nightstand rang.

Cal picked it up on the third ring. "Hello. Yes, I am. Oh, hey, Miss Ginger, sure we can be there in just a few minutes. Is everything okay? A gate behind the restaurant…all right, we'll all be there. Goodbye."

Cal placed the receiver slowly back down on the phone, looking to Jim and Donna. "That was Miss Ginger. She wants us to meet her at the restaurant right now."

"She does? But why?" Donna worriedly asked.

"I don't know. We're supposed to come to the back of the restaurant through a gate in a tall fence."

Jim piped up, "I don't like the sound of this. What if she's in cahoots with the Sawfish? She knows you two are the true owners of the *Donna Marie*. This could be a setup to get rid of anyone who could ruin their little operation."

"Oh, stop it. I don't believe she would be part anything of the sort," Donna admonished.

"Hey, look, we don't know anything about her. Money has a way of warping people."

"Look, we don't have time to be psychoanalyzing a rotund restaurant owner. Let's go and get Juky and J-Mac and hightail it over there. She sounded pretty emphatic about getting there right away."

"Well, okay. But that's *exactly* what someone would be like right before they…" He stopped and made an ominous slicing motion and sound at his throat.

Donna rolled her eyes. "Oh, stop that, ya drama queen. Miss Ginger isn't going to kill us."

Cal reached for the door pulling it all the way open. "C'mon, let's get going. She's not going to kill us…at least I hope not."

"Oh my god, *two* drama queens," Donna said, falling in behind Cal.

As she walked past Cal into the hallway, he added, "Well, we really don't know her. Juky could have made up that whole story about saving her daughters. Heck, maybe he's in on it too."

Donna didn't even look back. "Good Lord, have you two lost your marbles?"

Standing next to Cal, Jim said, "Hey, maybe this has something to do with that yacht that came in all shot up."

Cal quickly questioned, "What yacht?"

"Maybe," Donna began thoughtfully. "I did see a young boy take off running up the docks for shore as that thing entered the marina."

Frustrated, Cal snapped, "Again, what yacht?"

Jim and Donna both stopped. "That's right. We haven't told you about it or the British guy that actually stole our boat—he wants Jim here to fly him and his pals to Grand Bahama."

Looking quite perplexed, Cal stood slack-jawed for a moment. He then shook his head, then continued walking. "C'mon, tell me about it on the way to see Miss Ginger. Maybe whatever she has to say will make sense of all of this."

"Maybe, or else it's…*schlick*," Jim said, slicing his finger across his throat again.

"Oh, for Pete's sake, will you stop doing that? She is not going to kill us."

Arriving at Juky and Johnny Mac's room, Jim knocked on the door. When no one opened the door, he twisted the doorknob; it wasn't locked. Pushing it slowly open, they found the room empty. Entering the room, they immediately noticed something didn't look right. The beds were disturbed like they had been laid on, which was to be expected. However, the nightstand and dresser drawers were all pulled open. Jim walked on into the room but motioned for Donna and Cal to hang back by the door. Jim pointed to Johnny Mac's small travel bag sitting in a chair in the corner of the room. It too looked to have been rifled through.

Suddenly the bathroom door was slammed shut and locked, startling them all. Donna let out a short shriek while grabbing Cal's arm. A pounding noise erupted from the other side of the door. Jim froze for a second looking back at Cal and Donna, and then lunged for the door. Grabbing the doorknob, he threw his shoulder into the door. The pounding became louder and more urgent. Jim hit the door harder, shouting, "Who's in there? Unlock this door now!"

The pounding abruptly halted but was quickly followed by a few seconds of scuffling and grunting and then…silence. Cal hurried to join Jim's effort to bust through the door. On the third attempt with both men ramming their shoulders at the door, it burst open hurling splinters of wood and plaster into the bathroom. Quickly both men looked left and right, but there was no one. Cal glanced up over Jim's head and pointed to a window which hung ajar. The window was six feet or so off the floor. Jim pointed at some sand and grit on the edge of the sink.

"Check that out. It's the only way to be able to reach that window," Jim said.

"What's going on? Who was in here?" Donna asked, peeking around the edge of the door.

"Don't know, baby. Whoever it was must have stood on the edge of the sink and escaped through the window."

"That window? It can't be but sixteen inches high and not much wider than that. Must be a small person."

Jim climbed up on the edge of the sink to take a look. "Well, it appears that once they slid the hasp open, they found that it had been painted over and had to pound on it to get it open."

"Well, that explains all the racket. But why were they in here, and where the heck are Johnny Mac and Juky?" Cal mused.

Suddenly a man's voice called from the open door. "Well, we are right here."

Startled, Donna spun around to see Johnny Mac and Juky standing by the room door. "But what in heaven's sake are you all doing in the bathroom?"

"We came to get you two. But when we got here, we found someone in your room. They escaped through the bathroom window," Donna said, pointing to the window.

"Wow, must be a small guy," Johnny Mac declared.

"Et was probably one of the local boys. De Sawfish, he will pay dem to do tings such as dis to find out who people are."

"But why would he want to know about you two?" Cal asked, exiting the bathroom.

"I suspect et es not Johnny Mac as much as et es me," Juky lamented.

"You again?" Cal snorted. "You sure are a popular guy around these parts."

"Well, I think 'e es trying to see if I am de one who caused some trouble for him a while ago."

"So this guy knows you?"

"No, not really. Until today, 'e 'as only seen me once from afar…and dat was years ago. Dat es why he questioned me about what island I was from—'e is trying to remember."

"Remember what?" Donna asked.

Cal shook his head then glanced down at his watch. "Look, we don't have time for that. We need to get over to see Miss Ginger. Maybe she can shed some light on all of this. And you," he said, pointing at Juky, "on the way there, you can come clean about your past—all of it! Understand? 'Cause I'll be dammed if I'm going to get cut into fish bait on account of something you did. Now let's go."

Taking Donna by the hand, Cal threaded their way past Johnny Mac and Juky. Going past Juky, he added, "So help me, if something you did years ago screws up getting the *Donna Marie* back, you won't have to worry about the Sawfish hacking you up, 'cause I'll have already beaten him to it."

Jerking Cal's arm, Donna fussed, "Walter Caleb Arnold, you stop talking that way! I swear at times I don't know what gets into you."

"Look, can we please just get going? I got a feeling things are going to get weirder with all that's going on."

Johnny Mac fell in behind Donna and said off-handedly, "Boy, you don't know how true that is."

Cal stopped out in the hallway and waited for everyone. Jim was the last one out. Closing the door behind him, he said, "Okay, let's go. I want to see what Miss Ginger has to say, 'cause if isn't good, me and the Water Lily will be in the air fifteen minutes later."

"Hold on a second, everyone." Cal then looked pointedly at Johnny Mac. "J-Mac, just what did you mean just now? Do you know something, 'cause if you do, I want to know what it is right now."

Johnny Mac stared back at Cal. "Look, Cal…all of you. There are many paths that can be taken, and each will have a different result. Miss Ginger is going to try and help us get the *Donna Marie* back. But her influence is limited, and our success hinges on other elements too."

Cal stared hard into Johnny Mac's eyes. "You mean like the Sawfish?"

Johnny Mac gave a small nod. "And the ones on the yacht."

Jim stopped. "Hey, wait, how do you know about the yacht?" then snapped his fingers. "That's right, you're that—"

Cal cut him off. "Hold it, don't say it. Let's not get that whole thing going again. Johnny Mac, so it's those two that are our big concern here?"

Shaking his head "no," Johnny Mac pointed his index finger up at the ceiling making a swirling motion and said, "No, there are natural elements that could affect everything."

Cal widened his eyes. "Well, enlighten us."

Johnny Mac crinkled his brow. "Have you all forgotten?" he said, drifting his gaze around at them. "It's still hurricane season."

Cal rubbed his hand down his face. "Jesus, that's right, so is one heading our way right now?"

Johnny Mac started walking down the hallway. "C'mon, let's go see Miss Ginger. Timing *is* everything, especially in this case."

Everyone stood for a second watching him head down the hallway. Then in unison, they started after him peppering him with questions and concerns all at the same time.

"I've gotta get my plane outta here."

"Cal, we can't leave her here, not with a storm."

"Wait, J-Mac, just tell me if the storm is…"

Never looking back, Johnny Mac made a big forward sweep with his arm and kept walking. "The future is this way!"

Chapter 42

Kevin eyed the man walking with purpose up to the bar. He wasn't a regular. His thinning combed-backed salt-and-pepper hair, khaki slacks, and polo shirt told him he wasn't here for the fishing or scuba diving either. Probably another salesman, he thought. "Welcome to the Salty Anchor, what can I do for you?" Kevin said while serving a customer's glass of beer.

"Well, for one, I'll take a Pabst to drink, and then can you tell me where I can find a guy by the name of Kevin Arnold?"

Kevin nodded. "Easy enough." He filled the chilled beer glass and placed it in front of the man. "Here's your beer, and you have found Kevin Arnold. Now what can I do for you, Mister…"

Taking a quick sip and wiping beer foam from his upper lip, Roger smiled and stared into his face. "Oh yeah, I guess you are. I can see the resemblance now. You got your mother's eyes, all right."

Kevin crinkled his brow. "You know my mother?"

"Know her? I guess you could say that. I flew her to Rum Cay a couple of days ago. The name's Roger Strader. I own Strader Airways."

Kevin's eyes flew open. Instantly he shot rapid-fire questions as Roger took sips of beer. "You did? Is she okay? Is she still there? Is my dad with her?"

Swallowing hard, Roger held up a hand then choked out, "Hold on, hold on.'" Wiping his mouth with the back of his hand, Roger began telling Kevin all that he knew, starting first with the most recent message he got while flying past Pirates Well the day before.

"Okay, okay, so Dad is with Mom, and they have found the *Donna Marie*. Did she say if they were on their way back now?"

"Well, from what I gather, they don't have possession of her yet. But they expect to soon. Seems there was some damage to her that may need to be repaired before they can start back, is what I got."

"Damage? Did the pirates do something to it?"

"Not sure who did what. All your mom said was that it might need to be taken care of before they headed home."

Kevin shook his head. Just then Tammy sidled up next to Kevin at the beer taps nudging Kevin over a little so she could fill a beer glass. Smiling big, she said, "What's up? You look like you've seen a ghost."

Kevin turned to look at Tammy. "It's Mom and Dad—they found the *Donna Marie*—it's at a place called Pirates Well. That's the good news. The bad news is it has damage that needs to be repaired before they can start for home."

Tammy fumbled with the beer glass she was filling nearly dropping it. "Oh my god! Mom and Dad, are they all right? Where are they?"

Roger rolled his eyes. "Hold on, hold on, miss. You need to work on your delivery," he said, looking at Kevin. "They're fine. They found the boat already in that condition."

"Oh, thank God! When are they heading back?"

"Don't know yet," Kevin replied.

"I don't like this, Kevin. We need to call there and tell them to just come home."

Roger gave Tammy a sympathetic look. "I'm afraid you can't. No phones to the island, just ship-to-shore and shortwave radio. Heck, they had to raise me on my plane's radio as I was flying past, by calling me from another plane—which was pretty smart, I'd say."

"You say she did that from another plane?"

"Yeah, it was Jim Abbot's. He flies supplies and fisherman to the islands."

Kevin acknowledged that with a nod, adding, "Yeah, he flew Dad and another man to, I thought, Rum Cay."

Kevin caught Roger's puzzled look and asked, "What's the matter? You did fly Mom to Rum Cay, right?"

Chugging the last of his beer, he set the glass down. Talking as he combed beer foam off his big mustache with his fingers, he said, "Oh yeah, I flew your mom there, and I flew her out the next day too."

"What? To where?" Tammy asked.

"To the Exuma airport. I believe she was going to Rokers Point settlement."

"Why there?"

"Well, she believed your dad was there, and she was going there to meet him. She also told me all about what was going on with your sailboat too. Bloody pirates."

Tammy looked at Kevin, her face and voice heavy with worry. "Kevin, we have to do something. I think we should call the Coast Guard or the FBI—someone. We can't just let them be out there facing this alone. I mean there is damage to the *Donna Marie* from god knows what, and you know she's not telling us everything."

Pressing his lips tight not wanting to say what he was about to, Roger took a breath then spoke to them both. "Look, you two can call the authorities, *and* maybe you should. But understand they can't do anything. Your parents—they are not in U.S. waters. The FBI might let Interpol know about them, and if you're lucky, the bureau might inform the State Department about the situation. But other than that, I'm afraid they are on their own."

Roger stood up to leave. "Don't you two worry. I'm sure everything is going to be fine, but it probably wouldn't hurt to make those calls to the authorities."

Tammy and Kevin wordlessly nodded. Tammy looked at Kevin and said, "We both know that they're not coming back without the *Donna Marie*."

"Yeah, I was kinda thinking the same thing. When those two get something in their heads, you have to move heaven and earth to change their minds," Kevin added.

Roger saw the worry return to both their faces. "Hey, look, don't worry too much. Between me and Jim, we'll get them home even if we have to hog-tie and kidnap them to do it."

Hearing this, Tammy could barely contain her emotions it was all she could do to not burst out crying. Leaning into Kevin's side, her voice brittle and broken, she said, "Thanks for coming and letting us know what's going on."

"No problem. I'm a phone call away." Roger handed then a business card, gave a short wave, and left.

Tammy put her hand on Kevin's arm. "Kevin, I don't to wait to see if they make it back in two days. We have to do something now. We couldn't live with ourselves if something awful happened to them and we just sat here doing nothing."

"I know, sweetheart. We'll make some calls."

Chapter 43

Cal cautiously eased the heavy gate open. Warily he surveyed the enclosed courtyard, taking note of several things. The gate along with the high fence that surrounded the courtyard looked to be made from wood salvaged from old boat hulls. The evidence of that was shown in the different colors of weathered paint, worm holes, and barnacle remnants on it.

Not unusual to see that, he thought. Heck, even back home in the Florida Keys, there was a time when the residents of that island chain would purposely lure ships into the reefs in order to wreck them on the reefs and then plunder everything they could before it broke up.

He knew too that building materials are hard to come by in the islands, especially wood and concrete. So the islanders repurpose practically everything from boat hulls to whatever washes up on shore. What *was* a bit unusual to him was that the whole courtyard was filled with all manner of things. Stepping on into the courtyard area, being closely followed by Donna, she exclaimed, "Wow this place, is filled with stuff."

Juky, Johnny Mac, and Jim trailed in and likewise stood taking in the plethora of random items that were lined up in rows like an outdoor market, some of it covered in heavy tarps. There were stacks of lumber, crates filled with pipe fittings, spools of electrical wire, a wooden barrel with rakes and shovels stored in it, and even a washing machine.

Cal motioned for them to follow him to a covered porch. Moving through the stuff, Donna questioned out loud to no one in particular, "Where in the heck did she get all of this stuff? What could she be doing with it?"

Juky answered, "Et es sea salvage, whatever washes up on de beaches or found floating in de ocean."

Donna questioned him further while stopping to dig in a wooden crate filled with new beach balls still folded in their plastic packaging, "My gosh, when does she have the time to do this and run a restaurant?"

Juky laughed. "Oh, she does not gather dis stuff herself. She may buy some of it. But I'm sure she has some of de young boys on de island scouring the surrounding waters and beaches for whatever dey can find and pays dem a finder's fee."

Donna then stepped up to a mysterious crate. It was about six feet long, three feet high, and four-feet wide. Flipping up the rusty metal hasp, she then grabbed two thick leather loop handles to lift it open. The lid was fairly heavy she struggled a bit to lift the lid up high enough to get a glimpse of what was inside.

Looking down as soon as the lid cleared her face, she suddenly shrieked letting it slam back down. A look of horror tore across her face. Her words draped in terror came like she was trying to keep from being sick. "Oh my god! There are body parts in there!" Pointing a condemning finger at the crate, she backpedaled away from it falling backward into a large stack of new plastic gas cans that swallowed her in a sea of red.

Almost to the porch when she screamed, Cal turned, racing back the short distance to the gaggle of plastic gas cans she had disappeared into. Skidding to a stop, he reached for a lone hand haplessly jutting from jumble of red plastic. Lying on her back, she furiously shoved and kicked at the attacking gas cans.

Grasping her hand, Cal firmly pulled her to her feet, bursting into laughter as she emerged from what was once a neatly stacked display. Her hair was draped over her face, her pants were dusty, and the purple Mork and Mindy T-shirt she wore was twisted halfway around.

"Donna, what the heck is all the commotion about? Why are you yelling about body parts?"

Swiping the hair out of her face and straightening her T-shirt, she pointed at the crate behind him. "That big crate has human body parts in it."

"What? Oh, come on, Donna, that's ridiculous."

Continuing to dust herself off, she stopped long enough to point a finger back and forth the length of the crate. "No, it's not! Look for yourself. I'm telling you there are legs and arms and…God only knows what else might be in there."

Cal rolled his eyes at her. "Donna, c'mon, do you really think Miss Ginger is going to be keeping body parts in her backyard? That is as crazy as that purple T-shirt you're wearing. Look, I'll show you. Stepping up to the weathered crate, he grabbed the leather handles and was about to lift it open when Jim suddenly spoke up.

"Hey, Cal, what if that's where that Sawfish character stashes his victims' sawed-off arms and legs?"

Cal shot a look at him. "Not you too."

"Hey, you never know. There are some crazy-ass people in these islands."

Cal just shook his head then lifted the lid. Standing it open, he hesitated a second or two. Then before reaching down into the crate, he yelled out, "Oh my god, Donna, you were right! There *are* body parts in here." He then reached into the crate.

"Oh my god, Cal, what are you doing! Don't touch them!" Donna shrieked.

In the next instant, Cal whirled around holding up a human leg. Donna screamed, turning quickly away. Cal burst out laughing. "Relax, Donna, it's a leg all right—an artificial one! And a good one too. It even has hair on it. They're mannequin parts," he said, laughing harder now.

Donna turned partway around, still not sure she wanted to see it, even if it *was* fake.

"Cal, put it down. It's nasty-looking, and it's giving me the creeps," she said, while averting her eyes.

"Oh, come on, these would be great for Halloween, wouldn't they, Jim?"

"Yeah, sure, if you live at the Bates Hotel," he deadpanned.

Donna turned away and kept patting the dust off herself and trying to get some control of her hair. During all the commotion, no one had noticed Miss Ginger's arrival on the porch. She startled them all when she called out to them. "'Ave you all found something you want? Or are you just making a mess?"

Donna looked at Miss Ginger, then quickly to Cal pointing a finger at him. "Don't you dare say you found something you want!"

"What? Come on, it'd look great hanging on the wall in the Salty Anchor. Heck, we could even put a shoe—no, no, a pirate's boot on it."

Donna tilted her head giving him one of her "this conversation's over" glares.

Cal arched his eyebrows high. "Ohhh, okay, I'll put it back. But so help me, if I get the chance to buy another mannequin leg on this journey, it's going home with us."

"You do, and it'll be the only thing you'll be going home with."

Jim, Juky, and Johnny Mac all snickered and guffawed. Still laughing, Jim said, "Hey, Cal, you'd best stick with the two legs you got. She sounds pretty serious."

Cal tossed the leg back into the crate and closed the lid. "Yeah, I think you're right. Let's go. We've had some fun. Now let's go see what Miss Ginger has to say."

Miss Ginger called again to them, "Hurry along please. We don't 'ave much time."

With a sweeping wave of his arm, Cal called out, "Let's get moving, troops. Our operations commander calls."

The silliness of a moment ago quickly vanished, as the reality of why they were here came crashing back. Cal immediately began mentally putting together all the hurdles he felt had to be overcome in order to gain possession of the *Donna Marie*.

He understood full well that they were putting all their trust and hope in just one person—a person whom they didn't even know, other than she is an owner of a café and outdoor junk shop. He didn't like the fact that she was holding all the cards with no idea what cards were about to be dealt them. Hopefully, he thought, it wasn't going to be aces and eights.

*****

Michael and Terry were below deck gathering their things and cleaning up the shattered glass from the shot-out port window.

Terry spoke while gingerly picking up the shards of glass. "So what did that bloke with the plane tell you, Michael, is 'e gonna fly us outta 'ear?"

"He said had some other clients he might have to fly out. Said he'd let me know sometime later today."

Martin was topside working to re-rig the smaller sails. "Aye, Michael, did ya see that yacht what we got in to spars with last night just docked here. What are we going to do about it?"

"Yeah, I saw it when they slithered in. They was eyeing this tub like sharks. But we ain't gonna do nothing, ya hear, nothing. We're gonna do what the buyer told us: get our stuff off this boat and then we fly the hell outta here, got it?"

"Those bloody Russian mingers. They would be really stupid to try something right in port 'ear," Terry added.

"I suppose, but just the same, I'm keepin' me piece right 'ear," Martin said, patting his pants where the handle of his pistol poked out above his belt.

"Yeah, well, don't ya go wav'n' that bloody thing around. Nobody 'as any suspicions about us or this damn boat, so let's keep it that way."

"Yeah, sure, Michael. I got no desire to be shoot'n' it out with that ball-headed blighter again, that's for sure."

Just then then someone called out to Martin from the dock. "Aye, Mon, we 'ave come for de boat."

Startled, Martin stepped back and away from the hatchway to see two of the men who had accompanied Caesar earlier. The taller one spoke again, adding, "De boss man, he want it to go to de other side of de island fo-ah repairs for de crossing. We will help you with yo-ah things now."

Michael called up through the open hatchway door, "Who is that, Martin?"

"It's two of our contact's, men. They are 'ear for de boat, Michael."

Michael tromped his way up onto the deck. Eyeing the two men, he said, "Aye, mates. I, uh…I thought he was giv'n' us the day for to clean up a bit and get our things. We still need to arrange a way off this island."

"He worries about a storm dat might be coming. He wants 'et on de leeward side of de island to help protect et from further damage."

"I see." Michael turned and looked at his shipmates. "Well, you heard 'em blokes. Time for us to be landlubbers again. Let's get our stuff and be on our way. I need to find that bleed'n' pilot. He's gotta fly us off this pile of sand."

Chapter 44

Miss Ginger ushered them into her small living room. Donna noted that it was clean and neat and eclectically appointed, probably again from whatever they had scrounged from the sea over the years. They all noticed the smell of fried food which permeated the atmosphere. It was then that they all realized that her home was on the other side of a wall that separated it from the Conch Shell Café. She literally lived between her two businesses.

"Please 'ave a seat. We need to be quick about dis. Ma cousin is on his way back from de other side of de island. And please no one talk until I 'ave finished. First tings first, we 'ave a storm coming which is going to 'elp us get you boat back."

"But how is—"

Miss Ginger cut Cal off. "Listen please, we 'ave vury little time. My cousin's men are moving yo-ah boat to Abraham's Bay now to protect et from de storm ef it comes our way. I em told that yo-ah boat es seaworthy, only needing some of de small sails rigged with new rope. De mainsails were free-dropped, so maybe de hoist cable only needs untangling. De damage from de bullets will not affect de seaworthiness. Dees things will be taken care of tonight by several of mah men. So you two can sail yo-ah boat straight away."

Donna shuddered hearing about the damage from bullets and drove home the seriousness of their situation. Johnny Mac spoke up, "What about us three, Miss Ginger, are we just supposed to stay here and get cut into fish bait?"

"No, you need to split up. You," she said, looking at Jim, "I suggest you fly out just as soon as possible. And you"—pointing to Juky—"mah cousin will suspect you are de one who has taken de boat. I will make sure he believe dat aund dat you are heading north to Crooked Island, but you need to be on this maun's plane when he leaves," she said, pointing to Jim.

Looking worried, Johnny Mac again asked, "But what about me? Where am I to go?"

Miss Ginger looked Jonny Mac straight in the eye. "You may go in any direction you want. However, I suspect yo-ah already know which way es best for you."

Johnny Mac smiled and nodded but said nothing.

Finally, Cal, who had been listening intently and accessing her plan, spoke up. "Sounds like a good plan, Miss Ginger, risky but good. Miss Ginger, I see what you are doing. This is like a play in a football game. You are giving Caesar too many points to try and cover all at once. So he's going to be left with having to choose which way to go. Am I right?"

"Yes, but my task will be to make sure he doesn't choose de right one. Ma cousin is no fool."

Always one to think of others, Donna asked, "What about you? What if your cousin finds out it was you who helped us?"

Patting the back of Donna's hand, Miss Ginger smiled broadly. "Don't you worry about hem. I let hem think he run things around he-ah."

Just then a knock and call to Miss Ginger came at the door. Miss Ginger motioned to Jim who was standing next to it to open it. Jim slowly opened the door to reveal a lanky young man who spoke quickly to her. "Miss Ginger, de boat es on et's way to Abraham's Bay."

Hearing that bit of news, Donna became worried and nervous. She slipped her hand into Cal's, squeezing it tightly. Cal gave her a sideways glance. He knew how she felt at the moment, and he was right there with her.

This suddenly had gotten very real, Cal thought. There were so many different elements of danger involved in what they were about to do. Cal squeezed her hand back. His biggest concern was the safety of his wife. She mattered more to him than anything in the world. Without her by his side, he thought, life would not be worth living. Giving her another look, he decided right then that she would fly back with Jim. And he and Johnny Mac would sail the *Donna Marie* back home, that is if they could survive being drowned by a hurricane or shot by pirates.

Miss Ginger gave the young man some further instructions on the supplies to put on the *Donna Marie* during the night. She then reached and pulled open a drawer in the end table next to where she sat. From it she retrieved a notebook-sized paper. Unfolding the yellowed paper, Cal saw that it was a sea chart.

She called Cal over to her. Easing his way over to where she sat, he knelt down beside the end table peering under the lampshade at the chart. She angled it toward him and began explaining it to him. Cal figured it to be a pre-plotted course but said nothing.

What he *didn't* know, but Miss Ginger did and was beginning to explain, was just how dangerous the first part of the course was going to be. "Mista Cal, do not go sail straight out of Abraham's Bay. See des two *X*s here aund here." Cal nodded. "Dey are de entry and exit points through a coral reefs dat runs along dat side of de island."

Cal's eyes widened as he stared at the chart. The path made an L shape and was canted about thirty degrees to the direction of the reef. She pointed to some numbers. "Des numbers are de distance you must go through de coral and de width of the passage."

Cal gazed at the chart a moment more taking note of what looked to be a channel that ran next to the island straight into Abraham's Bay. He then asked the obvious question: "Miss Ginger, why not take the channel back north and then go west out to sea? Why take a dangerously narrow and long path through a coral reef?"

Miss Ginger turned herself on the couch to look at Cal. "Because going through the reef es de last place he would expect you go. He would expect you to use the big channel leaving de cove, so he will naturally go der first. But de one route he would least expect someone to be brave enough to try is de old pirates' path."

"Pirates' path?" Donna asked.

"Yes, et es a path de pirates discovered more den two centuries ago. Et es 'ow dey brought der booty to shore."

"They sailed their ships through that path?" Johnny Mac asked.

"Oh goodness, no, dat would be not only crazy but impossible. No, dey used der launches to go through de reef."

"Well then, how do you expect Cal and Donna here to sail through it?" Jim asked.

Cal spoke up. "Our boat is big, but not as big as a pirate ship, plus we have a diesel engine. That's how." Cal went on to ask, "Those other numbers I see, those are compass coordinates?"

"Yes, de ones dat are circled in black are places where de coral 'as grown back in some. So de path can be quite narrow, and de one's dat are underlined in red are course changes you must make, and you must make them exactly right and at de right times."

Cal straightened up, taking a deep breath. Looking back down at Miss Ginger who was folding the chart, he asked, "And there is no other way out of where the *Donna Marie* has been taken?"

"I'm afraid not. Et seems dat you 'ave three choices. Take dis way"—she held up the chart, then pointed the chart toward the north wall of her house—"or sail straight out of Abrahams Bay and be run down by Caesar's men before you get five miles out to sea."

Donna asked as she handed the chart to Cal, "That's two, and the third?"

Miss Ginger looked at her then to Cal. "De third choice is to leave yo-ah boat and go home." Just then a small bell rang over a door in the far corner of the room. Miss Ginger stood immediately up. "You must excuse me. My girls must be getting busy in de café. I must go and help dem. But yo-ah are welcome to stay he-ah and talk dis over."

Cal and the others somberly nodded acceptance of her invitation. Just as she pulled open the door to leave, Cal asked, "How much time do we have before we pull the trigger on this operation?"

Miss Ginger stopped, looking back over her shoulder as she said, "De storm will tell us. So you must be ready to go at a moment's notice."

"But how will we know when that is, Miss Ginger?" Donna implored.

Miss Ginger smiled broadly. "Don't you worry, ma sweet one. When yo-ah finished talking, go back to de motel, gather yo-ah tings.

259

When de time is right, de same man you saw at my door a moment ago will come for you. But do not delay. Go immediately with hem."

Jim quickly asked, "Hey, wait, just one more thing—am I to fly out when they leave too?"

"No, you need to be getting ready now and leave as soon as you feel you are prepared to go. I 'ope you 'ave enough fuel, for der es none on de island."

Jim nodded. "No, I'm good on fuel."

A voice called from the other side of the door. "Mama, we need yo-ah 'elp please!"

"No more questions. I must go and help my daughters now." And with that she disappeared through the door.

The room was quiet except for the murmur of voices coming from the café on the other side of the wall. No one spoke for a long moment. Each knew how serious this had gotten. Finally, Cal turned around to face them all.

Grimacing, he said, "Well, gang, do we leave her and go home?"

Donna quickly spoke up. "No, we don't leave her. We've come this far. She is literally in our midst. That'd be like leaving your child to drown just because the water looks rough."

No one said a word for a long moment. Johnny Mac stood near the door to the courtyard. Reaching for the door, he abruptly stopped and turned to face them. Confused, they all looked at him wondering what was going on. Cal though saw it on his face. "What is it, Johnny Mac? You know something don't you?"

Johnny Mac who had been uncharacteristically quiet with his predictions since starting this journey, Cal's question brought a rapid change to his whole manner. When he spoke, it was even and low. "The stakes are high. The bet you make determines the path you take."

Jim stared at him wide-eyed a moment then flatly said, "Man, that is some weird stuff."

Johnny Mac simply replied, "Yeah, I get that a lot."

Cal, who was far more used to and comfortable with Johnny Mac's cryptic manner, asked him, "So we take her through the reef, huh? And we'll make it safely?"

Johnny Mac made no indication of agreement on Cal's comment. Looking around at each of them, he said, "Fate has dealt the hand. There is risk in everything. It's time to ante-up or fold."

Donna glared at Johnny Mac then at Cal. "Why does everything about this darn sailboat have to circle around a darn poker game?"

A smile came to Johnny Mac as he said, "Well, it is how she came to be in your lives, *and* it is how that Texan Cal won her from acquired her as well."

Donna's eyes widened as she glared at Cal. "Oh my god, Cal! That's just great. You know, you should have named her the Mirage or the Golden Nugget for all the gambling that boat has seen."

Cal, growing annoyed with this diversion from their present situation and his wife's aversion to all things gambling, said, "Look, let's all go back to the motel room. I need to look this chart over, and you and I need to talk about a few things before any of this goes down."

"What *few things*?" Donna questioned.

"I don't know exactly. Something feels wrong, and I can't put my finger on it. I just need to get some place quiet and do some thinking."

Donna gave him a wary stare but said nothing. However, she knew him like a book. His first inclinations were always to protect her. Because of that, she knew he was going to try and send her back on Jim's plane. She resolved right then that there was no way she was doing that. Not sure how, but she was going with him. She reasoned that she had gotten them into this mess, and by golly, she was going to help get them out of it. And they would sail the *Donna Marie* through coral reefs, hurricanes, or hell if they had to, but they were going to do it together.

Chapter 45

As expected, Cal insisted Donna fly out with Jim, and Johnny Mac. She gave in after giving him just enough resistance to make it believable. Cal changed who was going to help him sail the *Donna Marie* through the treacherous coral reef; Juky was the logical choice.

With this all settled, Jim told Cal that he needed to go and do some flight checks before they took off. He suggested that Donna and Johnny Mac put their things on the plane now because it was likely they'd be taking off on short notice. Cal agreed. Jim took off for the docks to ready the Water Lily for a quick takeoff. Johnny Mac and Juky went back to their room to gather their things. Cal and Donna were alone in the room. Cal watched her as she silently went about packing the few things she had pulled out of her suit case.

"Donna, I know you're upset with me. But you have to understand, taking a vessel the size of the *Donna Marie* through a gap in a coral reef is off the charts crazy and dangerous. If something goes wrong, the kids will need you. They can't lose both of us."

Hearing that, Donna turned from her slow-motion packing to face Cal. "And what, they don't need you? You act like they don't love you or need you just as much. That's just a load of bull, Cal, and you know it, and what about me, huh? You think that if the worst happens to you that I'll just go on with my life like you were just some brief aberration, just a hiccup? For God's sake, Cal, we've had a life together. We have ridden out so many of life's storms, and you know what? We did it together."

Cal didn't say anything for a long moment. He stood just looking at Donna. She was right, of course. However, this was a far, far different situation than they had ever been in before, and the stakes were higher than he even wanted to think about.

"Donna…sweetheart, you're right about all of that. We have faced all the ups and downs life can throw at two people. But this one is different, and you know that. We both need to think about the future. Look, I can't take you. I just can't."

"But why? I can sail as good as Juky can."

"Donna, I know that, but I may need his physical strength to help me get through that reef. There are some real close spots along the way I have no idea if the *Donna Marie* can react that quick, and he may need to keep us pushed off the reef if need be."

Donna's heart sank. She knew he was right. But it was tearing her apart to think she could leave him behind to an unknown fate. While logic told her she should fly home, her heart was telling her to stick by her husband. She had no sooner thought that when the Tammy Wynette song "Stand by Your Man" popped to mind. Without thinking, she began humming the tune and resumed her packing.

Cal, however, not paying much mind to the tune, took her humming as her way of dealing with a tough situation and began tossing his things in his duffel bag. With each item he stuffed in the duffel bag, he threw quick glances at the chart that lay folded next to the duffel bag. His mind was spinning trying to reason this out.

Suddenly, he stopped and grabbed the chart, turned, and plopped down on the edge of the bed. Unfolding the chart, he began running his finger along the plotted course through the coral reef, then along the channel that ran north from the docks at Abraham's Bay.

Abruptly he stood and went to a small secretary's desk and laid the chart out flat. Turning on a lamp, he then opened a drawer to retrieve a notepad and pen. Donna was watching him out of the corner of her eye while she folded a blouse. She saw him furiously jotting something down on the notepad. She had to ask. "Cal? What is it? What are you doing?"

Without speaking, he held up the palm of his left hand near his face with a little jiggle and continued with his intense scribbling.

Donna dropped the blouse she was folding on the bed and stepped over to see what had suddenly so engrossed him. Leaning over his shoulder, she saw that he had a series of numbers in two different columns that he was adding up.

She watched as he underscored the sum of one of the columns. "Aha! There, you see? It can be done," he announced triumphantly.

Donna furrowed her brow as she studied all the numbers written on the pad. She then glanced at the chart. It was then that she saw what he was doing. "Cal honey, do you really think that it will work? The path through the reef *is* shorter."

"Ah, shorter, yes. But since I'm not familiar with that route, plus with the size of the *Donna Marie,* it will require that I go very slow through the reef. So I think it's better to run the channel straight out of Abraham's Bay."

"But what about the Sawfish and his men? Miss Ginger said that he would expect someone to sail out from Abraham's Bay."

"That's true, baby, but listen, if I can make him believe we left through the reef, he will be sitting *there* waiting for us instead of Abraham's Bay, and he'll be waiting there a long time. Meanwhile, the *Donna Marie* will be out of sight of land in plenty of time to keep him from figuring out which direction we went."

"So how do you get him to believe that?"

"That is where Miss Ginger's man comes in. I bet for fifty bucks he'll do a great job of convincing her cousin. And you know what all this means?" Donna shook head no. "It means that you and I are sailing straight for home!"

Chapter 46

Unaware of Cal's change of plans, Jim was busy going through his preflight checks. He had more than enough fuel to get back home to Marathon Key and hopefully a normal life again. While he was worried about Cal and Juky trying to navigate a sailboat the size of the *Donna Marie* through a coral reef, he figured Cal wouldn't do it if he wasn't sure he could make it. This notion was held more as a hope rather than anything he knew about Cal and his abilities to sail. He was about to wrap up the preflight checks when he heard the British guy he spoke to earlier call from the rear door. "Aye, mate, got minute to talk?"

Jim glanced down at the box where he kept his gun but elected to leave it where it was and instead heaved himself out the pilot's seat calling back to the man as he went, "Hold on, I'm coming back there."

Michael spoke pleasantly to Jim as he arrived by the doorway. "'Eh, mate, listen, I was wonder'n' if you gave any more thought to flying me and me chums back to the big island. What with that blink'n' storm, it looks as though the fish'n's gone for pots and dogs I'm afraid."

Jim lifted his ball cap a bit and scratched his head quickly trying to think of how to answer him. He then thought of the money the man had offered him earlier and that he'd be flying with Donna and that swami guy. "Get your things and toss them over there," he said, pointing to the rear of the plane. "Oh, and just like the big boys, all flights are paid in advance of takeoff."

Michael nodded agreement. "Yeah, sure, mate, you said a thousand bucks, right?"

Jim nodded. "Yup, just have it when I come back here, and listen, be ready to go. We will be cutting it close, so I have no time to wait, understood?"

Michael smiled broadly. "Oh, yes, sir mate, we'll be ready, all right. You can bet your mum's knickers on it, mate."

"Where are you staying?"

Scratching his forehead, Michael said frankly, "Well, mate, that's the rub. We was staying on that sailboat two slips away," he said, pointing back out the doorway. "We was hired to bring her to a fellow what bought her. His men are getting ready to take 'er to the other side of the island for protection from this storm what be coming."

Jim peeked around him out the door like he didn't already know to which boat he was referring. "Wow, she is a beauty. You must have been paid a pretty penny to transport her."

Dropping his guard a little, Michael looked out the doorway and matter-of-factly replied, "Yeah, well, I coulda got a bit more, but we 'ad a bit of a scrub with some blokes who tried to take 'er from us last night."

Jim was surprised. "Really?"

Michael pointed to the *Donna Marie*. "Oh yeah, 'ave a look, mate. See the splintered wood and the shattered port window? The bloody mingers tossed a spotlight on us and started firing at me and me shipmates."

Jim peered out the fuselage doorway and shook his head. "What did you do to stop them?"

Pointing with his whole arm back out the door, he gave a huffing laugh as he declared, "We shot out their bloody spotlight and then we shot the shit out of them, right at their waterline."

"You tried to sink them, huh?"

"We gave it our best shot, no pun intended, but that bloody yacht 'ad a bilge system that could water a wheat field. Plus, we needed to save our ammo. We slowed them down enough for us to get away. That's their rig over there near the shore, at the last slip next dock over."

Jim shaded his eyes, squinting into the distance to see which boat Michael was pointing at. "Wow, she's big and beautiful, gotta have twin diesels to push something that big through the water."

"That she does."

"Aren't you worried about them coming after you?"

Turning back to look at Jim, Michael said, "I don't think they will try anything here, mate. What they are really after is that sailboat. But just the same, me and my buds would feel a lot better putting some distance between them and us. Besides, they 'ave to worry about the bloke what paid us. 'E's one not to be trifled with. I'm told 'e uses some rather gruesome ways of dealing with blokes what get in es way."

Jim glanced out the doorway again to look at the *Donna Marie*. "She's a gorgeous sailboat. But she sure seems to attract a lot of attention. Too much for me, that's for sure."

Michael looked back over his shoulder at the *Donna Marie* and wistfully said, "Yeah, it was a bit more than we bargained for too."

Just then a gust of hot, humid air blew hard against the Water Lily pulling her hard against the dock lines. Looking in the direction from which the wind had come, his voice tinged with concern, Jim said, "Look, I've got to go back to my room and grab my stuff and round up my other passengers. I think it's time we get airborne. I'll be back here in a half hour on the dot. I'm not going to wait on you, understood?"

"That I do. We'll be 'ere with bloody bells on, mate."

"All right, see you then." With that, Jim stepped through door onto the dock, closing the fuselage door. The two of them shook hands and started off down the dock. Nearing the slip where the *Donna Marie* was moored, Michael commented, "She's a beautiful lady. Would love to 'ave a boat like 'er someday."

"Me too. Where did you have to sail her from?"

Michael grew uncomfortable with the questioning but remained pleasant. "Oh...well, the owner doesn't want that get'n' out. Yeah, 'e's a weird duck, a very private nob what don't like people much. Yeah, we never even saw 'em ourselves."

"Huh, is that so. Hey, maybe it's Howard Hughes. I hear nobody sees him anymore," Jim said, knowing full well Hughes had died seven years earlier in 1976.

Michael snapped his fingers, saying, "You know, that could be the bloke. He 'ad a right big 'ome, a, a mansion, you know, with servants and such all run'n' about."

Jim gave a crooked smile then said, "Yeah, that sounds like Hughes, all right. Okay, well, I'll see you in a bit."

Michael, glad to be done with this conversation, simply waved and stepped aboard the *Donna Marie*. Jim turned and walked on down the dock. He mouthed to himself, "Ya lying sack of crap." He had decided it might be better that Donna go with Cal instead. He didn't know how yet, but he was going to fly these guys right to the authorities on Grand Bahama, and he didn't want her along in case things got ugly.

Cal's decision for Donna to accompany him, and with their things packed, all they could do now was wait for Miss Ginger's man to come and take them to Abraham's Bay. Jim had stopped by their room to discuss his concern that Donna not fly back with him and why. He was relieved to learn that they had already made that decision.

Cal questioned him about how he was going to get word to the authorities about the three men who stole the *Donna Marie* with them on the plane. "I figure I'll radio the tower when I get close to Grand Bahama and tell them I have an in-flight emergency. Besides, I'll have Juky as my copilot and bodyguard."

Cal's eyes widened. "Ah, hey, General Eisenhower, your plan has one big flaw: They know Juky. They tried to kill him, remember?"

Jim's face dropped when he realized his error. "Oh, yeah, I guess you're right. I had forgotten about that. Well then, I go it alone. That Michael fellow has no idea that I know what they did."

Cal smiled and placed a hand on his shoulder. "Look, Jim, you've done enough already. How about just flying those cretins to the big island and then go home. Donna and me, we'll be quite happy to just have the *Donna Marie* back so we can sail her home and put this whole ordeal behind us."

"So you're just going to let these guys get away with this?"

"Jim ole buddy, you know the saying about picking your battles? I think trying to make those jackasses pay for stealing our boat just seems like the wrong battle to take on right now. We have enough to think about with just trying to elude someone who likes to saw people into fish bait while outrunning a tropical storm that could be heading this way."

Jim gave Cal a somber look. He wanted to tell him he was wrong, but he knew he was right. Sometimes leaving people to their own fate is a better punishment. Nodding, he said, "Okay, I guess you're right. But if I get the chance—"

A knock came at the door ending Jim's proclamation.

They exchanged glances as another more urgent rap came. Cal stepped over and opened the door, saying, "Well, gang, it looks like our moment of truth has arrived."

Miss Ginger's man was very insistent that they get going, rushing them to a Mini Moke in the motel's portico. Jim and Juky watched Cal and Donna toss their things in the back of the Moke.

"Cal, you sure about what you're doing?" Jim worriedly asked.

Cal turned to face him. "Am I sure? Hell no. But we are going to make a run for it, hell yeah! Besides, with the wind picking up, I can make the *Donna Marie* really fly. We'll be miles away before they even know she's gone."

Donna gave Jim and Juky a hug telling them to be careful. Suddenly, Miss Ginger's man called excitedly to them, "Please, we must be going!"

Cal shook hands with Jim and Juky, then he realized as they all did at the same moment that Johnny Mac was nowhere in sight. Queries of his whereabouts rapidly flew between them, with each thinking he had been with the other.

Panic in her voice, Donna exclaimed, "Cal, where is he? We can't just leave him here."

Cal looked at Jim. "Wasn't he flying back with you, Jim?"

Rubbing the back of his neck in thought, Jim said, "I thought so. It's what we said when we first planned this out. Could be he's waiting on me now. We did kinda change things up at the last minute."

"Please, get in de car. We must go now!" Miss Ginger's man implored.

Cal threw quick glances at each of them, then forcefully stated, "We don't have time to look for him now. He's a grown man who's been through far worse than being left on a tropical island. We have to go now!"

With that, he turned toward Donna, cupped her elbow in his hand, and urged her to get in the Moke, telling her, "Look, don't worry about J-Mac. He is a wily old coot. I'm sure he can find his way home. We have to go now, Donna, or call this whole thing off."

Miss Ginger's man started the Moke while imploring them to get in. Donna gave Cal a short nod then sat down. Cal looked back one more time at Jim and Juky, gave a quick wave, and simply said, "Good luck, boys."

In that split second, both Jim and Cal had that same gut feeling hit them as they did during the war whenever the trigger was pulled on a big operation. It was an odd mix of excitement and dread. They both knew that those missions seldom went off without a hitch. Cal hopped into the Mini Moke, and before anything else could be said, it was tossed into gear. Jim and Juky stood staring after them as they raced away in a puff of dust and tire-tossed gravel.

Chapter 47

Bouncing along in the Mini Moke, Cal and Donna could feel that the air had grown warmer and much more humid in the last hour. Cal questioned their driver about the storm's strength and position. Because of the engine noise, strong breeze, and his heavy island accent, he had to have him repeat himself a couple of times. From what he could make out, the storm had yet to strengthen beyond a minimal tropical storm. Which was still not to be taken lightly. Another stroke of good look was that its track was taking the center of the storm north of the island, which meant they would have a strong following wind.

The drive to Abraham's Bay wasn't long, taking just ten minutes or so. Cal and Donna were both surprised to see an airport along their way, for no one had mentioned one. And like so many others in the islands, it wasn't much more than an unpaved landing strip.

It wasn't long before they were zooming through the town square of Abraham's Bay. It was the only place where the streets were paved, which was a welcome break from the dust and shell road they had been careening down with their Mario Andretti-possessed driver.

In the center of town, without warning, the driver made a hard right turn never slowing down. Donna let out a scream, frantically grabbing for one of the roof posts that held up the colorful blue-and-white striped canvas top.

Miss Ginger's man continued to drive with wild-eyed abandon on the narrow roads, and being in an open-sided vehicle with trees, fences, and mailboxes whizzing past just inches away gave the impression that they were going much faster than they were.

Leaning forward and holding the back of Cal's seat, Donna pointed straight ahead. Cal drew his attention to where she was pointing. A slight chill ran through him at what he saw. There, poking just above the hill they were approaching were the twin masts of the *Donna Marie.* The seriousness of what he and Donna were about to do weighed heavy on him now. Cresting the hill, the landscape dropped quickly away revealing the placid waters of Abraham's Bay. It was easy to see why they brought her here. Land rose up and encircled the entire bay, effectively blocking the stronger winds.

Donna placed a hand on Cal's shoulder giving him a reassuring squeeze. She knew a thousand things were going through his mind at the moment. Finally, their driver slowed as he neared the dock. Swinging out wide, he made a sharp U-turn and came to a tire skidding stop right at the end of a short dock that led to the *Donna Marie.*

The Mini Moke had not even ceased rocking back and forth before Miss Ginger's man hurried to get out, but Cal grabbed his shoulder stopping before he did so. "Hold on, hold on. Listen, I need you to do me a big favor. I want you to get word to Miss Ginger's cousin that we are sailing through the coral reef cut. Understand? And here's fifty bucks for your trouble, okay?"

Giving Cal a rapid nod, he took the money then shot off the Mini Moke, grabbing their things from the back while telling them that there was food and water along with other supplies onboard the *Donna Marie*; he didn't elaborate on what that might be.

Donna and Cal went to stand by their bags. Cal went to restate his request, but the panicked man was in the Moke and rolling before Cal could even take a step toward him. Donna and Cal both stood watching as the little blue car disappeared over the hill leaving only a windblown dust trail as any evidence that he had ever been there.

Donna reached down to pick up her suitcase, saying as she did so, "Disney's Mister Toad's Wild Ride sure hasn't got anything on what he just took us on."

Cal turned to face her. "Yeah, or the one we're about to."

Reaching down to grab her other suitcase and his duffel bag, Cal questioned, "Did it seem weird to you that Miss Ginger's man was in such a panic over a minimal tropical storm?"

"Yeah, maybe, or maybe he knows something else."

"What do you mean?"

"I'm not sure. But my gut is telling me we need to be extra careful. Come on, let's get this stuff on the *DM* and get her underway. I want to put as much water between here and…hell, I don't have the foggiest idea of where we are heading."

Donna gazed up at the wisps of clouds blowing rapidly across the sky. "I don't think it matters at this point. We just need to get going." With that, she stepped from the dock onto the *Donna Marie's* deck. The moment she did so, a sense of exhilaration shot through her. The feeling was driven by the known danger of the storm that they were sailing away from and amplified by the unknown danger they may be sailing directly toward.

Cal tossed his duffel bag on the deck and hurried aboard. The moment he did so, he was already giving Donna orders to stow the middle dock lines. Hopping down into the seat-well, he took his position at the helm. After stowing the lines, Donna went straight to the bow and waited for him to fire up the diesel engine. Cal ran the block heaters for a few seconds then hit the starter.

In the next instant, the four-cylinder Perkins diesel rumbled to life. Cal idled it up a bit to let it warm for a moment. Donna kept an eye on Cal. When he looked up from the control panel, he idled down the engine and gazed the length of the *Donna Marie* looking for anything untoward. Not seeing anything that troubled him, he then shouted out to Donna, "Cast off!"

Donna immediately reached for the bowline, and with both hands, she gave a firm pull to draw them closer to the dock. The moment the line went slack, she deftly flipped the rope up off the dock piling in one motion. Cal did likewise at the stern. Cal's order to cast off carried with it more than a simple command to follow. Those two words meant that he and the woman he loved were heading into an unknown fate.

The *Donna Marie* glided away from the dock. She was free and now finally in the hands of her rightful owners. Cal eased her back far enough to bring the bow around to clear the end of the dock. Spinning the ship's wheel fast to the right, he shifted from reverse to neutral for a few seconds then eased them into forward, ramping up the throttle to half speed. The *Donna Marie*'s backward inertia slowed as the water at the stern rolled and bubbled in protest to the change of direction. It took only a few seconds for the propeller to overcome the backward motion and begin to slowly move them forward.

Running on the diesel engine until they neared the mouth of the bay, Donna had remained on the bow. She loved feeling the gentleness of the *Donna Marie*'s movements. For now, the water piled against the bow in small ripples. But once under full sail, the sea would roll, fold, and splash against her hull with a grace that only a sailboat the likes of the *Donna Marie* could command.

With the smell of the salt air and the wind in her face, Donna was feeling reinvigorated and relieved to be heading for home. Turning to look back at Cal, it was easy to see he was feeling much the same way. She then said a little prayer for everyone to make it home safe. Cal smiled seeing the relief on her face. He then motioned for her to come take the wheel so he could begin to hoist the sails before they cleared the mouth of the inlet.

Donna came quickly to his side at the helm. Cal stepped aside letting her take the ship's wheel. He pointed to the heading on the compass. "Hold us on this heading. Once I have the mainsails up, I'll signal you to cut the engine."

"Aye, aye, Cap'n," came her jocular reply.

Cal grimaced, saying, "Donna, this is serious, stop joking around."

Looking only a little apologetic, she replied, "Cal honey, I know it is. I'm just trying to deal with what we are doing, that's all, so don't get your knickers in a knot."

Cal gazed into her eyes for a long moment. She was half expecting him to give her some more static about her joking around, but as husbands and wives are apt to do from time to time, he surprised her.

Looking her straight in the eye with a softening expression, he said, "I love you, Donna. I understand." With that, he patted her forearm and quickly stepped up out of the seat-well and trotted toward the main mast. Reaching the mast, he immediately began releasing the ropes that bound the sail to the spar. Donna watched the man she had fallen in love with more than thirty years ago rapidly cranking the mainsail up into position.

With the mouth of the inlet drawing nearer by the minute, Donna made the sign of the cross while saying another small prayer. Checking the compass, she made a small course correction. There was still a lot of canvas to hang, and she didn't see how he was going to have the *Donna Marie* fully rigged by the time they exited the inlet.

"Cal! Do you want me to slow us down?" she called out.

Cal briefly ceased his efforts to check their position. Reluctantly, he called back to her to cut the engine speed by a third. Even with that, he knew he wouldn't make it before they were smacked with the stiff breeze that was blowing just beyond the inlet. With them being barely a quarter mile from the dock, he shelved the idea of stopping long enough for him finish the main mast and foremast rigged before they left the protected bay waters.

Donna did as he said and cut their forward speed, but she too knew that the best he could get done was the two mainsails. Time was their enemy at the moment; they desperately needed another pair of hands if they were going to make it.

Placing her hand on the throttle, Donna contemplated dropping their speed a bit more to try and give Cal a little more time but worried that he would get upset with her. She was about to do just that when someone called out from the cabin door just in front of her.

"Hey, what's with all the yelling about up here?"

Chapter 48

The notion of just letting these guys get away with stealing the *Donna Marie* just didn't sit well with Jim. Back in the hotel room Juky was packing the last of his stuff, but since Cal had switched things around, he had no idea of where he was going to go or what he was going to do. He and Jim talked while Jim grabbed the last of his things.

Juky knew it was only a matter of time before Cesar figured out who he was, so staying on Mayaguana was out of the question. And flying out with Jim didn't seem a good option either due to who his passengers were. Juky was musing out loud about his lack of options when Jim suddenly snapped his fingers.

"Hold on a second." Glancing at his watch, Jim exclaimed, "Look, those guys are supposed to meet me at the plane in twenty minutes. You have time if you hurry to get to the plane. You can hide in the cockpit."

"But 'ow? Dey will see me walking down de dock."

"That's right—walking *on top* of the dock they will. But if you swim underneath it out to the Water Lily, they won't."

Juky stopped and thought for a moment then said, "What about my things—dey will get wet and so will I."

"Don't worry about your stuff. I'll take it with mine. And as far as you…" Jim gazed around the room then spied a trash can by the desk. "Perfect, go and get a towel from the bathroom."

Jim grabbed the trash can while Juky retrieved a towel. Dumping out a few wadded-up pieces of note paper, he removed the plastic trash bag. Taking the bath towel from Juky, he rolled it up tightly and placed it in the trash bag and knotted the end.

"There. When you get in the plane, you dry off."

"Wait, I 'ave a pair of shorts and a T-shirt in my things as well."

"All right, fine, but let's hurry. Listen, I'm going ahead and stall them, if I need to. But give me about five minutes then you need to get moving. And listen, if you're not there, I can't wait. I've got to get airborne in the next twenty minutes, understood?"

"Yes, I understand. I'll be der, don't you worry."

"Okay then. I'll see you in the plane." Jim gave Juky a pat on the shoulder and left for the dock.

Juky quickly added his shorts and shirt to the plastic bag, waited a couple of minutes, and then left for the docks. On his way to the marina, he saw Jim at a small grocery story with the three Brits. A chill ran through him remembering just how close he came to being shark bait because of them. Arriving at the docks, that dreadful memory was reinforced the moment his feet touched the water. The only way he could keep going was to think about Cesar, and what he would do if he remembered that it was Juky who had caused him to miss out on thousands of dollars on a smuggling operation.

With the fear of Cesar stronger than the memory of the sharks, Juky sank down into the water. The water was clear, but the shade of the dock kept him from being seen unless you were close by. Diving under the surface, he pulled himself along by grabbing the pilings and shoving his way forward. The dock was a hundred and fifty feet long, so it required him coming up for air every so often. At last, with just thirty feet to go, he came to the surface to check out where Jim and the three Brits were. Easing out from under the dock, he pawed the salt water from his face and eyes. Blinking several times, he was finally able to zero in on them.

Good, he thought. *They just stepped onto the dock.* Since it was unlikely they could see him, there was no need to dive under water any-more, returning beneath the dock, he finished pulling his way to where the Water Lily was tied off. Several large fish hovering in the shadow of the big plane shot away as he approached. Suddenly he realized he had bit of a problem. The water level was nearly four feet below the top of the dock. Not seeing any kind of ladder nearby, there was no easy way to get out of the water. Jim and the Brits would be here soon. He had to find a way to get out of the water and in the plane and fast, but how?

Trying not to panic, he rapidly scoured the plane's fuselage for some kind of toehold but found nothing. The wind was keeping the plane pushed away from the dock; this kept the ropes out of reach as well. He tried shoving the plane with hands toward the dock; however, being in the water with nothing to brace himself against, the laws of physics weren't cooperating.

With his spirits sagging and feeling he was going to watch his best hope of getting off the island literally fly away; in desperation, he made a last-ditch effort to move the big plane. Swimming to the outside of the plane about thirty feet away, he reasoned that he might be able to muster enough speed to give the plane one good hard push. His hope was the inertia would hold it next to the dock long enough for him to grab a rope. Taking in a deep breath, he shot forward with powerful thrusts from his legs and arms.

It took only seconds to cover the distance. Squinting through the frothing water, he had to time his shove against the plane just right. Nearing the fuselage, he rolled under, turning himself the opposite direction, and like an Olympic swimmer, he shoved his feet hard against the fuselage.

He broke the water's surface just in time to see the big aircraft drifting toward the dock. Instantly he dove back under and began a panicked charge for the plane, kicking and thrusting his way through the crystal-clear water. Suddenly he saw it, one of the dock ropes dipping into the water's surface. Fighting against the pain in his ribs, he gave one last mighty thrust straight for the partially submerged rope.

Adrenalin-charged seconds passed as he tore through the water. His hand outstretched, he clawed for the rope grasping it at the last second. His heart was pounding as he pulled on the end attached to the dock.

Pulling on the rope with all his strength, he managed to haul himself up high enough to get a handhold on a crossbeam that ran five feet below the deck boards. Winding the rope around his forearm, he pulled on the rope until he could get his feet on top of the crossbeam so he could stand on it. Struggling and grunting and spitting salt water, he was finally able to take a very needed but short breather.

Huffing and wiping salt water from his face, he gathered his wits and swiftly tied a loop in the rope to shorten its length, which kept the rear of the plane from drifting away from the dock again. The Water Lily now rested about two and a half feet from the dock. This afforded him enough room to stand on the crossbeam and poke his head up just high enough to peer back down the dock's surface to check on Jim and the Brits progress.

What he saw wasn't good. They were about halfway now, more than close enough for them to see him get in the plane. He had to get Jim's attention somehow. Every second brought them closer. Juky noticed that even though Jim was conversing with the others, he kept his focus on the end of the dock while the three Brits took random glances around as they walked. All he needed was a split second or two for them all to be looking away so he could signal Jim.

The moments that he waited for this to happen dragged and yet speed past at the same time. "C'mon, c'mon," Juky quietly pled. Just then it happened; he saw his opportunity. With the others looking away, he poked his head up above the dock and waved with his right arm while keeping a close eye on the Brits. Frantically he waved.

"C'mon, dammit, Jim, let me know you see me." Suddenly Michael tuned back to look at Jim while pointing at the end of the dock! Juky instantly dropped below the dock's edge, his mind racing. Had Michael spotted him? Did Jim see him? He frantically wondered what to do next…what *could* he do?

Chapter 49

Donna couldn't believe her eyes and gawked at the sight of Johnny Mac coming up from the cabin hatchway menacingly waving around the same damn mannequin leg from Miss Ginger's like he had just pulled Excalibur from the rock. He let it fall to his side upon seeing Donna.

In unison, they questioned each other, "What are you doing here?"

Johnny Mac immediately began launching into to why he was onboard the *Donna Marie*. But Donna cut him off, yelling at him, "Johnny Mac! Never mind that. Drop the damn leg and go help Cal with the sails. Hurry! Go!"

Still confused, Johnny Mac shot hurried glances around the deck trying to find a place to toss the mannequin leg. Frustrated, Donna yelled at him again, "Just drop the damn leg and get to the forward mast now! Go!"

Johnny Mac looked toward the bow then tossed the leg in the cabin doorway and hurried his way forward. Donna shook her head seeing the mannequin's foot still poking out of the doorway and mused to herself, "Well, that had to be the weirdest order ever uttered in all of sailing history."

Cal was busy spinning the handle to the mainsail's winch. Donna's yelling had been drowned out by the loud clacking of the sails winch, so Johnny Mac's arrival was unseen and heard. Cautiously, Johnny Mac tapped Cal on the shoulder and shouting, "Donna sent me to help you with the sails."

Startled, Cal jerked quickly around. "Johnny Mac? What the hell are you doing here?" he bawled.

Urgently, he pointed back to Donna. "I don't know. She sent me here to help you!"

"Cal, let him help you. We have to hurry!" Donna shouted.

Cal glanced back to Donna and then back to Johnny Mac. Urgently, he said, "Grab the end of that rope and be ready to cinch it around the mast cleat when I tell ya."

"Aye, aye, Cap'n," he said with sharp salute.

"Knock it off. This is serious, Johnny Mac."

"Okay, okay, don't get your panties in a bunch, Cap'n."

Cal rolled his eyes then continued cranking the foresail into position. With a few more hurried rotations of the crank handle, the sail reached the top of the mast. Johnny Mac quickly cinched the rope to the mast cleat. Cal then took off waving for Johnny Mac to follow.

Cal quickly began raising the top and staysails. After a few tense wordless moments, they had the last one, the top jib, in position as well. Cal took a quick look back down the length of the *Donna Marie* making sure all was right. Turning back toward the bow, he saw they were nearing the mouth of the inlet. He also saw the whitecaps from the brisk wind that blew just beyond.

Johnny Mac nervously watched as they neared the mouth of the inlet. Donna nudged the throttle up to gain more forward inertia before she shut the diesel down. She knew the wind would grab the *Donna Marie* when they hit the open water and needed to counteract some of the list and starboard-side shove the wind would give the *Donna Marie*. "Hang on, you two, we're about to hit open water."

Cal spun around and took off for the helm leaving Johnny Mac at the bow. Moving quickly along the gunnels nearing the stern, he cut across the deck hopping into the seat-well behind Donna. She, however, kept attention locked on the open waters beyond the mouth of the inlet. She called out to him asking if he was going to take over. Stepping up next to her, he put a hand on her shoulder and simply said, "No, you got this."

Seconds later the bow of the *Donna Marie* cleared the mouth of the inlet. The wind began snapping the topsail and jib. Cal remained standing next to Donna but turned his gaze upward. The big foresail and mainsail still rolled and rippled in the last seconds of flaccid air.

Clearing the mouth of the inlet, he saw what he always loved to see—the *Donna Marie* take in her first full breath. And what a breath it was. Entering the open water, the wind poured into the foresail and mainsail with gusto, snapping the canvas tight and listing her starboard. Cal dropped his gaze from the sails to Donna to see her doing the same thing with a smile as big as life.

Cal shouted out to Johnny Mac, "Pretty good job there for a swabbie. C'mon, let's me and you check things out and make sure all is well. Donna, you okay here?"

"Yeah," she said with a broad smile.

"Good. Keep her on this same heading while J-Mac and I check the rigging."

Donna replied, "Aye, aye, Captain," followed by a little salute.

Cal cut his eyes to Johnny Mac. "Great, now you've got her doing that. C'mon, ya swabbie, let's go check things out."

Donna kept a firm hand at the helm. A steady fifteen-knot breeze blew with occasional stronger gusts that pushed hard at the *Donna Marie*'s hull, keeping her busy with staying on course. Cal and Johnny Mac went about making adjustments to the sails in an effort to build as much speed as possible.

Finally satisfied that they were getting all they could out of her, Cal returned to the helm to stand by Donna. Both had broad smiles. It had been a long while since they had been on the *Donna Marie* in conditions like this. It was a bit intimidating yet exhilarating at the same time. Cal had carefully plotted a course that would take them due west for a couple of hours then turn to make a long arc back toward the Florida Keys and home.

The storm's track was taking it well north of the island, so as they sailed farther from Pirates Well and the island of Mayaguana, the wind from the tropical storm would shift to come from a more southwesterly direction which would help them maintain a brisk pace all the way home.

Cal dropped his gaze for moment from the bellowed sails to the cabin hatchway. It took a second or two for it to register, but when it did, he threw a sideways glance at Donna. She wondered how long it was going to be before he noticed it.

"Donna, what the heck is that poking out of the cabin door?"

"You remember that mannequin leg you were holding back at Miss Ginger's outdoor emporium, or whatever you want to call that place?"

Puzzled, he simply said, "Yeah."

Pointing toward the cabin doorway, she said, "Well…there it is."

"What? But…but how did it get here? It's not possessed and gimped its way here, did it?" He laughed.

Donna snickered at the thought of that thing scrunching its way along inchworm-like to the *Donna Marie*. With a chuckle, she pointed to Johnny Mac sitting on the cabin roof near the bow. "It did sort of gimp its way here."

"Johnny Mac brought it onboard?" Cal questioned with surprise.

"Yup, he came up from below deck waving that thing like King Arthur's sword. I had to yell at him twice to drop the damn thing to go and help you with the sails. Had to be the weirdest order that's ever been given on the deck of a sailboat."

Piecing the whole scene together in his mind, Cal suddenly burst out laughing. "So…so he comes up from…from below deck and…and you…you ordered him to drop the leg to come help me?"

Donna glanced again at the foot still jutting from the hatchway. She burst out laughing with Cal. Their raucous laughter was as much about the situational humor as it was relief from trying to outrace a storm and Miss Ginger's cousin.

Johnny Mac suddenly stood and began making his way to the stern. Still laughing about the leg, Cal and Donna began shouting sailing commands like old movie pirates involving the leg, making them laugh and giggle like school kids. "Avast, ye swab!" Cal shouted out. "Drop that leg, sailor, and man the crow's nest before I 'ave ye keel-hauled!"

Donna responded by giving a sharp salute, saying. "Aye, aye, sir, I just…could you give me a leg up, sir?"

Johnny Mac came to a stop at the helm and stared at them for a moment listening to they're giggling and laughing about the mannequin leg. Catching them in a break from their silliness, he spoke out over the wind, asking, "Why are we going the wrong direction?"

Cal and Donna ceased their silliness but still held grins as Cal asked, "What are you talking about, J-Mac? We *are* right on course."

"You are if you want to be overrun by vultures."

Cal and Donna gave puzzled looks. Cal questioned him further, "J-Mac, what in the hell are you talking about? There aren't any vultures at sea."

"Not the kind that fly but the ones that float. We have trouble coming."

Cal and Donna shot worried looks to Johnny Mac and then to each other. Cal abruptly bent down to reach below the ship's wheel opening a storage compartment retrieving a spyglass. Standing next to Donna, he began scanning the open waters.

He had hoped the threat of a storm would keep people off the water, especially any modern-day pirates. He knew that pirates, like any other criminal, are opportunists, and attempting to commandeer a vessel in rough seas would be risky. With the popularity of the Caribbean Island chain, hapless prey was far easier to come by, and good weather made engaging in it much less risky, and unlike in Blackbeard's day, modern-day victims of it don't have cannons.

Seeing no one at the moment, Cal dropped the spyglass away, collapsing it. He began pointing around at the ocean while talking out loud. "Looks like we are alone out here. I didn't see anyone, Johnny Mac."

Adamantly, Johnny Mac warned, "You should be turning south now before they see us."

"Dammit, who, Johnny Mac? I just told you that I didn't see a soul out there."

"Look, Cal, radar has been around for a long time now. So you know that it will see you long before you see it."

"Radar…" Cal stopped to think for a moment. He then stared wide-eyed at Johnny Mac. "Is it that big-ass yacht we saw yesterday?"

Chapter 50

Jim had indeed seen Juky wave at him. Thinking quickly, he stopped dead in his tracks causing all three of the Brits to turn to face him. Suspecting that they weren't too savvy about traveling in the islands, he spit out a total line of BS.

"Oh, hey, guys, I almost forgot to ask, do you all have your inter-island travel visas?"

"Oh, yeah, mate, we 'ave our passports, if that's what you be talk'n' 'bout," Michael said, reaching for his.

"Oh, yeah, you need those, but you also need what's called a Bahamian inter-island travel visa."

"What? Why, we don't 'ave no such thing. No one told us about it."

"Hmm. I'm surprised no one asked to see it when you docked here. Ah, well, some of these smaller islands aren't as formal as the bigger, more populated ones, like Grand Bahama. They for sure will ask for it when we land."

Jim peeked over the shoulders of the three of them as he pointed out what their options might be. Juky saw what was going on and quickly pulled himself up out of the water, making his way quickly into the plane.

Jim kept up the phony visa ruse a moment more to give Juky time to change out of his wet shirt and shorts and get in the cockpit. He then abruptly snapped his fingers as though he just remembered something. "Oh, hold on a second. I just remembered I got a connection on the big island that can walk us right through this little issue. It'll be no problem. Now c'mon, we got a flight to catch."

Jim led the way to the plane. Reaching the door to the Water Lily, he pulled it open, hoping that Juky was nowhere in sight. Stepping in first, he asked for one of the Brits to untie the Lily from the dock. Michael told Terry to do as Jim requested while he held the plane close to the dock.

While Michael waited for Terry to untie the plane and come aboard, he noticed water all over the dock right in front of the plane's door. He then followed wet footprints amid drips of water all the way up the aisleway straight to the cockpit door. Curious, he shouted out to Jim questioning him about it.

"Hey, mate, looks like someone has been traipsing all wet through your bloody plane. What gives?"

Looking back down the aisleway through the partially open cockpit door, he saw what he hoped they would pay no attention to when entering the plane. Again, he had to think quick and come up with a plausible reason for the water being there. Just then he spotted a small squeegee that he used on the inside of the front windows when they would fog up.

Grabbing it off the cabin wall behind his seat, he waved it out the door, saying, "Oh, that, yeah, uh, well, I have a couple of the locals get in the water and squeegee off the part of the fuselage the sits in the water before I take off so any of the little critters that like make a home on it are knocked off. It's much easier this way than when they get all dried on after flying. It's a maintenance thing."

Michael gave a knowing nod then added, "Guess someone should show those blokes how to mop up all the water. A bloke could slip and fall. Ya wouldn't want that now, would ya, mate?"

Jim glanced down the length of the aisleway and said, "Oh, yeah, guess you're right about that. I'll have to get after them about that next time. Is the door closed and latched?"

"Yup, she sure is, mate. Now get us in the air and to hell away from 'ear. Don't care much if I ever put me peepers on this pile of weed-covered sand again."

"Sure thing. Everyone stay seated and belted in. We're tak'n' off momentarily."

Jim closed the cockpit door and gave Juky a wide-eyed look then said, "Well, that was a butt load of fun now, wasn't it?"

Juky nodded and whispered, "Dat kind of fun I kin do without."

"Yeah, me too. Let's just hope we don't have any more of that before we get to the big island."

Jim began his prefight checks across the instrument panel. A moment later he glanced to his right, flipping a toggle switch then pressed the right engine starter button. Instantly the big prop made two halting rotations then the nine-cylinder radial engine burst to life, shuddering the whole fuselage.

Looking left, he repeated the same procedure. The engine popped and sputtered then spun to life adding to the vibrating rumble that ran up and down the entire aircraft. Reaching up, he gripped the throttles easing them forward. Deftly he eased the big aircraft out well away from the main dock area. The slowly approaching storm had a steady wind blowing now. Jim rotated the Water Lily around pointing her nose directly into the wind. Speaking on the intercom, he told his passengers, "All right, everyone, hold on. Takeoff will be a bit bumpy due to the wind and the chop on the water."

Glancing over the instrument panel again and satisfied that all systems were good to go, he pushed the throttles forward. The big 1,450 HP engine's rpm ramped up and rapidly began moving them forward blowing clouds of mist off the tops of the waves.

Michael gazed out the window. This was pretty cool, he thought. He'd never done anything like this before. The two-foot waves began pounding against the fuselage the same way they would pound any boat. Quickly gaining speed, the bouncing began to smooth out. Michael smiled. He was now moving faster across the water than he had ever gone before. He had no sooner thought that when he felt himself being pressed down hard in the seat. The big bird lifted off the water, and they were airborne.

A wave of relief washed over them with each looking away from the windows flashing big smiles at each other. Michael spoke up. "Look at that, mates, we did it! Dammit, we did it!"

"Yeah, we sure did. It was a bit of a pinch there at the end, but we're still 'ear, breath'n' and with a fair bit a quid in our bloody pockets to boot," Terry gleefully stated.

"Yeah, we did, but I don't think I'll be try'n' that again," Martin deadpanned.

Michael guffawed, saying, "Oh, what ya talk'n' 'bout, mate? Look, we outfoxed a bunch of Russian blighters who had us outgunned and outrun what with that bleed'n' super yacht of theirs, but we outsmarted them. And now we be off to do us some drinking, gambling, and chasing some birds around. Now if that don't put some pepper in your grinder, then I don't know what will."

Both Martin and Terry snickered and elbowed each other hearing Michael's pep talk. Terry took a long gaze out the window hoping to spot the big yacht if for no other reason than cement in his mind they had indeed beaten the odds. Scanning the docks, which grew smaller as they gained altitude, he double-checked, looking over the whole marina. Sure enough, the yacht was no longer there. "Eh, mates, that bleed'n' yacht's not in the marina anymore. I don't see it anywhere."

"What are you talking about? We just walked past it not fifteen minutes ago," Michael fussed, getting up to look out the same window as Terry.

Terry leaned well back in his seat while pointing out the window. "See for yourself. It's not there."

Michael bent low to peer out the window. He quickly spotted where the yacht should've been. But just as Terry had said, it was gone. Continuing to scan the docks below, he suddenly saw the telltale prop wash trail in the water leading out of the marina, losing sight of it as went it underneath the plane.

Stepping to the opposite side of the plane, he gazed out the window and found not only the wake but the yacht as well. "'Ear they are, mates, and from the look of it, they are running full-out. That water's really boiling in her wake. Must be bug'n' out 'cause of that storm."

"Yeah, well, let's 'ope they're not going to the same place we are," Terry lamented.

"Naw, don't worry 'bout that, Terry. Looks like they're turning southwest and head'n' for the west side of the island. Prolly going to that same protected cove what they took the sailboat."

Martin turned his gaze to look out the window. He let go a sigh of relief glad to see that dreadful yacht disappearing from view. He then thought of how he had one heck of a story to tell from now on. Of course, he'd have to modify it a little to leave out the part about stealing the sailboat they were on when they outfoxed those ruddy Russians.

Just as he was about to say what he was thinking to Terry and Michael, he spotted something else well in the distance. "Eh, mates, 'ave a look-see out the window."

"Why, what is it?" Michael queried.

"Well, it looks like sails way out on the horizon."

"Where? I don't see noth'n'," Terry said, while gyrating his head trying to catch a glimpse.

"Right there, see where the land rises up high on the island? Follow that point straight out about for about two kilometers and you'll see it."

Michael quickly joined in the search. Doing as Martin had suggested, he traced his finger on the window from the point where the land ended straight out. "Eh, yeah, I see it now." He stared at it for a long moment trying to make it out, but with the distance and the broken cloud cover interrupting his line of sight, all he could really see were the two masts and sails and not much more.

Terry turned away from the window and, with a chuckle, said, "Eh, you don't suppose those Russian blokes are going after that sailboat, do ya?"

"Well, if they are, I wouldn't want to be the blokes what be on that sailboat 'cause I doubt that pack of hyenas will be in a mood to miss out on a second sailboat, that's for sure." Turning away from the window, Michael sat back in the seat closing his eyes. He said aloud, "Forget them. Let's get some sleep. We gotta get our rest so's we can chase all them bikini-clad birds that'll be all over those casinos in Freeport."

Martin looked back between the seats at Michael. "Eh, you two can 'ave a go at the tables and the birds and lose all your money. Me, I'm gonna find a nice, quiet swimming pool to lie by, get some sun, and watch those birds parade by me with 'ardly nuthin' on."

Terry's smile blossomed wide on his narrow face. "Eh, now I like the sound o' that."

With eyes closed, Michael chided Terry, "Oh, what are you talk'n' 'bout? With that mug of yours, the only birds that'd come near you'd be some old crow wear'n' her mum's bloomers."

Martin burst out laughing and pointing at Terry. "Eh, 'e's got ya there, Terry. Go find your own pool to sit by. I don't want you ruining me chances for a little leg-over action, mate."

Terry leaned forward in his seat. "Oh, shut yer piehole, Martin. I do just as good with the birds as you."

"Knock it off, you two, before I toss the both of you in the drink. I swear you two would argue over who gets the first bite of a bleed'n' turd pie ya would. Now shut up, the both of ya!"

Terry and Martin both made faces at one another before looking away. Turning his attention to look back out the window, Terry saw the wake of the yacht now was nothing but a distant line in the water. Closing his eyes, he peacefully remarked, "Yup, trouble be com'n' their way, but for us, it be smooth sailing from 'ear on out."

"Yeah, yeah, whatever, just shut up so's I can catch some shut-eye, will ya, Terry?" Michael begged.

The drone of the radial engines began to lull each of them soundly to sleep. After about a half hour, Jim took a peek out the cockpit door to see them all sleeping. Closing the door, he began discussing with Juky how they were going to deal with his passengers when they contacted the tower on the big island. He wanted to be sure the authorities nabbed these guys at the airport.

Juky pointed out that they really had nothing to prove that Jim's passengers did anything wrong; it was just Juky's word against theirs.

"Hey, wait a minute, Juky. What about that boat captain whose boat you got hauled aboard?" Jim happily remembered.

"Yes, dat es right, but he never saw me on de *Donna Marie*…wait, de man dat came to fix de compass, 'e saw me onboard the *Donna Marie*, but even if we find him, I doubt he will go to the big island."

Juky stared thoughtfully out the cockpit a long moment wondering how to get the witnesses to Grand Bahama. Still lost in thought, he wistfully commented, "Yo-ah plane's engines run so smoothly."

"Yeah, they do sound sweet, don't they? I take great care of them."

"Has one ever quit on you?"

"No, the Water Lily's never had that happen, but I've limped more than one B-17 home with fewer engines running than I took off with. Brought one in with only two engines running once and both on the left wing. We looked like a damn crab running approaching the runway, straightened her up just before we touched down."

Jim's face brightened. "Oh, now I am a devious devil." Giving Juky a sideways, he said, "Juky, my man, we don't need to take anyone to Grand Bahama. Look, everyone that can verify your story is at Rokers Point, right?" Juky nodded. "Then we land this bird there and let the authorities there deal with them."

"But deh will be angry dat you did not fly dem to Grand Bahama. You forget they have guns."

"Yeah, well, so do I. But I have a little trick up my sleeve that will make them damn glad to be landing on any damn island we can find."

Confused, Juky asked, "But how? I do not understand what could make dem do such a thing."

A big smile spread across Jim's face as he pointed past Juky to the right engine. "Juky, I get the feeling we are about to have some engine trouble."

Juky snapped his head around to glare wide-eyed at the smoothly running engine. "What is it? What es wrong?"

Jim patted him on the shoulder. "Relax, nothing is wrong yet. I have the perfect plan that's going to make those guys believe something is very wrong. And they won't care where we land."

Juky turned back from the window. "I sure hope you know what yo-ah doing."

Jim smiled then pointed to the instrument panel. "See that little lever labeled 'fuel mixture.'" Juky nodded. "That, my friend, is what will make those dimwits think they're about to meet their maker."

Juky was about to question him further, but Jim stopped. "Look, you don't have to worry about how, just relax and enjoy the ride."

Jim had some concern; their new destination might still have them in the storm's projected path. This wasn't a big deal as long as it didn't strengthen into a full-blown hurricane on its way to the upper islands. If it did, that could change things, and change things a lot, like heading straight for home.

Taking his attention from the window, he reflexively scanned the instrument panel. Finding all in order, he then reached back and cracked open the cockpit door just enough to see that all of his passengers were still sleeping. Easing the door closed, he smiled and mumbled to himself, "Those boys are sure going to get a rude awakening in a little while."

Scanning the vastness of the ocean below, Jim thought about Cal and Donna. "Sure hope you two know what you're doing down there, 'cause mistakes out there sure have a high price." Looking upward through the cockpit window while rubbing a Saint Christopher medallion that hung from a window post, he added, "Let's have a good end to this mission, 'cause I've seen enough of the other kind."

*****

"How did Cesar know de boat has left?" Miss Ginger angrily asked the tall and very nervous man, an employee of hers.

"I see Tomas going into his house after he had taken de two people to de boat."

Miss Ginger slapped the top of the table she sat at in anger. "Tomas, you say? I 'ave often wondered about hem. Dis make me vury angry—do I not pay well? Have Cesar's men left in der speed boats?"

"I...I do not know, Miss Ginger, I...I came he-ah straight away to tell you what I see. But der is more I must tell you."

"More? Well, out with it, maun!"

Nervously, he added, "De big boat de…de yacht et left vury quickly."

"How long ago, Samuel?"

"Maybe twenty minutes."

Miss Ginger abruptly stood up from her kitchen table startling the informant who fearfully backed away. "Relax, Samuel, I em not angry with you. But Tomas is another matter. Say nothing of this to Tomas, do you understand? He may be useful doing exactly what he is doing. Information is only good if et es accurate. We have to get word to dos people on de boat. Find Michel and take two of my boats and take your guns—you may need dem." She then began hurriedly jotting down something on a piece of paper. Underlining what she had written three times, she folded it, handing it to Samuel. "Now 'urry. Give dis to Cesar."

Taking the note, he quickly left her standing at the table. Watching him close the door, she shook her head, saying, "Cesar, it is time you repay de favor you owe me."

Chapter 51

The hasty repairs made to the yacht's hull were holding for now. The burly Russian paced the whole deck walking laps around it, thinking and muttering to himself. He fumed about being bested by three British dimwits. Whomever they had turned that sailboat over to was not going to find it so easy to run from him. He was going to have that sailboat or sink it and all aboard.

He had been informed it was taken to Abraham's Bay. Soon they would clear the western side of the island, and his expectation was to find that sailboat there. If true, then taking it would be far less troublesome. However, if it had put to sea, then so be it. In either case, it would soon be in his possession. Ceasing his intense pacing at the very point of the bow, he rigidly stood watching the high land mass scroll past. His anticipation grew by the minute at waiting to see his quarry come into view.

Signaling the helmsman to slow for the turn toward the mouth of the cove, he froze watching the land draw back like a curtain, slowly revealing the entirety of the protected bay. The Russian captain drew a tense breath while rapidly scanning the whole area. Clenching his jaw, his eyes narrowed at seeing nothing! Nothing but a couple of small runabouts and a dingy lying upside down onshore. But no sailboat! Spinning on his heels, he shouted for binoculars to be brought to him, cursing and stomping in a circle while waiting.

A moment later a crewman raced up to him, his arm outstretched presenting the binoculars. Snatching them from his hand amid curses, he ordered the helmsman to bring them to a complete halt. He widened his stance on the bow steadying himself from the change in the forward inertia. Putting the binoculars to his eyes, he did a quick sweep of the horizon. Seeing nothing but ocean, he dropped the binoculars away to look to his left and right, then took off for the flying bridge. He needed elevation.

That damn sailboat couldn't be far, he thought, and he wasn't going to rest until he had found it and taken it, by any means necessary. The binoculars dangled from his neck while climbing the narrow ladder to the roof of the flying bridge. Struggling to steady himself, his pants and shirt ruffled in the stiff breeze. Nearly twenty-five feet above the surface of the water, he had a much better vantage point. Tense minutes passed while conducting his methodical search. The helmsman was kept busy trying to keep a vessel this size steady in the wind.

Dropping the binoculars down to his chest but still tightly gripping them, he glanced back at the bay, then back out to sea. His mind raced, thinking of what he would do if it were he sailing that boat. Suddenly he shouted for the helmsman to take a heading of due west at a slow speed. Bringing the binoculars back up, he scanned a narrow path straight in front of him.

All eyes of the crew were on him; the tension among the crew was thick. Their captain was an ill-tempered man who ran things with an iron fist. Diligent compliance to his orders were all that kept his violent temper at bay. To a man, they prayed he would find that boat, knowing if he didn't, then all would relive the blind rage he flew into the night before.

Continually adjusting the binoculars' focus, he slowly swept the horizon just a few degrees left and right. Suddenly he stopped. "There!" he shouted. Instantly the crew scrambled their way on deck to look in the same direction. Without looking, his shouted out orders struck like a blacksmith's hammer on hot steel. "Оставайтесь на курсе! Полная скорость впереди!" ("Stay on course! Full speed ahead!")

Looking down from the roof of the flying bridge at his crew standing on the bow, a huge smile chiseled its way into his jutting jaw. He again shouted out to them, "Мы снова играем в кошки-мышки!" ("We play cat and mouse again!")

Having not seen anyone on the water, Cal had a hard time accepting Johnny Mac's claim that someone was coming after them. Cal pressed him for more information. Johnny Mac could only say that the one who was coming had great anger within him, that his heart was as black as the clothes he wore.

Hearing this, Donna and Cal threw worried glances at each other. Johnny Mac then added, "One we know of is also coming."

"What? Who else could be coming after us?"

Johnny Mac stroked his long beard straight from the buffeting wind then said, "Could be that Sawfish guy."

Cal cursed, "Shit!" He threw a panicked look at Donna then up at the small crow's nest. "I'm going up. Donna, you and J-Mac get ready to make some rapid course changes."

Donna worriedly nodded, telling him, "Please be careful up there."

"Being up there doesn't bother me. It's the trip up and down that'll give ya a little nerve gas."

The seriousness of Johnny Mac's information kept Donna's usual feigned repugnance and retort at Cal's reference to getting the farts at bay. She knew that he often used humor to deal with stressful situations. However, this was too off the charts for her to engage in their usual husband-and-wife banter. Just as Cal started for the main mast, Johnny Mac stopped him, grabbing his shoulder urgently and saying, "Wait! No need to go up there—we must stay on course now."

"What, are you crazy? I need to try and make some evasive maneuvers and soon!"

"No, we don't. Help is also on its way."

"What kind of help, J-Mac, the police? Who?"

"I don't know exactly. I just know we need to stay on course and let things unfold."

Cal turned to face Johnny Mac placing both hands on his shoulders and looking him directly in the eyes. "Johnny Mac, you know I want to trust you, but this is our lives we are talking about here. Are you sure about what you're saying?"

Johnny Mac gave Cal an emphatic look. "As sure as I have ever been, Cal. We must stay on course."

"What are we supposed to do, just let them catch us and take the *Donna Marie*?"

"Just remember what you used to do when you were young."

Cal's worry was evident. "Look, Johnny Mac, I was young, and I used to pull con jobs on people sometimes, even on other con artists, but—"

Johnny Mac stopped him. "Well, it could be that you are going to have to con our way out of this."

"But how? I don't know who the mark is or what I'm doing in it, or even who else is involved. These things are like plays, J-Mac—everyone in on the con has to know their role."

"I think you'll know. It will come to you. Just trust in what you once were."

Cal continued to stare into Johnny Mac's face. Somberly, he said, "J-Mac, that was a long time ago. I'm not that person anymore."

"Cal, you need to be that person again. I think it's what's going to save us."

"But how? This is crazy."

"Cal, these visions I have are like road maps. If all stay on the right roads, then you reach your destination, but if anyone takes a different path, then it changes everything. That's why it is so important for you to find the path of the 'old you' and stay on it."

Cal turned away and looked at Donna; the worry on her face only made things worse. His logical mind gnawed at him to try and do something to evade their pursuers. Donna had heard all of what was said. She knew he was worried about her more than anything else. Looking intently into his face, she said, "Cal, we can't outrun them. Stop worrying about me. Listen to what Johnny Mac is saying and be the old Cal again, the one who'd take a gamble and win."

"Donna…that was so long ago. I don't know if I can pull it off anymore. Worse, I don't even know what the game is. We have no idea what's going to happen—you know that."

"No, we don't, but we didn't know what was going to happen to us when got married either. Heck, Daddy was convinced I'd be visiting you in prison. But look how that turned out."

Cal smirked remembering her dad's extremely low opinion of him. It was that low opinion that had driven Cal to prove him wrong. Years later her dad admitted to Donna that he was wrong about her choice of a husband, though he never said so to him.

Oddly, it was again the thought of her dad's low opinion of him that helped to make his decision of what to do right now.

Donna queried, "So what is it, baby? Run from the foxhounds? Or outfox them?"

Donna saw his expression begin to change, seeing what she had seen in him when they first met. The look of cool confidence told her what he was going to say before he said it.

"We outfox the bastards, that's what we're going to do."

Donna smiled and saluted him. "Aye, Cap'n."

Cal turned to Johnny Mac. "J-Mac, I want you to go below and stay there. Donna, I want you and me to look like two hapless schlubs on a sailboat. Now listen, Johnny Mac, in case we get into some kind of Mexican standoff with these guys, there's a radio down there. Get on and send out an SOS giving our coordinates. Then here, take this key. It goes to a wooden box under the bed. I keep a nine-shot Ruger pistol in it."

Taking the key, Johnny Mac nervously said, "Cal, I...I don't know. I haven't had a gun in my hand since Nam. And as you can see, I wasn't too damn good with that one either."

"Look, you were surrounded back then. I think the odds might be a little different this time. Besides, if everyone stays on their road map, there won't be any need for guns, right?"

Johnny Mac tossed the key up and down in the palm of his hand. "Yeah, I suppose. Let's hope everyone is looking at the same road map I was."

"I think that's where I come in, right?"

Johnny Mac gave a nod and half smile then turned to go below. Cal went and stood next to Donna contemplating whether he should take the helm or let Donna stay with it, finally settling on her staying at the helm so he would be free to move around if needed. Cal gazed at Donna; the wind blew her hair from her face showing her profile. Though a few gray hairs trailed through it now, to him she was still as beautiful as ever. And seeing her guiding the *Donna Marie* with stiff-jawed determination straight into an uncertain future served to steel his resolve to make damn sure they all still had one.

Cal wrapped his hand over Donna's hand still gripped on the ship's wheel, saying, "Donna." She turned to look at him. "I still need to go up the mast. I have to try and see just who's coming, how many, and how close they are. I need to try and get a feel for what's about to happen. You okay here?"

Donna placed her hand over his and gave it a firm squeeze. "I'm fine. Do what you need to do, just please be careful. You know the wind can take you right off that mast."

"Don't you worry. I won't make it that easy for these sons-of-bitches."

Donna's face softened with a warm smile. "Now that's the old Cal I knew, but listen. Don't let him get too used to the sunlight. I prefer my fifty-something Cal."

Leaning into her, he placed a firm kiss square on her lips, and then said, "Who are you kidd'n'? It was this bad boy that attracted you in the first place."

Pleasantly surprised by the kiss though raising an eyebrow at what he said, she countered, "Listen here, *bad boy*, I was twenty then. Now climb your old ass up that mast before I do it myself."

"Ooh, look who's a bad girl now. Looks like we've changed roles in our old age."

Donna dropped a hand from the ship's wheel and smacked Cal on the butt as he left, saying, "Old age! Cal, get up that mast now! *Old age*." She muttered, "I'll show you 'old age' when this is over, ya old coot."

Cal laughed out loud, yelling back without looking, "That's what I'm hoping, baby. That's what I'm hoping!"

Donna just shook her head listening to him laugh his way to the mast. The brief moment of levity took some of the edge off what may be about to happen. However, watching him climbing a sailboat mast in a strong wind brought the seriousness of their situation crashing right back down. Checking the compass heading, she made a small course correction. Looking back to check Cal's progress, she was more than a little surprised to see he was already up the ladder and in the crow's nest. "That man never ceases to amaze me," she said to herself. Turning her eyes up to the graying skies above, she made the sign of the cross while quietly saying, "Lord, please watch over us."

Suddenly Cal's shouts snapped her out of her solemn moment. "Holy cow! We got more boats coming at us than a school of tuna! One of them is that big-ass yacht we saw at the marina in Pirates Well!"

A jolt of fear shook her remembering how those men appeared standing around the deck of that intimidating-looking yacht. Nothing about it or them was good, she thought. Donna cut a sideways glance up at the sky again adding to her earlier supplication. "I know you don't like lying, Lord." She paused to cut her eyes to Cal coming down the mast then back skyward. "But could you help him do a really good job of it just this once? Amen."

She watched as Cal hurriedly made his way back to her. Stepping down into the seat-well behind the helm, he filled her in on all that he had seen. "Donna, that yacht isn't the only boat I saw coming our direction."

Donna turned halfway around to look at Cal. "How many?"

"Looked like maybe four or five."

"How long before they reach to us?"

"The yacht is maybe a couple of miles to the east, and it appears to be running full-out. But there are two runabouts just clearing the mouth of the inlet we came out of at Abraham's Bay."

"And the others?"

"It's a pair of cigarette boats that are coming fast from south of Abraham's Bay. Looks like they're coming from the coral reef area Miss Ginger told us to navigate through."

"What?"

"Yup, it looks like our plan to throw him off track worked. But what I didn't figure on was his having boats like that!" Donna faced forward again. Cal moved to stand beside her putting his arm around her. She leaned into him.

"Cal, I am very worried, but I keep getting this feeling it's going to be okay. Must be my woman's intuition, I guess."

"Well, I hope your feelings are right, but I'm not ready to hang our fate on your woman's intuition just yet."

Scrunching her face, Donna pulled back a bit to look at him. "And why not?" Pointing at the cabin hatchway, she exclaimed, "You don't have any problem following our bearded, Hawaiian-shirt-wearing Edgar Cayce in there."

"Donna, now is not the time for this. Right now, I need to focus on what we are going to do when they reach us." Just then the shrill sound of a bullhorn crackled across the water telling them to trim sail and slow down. Startled, both turned to see the two cigarette boats about two hundred yards out racing up from the southeast.

Donna gripped Cal's hand. This was it, she thought, the moment of truth.

Cal stepped away from Donna just in case these guys were of the "shoot first and ask questions later" type. He hollered to Johnny Mac, "Get ready in there, J-Mac, our guests are arriving!"

Chapter 52

In no time, the cigarette boats pulled along the *Donna Marie*'s port and starboard sides. Again, they were ordered to slow the *Donna Marie*, this time accompanied by a burst of gunfire into the air from one of Cesar's Uzi-wielding men.

Cal quickly went to comply with their orders while yelling out, "Okay, okay, keep your shirt on. I'm just one man. It takes a few minutes." Cal began to do as asked but kept glancing over at Cesar who stood smiling back at him like a Cheshire cat. Cal stopped for a moment and shouted out to him, "Hey, you need to back off some. It's going to get harder to maintain our course in this crosswind. We could collide."

Nodding agreement, Cesar raised the bullhorn, calling out, "Very well, but first I'm going to put two of mah men aboard yo-ah vessel to help with de sails. Hold yo-ah course."

Cal shot Donna a quick look. "You ok, Donna? You still have her under control?" Donna gave a rapid nod yes.

Cesar, seeing her response, gave a couple of quick hand gestures to his helmsman. The sound of the sleek cigarette boat's powerful engines ramped up and down as he matched the *Donna Marie*'s forward speed exactly. He then deftly moved parallel with the *Donna Marie*'s starboard side until they were barely three feet apart.

Two of Cesar's men waited until the motions of the two vessels fell into unison. At the same moment, both men jumped, landing hard on the *Donna Marie*'s deck. Quickly getting their footing, they took a defensive stance each pointing their Uzis, one at Cal the other at Donna.

Cal's temper flared, shouting at Cesar. "What the hell! Tell him to stop pointing that damn thing at my wife. Point it at me if you want, but leave her the hell out of this!"

A wide grin spread across Cesar's face admiring Cal's defiance and concern for his wife's safety. "Very well, Zidane, place yo-ah gun on de cabin roof and assist de gentleman with de sails. Jaden, keep yo-ah attention on de gentleman. Now, es dis better, my American friend?"

Cal only tersely nodded. He then waved at the now gunless Zidane to come to where he stood. Cal eyed the Uzi lying on the roof of the cabin just inches from the cabin doorway. If only he could get word to Johnny Mac; however, he reasoned it would make things get instantly worse. The gunman, Zidane, came up to Cal. He spoke English but with a very heavy island accent.

"Sho me whut et es yo-ah need'n' dun quickly!"

Reluctantly, Cal began showing him what he needed to do. As they worked to lower the foresails and jib, Cesar and his men kept a steady vigil on Cal's every move. Soon the *Donna Marie*'s forward speed dropped off. Cal estimated they were only making three knots or so. He took a look back at Donna. "How does she feel, Donna?" he shouted.

"A little muddy, it's getting more difficult to maintain our course."

"Cesar, you heard her, right? I can't do anymore, or we'll begin sidetracking."

"Vury well, do as yo-ah think best. 'Old steady now. My man Zidane will take de helm."

Hearing that made Cal's blood boil. "No, he won't. I'll take the helm." He wanted nothing more than to run for that Uzi on the cabin roof and tell them all to go to hell. Cal threw a worried glance toward Donna. She was his biggest concern. He wanted her as far away from these men as he could keep her. Donna saw the look of consternation on his face as he made his way to her. Cesar's man, Zidane, trailed along a few steps behind him.

Passing the Uzi laying on the cabin roof, Cal again fought the urge to make a leap for it. But something told at him to just stay with what was going on. Walking past the gun, Cal heard Zidane hop onto the cabin roof to grab the Uzi. *There goes that temptation,* he thought. Arriving at the helm, he said, "I'll take it from here, sweetheart. It's going to be a bit sketchy running these boats so close in these seas."

Donna gave him a worried look then relinquished the helm to him but stayed by his side. "Donna, please go in the cabin. I'll be okay."

"Nothing do'n', mister. I didn't say 'I do' from a distance. I said it right by your side, and that's where I belong."

Cal turned to look at her, his lips pressed tight, eyes moistened. Somberly he nodded, then with the back of his fingers, he traced the side of her cheek and gave her a kiss. Somehow, he had to get them out of a hopeless situation, but how? Johnny Mac's vision left a lot unanswered. He had no idea what was going to happen next. And even if he did know, what the hell was he to do about it?

Donna drew Cal's attention over to the boat that Cesar was on; they both watched it draw closer and closer to the *Donna Marie.* Suddenly, one of Cesar's men hurried up to him talking excitedly and frantically pointing behind them to the east. Cal and Donna both turned to see two runabouts with a man standing on the bow of one of the boats, yelling and waving something he held in his hand.

Cal stared for a moment at what was happening. Out of the corner of his mouth, he quietly said to Donna, "Donna, I think things are about to change." Cal had a gut feeling that the scales were about to tip in their favor. He had no idea how; he just knew he had to be very focused and ready to roll with the punches.

The runabout pulled right alongside of Cesar's boat with the man still waving what was apparently a piece of paper tightly clutched in his hand. He animatedly spoke in an Antillean Creole language, so neither Cal nor Donna had any idea what was being said. All they had to go on was Cesar's reactions, and at the moment, he didn't have any. However, it was apparent that he knew the men on the runabouts.

Retrieving the paper from the man, Cesar unfolded it and began reading. The paper flapped and folded over his hands as he worked to read it in the steady crosswind. Suddenly he threw a hard glare over at Cal and Donna. His face was straight and unflinching. He then slowly traced his glare up and down the length of the *Donna Marie* then back to them. Abruptly he turned and again spoke to the man on the runabout in the language that to Cal's ear sounded like nothing more than baby-talk gibberish. However, the tone and cadence of their words clearly indicated it was all very serious between them.

Cesar turned halfway around to face Cal and Donna. He shouted a single command, "I'm coming aboard!" He then motioned for the runabout to come alongside of his boat. With both boats bobbing precariously in the waves, he was assisted onboard the runabout. He then nodded toward the *Donna Marie*.

The runabout was quickly maneuvered along the *Donna Marie*'s side near the stern. Jaden and Zidane laid their weapons down and rushed to help their boss aboard. Once onboard, Cesar came quickly to where Cal and Donna stood. He gave them an assessing stare for a moment. He then said, "De note es from Miss Ginger." He was about to tell them what it said when machine-gun fire ripped across the water fifty feet short of the *Donna Marie*'s stern spraying water high into the air and causing everyone to dive for cover.

Cal and Cesar warily popped their heads back up to see from which direction it had come. Cesar's men were already up and about to return fire when Cesar shouted for his men to hold their fire. Cal and Cesar both stood to see the yacht from the marina at Pirates Well heading straight for them. On its bow standing spread-legged was a defiant-looking bald man dressed in black, holding a machine gun pointed in their general direction. The Russian captain brought an arm halfway up making a hand motion to slow down. Instantly water piled high at the bow as the big yacht quickly slowed.

Cesar immediately ordered his boats and the runabouts to swing around to the *Donna Marie*'s portside. Cal didn't like this one bit. It left the *Donna Marie* completely exposed on the starboard side. However, he understood the tactical maneuver. Cesar then ordered his cigarette boats to keep a distance off the *Donna Marie*'s bow and stern fifty yards or so and remain there. He then told the runabouts to stay about a hundred feet away but remain in the *Donna Marie*'s shadow.

The yacht turned to run parallel with the *Donna Marie* and the small armada of boats. Now only fifty or sixty feet away. The big Russian shouted out to Cesar, although not by name, for he knew no one on any of the corralled vessels before him.

"You, in da white pants, you vill surrender da sailboat to me now!"

Cesar went to stand on the *Donna Marie*'s cabin roof taking Zidane's Uzi as he went. Everyone was frozen in place watching Cesar take an equally defiant stance facing the stone-faced Russian. Cesar's answer was as defiant as his stance; his deep voice punched his words through the wind and rumble of the high-powered boat engines surrounding them. "'Et es not mine to give, not yet anyway, but if 'et were, why should I allow that, Russian?"

The Russian laughed out loud, his hubris draped reply echoing off the water and boats. "Ahh, so you know something of me, I see. So then you should know zat I get what I vant."

Cesar's reply came quickly. "I know about ever-ting and ever'one dat comes into my waters, Russian. Yo-ah activities in de lower islands es known to me, yes. And dat es precisely where dey should 'ave stayed."

Again, more laughter erupted from the Russian. "Is zat so? Perhaps it is time for me to expand my operations. And if you know of me as you say, zen you know it is a fatal mistake to resist me. Yes?"

This time it was Cesar who laughed boisterously. "Russian, I'm afraid et es you who has made de mistake. You 'ave no chance of taking dis or any other boat in my waters."

Cal's hand touched something he had forgotten about in the pocket of his cargo shorts, and instantly, inspiration hit. Suddenly he shouted out to everyone, "Hold on, hold on! Wait just a damn minute!" Cal shot Donna a rapid glance, saying, "Take the helm." Leaving her side, he stepped up onto the roof of the cabin. All eyes were on Cal now. He then continued, speaking to both Cesar and the Russian.

"Look here, you both are making a *huge* mistake here."

Cesar turned halfway around to face Cal, saying nothing. The Russian's voice resounded loudly across the water. "Oh, is zis so? And just what would zat mistake be, American?"

Cal took in a big breath. He knew he was about to tell one whopper of a lie, with not much to hang it on either. However, the way he saw it, this was their only chance at getting out of this with their skin intact. Taking a quick glance at Cesar, then to the Russian, he said with utter and complete confidence, "Neither of you want to take this boat. I was just about to inform our friend here—" he pointed at Cesar, "why when you made your grand entrance."

A suspicious expression drew across the Russian's face, his voice reflecting the same in tone. "I grow tired of zis. Tell me why, American."

"Because, my friends, there are a hundred and fifty kilos of high-quality cocaine in the hold of this boat. That's why. I'm a drug enforcement officer with Interpol. We are currently working on a very big drug smuggling operation of which I was on my way to the rendezvous point, that is until all you water-bound leeches decided to show up."

"Zat is bullshit. I don't believe you. Where is your ID?" the Russian's incensed reply came with the machine gun being brought to bear directly on Cal. A surge of adrenaline hit Cal; however, it neither showed in his posture or voice. A long ago memory flashed through his mind of two cops with their guns drawn and pointed at him over a still in the woods.

That memory helped to strengthen his confidence in his little charade. "Look, you should be smart enough to know I wouldn't keep my badge on me while running a sting operation. These drug dealers are way too smart and suspicious for that."

"Ha, just as I suspected," the Russian mocked. "You have nothing, nothing but a big lie you use to try and save your ass."

Cal couldn't let this guy think he was intimidating him, so he gave the same kind of cockiness he was getting right back at him. "Tell me, are all you Ivans as shortsighted as you? 'Cause if they are, then the cold war is looking a lot better for the West. Look, I didn't say I didn't *have* a badge. It's in the cubby of the console below the ship's wheel. Let me go get it and I'll show it to you."

"No! Have da woman bring it. I don't trust you," he shouted back.

Donna started to do what he said, but Cal stopped her cold.

"This is bullshit! Stay where you are. In fact, everyone stay put. I'll get it!" Cal shouted out.

"Make a move and I vill put many holes in you, like screen door!" He snarled, re-aiming the machine gun squarely on Cal's head.

In frustrated disbelief, Cal turned his head slightly away then back, firing right back at him.

"Well, dammit, shoot me then! But know this—this tub is wired for sound, and everything we are saying right now is being monitored. Just how damn stupid do you think we are? Now I'm going to walk back there and get my badge."

Without wanting or waiting for a response, he stormed his way back to the helm. He had to think quickly though. The badge was actually already in his zippered left front pocket. He was going to have to make it look as though he were bringing it up out of the console cubby. For once he was glad for his forgetfulness; otherwise, the badge would be back in Rokers Point with its rightful owner.

Reaching the helm, he crouched slightly to cover his left leg by the console. The Russian captain kept the machine gun trained on Cal. Donna moved aside to let him get to the console's cubby but kept a hand on the ship's wheel. Out of her mind with worry, she nervously watched Cal in silence. Every nerve in her body was on fire. She didn't know how Cal was able to seem so calm and in charge. She had never seen him quite like this and figured him to be reaching deep into his old personality to appear so calm and cool.

She watched him slip the badge from his pocket then fumble around like he was looking for it while he pinned it to the inside of his wallet. Suddenly he triumphantly stood up flashing it at the suspicious Russian. She was utterly amazed at his rapid sleight of hand; it was so smooth and seamless.

The Russian lowered the gun a little straining to see it. He then shouted out, "You!" he barked at Cesar. "Go and check it out. I still don't trust him."

Cal called out, "Just stay there, I'll come to you." Again, he didn't wait for agreement from the Russian. He did this to shift the sense of who had more authority at the moment. Cal handed his wallet to Cesar, who eyed the badge with a clear look of admiration and curiosity. Even he was beginning to believe Cal was who he said he was. After all, they all arrived on big seaplane; they had not come there on this sailboat but were leaving on it.

Looking over at the Russian captain, Cesar shouted to him, "It appears he es telling de truth. De badge is real. I have seen them a time or two in de past."

Again, curse words spewed from his mouth as he stormed around the bow in a tight circle. Suddenly he stopped. With his earlier defiance returning, he brought the machine gun to bear on Cesar, yelling out a new demand, "De kilos of drugs, show it to me—show it to me now! You go below and bring some on deck now. Do it now!"

Cal's mind raced; there was, of course, no kilos of cocaine in the cabin of the *Donna Marie*, just a bearded psychic in the form of one Johnny Mac, whom he hoped had been listening to all that was going on and done as Cal had instructed if things took a turn for the worse.

Cesar, thinking Cal *was* with Interpol, gave him a look as if wanting his approval to go below. Cal, just like being in a high stakes poker game, gave him an expressionless nod, saying, "Sure, go have a look." Cal appeared to be calm and unruffled by this latest development. However, he was anything but; his mind was on fire trying to think of what to do next.

He knew damn well that Cesar was going to come back on deck empty-handed. Cal looked back at Donna. What was he going to do to protect her now? He turned back in time to see Cesar disappear through the hatchway into the cabin. This was it, he thought.

Chapter 53

Cesar entered the cabin stopping a moment to take it all in. He marveled that in spite of a couple of bullet holes and a broken window, it still looked really nice. Much of the wood used for trim appeared to be Brazilian rosewood. The mahogany floors were stunning. The wood cabinetry was of the kind one would find in only the finest of homes.

Clearly this was no ordinary sailboat; it was easy to see that this was a very expensive and well-made vessel. Taking a breath, he continued forward toward a closed door presumably where the cocaine was being stashed. Just as he neared the door, it eased partway open. Startled, he froze; he thought no one else was aboard. Now he was even more certain that Cal was who he said he was. Just then the barrel of a gun appeared in the two-inch gap between the door and the jamb. A voice quickly accompanied the gun's appearance.

"Just hold it right there. I know what you came looking for. I've heard everything going on up there. Now back up. I've got what that cocky loudmouth wants to see.

Cesar did as he was ordered and backed away. The door eased slowly open to reveal Johnny Mac holding the gun in one hand and a small rectangular package wrapped in plastic and duct tape in the other. Keeping the gun on Cesar, he held out the taped-up package for Cesar to take.

Cautiously, Cesar grabbed the brick-like package. Looking curiously at how Johnny Mac was attired, he questioned, "Yo-ah don't look like a drug agent, but ef so, then know this: I want no part of dis," palming the taped-up bundle in his big hand.

Just then the Russian captain could be heard shouting, "'Vat is taking so long? Get up here now!"

Cesar cut his eyes in the direction of the Russian's voice. "I will go and show de loudmouth. It es best dat he leave while he still can."

Johnny Mac quickly said, "Listen, when you go out there, you didn't see me, and that package *is* cocaine, understand?"

Cesar glanced at the package in his hands then at Johnny Mac's fingers holding the gun on him. "I suppose dat is cocaine all over yo-ah fingers too."

Johnny Mac smiled at him then said, "It is today, my friend, and you better make him believe it too."

"What es et really?"

Johnny Mac smirked. "Pancake mix and powdered sugar. Why?"

"Just curious. I like to know what et es I'm selling."

Suddenly machine-gun fire erupted as a rake of bullets exploded in the water parallel to the *Donna Marie*'s hull, with the Russian captain screaming at Cesar to show himself. Cesar took off for the cabin hatchway waving the package over his head as he came out on deck.

"Here, here! The door was locked. I had to break into it! Look, here it is!" Cesar shouted.

The Russian glared at Cesar holding the package then threw a hard stare at Cal.

"How much is aboard?" he tersely questioned.

Cesar matter-of-factly stated, "It is as de officer here claims, about a hundred and fifty kilos."

The ever-suspicious Russian captain abruptly ordered Cesar to open the package. "Open it. Open it, I say. I vaunt to see it."

Cal realized then that Johnny Mac had indeed been listening to what was happening but was now worried about what was actually in the mysterious package. With no idea what had been used to make what Cesar was holding, he decided it was time to turn up the heat on the hotheaded Russian.

"Now wait just a damn minute," Cal barked. "Look, enough! You know I'm an officer with Interpol. I told you what we are engaged in here. Now unless you want to be sitting in a prison cell, you need to shut up and go away. I told you this is all being monitored. Now what's it going to be, Ivan?"

"He es telling de truth, Russian. I saw de radio equipment, aund I heard someone attempting to raise them. I believe et wise to let dis fish return to de sea."

Everyone was still and quiet for a long moment waiting for the Russian's response. A gust of wind blew hard against the rigging in the masts. Donna finally worked up the nerve to speak, vacillating a split second with on how to address her husband, finally opting to roll with the Interpol ruse. "Lieutenant, I can't keep our heading, sir. The winds have picked up. We're cross-tracking. Somebody is going to get run into here. We either need to build our speed up, or these guys are going to have to back off."

Cal spun to face Donna. He fought back the urge to give her big smile. He did give her a playful wink, and then a nod. Turning back quickly to face the Russian, he mustered all the authority in his voice he could and boldly stated, "That's it, boys. This party is over! You, *Ivan*, you need to take your happy ass back to Moscow and stay the hell out of these waters. Now lower your weapon and tell all your boys to do the same."

The Russian captain gave a small haughty chuckle. "And ef I refuse, vat zen? I could sink ze sailboat and you along with it."

Cal's frustrations became more real and less of an act now, looking away then quickly back to the Russian. "Man, you are one stupid Ivan." Cal then made an obvious check of his wrist watch. "Look, you have delayed us by twenty minutes. You heard him say he heard someone trying raise us on our radio," he stated, pointing at Cesar.

"Now because of *you,* we couldn't respond, so guess what, shit-for-brains? There is a U.S. Coast Guard cutter heading our way at top speed right now. So are you going to keep being hardheaded, or do you want to get a free ride to the U.S. naval station in Key West?

The Russian glared hard at Cal for a long moment. Dropping his head, he spun around and spat out orders intermixed with curses, all in Russian.

He then spun back to face Cal and Cesar. His face went purple with rage as he screamed out at everyone, "Zis is not over, do you understand! I still think you bluff, so watch your back!"

Cal tired of being threatened stepped to the starboard rail in defiance of the Russian's rage and threats. He leaned toward the fuming man, arrogantly shouting back, "Blow it out yer Commie ass!"

Hearing Cal's taunt, he stood for a moment just seething and clenching his jaw in anger. Abruptly his eyes bulged. He became so enraged he let out a violent scream, spat directly Cal. The full fury of his anger then erupted. Lifting the machine gun, he pointed it squarely at Cal. Utter terror gripped Donna as she screamed out Cal's name.

A fraction of second before triggering the weapon, the Russian shifted his aim from Cal to the boat. Suddenly flame burst from the barrel of the gun as bullets ripped along the cabin walls then chased their way snakelike up the mainsail mast. Splinters of wood flew in all directions raining back down onto the deck and into the water. He ceased his crazed hapless firing and in one smooth motion, he let the gun's strap fall from his shoulder to grab it by its still smoking barrel. Then in a final curse-filled exhibition of out-of-control rage, he hurled it through the air directly at Cal.

The machine gun somersaulted slow-motion-like over the gap of water between the two boats. Cal ducked, turning away in time to see the gun hit the *Donna Marie*'s deck, leaving deep gouges as it slid to a grinding halt.

A split second later the sound of the yacht's twin diesel engines ramped up to full throttle. Everyone slowly rose up from the cover they had taken in time to see the bow of the huge yacht lift sharply up out of the sea. Its huge props clawed at the ocean shoving a massive wave aft of her stern, followed by roiling black smoke bellowing from her exhaust ports. Then, reminiscent of a school-yard bully defiantly kicking sand at a victorious opponent, the helmsman cut a hard sharp turn away, blasting the turbulent prop wash and exhaust smoke directly at the *Donna Marie*.

Cal spun back to face the rapidly departing yacht. Through the bellows of exhaust and sea spray, he read its name, the *Akula*. He then glanced to his left at Cesar widening his eyes. He said, "If *Akula* means asshole, then that tub is aptly named."

Cesar laughed out loud, then started walking toward Cal, saying, "De name es Russian for *shark*. As I said, I know of his activities among de islands. So yo-ah name es Cal?" Cal nodded yes. "Well, Mista Cal, what you did was either de bravest thing I have ev-ah seen or de craziest, aund only de real owner of this vessel would do such a thing."

Cesar stopped a few feet from Cal. Donna wanted desperately to be by Cal's side; she began to tremble. Cal saw this and went quickly to her side putting his arm around her shoulders. He then looked Cesar directly in his eyes. With a good deal of exasperation in his voice, he said, "Well, Cesar, do I have to do any more brave or crazy things here? You still planning on taking our boat?"

Cesar crinkled his brow in confusion for a second or two in contemplation of what to say about his showing up and basically commandeering their boat, electing to hold back on the truth and only tell them what he felt they needed to know. Reaching into his pocket, he retrieved Miss Ginger's note and handed it to Cal. Taking it, he quickly read it.

> *My dear cousin, you owe me one. Do these people no harm and see to their safe passage home on their sailboat. We have things to discuss when you return.*

Cal looked up from reading the note. "So because of this note, you're not going to take the *Donna Marie* from us?"

"Dat es correct. I will honor my cousin's request. Today es yo-ah lucky day."

The effects of the adrenaline that had been pumping through Donna began rapidly dissipating. Her legs went suddenly weak; in fact, her entire body felt like rubber, and she began to slump toward the deck. Cal immediately caught her under one arm while Cesar reached and caught her under the other. She tried to stand, but it felt as if there wasn't a solid bone in her entire body. Cesar called for Jaden to take the helm so she could be taken to the cabin.

Coming through the cabin door, Cal called out to Johnny Mac. "J-Mac, quick, get Donna some water!" Cal and Cesar moved her to the couch and eased her down to sit, then helped her to lie down.

Johnny Mac came quickly with a glass of water. "Is she okay, Cal? Did she get hurt?"

"No, no, it's just the effects of all the adrenaline leaving her. She's never been in a situation like this before. Fact is, neither have I...well, not quite like this anyway."

Johnny Mac nodded, saying as he went to sit back down at the galley table, "Yeah, I kinda know the feeling."

Cal put his arm under her shoulders lifting her up a little so she could drink some water. Wearily, she took a few sips then dropped back down on the couch. She lay there staring at the ceiling. Gradually her breathing began returning to normal. The moments ticked slowly by, but with each passing minute, her heart rate slowed, and she felt herself returning to normal.

Rubbing at her face and eyes, she finally took a deep breath then raised up on her elbows. Cal was kneeling on one knee right by her side still holding the glass of water. She blinked her eyes a couple of times and asked for another sip of water; Cal held the glass to her lips. While taking a few more sips, she drew her eyes around the cabin. Suddenly she stopped drinking. Cal had no sooner pulled the glass from her lips when she blurted out, "That Russian ass shot the hell out of our boat, Cal!"

It was then that Cal and Cesar threw glances around the cabin. "My word, dat SOB really did a number on yo-ah boat. I'll go topside and have my men check de whole vessel fo-ah any serious damage. If der is, you will need to return to Abraham's Bay."

Cal nodded then stood. "Thank you, you really came through for us."

Cesar gave short laugh. "'Twas not me. Et was you who made him back off. He wanted nothing to do with an Interpol officer, dat es for sure."

Cal smirked. "Ah, well…about that. I'm *not* an officer with Interpol. I made that whole thing up."

Cesar stopped midway out the cabin doorway to look back at Cal. "So yo-ah not a real Interpol officer? Is de badge phony as well?"

Cal smirked. "No, the badge is real. The rest of it was total bullshit. Actually, my wife Donna and I, we are just the owners of a marina in the Florida Keys, Ramrod Key to be specific."

Cesar remained in the doorway a moment. His expression was one of amazed disbelief. "Aund just when did you concoct dat story of having de drugs onboard?"

Cal pressed his lips tight, raising his brow high. Sheepishly, he admitted, "About ten seconds after I flashed that loudmouthed Ivan the badge."

A perplexed look came to Cesar's face trying sort out all of what just happened. "So de three of you made all of it up on de fly?"

"Yup, 'fraid so," Cal replied.

Donna spoke out, "Hold on, that's not true. Cal honey, that was all you. We all just played along."

Cesar shot Cal a look of surprise then said, "Ma friend, remind me to never play a game of poker with you."

Hearing that, Donna suddenly tossed her legs over the edge of the couch and quickly sat up, interjecting, "You can say that again. How do you think we got this sailboat?" she said with a proud pat on Cal's thigh. Cal gave her a confused sideways glance. It was the first and only time she had ever seemed impressed with how he had won the *Donna Marie* in a game of poker.

Cesar's mouth dropped open a bit as he threw a quick look around the interior of the cabin then back at Cal and Donna. "Of dis I have no doubt. Anyone who could be dat calm while a crazy man points a machine gun at them es too cool a card player fo-ah me. Now let me go aund see about yo-ah vessel."

Donna and Cal both watched as Cesar went topside giving orders as he went. Donna turned her eyes to meet Cal's, still trying to wrap her mind around all of what had just happened. She shook her head seeing sharp beams of sunlight pouring through the bullet holes in the cabin walls. One of the galley cabinet doors drooped open to hang on only one hinge, the dishes inside shattered.

Cal gazed around at the damage too. "Looks like about six bullet holes, and that's not even counting the—" He suddenly stopped remembering the trail of bullets up the main mast. Spinning around, he put his hands on Donna's shoulders. "Stay here, baby, I've got to go topside and check out the main mast. That asshole blasted it pretty good. We may have to turn around and head back to Abraham's Bay."

Donna's heart sank. That was *not* what she wanted to hear. She wanted desperately to go home and try and put all this craziness behind them and just be two marina owners again. Donna nodded and watched Cal disappear through the hatchway. When she turned back, she noticed Johnny Mac, who had been oddly quiet, sitting alone at the galley table. Other than the wind blowing through one of the shattered porthole windows, it was quiet in the cabin. She went and sat down opposite Johnny Mac. It was clear that the shattered inside of the cabin wasn't the only thing that had suffered from the effects of the hail of bullets.

Chapter 54

Johnny Mac sat with his hands folded before him just staring blankly down at the tabletop. It was then that Donna realized that in the jubilation of seeing the Russian turn tail and run, everyone had forgotten that Johnny Mac had been in the cabin when it was shot up. She gently placed her hands over his and spoke softly. "Johnny Mac, you okay? You're not hurt, are you?"

Only a wordless minor nod came. His gaze remained fixed on the tabletop. Donna squeezed his hands; it was then that she became acutely aware of the horrible scars all over his hands and the missing ends of two fingers. A chill ran through her recalling what Cal had told her about Johnny Mac's time in Vietnam. Gently squeezing his hand again, she spoke to him. "John, talk to me." Donna suspected that the machine-gun fire had triggered the memories of his being horribly wounded and nearly dying in Nam.

They both sat in silence for a moment more. Johnny Mac slowly lifted his head bringing his eyes to meet Donna's. His gaze remained frozen on her for a long moment, then almost in a whisper, he spoke. "No one calls me John anymore. Sometimes…I really miss just being John Daniels." He took a troubled breath. "People think that I survived that damn war." Slowly shaking his head, he added, "But that nineteen-year-old kid, John McKenzie Daniels, died that day. Only his ghost survived."

Donna choked back tears as a knot built in her throat. "John, that's not so. *You* did survive. You survived for just such a moment as this. If it weren't for you, *all* of you, right here right now, we would all likely be dead. And it wasn't the Key West prophet that did it. It was you, John Daniels, that figured out what to do at a critical moment in all of our lives."

Johnny Mac gave a small smile. "How? With some pancake mix and sugar in a taped-up trash bag?"

A puzzled look came to Donna's face. "Is that what that was?" Johnny Mac gave a small smile and nod. Donna continued, "Well then, that really *was* quick thinking. *And* it convinced everyone that the pile of bull crap my husband was selling them was true. Listen, my husband is a pretty good liar, but that crazy Russian was having a hard time buying what he was selling, that is, until Cesar came on deck waving around what you had made."

Johnny Mac's smile deepened, and his face brightened. "I'm just glad he didn't want to sample it. Cal really did a great job of BS-ing that guy to keep that from happening."

Donna patted Johnny Mac's hand and said, "Well, like I said, my man can really lie when he wants to." Scrunching her face, she looked toward the cabin hatchway. "You know, I'm not quite sure how I feel about that—makes me wonder about him."

Johnny Mac looked up at the cabin wall next to him and put a finger into one of the bullet holes. His smile drifted away. Staring at the large hole, he rubbed its splintered edges. Without looking away, he quietly said, "What is it that makes human beings want to be so cruel to one another?"

Donna's heart was aching for him. "John, if I knew the answer to that, I could solve all the world's problems. But there is one thing I think *is* the root cause of all of our troubles, and it is jealousy. To me, it seems every problem we have is spawned from that one human flaw."

Johnny Mac looked away from rubbing the bullet hole to Donna in consideration of what she had said. "You know, Mrs. Arnold, I think you are exactly right. It is after all the reason the very first murder was committed."

His reference to Cain and Abel surprised her a little and served to wash away the last of any misgivings she still held about him and his prophetic abilities. For the first time, the man sitting across from her, she felt, was truly a remarkable man who had a gift that he never once used maliciously. He was a good man.

"You know something, John, I think you need to start focusing on all the good you do in this world with that God-given ability you have. I think that will really help to heal the wounds that can't be seen."

Smiling again, he said, "You think so?"

"I know so."

Johnny Mac gave her a small smile and laugh and said, "One thing though, if my gift is as you say, 'God-given,' I sure wish he had used the U.S. mail to deliver it instead of bullets and shrapnel."

Donna looked at him with, at first, surprise, then a motherly countenance came to her face. Her tone of voice matched her look as she replied, "John, I don't think that's so. I think it was the love and kindness of total strangers who risked all of their lives to try and save yours. And love, my friend, will always be more powerful than bullets and hate."

Right then Johnny Mac felt as though a great weight had been lifted from him. Standing up from the table, he took a couple of steps away. Donna did likewise. When their eyes met, he gave her a soft smile then simply said, "Thanks." He leaned in and gave her a long hug to which Donna reciprocated.

They were still in their embrace when suddenly Cal burst through the cabin hatchway talking loudly as he came. "Hey, it looks like we're going to have to head south. That storm has strengthened, and it is heading due east now and—" Stopping in mid-sentence, he loudly exclaimed, "Hey, what's going on here!"

Donna and Johnny Mac broke off their hug and turned to face Cal. Donna sarcastically replied, "Nothing is *going on*, Cal. John and I were just having nice conversation, that's all."

"A conversation? You two sure got a funny way of talking."

"Relax, Cal, I'm not trying to take your girl. But you sure are one lucky SOB, that's for sure."

A bit confused and annoyed, he still wanted to go over what he had to tell them, so he launched right back into it. "Look, I don't know what's going on, but that will have to wait. I'm taking us due south. I'm worried about the integrity of the main mast—that Ivan put two or three good sized holes in it. We can't risk being in heavy seas and wind with it."

Donna stepped toward Cal. "What...no, no, we need to go home, Cal. Are you sure about the mast?"

"No, Donna, I'm not. That's the problem. We can't go sailing into rough weather with a compromised mast. If it fails, it will take everything else with it. No, we have to head south and right now. Now come on, I need both of you topside. That is, if you two are done with whatever it was I walked in on."

Johnny Mac smiled and shook his head then looked at Donna. "You know, Donna, you are a hundred percent right about jealously being the problem."

Donna gave Johnny Mac a sideways glance then looked back to Cal. "Well, sometimes a little of it is a good thing. Lord knows that old buzzard of mine could use a dose of it now and again." Contemptuously, Cal swatted his hands in their direction, turned in a huff, and disappeared back through the hatchway mumbling and grousing the whole way.

Putting a hand to her mouth, Donna began snickering. Johnny Mac let go a good laugh too then said, "Boy, that sure got under his skin. I never knew he was so jealous of you, Donna."

With a big smile, Donna started for the hatchway, saying as she went, "That? That was nothing. He was awful when we first got together. He wanted to whip any guy who even made a sideways glance at me. His mother and I finally had to plot against him to get him to stop."

"What did you do?"

"Well...his mother got one of the cute young girls at the five and dime where she worked at to corner Cal in the stock room one day. She began talking very saucy and friendly like and moving closer and closer to Cal until she had him cornered and just inches apart. Then at just the right moment, her very big and muscular boyfriend burst in on them."

Donna let go a deep laugh at the memory of it all. Through chuckles and snorts, Donna continued. "What my very fast talking and backpedaling future husband didn't know was that the 'boyfriend' was actually her older brother who played college football. They both played it off so perfectly she kept yelling for him not hurt Cal, and her brother kept trying get around her while taking wild wide swings at Cal who was sputtering words out like an old teletype machine. Cal was looking for any way out of this predicament.

"His mother and I were peeking through the swinging stock room doors trying desperately to hold back our laughter. Finally, when we couldn't take it any longer, we stepped through the doors. I don't think that man of mine was ever more relieved to see his mother and me, that's until we all busted out laughing at him."

Johnny Mac and Donna both laughed out loud. Johnny Mac, still laughing, asked, "What...what did Cal do?"

"Oh, he got pissed off and stormed out of there right past his mother and me. We tried to stop him to explain, but he just stormed right out of the store. He didn't talk to me for three days. He finally came by the house one day, and we had a very good talk, and I gotta say he's been very good ever since—almost too good."

Reaching the hatchway, Johnny Mac queried her, "What do you mean by 'too good'?"

Donna looked back at Johnny Mac with a wry grin. "Well, every girl still wants to know that her man will fight for her now and again."

Johnny Mac gave a short laugh, saying as they stepped out onto the deck, "You women, you got us guys figured out like a road map."

"Pffft, a road map? Guys are much simpler to figure out than that. Men have three basic needs: something to eat, a place to sleep, and that *other* thing taken care of."

Johnny Mac questioned her, "What *other* thing?"

Donna turned halfway around grimacing at him; never saying a word, she shot a quick glance down at Johnny Mac's crotch. Johnny followed her eyes down, then quickly back up. "Oh...oh, uh, huh, yeah. Guess that would be other thing."

Donna and Johnny Mac emerged on deck to find Cal and Cesar talking at the helm. Donna was pleased to see that all of his men were off the *Donna Marie*. Likewise, Miss Ginger's small speedboats and men were gone as well.

Both Johnny Mac and Donna eased their way to where Cal and Cesar stood. The *Donna Marie's* deck was pitching and rolling more in the building seas, requiring more effort to walk. Just as Donna and Johnny Mac walked up, Cesar turned to face the cigarette boat he had arrived on. He shouted to them and the others to head back to Abraham's Bay, telling them that he was staying aboard the *Donna Marie*.

Donna looked at Cal in total shock at this new development. This added to her frustration about not heading home. Glaring at Cesar, she snappishly blurted out, shouting over the wind, "Why? Why are you staying aboard? Are you just planning on stealing the *Donna Marie* from us in a more convenient place?"

Cesar laughed out loud while clapping his big hands in front of his chest. He then spoke directly to Donna, his deep voice easily penetrating the wind, "My dear, dear lady, no. A deal is a deal. I have no intention of taking yo-ah vessel. The mast is in need of repair, aund de maun who can best do dis for you lives in Cockburn Town. He should be able to repair it."

Donna cast a stern look in Cal's direction. Cal knew she was looking to him to ease her mind about all of this. "Donna, look," he began, "we really have no choice. We simply can't risk making a run for home just yet. Besides the mast, the mainsail has a couple of holes shot in it too. If we get into wind much stronger than what we are in now…well…you know what will happen."

Donna wanted to just burst out crying. Instead of going home, they were heading farther away. Worse, she didn't even know how much farther or how long the repairs would take, compounding her anxiety. Having a man onboard with a reputation like Cesar's didn't help matters either.

Cesar saw the expression on her face and immediately understood all of her concerns. Hoping to ease her mind, he looked her right in the eyes; his expression was soft, almost fatherly, and his tone was similar as he began. "Look, Miss Donna—if I may address you dat way." She nodded; he smiled. "I know you are worried about me, but please do not worry. I'm going with you for yo-ah protection. I am known well in de lower islands, and dis can be vury useful to you."

Donna held her gaze on him and, without fear, said, "It's your reputation that worries me. I mean, for God's sake, you are known as the 'Sawfish,' are you not?"

Cesar gave a chuckle before he spoke. "Yes, dat es true, but a well-known reputation, even a bad one, can be used to do good."

"So essentially you are asking me, us"—she pointed to Cal—"to make a deal with the devil."

"Oh, Miss Donna, is dat 'ow you see me? Ah, you 'urt me to my soul, and yes, I do 'ave one. Listen, de waters of des islands can have some vury nasty people in dem. My 'Sawfish' reputation es ninety percent, ah, ah, bullshit, as you Americans say. I have crafted et for a particular interest and for my family—Miss Ginger and her daughters, for instance."

Cal finally broke in to the conversation. "Donna, look, we are losing precious time here. I trust Cesar to do exactly as he says, which is to help us to get the repairs done so we can be on our way home. Look, he said that Sawfish thing is BS, right? So we have nothing to worry about, okay?"

Donna raised one eyebrow and then looked to Johnny Mac. "What's your thoughts about all of this?"

Johnny Mac trailed his eyes around to each of them, stopping on Donna. "A chameleon uses their abilities for protection. I suggest we let this one use his to do the same."

"He said it was *ninety percent* BS, Donna," Cal reiterated.

She cut her eyes to Cesar then back to Cal. "Yeah, well, ten percent of a snake bite is still a snake bite, but I guess we really have no choice now but to trust him." Donna threw up her hands. "All right, let's get this girl headed to…to wherever, and the sooner we get there, the sooner we can go home, and I mean home, Cal."

"Et es Cockburn Town, Miss Donna, and et es not too far south."

Donna gave a stern look at Cal, telling him, "I'll take the helm. What are the coordinates for this Cockburn Town anyway, and what kind of damn name *is* that anyway? Cockburn…must have been a sailor that named the damn place."

Without another word, she placed her hands on the ship's wheel practically shoving Cal's out of the way. He relinquished the helm to her knowing full well that she was in no mood for any comment from him. Instead he opened the cubby below the ship's wheel to retrieve the map. But before he could unfold it, Cesar was giving her the coordinates.

Donna gave Cesar a terse nod and began turning them south. She gazed around at the three men staring at her. "The three of you, don't just stand there gawking at me. Rig her out to make some speed. Leave the mainsail with a bit more slack so maybe the bullet holes don't tear into big holes. Move it! Let's go!"

Without a word of protest, all three of them scrambled to do as ordered. Cal and Cesar went to the mainsail while Johnny Mac headed for the jib. As Cal and Cesar worked the lines, Cesar commented to Cal, "Yo-ah woman, she is very impressive. She is vury strong in her mind."

Cal looked back at his wife while pressing a tight smile of admiration. "Yeah, and her mind isn't only thing that's strong. She'll kick yer ass if you put her in the mood for it, which I try to avoid. That girl is like a wildcat when she gets pissed off."

A deep laugh erupted from Cesar that cut through the wind before he spoke. "Ah, so you 'ave 'ad experience with dis?"

"Not me, but I've seen her take down a drunk at our restaurant one time that got too fresh with her. That guy was on his back looking at the ceiling before he could even blink an eye."

Cesar burst out laughing again. He put a hand on Cal's shoulder and was about to speak when a shout came from the stern. "Hey, you two, we need the sails flappin', not yer mouths!"

Neither one looked back but jumped right back to the task at hand, chuckling and laughing as they went about resetting the sails. Quickly though, Cal's mind was back on the seriousness of their present situation. They had come within a hair's width of being made into fish bait by that crazy Russian, but something about why he shot up the mast and sail kept spooling around in the back of his mind. He had a strong feeling that they had not seen the last of him. The moment he thought that, he drew his eyes over the mast and mainsail again. Suddenly it hit him—*That crazy-ass bastard did it on purpose. He knows where we are going now. He likely knows the same people Cesar does who can fix this kind of damage.*

Cal, while cinching a rope line, told Cesar what he had been thinking. Cesar ceased knotting a line while in consideration of Cal's deductions. His face abruptly went straight; fixing his eyes firmly on Cal, he earnestly stated, "Den we must make Cockburn Town vury quickly, ma friend, but we must not be predictable. He will be expecting us to take de shortest route to de island. We must be clever like de fox."

Cal understood and gave a nod of agreement. However, he had no idea how or what could be done to throw the Russian off their trail. For now, it appeared as though they were completely dependent upon the nefarious reputation of the man known as the Sawfish—a reputation that he hoped the population of Cockburn Town knew and feared but were not out to have him or whoever was with him arrested, or worse.

Completing the task of rigging the *Donna Marie* for as much speed as she could make, Cal took a moment to look back at his wife at the helm. Her steeled expression told him that she had but one thing on her mind, to head home, and the sooner the better. A smile pulled into his cheek while speaking to himself, "Well, baby, you wanted us to have a Caribbean adventure. By golly, we are smack in the middle of one now."

Chapter 55

With the sails set and the *Donna Marie* making good time, Cal went to check out the severity of the holes shot in the side of the cabin. Johnny Mac went to where Cal had squatted down to examine the half-dozen holes that trailed snakelike down the side of the cabin. Fingering one of the holes, he spoke out loud. "That son-of-a-bitch shot the crap out of my damn boat!"

"Yeah, he damn near shot the crap out of me too. I hit deck just as those bullets zipped over my head!"

Cal looked up at Johnny Mac. It was then that he realized what he had walked in on with him and Donna. Standing to face Johnny Mac, he said, "I'm sorry about that, man. I had no idea that crazy bastard was going to react that way. I should've picked up that damn gun and shot his sorry Ivan ass."

Just then his eye caught the image of the machine gun lying past Johnny Mac still lying right where it had skidded to a stop. Cal then fixed his eyes on it and began quickly heading for it, followed by Johnny Mac. Stepping up to it, Cal bent to pick it up. Examining it, he rubbed his fingers over the name stamped into the barrel's side.

Cesar also joined Cal and Johnny Mac who stood carefully examining of the rather odd-looking weapon. Johnny Mac didn't touch it but quickly identified it. "It's a Chinese-made Norinco Type 56."

Cal ejected the ammo clip and began removing the remaining bullets, counting as he went. "Looks like seven. Too bad I didn't make that crazy bastard angrier. He might have tossed over another clip of ammo to go with it," he said with a laugh.

Cesar laughed out loud. "Or he may 'ave put some holes in you too, ma friend. Dat one es vury unpredictable, and not to be trifled with, to be sure. If et es as you think, Mista Cal, dat 'e goes to where we are going, den 'e will not be fooled again."

Cal agreed. He then looked back at Donna at the helm. His concern for her safety was all he could think of at the moment. He had been in some rather tight situations in his younger days, but none quite like this, he thought. Back then he always had an escape route if things didn't go as planned. But that was on land and in neighborhoods he knew like the back of his hand. Still wandering through the thoughts of his misspent youth, he drew his eyes upon the endless horizon of sea and sky. Shaking his head, he murmured to himself, "No place to run out here. It's just wits and luck out here, mostly luck."

Just then his eyes fixed on something on the distant horizon. Squinting into the distance, he hooded his eyes with one hand. Without looking away, he spoke out to Cesar, "Hey, do cruise ships make any stops where we are going?"

"Well, yes, some do. Dey use de old supply docks de American military built many years ago. Why?"

Pointing at the horizon, he said, "I think we may have a safe way to make it to Cockburn Town. Look way out on the horizon, does that look like a cruise ship to you?"

Cesar looked to where Cal was pointing. It took a moment for his eyes to find and focus on what Cal was pointing at, but sure enough, it was a ship and a rather large one to boot. "Yes, yes, I believe it es one. Aund I know what yo-ah thinking, Mista Cal." Cal looked back at Donna again and started for the helm.

The tricky part in what he was planning was the timing. They were going to have to run an intersecting course with the cruise ship and then at the right moment make a turn to run parallel with it. This wasn't too difficult a maneuver, he thought, as long as the cruise ship didn't alter its course at the last minute, which could throw off the timing with perhaps disastrous results.

*****

Jim readied himself for handling the Water Lily to fly with only one engine running properly. He had already radioed the Exuma airport notifying them that he was experiencing engine trouble. A general call was made to air traffic in the area to maintain a holding pattern around the island until the Water Lily could attempt to make an emergency landing.

Soon he radioed Exuma to say that he was about to turn onto his final approach. He gave Juky a furtive glance then reached up and began to slowly adjust the starboard engine's fuel and air mixtures so that it began to run rough; large amounts of black smoke began bellowing from its exhaust. The aircraft slowed precipitously, becoming more difficult to maintain level flight. The whole airframe vibrated and shook.

The sound of the sputtering engine and shaking fuselage woke all three sleeping passengers. Hurriedly rubbing the sleep from their eyes, they peered out the window to see black smoke boiling and rolling past their windows with the prop struggling to keep spinning. Terry stared wide-eyed out the window. His voice quavered with nervous panic as he shouted out, "Michael, what's 'appen'n', why is the engine smoking?"

"'Ow the 'ell should I know, ya sprog! Stop 'av'n' a bloody fit!" Michael barked back. Standing up, he held on to whatever he could as he worked his way to the closed cabin door. Reaching the door, he tried the handle and found it locked. Banging on it with his fist, he shouted, "Ey, bloke, what the bloody 'ell is 'appen'n' with that bleed'n' engine?"

Jim grinned at Juky, then shouted out, "Go sit down and put on your seat belt! I'm trying to land this thing!"

Michael stood for a moment then looked back at his panicky cohorts and decided it was best to do as suggested. "Relax, mates, get yer seat belts on. We are about to land."

Terry began quickly buckling up while still nervously talking as Michael returned to his seat to do the same. "So 'e can land this bird with just one engine? We're not gonna crash?"

Michael plopped down in his seat and replied to Terry while fishing for his seat belt. "Sure, 'e can land this bird with just one bleed'n' engine. Remember, 'e told us he was a bomber pilot during the big one. Those blokes could land a B-17 with just one engine running, and they had four engines."

Martin added, "Yeah, Terry, those birds would be all shot up and on fire sometimes, and they could still land those things."

"Yeah, well, I still don't like it one bit. I got me a bad feeling about this."

"Oh, enough with the bad feelings. We are going to land on Grand Bahama island in a moment with our wallets fat with cash and pretty birds walking all around us with little bikinis on flirt'n' with us. What could go wrong? And so 'elp me, Terry, if you say one more word about us crashing, I'll twist that flap of leather you call a tongue out of your ruddy mouth, I will."

Terry stared at Michael with mouth agape, rolling his tongue around for a moment, then turned to stare out the window. Gripping the armrest of his seat, he watched the black smoke bellowing past the window.

Just then Jim came on the intercom. "Okay, everyone, stay seated. We are about to land. There is a crosswind, so it might be a rough landing. But stay seated until we come to a full stop."

Jim looked over to Juky after making the announcement and said with a smile, "Those boys don't know just how rough it's going to be for them once we stop, do they, Juky?"

Juky gave a wary smile back at Jim. "Lets 'ope dat de authorities will be der to meet us when we stop dis plane, and dat dey believed our story about kidnapping me aund stealing de sailboat."

Jim turned his full attention back to landing the Water Lily. Even though he had landed planes before with an engine out, it was still a risky maneuver. So to improve things, he planned to adjust fuel and air mixture on the misfiring engine to the correct settings on their final landing approach. This would give the engine time enough to clear and begin running smoothly again before touching down.

Making the turn to start their final approach, he made the adjustments to the fuel and air mixture. Leveling out and lining up on the runway, he expected the engine to begin to smooth out;

however, it continued to belch black smoke and struggle to continue running. Having to keep both hands on the controls, he quickly told Juky to make the further adjustments telling him the new settings.

Juky reached up to do as told. Suddenly, thick black smoke belched from the engines' exhaust, shuddering the plane violently as the prop's rotation began to slow! With the runway now only a mile or so ahead, there was no time to try and refire the engine. Jim cursed out loud, "Dammit! Now we really do have an emergency. Better belt in. This could get a little dicey."

Terry saw the prop come to a complete stop. With eyes frozen on the crippled engine, his voice quavered as he spoke out loud, "Aye, mates, that, that bleed'n' engine stopped. I—I don't like this one bit."

Martin barked back at him, "Be still, ya quid. I told ya it will be okay."

Michael looked out his window to see the engine's prop had indeed stopped. He never cared for flying much, never cared for the feeling of not being able to control what was happening. And right now, the feeling he had was worse than just being out of control.

Looking toward the closed cabin door, he hoped that their pilot knew how to land this beast on just one engine. Without warning, the plane suddenly crabbed sideways; instantly, the left engine revved higher, roaring loudly. Slowly their flight path straightened.

In the cockpit, Jim was very busy, his concentration level off the charts; that sudden crosswind caught him by surprise. Not because he didn't know there were crosswinds; he took note of the wind sock on his approach. What had surprised him was the intensity of the sudden blast of air. He remembered then about that cursed tropical storm swirling to their south.

"That's great," he said out loud.

Juky was watching him and knew he was really working to keep them flying. "What es et? What's de matter? Can I 'elp?"

Without looking at Juky, he answered, "It's that damn storm. It's spinning off gusts of wind. If we get a gust like that last one as we are about to touch down, we might wind up spinning like a top down the runway."

Jim shot a quick look at Juky and realized too late that he shouldn't have said that. He then added, "But don't worry. I'm not going to let that happen. I can't. The Lily is my lady. I take care of her, and she takes care of me."

Juky brought his eyes to meet his, giving Jim an affirmative nod. "I just 'ope that you two are not 'aving a lover's quarrel right now."

Jim gave a short laugh but remained focused on the task at hand, trying to land a seaplane on one engine in gusting crosswinds, a fact that also had the Exuma airport very nervous. Preparing for the worst, they cleared everyone off the tarmac and rolled out their one and only fire truck.

Beads of perspiration dotted Jim's forehead. At the moment, he had them lined up perfectly with the end of the runway. Skillfully working the lone engine's throttle, rudder, and flaps all at the same time, he had them lined up right at the end of the runway, less than a fifty feet above it.

Clearing the end of the runway, Jim pulled back on the throttle letting the big bird settle to just above the runway. Everything was looking good, just feet away from making a safe landing. Without warning, it happened again! The tail of the plane was abruptly shoved sideways!

Chapter 56

"Oh god, no!" Juky yelled. Instantly Jim throttled up the engine while mashing hard on the rudder peddle. The engine roared in response; the aircraft rose back up a few feet giving them precious few seconds to straighten out before the Water Lily dropped hard on the runway. The late touchdown left little room to slow and stop. Reversing the prop's pitch, he jammed on the brakes, knowing full well they were never designed to be used in this manner.

Holding onto the sides of his seat, Juky's eyes were wide with terror watching Jim, who appeared like a one-man band working all the controls. Juky looked away from Jim to see the end of the runway coming up fast. Reaching for the cowling above the instrument panel, he braced for the worst. The whole fuselage shuddered under the stress, careening back and forth across the runway. The Water Lily's forward inertia finally broke, with only a scant few feet to the end.

Rolling to a slow stop, the nosewheel came to rest five feet from disaster. The overheated brakes emanated curls of smoke up and around all the landing gear. Jim idled the lone running engine, letting it cool some before shutting it down. Juky slumped back in his seat and stared at the cockpit ceiling. Jim checked over the instrument panel, then to his right at the stalled engine's exhaust still trailing wisps of black smoke. He matter-of-factly stated, "Jeez, I musta ran it a little too rich."

Shutting down the left engine, it became quiet, but only for a moment. In the distance, the sound of sirens coming closer could be heard. Soon the Water Lily was surrounded by airport personnel who leapt from the beds of pickup trucks, small cars, and an old '70s-era American station wagons—an all-white one sporting a big red cross on its sides. The lone antiquated fire truck took a position in the grass a few yards in front of the Water Lily. Jim and Juky looked to see several men piling off the fire truck while grabbing all manner of gear and uncoiling reams of fire hose.

Jim looked around at the *Keystone Cops*-like calamity erupting all around the Water Lily. With a smirk and laugh, he said, "Damn, we musta scared the shit out them."

Juky brought his wide-open eyes around to meet Jim's. "Out of *them*?"

Jim reached over and patted Juky's shoulder. "What this?" he asked, gesturing around at the runway and the interior of the cockpit. "This? This was nothing. Try that stunt with a rack of bombs still swinging in your bomb bay. If that doesn't make you pinch some vinyl up between your butt-cheeks, *nothing* will."

Just then sharp raps came at the rear door followed by Michael's agitated voice. "Aye, can we please get off-a this crate before she catches bleed'n' fire and blows up?"

Jim widened his eyes looking at Juky. "Well, let's go see if we can ruin these guys' whirlwind vacation in the beautiful Bahamas. You wait here while I go to see if my buddy with the local police is here with the two witnesses. Without them, it's just our word against theirs. I'll give you a whistle to come out so we have all the players, all right?"

Juky scrunched back away from the cockpit door. Jim opened it just wide enough for him to squeeze through. Michael nervously commented, "Boy, that was a close one, one to tell the grandkids, aye? But we made it to Grand Bahama, didn't we, boys?"

Jim stopped unlatching the rear hatchway door to look back at the three of them. "Yeah, ah, about that, this isn't Grand Bahama island."

"What? I told you we wanted to go to the bleed'n' big island." Michael bent low to peer out a window.

"Well, if I had tried to make it there, we'd all be swimming with the sharks right now."

"Where the 'ell are we?" Michael barked.

"Great Exuma island. This is the Exuma airport."

"What? This is where we left a couple o' bloody days ago. How far is this from the big island?"

Just then someone began pounding on the door. "Look, let me deal with all of the commotion outside, then I'll work on getting you where you want to go, okay?"

Michael dropped his head a bit, rolling his eyes. "Looks like we don't 'ave a bloody choice now, do we, mate?"

More pounding came. "Sorta looks that way, I'm afraid." Jim finished unlatching the hatchway door. He shoved the bifurcating door open to reveal a throng of people surrounding the rear of the plane.

Stepping on the top step, he raised his arms and began shouting to everyone. "It's okay. Everything is fine. Nobody is hurt, so please everyone back away so my passengers can disembark, please!" He repeated this as he descended the steps to the ground. The whole time he kept searching the crowd for his friend. Not seeing him, he reluctantly called for his passengers to grab their things and come on out.

Frustrated by not finding his police contact, he worried that these three were going to get off scot-free, which was making him none too happy. Somehow, he had to find a way to keep them from catching another plane to the big island. Muttering to himself, he said, "Cal, sure wish I had your conniving ass here right now."

Chapter 57

The Russian captain sat below deck still stewing on what happened. Shooting up the mast on purpose was the best way to see if that was truly an Interpol officer. If he was, he would radio his fellow officers to inform them of what happened and likely return to Abraham's Bay, which is where they were headed. If they didn't show up there, then he was sure they were headed to Cockburn Town, then that was a safe bet he had been snookered.

He had a nagging feeling that something wasn't right when it was going down. But he couldn't take that chance. A knock came at his cabin door. The first mate spoke through the closed door. "Сэр судно здесь нет. Каковы ваши приказы сэр?" ("Sir, the vessel is not here. What are your orders?")

Without opening the door, he barked, "Немедленно возьмите курс на Кокберн-Таун и не дайте нам быть замеченными. Теперь поехали!" ("Set a course for Cockburn Town immediately, and do not let us be seen! Now go!")

Grim-faced and still brooding over what had happened, he stepped over to a liquor cabinet. Grabbing a bottle of vodka, he poured a flight of Russia's best and tossed it back and set down with a rap, a menacing smile pressed into thick jowls as he spoke. "Давайте посмотрим, если вы можете фигня ваш выход из того, что идет." ("Let's see if you can bullshit your way out of what's coming.")

*****

Cal maneuvered the *Donna Marie* to within a half mile of the cruise ship and began turning to run parallel to it. Donna stood beside him feeling much more relaxed to have the protection of so many witnesses but was still wanting very much to be heading home. She missed being at the Salty Anchor and worried about the kids. The second she thought of them, she remembered that she was going to be a grandmother; this only intensified her desire to return home as quick as they could.

It was easy for Cal to read her thoughts; he knew what she wanted; he wanted the same thing. It was in these last moments of calm that he found he was missing the old bait shop a lot more than he ever imagined he would. In fact, it was the day-to-day routine he was missing the most. It was then at that very moment he understood Donna's reluctance to sell the place. She always could see past the superficial things to what was really important.

Cal cut his eyes to see her standing with her face braced against the wind, eyes fixed on what lay ahead, showing not an ounce of fear. Just like her dad would say, never let 'em see you sweat. Donna felt Cal's stare on her and turned to look at him, exclaiming, "What? Why are you looking at me that way?"

"Oh, nothing, just thinking about home. I'm definitely ready to head back. I'm ready to be just a bait shop owner again."

Donna gave a small smile then lovingly said, "Cal…it's a whole lot more than that, and you know it."

He held her gaze for a moment, then put his arm around her, saying, "I know it is. And I promise the second that mast is repaired, we are heading straight back there." He then gave her a kiss on the forehead as if to punctuate his words.

The two of them had been so engrossed in each other they hadn't noticed Cesar's approach, who spoke out as he drew near. "You know, to watch you both, one would swear you two to be newlyweds."

Cal and Donna had a slight look of embarrassment at being "caught" in a private moment. Cesar apologized. "Please forgive me. Et was not my intention to intrude, but I thought you would like to know dat we are not far away from de island now. It should be coming into view vury soon."

An obvious wave of relief washed over them, bringing broad smiles and nods of approval. Cal questioned, "How much further do you think?"

Pointing toward the cruise ship, he said, "Oh, maybe ten miles or less. De cruise ship, she begins to slow now."

Cal and Donna, because of their attention on each other, hadn't noticed that they were beginning to outpace the big ship. Cal questioned Cesar, "Should we slow as well?"

Cesar's smile went quickly away. "No, no, do not worry about de Russian. We are close enough to de island dat he will not likely try anything now. Besides, if he has followed us here, he will wait until the mast has been repaired, den dat es when he could be a problem once again."

Cal nodded his agreement. Donna gave him a worried look. "Do you really think he's going to come after the *Donna Marie* again?"

"I don't know, but one thing's for sure: we better act like he is," Cal stated.

"Then what are we to do, how do we protect ourselves from that psychopathic SOB, Cal?"

"Donna sweetheart, I'm afraid we are going to have to take this one hurdle at a time, and the first hurdle is getting that mast repaired."

"'E es right, Miss Donna, that es first." Bringing his eyes to meet Cal's, he added, "Mista Cal, keep yo-ah eyes on de horizon. When you see de land, change yo-ah heading to due east. We must come to the eastern side of de island. There is a narrow cut which leads to a landlocked cove—dis es there we will find de man who can repair de mast."

"Who is this man? What's his name?" Donna asked.

Cesar let go a boisterous laugh. "Who es dis maun, you ask? Nobody really knows. All anyone knows es that 'e showed up on de island maybe ten years ago after a bad t'understorm. His boat was badly damaged. He repaired he's boat, and when de people saw how good de work was, well, de islanders began bringing em more and more boats to be repaired."

"So what's his name?" Cal asked, repeating Donna's other question.

Cesar widened his eyes looking to each before answering, then said, "De local's call em El Jurakan, de Storm God, because of the way 'e arrived on de island. No one knows 'is real name. In fact, 'e lets no one see em make de repairs either. He hides much of his work beneath a large canopy of tarps at the end of a lone pier."

Donna shook her head, saying, "Great, that's all we need—another mysterious kook to deal with."

Cal shot Donna a disapproving look then emphatically stated, "Donna, I don't care if he's Attila the Hun as long as he can repair the damn mast."

Donna pointed a finger at Cal and was about to rebuke him when Cesar stopped them both with an excited pronouncement. "Look! Der es da shoreline! Quickly, Mista Cal, make de turn east."

Cal did as instructed, making an easy turn to the east. Slowly the wind began shifting in the sails. With the change of direction, the *Donna Marie* made a slow roll to list from the starboard to her portside. Her sails rolled, curled, and popped, momentarily falling slack before fully clasping the wind once again.

Cal loved to hear the sound the sails and the rigging made whenever he made these kinds of course changes. The *Donna Marie* made it seem so harmonious and peaceful and fluid like music. The wind and the waves were like elemental fingers on the keys of a heavenly instrument, playing a concerto of the sea. Seeing the coastline grow larger on the horizon, Cal had no idea what lay ahead for them. However, one overriding thought permeated this moment of bliss. He *had* to get them home no matter what, and nobody, not even a crazy Russian, was going to stop him.

Chapter 58

Jim descended into the clamor and commotion of the crowd at the bottom of hatchway steps, fruitlessly trying to get everyone to cease their shouting and shoving. Frustrated he stepped back up onto the lower steps so all could see and hear him, and hear him they did! Waving his arms in the air, he yelled out over the crowd, "Stop it, everyone, just shut up. Everything is okay!"

The crowd quickly began to quiet down. In the moment of calm, he spoke out over them again. "Thank you. Now, if you all would move back so that my passengers can exit the plane, please."

Slowly, with Jim's continued coaxing, everyone began filtering back leaving a large empty space at the bottom of the steps. Jim turned halfway around and shouted up through hatchway door for the three Brits to come out. Turning back, he watched the retreating crowd; for the life of him, he couldn't figure out why everyone was so interested in staying around. There was nothing to see.

Stepping off the ladder, Jim moved into the center of the half circle of people who remained mostly quiet. It was weird, he thought, how everyone was acting. It was as if they were waiting for some movie star or the Beatles to come popping out of the doorway waving to their adoring fans. Michael was the first to appear; a murmur ran through the crowd. Looking quite bewildered at the scene before him, he slowly descended the steps to the ground followed by Terry and Martin.

They all stood for a moment wondering what the heck was going on, for the crowd remained as a solid ring around the four of them. Jim spoke up once again. "Okay, everyone, let these guys through. They still have to get to the big island."

Jim had taken a couple of steps toward the crowd when a voice called out from behind the ring of people. "Just one moment please, stay where you are." The crowd began parting like the Red Sea in front of Moses. Into the gap created by the parting crowd stepped three Exuma police officers.

The lead officers tersely asked, "Who es de pilot of de plane?"

Jim gave a wary wave, saying, "That'd be me, Officer."

The officer nodded then asked, "And des are yo-ah passengers?"

"Yes, sir, they asked me to fly them to the big island, but as you can see, we had a minor problem."

The officer nodded but said nothing more to him. He then turned his attention to the three Brits. Taking a notepad and pen from his shirt pocket, he asked, "What es yo-ah names? You first," he said, pointing to Terry.

Nervously Terry answered, "Ah, Terry, sir, ah, Terry Worthington." The officer then gave a stern expectant look at Martin, which was quickly understood by Martin who warily gave his name as Martin Holbrooke. Holbrooke was an alias he would sometimes use. The officer then looked to Michael.

Michael was far less intimidated than his companions. With a tilt of his head, he elected not to give his name. Instead, he queried the officer, "Ey, mate, what's this all about? We ain't done nothing wrong. Now what's going on?"

The officer lifted his eyes from the notepad. With the end of the pen, he pointed at Michael. "Dat remains to be seen. Now yo-ah name please."

"Uh-uh, no way, not until you blokes tell me what's going on 'ear."

The officer dropped his hands to his side, then pointing the end of the pen directly at Michael, he firmly stated, "Vury well then, have et yo-ah way. De three of you are being detained for suspicion of kidnapping and piracy." Giving a short quick side flick of his head, two officers moved toward Terry while removing handcuffs from their belts.

"Ey, ey now, 'old on 'ear. We ain't done nothing of the sorts. We came 'ear to do some bleed'n' fish'n'. Who's tell'n' you these lies?"

"We 'ave witness testimony. A marine mechanic who saw de kidnap victim, a man, on a sailboat with you. Dis same man was later rescued by a dive boat captain from de waters not far from where you had been anchored offshore."

"Now wait just a damn minute 'ere. You can't arrest us on flimsy-ass evidence like that. I don't see no bleed'n' witness, and where is this kidnap victim? All you got is 'earsay."

Michael backed away from the officer, yelling out, "You got no evidence of any of that!"

Suddenly from above his head, a voice called out loudly, "Oh yes, he does. I em yo-ah victim!"

Michael turned to look up at the open hatchway. His eyes widened in disbelief. "You? But, but 'ow?" Michael turned back to look at the officer, then at Jim who was sporting a huge smile. "Looks like you stole the wrong sailboat."

"This is crazy!" Michael roared at the officer. Terry and Martin began loudly pleading for Michael to do something. Just as the officer produced his pair of handcuffs, a wall of water came arching from high over the plane crashing down on everyone causing all to scatter in every direction.

Jim raced around to the front of the Water Lily to see three firemen hopelessly trying to get control of a fire hose running full blast that was shoving and whipping the lanky men in every direction as they struggled to zero the blast of water in on still smoking engine.

Jim tore off for the fire truck shouting out to them, "Control that hose!" Skidding to a stop at the rear of the truck, he saw to his astonishment two firemen yelling and pointing and frantically trying to find the handle to the shut-off valve that had fallen off in the muddy water in which they stood. Their efforts were being made worse from the hydra-like fire hose whipping back and forth sending intermittent torrents of water crashing down on them.

Drenched with water, Jim shook his head at the hysteria going on all around his plane. Rolling his eyes, he darted around to the driver's side of the running fire truck. Stepping up on the running board, he reached in the open cab door and twisted the ignition key off. Immediately the water pressure began to abate, and the fire hose's wild gyrations began to slow.

The remaining three firemen who had been running back and forth like barnyard chickens being chased by a fox trying grab the runaway hose finally threw themselves on the slithering beast. Then, like a dying anaconda, the hose went limp. The men who had been holding onto the business end of the hose dropped the nozzle and collapsed to the ground.

Gazing around, Jim pawed the water from his face. He shook his head thankful that his plane wasn't really on fire. Soaked to the bone, he trudged through the mud puddles toward the rear of the plane. Over the noise from the crowd of people all talking at once, he heard his name being shouted. Taking off in a trot, he splashed through the mud and water around the tail section of the plane.

Clearing the rudder, he came face-to-face with a panicked Juky, shouting, "Quickly, hurry, dey are gone!"

"Calm down, Juky. What are you saying? Who is gone?"

"De men who kidnapped me, in all of de confusion, dey took off running. Dey are gone!"

Chapter 59

Cal deftly maneuvered the *Donna Marie* into the mouth of the narrow cut. With sails stowed and running on the diesel engine, he had all eyes watching the water's depth. Donna was at the bow. Johnny Mac and Cesar were at the port and starboard sides.

Cal shouted out to Cesar, "How much farther?"

"All de way to de end of de pier, Mista Cal."

Cal mumbled to himself, "Great, that's what I thought you'd say."

"Our destination es straight ahead now. Aim for de square structure made of green army tarps."

"Roger that. All of you keep a sharp eye out."

Without taking her eyes off the water, Donna called back to Cal, "Cal honey, it looks like the deeper dark blue area of water is getting much wider now."

Johnny Mac snickered, saying, "Yeah, honey, it's getting a lot wider now."

"Just watch the water smart-ass," Cal deadpanned back.

"Okay, Mista Cal, slow down and stop about a hundred feet away from de dock."

"Why? Why not dock?"

"You'll see. Just bring us to a stop, Mista Cal, please."

"Aye, aye, Cap'n. Donna, does it look like we have enough room for me to make a loop here to burn off some of our speed? We are too close to just reverse the engine."

"Yeah, it looks like it, but make it tight just to be safe."

"Okay, everyone grab onto something. She's gonna list a little."

Cal reversed the prop while cutting the rudder hard left. This had the desired effect of momentarily plowing the *Donna Marie's* bow down deeper in the water helping her to make a much sharper turn. The *Donna Marie* listed hard to port.

Cesar had to steady himself with both hands on the cabin rails to keep from losing balance. "Whoa, Mista Cal, dat is a great maneuver. You are a vury skilled sailor, I see."

Donna had squatted down to hold onto the end of the bowsprit and looked back at Cal, watching him make the quick turn. She had seen him do this a time or two before, but she was always amazed at how he could handle the *Donna Marie* with such confidence and ease.

He deftly spun the *Donna Marie* in a complete circle, pointing her back toward the dock and the large tarp-covered area that sat off to one side of the pier. With their forward speed cut to a crawl, Cal called out to Cesar, "How much farther?"

Cesar stood with eyes fixed on the tarped area off the side of the pier. "Dis es good right he-ah. Bring us to a stop."

Cal reversed the engine until they came to a complete stop. He then asked, "So what do we do now?"

Cesar held up a hand and walked to the bow where Donna stood. Cupping his hands on either side of his mouth, he shouted across the open water, "Señor Jurakan, may we approach? I have a vessel in need of repair!"

The lap of waves along the shoreline and the laugh of seagulls pirouetting overhead filled the otherwise quite lagoon. Cal spoke out to Cesar again. "We're beginning to drift. I can give him a blast with the foghorn."

Cesar waved his hand behind his back then shouted as he had done before, "Señor Jurakan, may we approach? I hav—"

Suddenly, the end of the tarps parted revealing the sullen face of a man looking like the typical ruddy movie pirate. A scraggly beard hung long from the chin of his narrow, darkly tanned, and deeply lined face. Long gray hair trailed down to his shoulders with the rest barely contained underneath a faded red bandanna. Cesar started to repeat his request but was stopped short again. "Stop yer beller'n'. I heard ya the first time!"

In a lower voice, Cesar called back to simply ask, "May we approach, sir?"

"No, you may not! I'm busy. Now go away. Come back in a week or two. I'll see if I have time then. Now go!" With that, the tarp snapped closed.

The four of them looked around at each other. Cal then fixed his eyes on Cesar. "Well, what to do we do now, Batman?"

Cesar shrugged his shoulders. Donna looked expectantly at Cal for some kind of answer. Johnny Mac, however, began to make his way to Cal at the helm stopping a few feet short. Cal gave him a somber look then asked, "What do you think, J-Mac, do we split and make for home? We *could* run with just the foremast rigged and leave the mainsail stowed, though it'd be slow going."

Johnny Mac nodded in consideration of what Cal had said. He then gave Cal a thoughtful look and said, "I think ole Jurakan might be hiding behind a big false image. And images are like balloons. Sometimes they need to be popped."

"Then what are you suggesting we do, J-Mac?"

"Ease us closer to the dock. I have an idea."

"And that is?"

"Just follow my lead."

Chapter 60

Cal did as he was instructed, easing them to within fifty feet of the dock. Both Donna and Cesar came to the stern to see what was going on. Donna quickly asked, "What are you doing, Cal? That kook told us to leave. Why are you taking us closer?"

Cal smirked and simply pointed to Johnny Mac. Donna gave Johnny Mac a questioning look. His reply confused her even more. "Dear lady, we are popping balloons. Just follow my lead."

Donna looked back to Cal who only shrugged his shoulders. Cal had them barely moving toward the dock. Johnny Mac watched their progress then patted Cal on the shoulder, telling him, "Hold us right here."

Doing as asked, Cal brought the *Donna Marie* to a smooth stop. They were close enough now to hear the sound of a hammer tapping on metal along with a graveled voice held low singing of all things an Elton John song, "Tiny Dancer." The rhythmic sounds of hammering and singing comingled in an odd mechanical harmony.

Suddenly, without warning, Johnny Mac loudly blurted out, "C'mon, Cal, let's get going! That ole' dock crab probably can't pour mud out of his own boot, let alone know how to repair a sailboat the likes of the *Donna Marie*."

Instantly, Cal understood what Johnny Mac was doing, chiming right in with his own condescending remark, "Yeah, you're probably right. I've seen guys like him before. They're all hat and no cattle."

Cesar caught on as well. "I am sorry to have bought you he-ah, Mista Cal. Apparently I was misinformed about dis man's abilities."

Johnny Mac spoke out again, "Cesar, I hear there's another fellow around here that does just as good if not *better* work than this ole' deck swabbie."

Cesar threw a puzzled look at Johnny Mac, and for a second or two was not quite sure how to reply. Soon a large smile spread across his face as he said, "Yes, yes, I believe yo-ah correct. I should 'ave taken us to hem first."

The hammering and singing abruptly halted. Seconds later the tarp was again brusquely tossed wide open. "What the hell are you talk'n' about? You can't take a sailboat that beautiful to a shipworm like him. Why, he doesn't know a yardarm from a bowsprit."

Cesar replied, "But, sir, you 'ave left us no choice."

Cal quickly interjected, "He's is right, so I guess we'll be going."

Looking back into his tarp-shrouded world for a second or two, he then turned back to face them. While the grumpy sternness of before had drifted from his face, he was still not exuding a jubilant Miss Universe smile. What they did get was a halfhearted wave and a groused order of where to dock. "You can tie her off there," he said, thrusting a bony finger first at them, then at the dock.

Cal smiled and spoke under his breath to Johnny Mac, "Good call, J-Mac." Then to Donna and Cesar, he said, "You two get ready to tie us off." Cal eased the *Donna Marie* alongside of the dock. Donna and Cesar quickly looped ropes around the pilings and tied off. It was then that they all felt a little relief. They and the *Donna Marie* were safe, at least for the time being.

It was a moment before their crusty shipwright fully emerged from his olive-drab-colored world of canvas. When he did, he began a slow assessing stroll down the dock next to the *Donna Marie* with a bottle of Jack Daniels hanging from the fist of his left hand. Clad in a pair of threadbare cutoff jean shorts, Bob Marley graced an oversized faded purple tank-top that draped from his shoulders. Slowly he scuffed along the sun-bleached dock planks in leather sandals that looked as if they had been made during the time of Christ. His feet were the same hue of brown as his sandals, making them appear as though they were part of him rather than something he wore.

The four of them stood in silence watching him slowly amble alongside the *Donna Marie*, taking a few steps, then stopping to gaze up and down her masts then along her decks. Each time he stopped, he'd take a swig of Old No.7 before resuming his slow stroll again. Arriving at the bow, he turned on his heels to face them. He stared at each of them, then down the full length of the *Donna Marie*. Suddenly, without a word, he lifted the bottle to his lips and chugged what was left of Lynchburg's best.

Clutching the now empty bottle, he began meandering back toward the stern while holding his gaze on Cal. Halfway to the stern he stopped. With his words one sip of whisky away from being slurred, he spoke out while gesturing with his bottled-filled fist, waving it at all the damaged areas, as he croaked out, "I can fix it all, everything, even sew up them holes in the canvas too. But! It'll cost ye."

Cal stared at him in utter disbelief, thinking, *Is he kidding, "It'll cost ye?" This guy's a joke.* Cal remained silent though and waited until he finished his ambling walk toward the stern before asking the obvious question of cost. Showing no expression, Cal flatly asked, "So, just how much *will it* cost?"

A humph escaped through his thin barely parted lips. Lowering his head down to the dock, he then turned his head slightly up, cutting his eyes to meet Cal's. He chewed and rolled his bottom lip. He then rasped out, "Two thousand dollars." Lifting his head and fixing his gaze squarely on Cal, he added, "And that'd be American dollars too."

Straight-faced Cal stared at him a moment. Cal's eyes suddenly narrowed as he raised a pointed finger. "Why, you poor excuse for an out-of-work movie pirate! I'll be dammed if I'm paying the likes of you that much money to fix a few bullet holes, that's for damn sure."

"Bullet holes? Just what are you doing in these waters anyway? You all look like an unlikely lot to be traveling together," he said, turning to face Cesar. He then questioned Cesar. "You look familiar to me. You go by another name, I think."

Suddenly, Johnny Mac spoke up. "Yeah, that's right. He is known as the Sawfish! Right, Cesar?"

Cesar gave Johnny Mac a furtive look, and then to El Jurakan, but only nodded his agreement to Johnny Mac's statement. El Jurakan widen his eyes holding them on Cesar, then in a cautious tone said, "Yes, yes, that's right. I know of you in these parts, and so do a lot of other folks. So tell me, Sawfish, have you commandeered this vessel? Where are your men? I hear tell there's a bounty on your head. Could be I'd make a lot more money turning you into the authorities than I'd get out of fixing this tub."

Cal had had enough of this guy and shouted out to Cesar, "Screw this jerk. I wouldn't let that sunbaked goat humper on the *Donna Marie*'s decks if he paid *me* to fix it!"

Donna spun around to face Cal, exclaiming, "Cal! What kind of language is that?"

"Donna, now's not the time. Besides, that's what he is, a dried-up old goat humper."

"Cal!" Donna barked. "Don't say that again! It's disgusting!"

El Jurakan doubled over in laughter. Straightening up, he pointed at Cal with the empty bottle still hanging from his hand, saying, "Would you look at that. We know who the *real* captain of this tub is now, don't we?"

Donna threw a furious look back toward El Jurakan who had begun laughing and walking to just past the *Donna Marie*'s stern. "You listen to me," she began. Shaking with rage, she commanded, "You'll stop calling the *Donna Marie* a tub this instant! Do you hear me? You...you...you, uhhh...goat humper!"

Cal immediately threw a wide-eyed surprised look at Donna but held his tongue. Donna, her face flushed in anger, tossed a quick glance at Cal then said, "Well, you're right. That's what he is!" She then looked from Cal to see what El Jurakan was doing behind the *Donna Marie*.

He had knelt down on one knee a short distance behind the *Donna Marie*'s stern, laughing and repeating "goat humper" to himself. Leaning over the water, he promptly immersed the empty Jack Daniels bottle into the crystal-clear water, letting it fill completely. Holding it for brief moment, he then released it. Motionless and silent, he watched the bottle drift slowly from his hand; his gaze remained on it watching a school of tropical fish skitter from its path until it gently settled atop a large pile of empties just like it ten feet below.

Donna's eyes flew wide open. In the next instant, she was on the dock storming her way straight toward El Jurakan. Cal saw what was coming and likewise jumped onto the dock in front of her to block her storm-trooper march toward him. "Donna, hold now, just stop right there! Just hold it and calm down!"

"Cal! Out of my way! He's not a goat humper—he's a damn pig! No, wait! That'd be an insult to pigs too!"

Cal grabbed her by the shoulders stopping her and imploring her to calm down. She angrily tried to free herself. "Let me go! I'm going kick that scrawny old buzzard's ass in the water."

"Donna, calm down please. Look, we are leaving. We'll just have to sail back home with one mast rigged. We don't need this jerk's help."

Donna began to calm a little but pointed around Cal. "Do you see what he's doing?"

"Yes, and I don't like it either. But this is not the time for this battle. Look, we are smack in the middle of hurricane season. We've dodged one bullet, and you know as well as I do that at this time of year these storms can pop up every few days. It's going to be slow going to get back home from this far south."

El Jurakan remained squatted on one knee smiling and listening to Cal and Donna from behind. He was feeling pretty good at the ruckus he had caused between them. Johnny Mac likewise watched the goings-on, waiting for just the right moment to speak. And right about now, he thought, was that right moment. What he was about to say though could change things, hopefully for the better, or it could make it worse. It all hinged on just how this mysterious, cantankerous man known as El Jurakan could take hearing the truth!

Chapter 61

El Jurakan was seconds away from injecting himself into Cal and Donna's tête-à-tête when Johnny Mac spoke up, posing a question to him, one that froze him where he stood.

"So tell me, do you see her face every time you let that bottle drift from your hand, El Jurakan, or should I call by your real name Mr.—"

Abruptly he stood, whirled around, and began shouting back at Johnny Mac. "Shut your mouth! Don't you say another damn word, or I'll, I'll…"

"You'll do what?" Johnny Mac challenged. "Get another bottle of Jack and try to keep washing that memory away?" Johnny Mac threw a quick glance in the water then added, "Judging by that pile of empties, I'd say it's not working."

Staring at Johnny Mac, his face twisted in confusion. He then looked away, casting his gaze down into the water at the pile of empty bottles looming below. His expression rapidly changed to one of deep despair. Taking a couple of heavy steps to the very edge of the dock, he knelt on one knee again. Stirring the water with the tips of his fingers, he solemnly, softly, almost in a whisper spoke, never taking his eyes off the water-distorted image below, "I tried to save you, I did, but, but…the waves, they…they kept hitting us. I couldn't hold on…I—" Suddenly he stopped. Slowly he stood turning to face Johnny Mac. Confusion, tinged with anger, painted his face and colored his words. "Just who the hell are you?" Looking around to the others, he added, "In fact, who the hell are *all* of you?" Looking back to Johnny Mac, he questioned him, "Why did you say that? How did you recognize me? I don't look anything like I did in the newspaper stories from back then."

Johnny Mac gave him a warm sympathetic smile, answering, "I didn't recognize your face. It was your soul that gave you away. Ellie's too."

He staggered back upon hearing that name, staring wide-eyed at Johnny Mac. He again questioned, "How do you know that name? No one called her by that name except for me, and only in private. It was *never* in the papers."

Cesar suddenly spoke up. "He knows because he es de Key West prophet. He is known even among some of des islands. And I can tell you he es one to whom you should listen."

Suddenly he pressed a hand over his eyes. He then swept it up over his dew rag-covered head. Turning away he began walking slowly toward the same place he had emerged from in the canopy of tarps. Cal tossed a questioning look at Johnny Mac who returned an eye-widened shrug of the shoulders.

Reaching the tarp, he threw it open, stopping before going in. He stared back at Johnny Mac with a hopeless look in his eyes. Hesitating a split second more, he then took a step to go inside, but Johnny Mac spoke out again, solemnly telling him, "She says she knows you did all you could, but she hates what you are doing to yourself. Says that's not the man she married."

Remaining stock-still in the opening, he held his stare on Johnny Mac who in that moment saw his face transform; years of sullen indifference began to melt away. Eyes once squinted in surly contempt fell softly open rimming with tears. His voice tight with emotion, he asked, "You…you can hear my Ellie?"

Johnny Mac silently nodded yes. Rubbing at his eyes with the back of his hand, he coughed a couple of times, then gazed around to all, finally settling his stare on Cal. He then firmly stated, "I will fix it all. No charge. *But*"—pointing to Johnny Mac—"not before he comes in here and has a long talk with me. Agreed?"

Cal cut his eyes to Johnny Mac who gave him a small nod; Cal simply stated, "Agreed."

"Fine. Now all of you go away, except for him." Again, he pointed to Johnny Mac. "He stays."

Donna gave him a puzzled look, questioning, "Go where?"

Mildly irritated with the question, he snapped, "It's a dock, madam. There's a town at the end of it. Go spend the money I just saved your husband."

Instantly Donna's face flushed red. Raising a sharply pointed finger at him, she was about to launch into him. Cal quickly pleaded with her, "Donna, Donna, now, now hold on. Don't go all Sherman's army on him. The nice man has agreed to fix the damage to our boat. Now let's do as the nice man has suggested and go into town."

This brought an immediate laughter-soaked comment from El Jurakan. "Ahh, ha-ha, you two remind me of me and my…" His laughter faded his brow knitted in a frown. "Go on now, the three of you, and don't come back till I send for you."

"But how will you know where to find us?" Donna implored.

"It's a small island, missy. I'm sure I'll hear you yelling from here." With a flick of his hand, he added, "Now go on."

Donna positively bristled with indignation. Turning to face Cal, she demanded, "Are you going to just stand there and let him talk to me that way? Aren't you going to do something?"

"No, I'm not. I'm going to do as the *kind* gentlemen suggested and start heading down the dock to shore." With that Cal stepped around Donna and began walking down the dock. Donna stood in shocked disbelief watching Cal leisurely stroll down the dock as though he was on a sightseeing tour.

Thrusting her hands on her hips, she threw a glare at Cesar who shrugged his shoulders then sheepishly stated, "I'm going with him." Stepping quickly from the *Donna Marie* to the dock, he began quickly walking after Cal. Donna stood there a moment more. Finally taking an exasperated breath, she exhaled a single frustrated word, "Men!"

Dropping her arms to her side, she looked back over her shoulder to Johnny Mac then at the surly, contentious man who only gave her a haughty smile, then nodded in Cal and Cesar's direction with a broadening smile. Twisting her tightly pressed mouth sideways, she stomped her way down the dock in an arrow-straight march toward shore.

"Take it easy on the natives, ma'am," he shouted after her. "They respond to smiles better than scowls." Deep laughter followed his words.

Hearing his taunt from behind her, she growled to herself, "Walter Caleb Arnold, you better hope there's a hospital on this island, 'cause when I catch up to you, I'm gonna—" She suddenly froze in her tracks ceasing her solitary rant and march down the dock.

She stood a moment watching Cal and Cesar walking away. She slowly turned back to see Johnny Mac going into the rectangular canvas world of the strange man known as El Jurakan. It was then that all of what had just played out moments ago right in front of her suddenly hit home. Why it didn't at the time she wasn't sure and could only blame it on the stress of their present situation. But whatever the reason, she now only felt a deep sadness and pity for someone who obviously lost a wife he loved to some kind of accident for which he's been blaming himself for God only knows how long.

She considered going back to apologize, but seeing the flap of the tarp fold closed, she realized that whatever was about to take place in there was going to be far more beneficial than anything she could say. Slowly she turned back toward shore. Lost in the magnitude of the moment, she focused her eyes on Cal. She held her gaze on him for a long moment, just studying him, paying attention to the way he walked, the way he gestured with his hands while talking. And though he was too far away to be heard, she knew well the sound of his voice and manner of speaking. In fact, she thought, *I know that ornery old man better than anyone else in the world.*

She took a last quick look back at the tarps that rolled and flapped in the warm ocean breeze, then back to Cal and Cesar, who by now had reached the end of the dock. A rumpled smile drew across her face as she thought, *I think I need to hang onto that old coot as long as I can.* She took a deep breath, yelled out to Cal and Cesar to wait for her, then took off in a brisk trot. Suddenly she felt a powerful urge to do nothing more than wrap her arms around his waist and enjoy just being with him no matter what or where life led them.

*****

It was late afternoon when the Russian's yacht eased up to Cockburn Town's docks along Front Street. Yuri had gambled that they wouldn't take a chance on sailing on with all those bullet holes in their mast and sails. In need of fuel and supplies, he would take this time to figure out his next move. But first he needed to know if they had indeed come here for repairs. Standing at the stern, he brusquely ordered two of his men to go and search for the *Donna Marie*. A vessel such as that he thought should be easy to find.

Meanwhile he needed a bite to eat and a place to think. After barking some last-minute orders to the remaining crew, he departed for the center of town a short distance away. During his brief walk, he ruminated on his encounter with the supposed Interpol officer.

Finding a quaint restaurant and bar, he situated himself at a small table in a dimly lit corner facing the front door. He needed to relax and think. His order of fried calamari and wine was promptly served to him; he paid and tipped the waitress with a request to not be bothered anymore, for which she was all too happy to oblige the gruff foreigner's request.

Chewing slowly and taking small thoughtful sips of his wine, he dwelled on the encounter. Remembering the last minutes of their confrontation, he suddenly jammed the end of his fork into the wooden table, angry at himself for losing his temper that way. Because of that, he not only came away with nothing, but worse, he had essentially armed them with one of his own machine guns, albeit with not much ammo left.

Finishing the last bite of calamari, he promised himself he would not make those same mistakes again. Lifting his wine glass to enjoy a last long sip, he peered through the bottom of the glass toward the front door. Just as the last bit of wine drained from the glass, bright sunlight filled the goblet along with the distorted image of three people trailing in the door. He kept the wine glass to his mouth dropping it ever so slightly to peer over its rim. He couldn't believe his eyes! It was them, right here. He tensed a little waiting to see where they were going to sit. Dropping the glass slowly away from his face, a smile spread slowly across his wide square jaw.

Pouring the last of the wine into his glass, he quietly laughed to himself, thinking, *Yuri, it looks like your fortunes are about to change.* Lifting the glass, he gestured as if giving a toast to an unseen table mate, softly saying, "За второй шанс." ("Here's to second chances.)

Chapter 62

Kevin had just hung up the phone from talking to Jim who had called from the Exuma airport. In the call, Jim had informed him that they had indeed found the pirates who had taken the *Donna Marie*. He further informed him that his mom and dad were safe and safely aboard the *Donna Marie* and sailing for home; he, of course, knew nothing of their encounter with the yacht. However, that bit of good news gave Kevin wave of relief.

Jim also gave Kevin the Reader's Digest version of all the events that had led up to getting the *Donna Marie* back including the Keystone cop-like buffoonery that had occurred at the Exuma airport that resulted in the three crooks escaping after he had tricked them into landing there. He went on to say that one had already been captured with assurances from the authorities that it wouldn't be long before all were in custody.

During their conversation, Kevin elected to not reveal that he and Tammy had decided to get the authorities involved, after one of their regular customers who happened to be an FBI agent questioned as to where his parents were. And given that they hadn't heard anything more since the pilot who had flown his mom to Rokers Point had come in with an update, they felt they had no choice. In their conversation with the FBI agent, he informed them that he would make some inquires with the Bahamian authorities and Interpol to see what he could find out and ask them to keep an eye out for his parents.

With the knowledge now of what Jim had related to him about his mom and dad's location, he reckoned that they should be back in a couple of days. While he was relieved with the news about his mother and father both heading for home, he felt he couldn't relax until he saw them tying the *Donna Marie* to her berth. While thinking about all that had happened, he looked up to a picture hanging on the wall above the desk. In it were his parents standing in front of the *Donna Marie*, arms around each other with smiles as wide as the blue sky above them. He smirked as he spoke quietly to himself, "You two are in for the ass-chewing of your lives when get you back."

*****

Yuri had managed to ease his way into the kitchen without being seen and slip out the back door of the restaurant after handing the cook some cash to keep quiet about his departure. Hurrying back to the yacht, he wanted them out of port fast. Coming down the dock, Yuri was already barking orders at the crew. Men began quickly readying to leave port. The twin diesel engines rumbled to life as he stepped aboard. Dock lines were tossed away, running lights flashed on, shimmering on the water along with the dusky leftover light of a newly set sun.

His crew had, as usual, precisely followed his orders, refueled now, and restocked with provisions, including more ammo *and* another machine gun. That was the one thing Yuri loved about these islands; if you knew who and where to look, you could get just about anything you could ever want—for a price that is. Looking back toward shore, he smiled. They were ready to go.

Yuri wasted no time ascending to the bridge telling the helmsman to take them out as soon they cleared the dock. With the information he had from his scouts, he now knew where the *Donna Marie* was and that there was only one way in and out of the cove where she was berthed. He briefly considered just going in there and commandeering her but quickly thought better of that, reasoning that it was more prudent to let the repairs be made and not cause a scene. This would also allow him time to devise a plan for taking the *Donna Marie*, and then make for a rapid crossing of the southern Atlantic.

Yuri smiled while dwelling on just how much pleasure he was going to have making those aboard into shark bait, especially the one called Cal! The woman he considered could be of value in other ways. His eyes narrowed. A crooked and evil smile slithered across his face while saying, "Yes, she is quite attractive." His ruminations of Donna were interrupted when the helmsman asked for the coordinates of where he wanted them to go. Irritated with the interruption, he tersely stated, "It does not matter! Just take us out of sight of land."

A stiff nod was returned. The big yacht backed smoothly away from the dock. Clearing the end, it quickly spun away. A burst of turbulent water gushed from the wide stern as the powerful diesel's exhaust sent bellows of black smoke curling and rolling with the water.

Yuri turned back to watch the shoreline grow rapidly smaller. Soon, he thought, he would either have that sailboat, or it and all aboard would go to the bottom of the Caribbean Sea. At that moment he cared nothing about the money he would lose if the latter occurred. Only one thought consumed him now, and that was to pay back the son-of-a-bitch who had embarrassed him in front of his crew. That thought brought an immediate deep smile as he said to himself, "Yes, you *will* indeed pay."

Chapter 63

Pushing open the door of the police station to leave, Juky commented to Jim, "I suppose you will be flying back home in de morning?"

Walking side by side, Jim looked down at his feet in consideration of what Juky had said. He then thoughtfully replied, "Yeah, I suppose so. I mean there's no reason for me to hang around here, right?"

Juky likewise walked along looking down, his thoughts in pace with his slow purposeful steps. He suddenly stopped, wistfully asking, "Do you suppose dey are okay?"

Jim stopped a couple steps beyond Juky turning halfway around, peering at Juky for a moment before speaking. Then, sounding more like he was trying to convince himself than Juky, he said, "Oh, yeah, I'm sure they're fine. I mean they both know how to sail, and, well, they had enough supplies aboard, right?" Jim's eyes widened. "Hey, and look, Cal said they could make it back to the Salty Anchor in short order, right? So I wouldn't worry. Say, why don't you fly back with me? We'll get there before them and…and have a big welcome home party when they arrive, whaddya say?"

Juky held his eyes on Jim a moment, and a half-hearted smile came to his face. Nodding, he said, "Okay, I suppose you are right." Juky's face brightened, adding, "After all of dis, a party might be just what we all need."

"Great, let's go see about getting a room for the night, get some sleep, and head out in the morning."

Juky gave Jim a big smile, saying, "Sure, dat sounds like a good plan." Resuming their slow stroll in the dusky light of early evening, a pole light winked on as they strolled underneath. In that brief moment, the pyramid of light shone on them like Humphrey Bogart and Claude Rains in the last scene of *Casablanca*. And not unlike like their movie counterparts, they too were unsure of what the future held.

*****

Cal, Donna, and Cesar were confused when the young waitress, concerned for their safety, came to their table and informed them of what the brusque customer had done by slipping out through the kitchen. She told them that he gave the cook a big tip, telling him not to tell anyone about his being there. Cal asked her, "So if he said not to tell anyone, why did you pick us?"

She looked around the empty dining room, then like Vanna White, she spread her arms out wide, firmly stating, "Because you are de only *anyones* in here, and I worry dat he might harm you. He quickly left after you all took yo-ah seats. I get de bad feeling from hem."

"Do you know him? Cal asked.

"No, and I do not wish to. He seemed to be vury angry, dat one."

"What makes you say that, was he mean to you?"

"No. Abrupt and surly, yes. He paid right away, telling me to not bother hem anymore. But each time I pass by de table where he sat, I hear hem speaking to hem self in he's own language."

Cal's eyes widened. "In his own language? So it wasn't English?"

"Oh, heaven's sake, no." Her eyes widened with a laugh. "It sounded like Russian. Now I don't understand hem, but et was easy to know he was vury angry about something, so I put two aund two together as dey say, so here I am."

Cal and Donna's eyes met. Donna nervously said, "He's followed us here, Cal."

"Yeah, it sure looks that way."

"Do you have de problem with dis maun?"

"You could say that," Cal replied.

Donna quickly added, "He's trying to steal our sailboat is the problem."

The young waitress widened her eyes. "I see." Looking back to where the Russian had sat, she continued. "Where es your boat now?"

"It's in the cove getting some repairs done," Cal said, pointing in the general direction.

"Ah, so it is with El Jurakan. He es de best one for dat."

Donna rolled her eyes. "Yeah, well, he could use a few lessons in manners if you ask me."

The young waitress smiled, nodding her understanding. "Yes, he pinches at you like de crab with his words sometimes. But I know he only do dat so no one gets close to hem."

The waitress then looked to each of them, focusing her attention on Cesar. "You 'ave been here several times before. Where are de men who accompany you?" Not waiting for an answer, she cast a quick look at Cal and Donna, adding, "And why are you two with hem?"

Cal pressed his lips tight as he thought, and then said, "Well, young lady, it's kind of a long story, but the short of it is, someone stole our sailboat from us, and we came to get her back, which we have. But that Russian A-hole is trying to take it away from us now."

She threw a look to Cesar again, suspiciously asking, "Aund dis one is helping you?"

Cesar immediately laughed out loud. "Ah, I see you know my reputation, but it's not as you think. I am truly trying to help. As for my men, dey will be he-ah soon."

Cal gave him a curious look but elected to not question him about it right then. Instead he asked her, "Has that Russian been in here before?"

"Goodness no, well, at least not while I 'em working, but I can ask around de other bars and restaurants along de avenue aund see if anyone have seen hem before. He will be an easy one for de people to remember."

Cal thanked her and then asked where they could get a room for the night. She gave them two suggestions, both of which were a short distance away. She then added, "I am 'appy to help, but be careful of dis maun. I think hem to be a vury bad maun." She wrote a phone number on a scrap piece of paper and handed it to Cal. "Call me here about this time tomorrow. I may have information about hem by then."

Cal glanced at the number then folded it into his shirt pocket, saying, "Thanks, I'll do that."

Just then a large group of people came in the restaurant talking loudly and obviously on their way to being seriously drunk. Fortunately, they snaked their way through the tables and chairs to the opposite side of the dining room. The waitress rolled her eyes. "Uh-oh, looks like de fishing tournament people are coming back in. Dis is when et get crazy in dis place."

As she started to leave, Cal stopped her by asking, "Hold it, what is your name, young lady? Who do I ask for when I call?"

"Oh, I em so sorry," she said, laughing. "My name es Anya, Anya Brigitte."

Smiling broadly, Donna said, "What a pretty name." Anya's smile brightened as their eyes met. Then with a wag of her finger, she again admonished them to be careful about the Russian. She then excused herself to go and deal with the table of inebriated and sunburned patrons. She had no sooner walked away when three of Cesar's men appeared at the doorway; they quickly scanned the room locating Cesar. Two of them immediately took positions on either side of the doorway while the third came straightaway to their table.

Cesar's easygoing manner and smile vanished as the bodyguard arrived. Expressionless, the bodyguard glanced at Cal and Donna then bent down and spoke low into Cesar's ear. Cesar nodded, then whispered back into the man's ear who gave one firm nod then left the table. Cal and Donna watched him stop to speak to both men at the door. He then opened the door and left. One of the men at the door then walked to a darkened area of the dining room taking a ridged stance a few steps behind Cesar.

Cal and Donna watched this all take place and were actually a little impressed with it. Cal then gave Cesar a nod and smile, saying,

"Pretty impressive. You've done a good job. They seem well trained, Cesar."

Cesar laughed then said, "Well, I wish dat I could take all de credit, but several of my men also work for de police on some of de islands."

"Let me get this straight. You have cops working for you? How in the heck does that work if you are engaging in less than legal commerce?"

Cesar again laughed out loud. "Cal, ma friend, der es much you do not know about me. Des men do not make much money being police officers. So I 'elp them to 'ave better lives."

Call shook his head while answering, "I gotta say you folks' certainly have an odd sense of right and wrong."

A short laugh came with Cesar's reply. "Not really, ma friend. Des men know who de real criminals are, so all I'm doing is making it more difficult for dem, kind of like yo-ah Steve McQueen in de old TV show." Cesar snapped his fingers while struggling to remember the name of the TV show.

Cal scrunched his brow in thought trying to remember, then triumphantly said, "Oh, you mean that old show, *The Bounty Hunter*."

"Yes, yes, dat es de one. I em like hem. I make sure de police capture de bad ones."

Donna gave Cesar a head-tilted look, questioning him, "So you don't hack people up and feed them to the fish?"

"Oh, heaven's sakes, no, Miss Donna. But as I told you before, in de islands, a bad reputation can be your best weapon. You see, most of de criminals, dey like to prey on de weak and vulnerable as you have seen. So with my reputation together with ma men, I can operate with much freedom making it appear as though I am vury powerful and not to be trifled with. This has been vury effective."

"But Miss Ginger—the note she sent said not to harm us and to help us get home. So you were coming to take the *Donna Marie*."

Cesar laughed as he answered, "Miss Donna, my cousin thinks she knows everyt'ing goin' on in des island, but she doesn't know all about me."

"But she said you were coming to take our sailboat when that crazy Russian showed up, and it was Miss Ginger's note that changed your mind, right?"

Cesar again laughed as he answered, "Miss Donna, I guard my reputation like a fine jewel, even from dose such as ma dear sweet cousin. I'm sure you can understand why. I do it for her protection."

Cal finally interjected, "Look, honey, stop grilling him. I get what he is doing. Back during the war, there were all kinds of operations similar to what Cesar is doing."

Donna widened her eyes then said, "Well, it all seems so dangerous and convoluted to me."

"Look at it dis way, Miss Donna. I am not unlike de chameleon. I am adapting to de environment in which I live. De criminals, dey only see me as a criminal like demselves, so my reputation only adds to my camouflage."

Just then the bodyguard who had left returned and came immediately to Cesar and again whispered to him. Cesar nodded, answering in similar fashion. The bodyguard nodded, turned, and retreated to the front door and left.

"So what's going on, Cesar? Why all the mystery?" Call asked.

Cesar drifted his eyes to both of them and, with a somber look, said, "It appears as though our Russian friend 'as departed from de island."

Donna hopefully remarked, "So that's a good thing, right?"

Cesar somberly stated, "He has left the de island but not de surrounding waters. He sits about two kilometers offshore."

Cal let his hand drop hard on the table in frustration. "That Siberian bastard, what is his problem?"

"I suspect that you have injured his pride, and now he seeks revenge. Men such as hem have big egos and small minds."

Cal rolled his eyes, saying, "Great, we have a Slavic Tyrannosaurus rex chasing after us."

"Cal honey, what are we going to do?"

Cal's brow arched high. "Pray a meteor flames down to get the one dinosaur the last meteor missed."

"Stop joking, Cal, I'm serious. Even if that surly beach bum repairs the *Donna Marie* perfectly, we can't outrun that yacht."

Cal understood her worry. Patting the back of her hand, he said, "I know, sweetheart. I don't have an answer right now. I haven't had time to study the pieces on the board yet."

"The board? What are you talking about, Cal?"

"The chessboard. This is a game being played out, a high stakes game. So just like playing chess, you have to see several moves ahead of your opponent, and to do that, you have to study the board."

Cesar let go a short laugh while saying, "Yo-ah man is quite right. What you both need to do is go and get a room and relax."

"Relax!" Donna shot back.

"Why, sure. A relaxed mind always thinks clearer din one filled with de trouble."

Donna started to reply, but Cal stopped her. "Donna, he is right. We are both exhausted. Let's do as he suggested: get a room, relax, and catch some shut-eye. We'll feel much better in the morning.

"Cal, how am I supposed to relax enough to sleep knowing that Russian kook is out there waiting to kill us?"

Cal's eyes met Donna's as a big one-sided grin pressed deep into his cheek. "Well, I can think of one way that will relax you enough to sleep."

Donna's mouth and eyes flew open. "Walter Caleb Arnold! What kind of talk is that, and in front of a total stranger no less? Really, I don't know what gets into you sometimes. I'm not some little trollop that's gets twitterpated at such talk."

Cal held up a hand to her. "Easy, easy, honey, you're proving my point that you need to relax and get some rest. I'm not the enemy here. And Cesar isn't a stranger...well, not a total one anyway. Look, I'm sorry if I upset you. Come on, let's go get a room and get some sleep, okay?"

Suddenly Cesar pushed back from the table. "Look, I have some business to attend to. Miss Arnold, try not to be too hard on yo-ah husband. It es vury plain to see dat he loves you vury much."

Donna held her eyes on Cesar for a moment, then let go an exasperated breath and said, "I suppose you're both right. I am tired."

Giving Cal a sideways glance, she added, "C'mon, let's go find the place Anya told us about, it sounded nice."

Cal smiled and patted the back of her hand, saying, "Sounds good to me." Looking at Cesar, he said, "So where are you headed?"

"I have friends here on de island. I too need some rest. Perhaps we'll talk tomorrow or perhaps not. Our friend, El Jurakan, seems to be in control of things for de moment."

Cal gave him a smirk while saying, "It sure looks that way. Better him than that crazy-ass Russian."

Rolling her eyes, Donna added, "Boy, you can say that again."

Cal pushed back his chair while taking Donna's hand to stand. "Cesar, guess we'll see ya whenever, huh?"

"Of dat you can be sure. It won't be for more than a day. You two need to rest up and relax." Bringing his eyes to meet Donna's, he added, "By de way, dey have phone service to de States here. You can call home."

Donna's whole demeanor changed in an instant. "Really? Cal, did you hear that? We can call the kids."

"Yes, yes, sweetheart, but let's get a room first then we can see about calling them, okay?"

Barely able to contain her emotions, she put her hand to her mouth giving him short quick nods. Turning her to leave, Cal put his arm around her shoulders and started them toward the door. "C'mon, honey, let's go get a room."

She worriedly asked, "And then we can call the kids, right?"

Cal calmly replied, "One thing at a time, Mrs. Arnold, one thing at time."

Chapter 64

Closing the door of the restaurant behind them, Cal and Donna strolled along the sidewalk next to the docks both lost in their own thoughts. Donna's were of course on making that phone call home and trying think of what to say to them that wouldn't worry the hell out of them. Cal's thoughts, on the other hand, were focused on their immediate dilemma which had him taking repetitive glances out to the waters well beyond the docks.

Cal knew he had pissed the Russian off pretty bad, bad enough to know that another encounter with him would go much differently and no doubt with a grim outcome. Because of that, he knew it was time to send Donna home. Since this was one of the few islands that had phone service to the States, it would be no problem to call the pilot who had flown her to Rum Cay or even maybe to get Jim to fly down here and take her back home.

His problem was how to get her to go. He knew she would fight him like a wildcat about going home. Cal smirked while thinking about getting her plastered and then loading her on the plane after she passed out. After all, she didn't drink much, he thought, so it wouldn't take much. Taking a quick sideways glance at her, he knew that once she woke up, that poor pilot would catch hell. He let go a little chuckle, thinking, *Well, I could tie her up and gag her.*

Donna caught his little laugh. "You want to let me in on the joke?" Cal's eyes widened as he quickly thought of what to say.

"Oh, uh, just thinking about how mad the crazy-ass Russian was when he hurled that machine gun at me."

"And you think that's funny, Cal? He could have shot you instead of our sailboat."

"Yeah, but he didn't. That means I made him question himself, something I'm sure he's not accustomed to doing, and that is what I think really got to him."

Donna gave Cal a matter-of-fact look while stating, "Well, I doubt he'll be so pliable next time."

"No, you're right about that. But that Ivan SOB is a hardcore type-A personality. And if there is one thing I've learned, it's that type-A people can be easy to manipulate."

"What? How so? He seems like he doesn't take orders from anybody."

"You're right about that. But he is also predictable, and that temper of his is his Achilles' heel."

Donna stopped walking, making Cal stop as well. "So if he is so predictable, then you knew he was going to hurl that gun at you?"

Cal gave Donna a smiling arch of the eyes. "Well, let's just say I was pretty sure he wasn't going to shoot me."

"Pretty sure! That's a very thin line to risk your life on, Cal."

"Look, Donna, it's hard for me to explain, but most of the commanding officers I came across in the navy were type-A guys. They live by a rigid and ordered way of thinking. That's why when something comes along that doesn't fit with their method of dealing with things, they become frustrated, and *that* is when they can be manipulated."

Donna gave Cal an inquisitive look while questioning, "Is that so? So when did you learn so much about psychology, Mr. Arnold?"

Straight-faced he replied, "I learned it the hard way—growing up without a father." He then smiled, adding, "That and a *Reader's Digest* article I read last month on personality types."

Donna rolled her eyes. "Oh, great, that makes me feel so much better now. So," Donna began again while resuming their slow walk, "just what personality type am I, Dr. Arnold?"

Cal threw her a quick look, asking, "Do you really want me to answer that?"

"Sure, this should be very amusing."

Cal pressed his mouth tight before answering her then said, "Well, I'd have to say that you are…" Cal turned back to look at Donna again before finishing. "You sure you want to hear this?"

"Go on, spit it out," Donna implored.

Cal shook his head a little before finishing what he was about to say. "Okay, here goes. I'd have to say that after being married to you for all these years that you are a definite type-A personality."

Donna practically skidded to a stop. Cal stopped a couple more steps beyond her, turning back to face her. Donna stood frozen with her arms folded across her chest with her mouth open wide. Cal remained where he was and stared at her with a slight smile, waiting for what he figured was coming.

"Walter Caleb Arnold!" *Uh-oh*, he thought, *she used all three names. Better hold on.*

"I can't believe you think that I'm like that…that crazy, ill-tempered Russian. I don't go around yelling and barking orders at people and, and throwing things at people. Now you take that back this instant, do you hear me!"

Cal remained silent and smiling, letting what she had just said kind of float in the air between them. She held her hot stare on him a moment more, then in a calmer but stiff voice, she asked, "So you're just going to stand there giving me a stupid smile?"

Cal's eyes squinted as his smile broadened. He then simply said, "Well, *this* is what a type-B personality does, Donna."

Donna's arms dropped to her side like they weighed two tons. "Look, smarty-pants, for your information, I read that same article, and there is no way you're a type B. You're a, a…type Z or something beyond that, 'cause sometimes you are *way* out there in left field, buddy boy."

Cal gave her a knowing nod while rubbing his chin then said, "Yup, that's exactly how the article said a type-A person would react."

Donna stomped her foot while jamming her hands on her hips. "Caleb Arnold! Stop calling me that!"

Cal stood for a moment more looking at his fiery-tempered Irish wife, glad that she had not lost any of her passion about herself or life. If there was one person that was anchored in knowing exactly who they are and what they believe, it was Donna Marie Arnold. And that was one anchor he never wanted to be cut loose from, ever. Donna stood with her eyes fixed on him waiting for some kind of response.

Cal's eyes softened as he closed the three-foot gap between them. Donna remained rigidly in place not quite sure what he was going to do. In an instant, Cal took another step closer then tossed one arm around her shoulders and the other around her waist, spinning her partway around and down at the same time, while planting a long firm kiss squarely on her mouth!

Donna's arms hung limply down behind her for a second or two, but as the kiss lengthened in time and passion, her arms rose and drew tight around his shoulders pulling him tight to her. Suddenly ending the long and passionate kiss but remaining close to her face, he said, "Damn, I love it when you get mad, baby."

They remained in their embrace for a moment longer as Donna questioned, "What? Is that why you poke at me like you do? Just to see me get mad?"

Cal whirled her back upright before replying but remained close to her. "No, not really. It just seems to happen naturally, I guess." Taking a small step back and staring intently into her eyes, he continued with what he felt she needed to hear. "Donna, look, haven't you noticed how much you've been snapping at everyone? This isn't like you. It's easy to see that you are under a lot of pressure. So am I, but I have an edge over you when it comes to handling stressful situations like this, don't you see?"

Donna held her gaze on him for a moment longer. She knew he was right about her and his ability to deal with stressful situations. His life growing up had been tough, and on top of that, being in a world war had put him in situations she couldn't even imagine. While it was true that his life experiences had given him an edge dealing with stress, she, however, could read him like a book.

Dropping her arms from his waist but remaining close, she said, "Yes, I know. This whole thing has had me all keyed up. *But* I can tell you this right now, Mr. Arnold—you are *not* sending me home."

Cal widened his eyes. "Who said anything about sending you home, Donna Marie?"

Tilting her head, a small smile creased her cheek as she said, "Your little preamble about the effect all this stress is having on me. That was your warm-up act to 'Honey, I think its best that you go home' speech. Right?"

Cal smiled broadly while looking her right in the eye. "Hey, you are getting really good at imitating me—that even kinda sounded like me."

Suddenly Donna's smile grew wide while looking past his shoulder. Pointing past him, she said, "Hey, look, there's the motel Anya told us about. Let's go see about a room and make that call home."

Cal turned to look where she was pointing; sure enough, about half a block away sat the Seas Edge Cottages. Donna walked past Cal talking excitedly. "C'mon, they are so cute. They're like little houses. Oh, and look, they have flower boxes under the windows and cobblestone paths between them, and all of it shaded by big mahoe trees. Look at the blooms all over them. They're just like the one we have back home."

With Donna talking of home, Cal felt that this, plus a call to the kids, was what would seal the deal on her leaving for home. *But the trick was when to spring his sales pitch on his Irish-blooded wife. Should he butter her up before or after the call home?* Walking a step or two behind Donna, who, like a real estate agent trying to make a sale, found more homey touches to the cottages to point out. Cal however was paying only cursory attention to her. His thoughts were not on flower boxes or cobblestone paths and shade trees.

Nearing the door to the main office, Cal threw a long look out past the docks. Somewhere out beyond the horizon, the *Donna Marie*'s fate awaited a final outcome. Again, he was confronted with the notion of just leaving with *Donna*. As much as they both loved the *Donna Marie*, it simply wasn't worth risking people's lives trying to sail her back home.

The squeak of the screen door's hinges to the motel office drew him away from his somber ruminations of the moment. Donna pulled the screen door open holding it for Cal to grab while she opened the thick wooden door just behind it. Pushing it open, a refreshing whoosh of cool air swept past them as they entered the small lobby.

A warm hello greeted them from an older rotund island woman who wasn't much taller than the reception desk she stood behind. But with a bright smile and a welcoming demeanor, she and Donna quickly engaged in conversation about the adorable look of the cottages. Meanwhile, Cal thrust his hands in his pockets, taking in a deep breath, and waited for the conversational quilting bee to slow down long enough to get the process of getting a room started.

While waiting for the ladies to exhaust themselves of all things homey and comfortable, he stepped over to a window and stared out at the ocean. His thoughts were still of going home and abandoning the *Donna Marie* to her fate; however, spooling around in the back of his mind, he found he couldn't let go of the notion that he could somehow still bring her home safe and sound.

Staring past the activities of the day-to-day life happening all along the shore of the busy harbor, he began to think more and more about how to sail the *Donna Marie* right out of here without that crazy-ass Russian even knowing they were gone. A small smile came to him as he thought that what he needed was a diversion. Something that would stop the Russian from coming after them long enough to make it impossible for him to know what direction they had taken.

Cal's eyes were suddenly drawn to a large deep-sea fishing boat that was being loaded with buckets of bait for the next day's group of sunbaked day-trippers to use. Cal continued to watch as the deckhands, working in a chain of five men, switched from dumping buckets of bait into a large storage bin that sat just behind the pilothouse to buckets of ice.

Suddenly, Cal snapped his fingers. Without taking his eyes off the men passing buckets of ice from one to another, he moved to within inches of the window and spoke out low. "That's what I need—bait! But what?"

"Cal...Cal honey, I need your credit card."

Not looking away from the window and still engrossed with the happenings along the docks, he gave an absent-minded reply,

"What...oh, oh yeah, sure, here you go." Reaching in his back pocket, he pulled out his wallet holding it out behind his back while maintaining his stare out the window.

Donna, puzzled by his disinterested reply and what could have him so mesmerized out the window, decided to see if he was really listening to her at all. Stepping over to grab the wallet from him, she calmly stated, "Yeah, honey, these cottages are only three thousand bucks a night, so I booked us for three nights. Is that okay?"

Cal, still engrossed in everything that was taking place along the docks, gave a vacant reply, "Oh, yeah, okay, that sounds good, honey."

A giggled laugh erupted from the woman behind the counter as Donna spoke right next to Cal's ear. "That's *nine thousand dollars*, Mr. Arnold."

Instantly, Cal's thoughtful stare out the window fell apart. He quickly spun around, sputtering aloud, "Nine thousand dollars! For, for what? What are you talking about, Donna Marie?"

Donna and the desk clerk both burst out laughing. With credit card in hand, Donna spoke out while returning to the reception desk. "Just checking your hearing there, Mr. Arnold. Book us for two days please. Oh, and do you have phones in the rooms? I need to make a long-distance call home."

"Vury well, two days, and yes, ma'am, we 'ave de phones, but de calls will be on yo-ah bill when you check out." Donna nodded her approval while handing the broadly smiling desk clerk the credit card.

Still confused about what Donna had said, he simply shook his head and turned his attention and thoughts back out the window to the activity along the docks and of bait. He then recalled something con men used all the time, the bait and switch. Again, lost in thought, he spoke softly under his breath, "A bait and switch scheme—maybe that's what's needed."

Donna came up behind him. Threading her arm around his waist, she asked, "What has got you so transfixed out that window, Mr. Arnold?"

Cal drew a thought-clearing breath. Still holding his gaze out the window, he exhaled his reply. "Oh, nothing really, just watching some men load a boat with bait."

Donna gave him a curious look. She knew by his tone and facial expression that something was indeed noodling around in that head of his. But rather than question him about it now, she wanted nothing more than to get to their cottage and make that call home. Though she had no idea what she was going to tell the kids, that wasn't what was important to her. All she wanted at the moment was just to hear their voices.

With her arm still around his waist, she nudged him toward the door. "C'mon, Einstein, you need to relax that brain of yours. Let's get to our cottage where we can wash the salt spray off us and get some rest."

Cal gave her a thoughtful smile. "I suppose you're right. A hot shower would feel great right about now along with a stiff belt of scotch."

Donna opened the door to leave nodding her agreement while adding, "Mr. Arnold, after the events of today, I might just join you in a belt of scotch myself."

A surprised look drew across Cal's face. "You? Having a scotch? Well, now aren't we becoming quite the salty sailor now."

"Oh, stop it. You talk like I'll be hanging from a light pole drinking rum from a jug and singing pirate songs."

Easing their way along the cobblestone path toward their cottage, Cal gave her a kiss on top of her head, saying, "I don't know. I seem to remember a certain someone at a pool party who was trying to do the Rockettes kick step on the end of the diving board while holding a margarita in one hand."

Donna elbowed him in the side. "Caleb Arnold! That was my fortieth birthday party, and I wasn't drunk. I just lost my balance, that's all."

Cal let go a deep laugh, saying, "Oh yeah, you did. When your butt hit that diving board, you shot up in the air with your drink going one way and you the other. The look on your face was priceless. Never laughed so hard in all my life. The best part is, we got it all on a home movie."

Donna rolled her eyes with a smirk on her face. "Yes, how can I forget? You remind me practically every time I take a sip of alcohol."

"Oh, not *every* sip. Just the ones that make you want to dance on diving boards."

Donna, wanting to change the subject from her and drinking, asked, "Hey, just what was it that had you so interested in watching a boat being loaded with bait?"

Cal cut a quick glance to her then said, "Not sure really, but I think a hot shower and that scotch might help me figure out what to do about our Russian *friend* out there," pointing out to the bay.

Donna's face went straight. "Yeah, we can't forget about our ill-tempered buddy now, can we?"

"No, we can't, Donna, but for now, I need to relax and think about bait."

*****

Yuri paced the confines of his cabin, silent and brooding. His thoughts of course were on nothing more than obtaining that sailboat *and* getting even with the one who had embarrassed him in front of his men. Sitting still anchored offshore only stoked his impatience. A waning moon would rise late showing less than half its light.

That fact disturbed him; his concern was held in the knowledge that in the darkness that preceded the moon's rise a vessel, even as big the *Donna Marie* could, with running lights off slip out of the cove unseen. He had originally ordered that they anchor out of sight of land. But now standing and staring out the window of his cabin, it was easy to see the glow of Cockburn Town's lights in the total blackness that surrounded the island. And *that*, he thought, was also a problem, a big problem.

Breaking his gaze from the window, he resumed his pacing, once again in deep thought. If he chose to move close enough to the island to see the mouth of the inlet where the *Donna Marie* was docked, the lights of the island would reflect off the *Akula* and give away his position. Holding the elbow of his upturned arm in his cupped left hand, he tapped and rubbed his fingers on the stubble of his jaw.

What he needed, he thought, was a diversion, or a trap of some sort, something that would bait them into making a mistake. Just what that could be eluded him for the moment. But something he felt would surely come to mind. However, just sitting here and waiting for his quarry to make the first move wasn't an option. Knowing that the repairs to their vessel could take a couple of days, he decided it was time to take them back to port and dock there once again.

What drove this decision was his memory of a time he and his father were hunting pheasant. A large brood had taken refuge in a sizeable stand of underbrush. And while he wanted to make some noise to try and flush them out, his father took a completely different approach. Instead of trying to flush them out as he wanted to do, his father instead crouched down behind some brush motioning him to do likewise. Crouched beside his father, his father whispered to him, "Yuri, be still and silent, and your quarry will come to you."

Choosing to not follow his father's example exactly, he thought that while he didn't want to make any "noise" to try and flush them out, there was nothing wrong with making his quarry a little nervous. Yuri smiled. Speaking out into the quiet of his cabin, he said, "Yes, it is time to keep quiet but also to prepare for the kill."

Chapter 65

It was late when sleep finally overcame them. Donna and Cal had been able to talk to Kevin and Tammy earlier in the evening and successfully, *they hoped,* convince them that everything was okay, telling them that they had at the last minute decided to wait out the tail end of the squalls that had churned up the ocean from the retreating tropical storm making for smoother sailing on their return voyage.

Their conversation then drifted, of course, to the Salty Anchor. Kevin and Tammy were both very anxious for them to return home because things were becoming very busy with lobster season underway. After talking business, Donna took control of the phone from Cal and turned the conversation to Tammy and her first prenatal visit with her doctor. Cal lay beside her and thought about bait again while they talked about pregnancy and things he didn't understand until he drifted off to sleep.

Donna reluctantly ended the call thinking she had convinced them that all was well. Hanging up the phone, Kevin and Tammy both looked at each other. Kevin gave Tammy a skeptical look, asking, "Tammy, did you believe any of that bull about wanting to wait until the seas calmed down before sailing for home?"

"Not a word of it. Your mom tends to use the word *see* a lot when she's not comfortable with what she is saying."

"Really? I've never noticed that."

"C'mon, Kev. Didn't you hear her? It was, 'See, we decided to wait and let things calm down see, and you see, Dad thinks it will make for a faster trip see.' She must have said 'see' ten times. There's something going on, Kevin. I can feel it."

Kevin held his gaze on her for a long moment. Picking up the phone again he said, "I'm calling the FBI agent we talked to the other day and tell him all about this. At least we know where to tell him they are now. But Tammy, I don't know if telling him that Mom says 'see' a lot when she's uncomfortable is going to be of much help."

"Kevin, I don't care what we have to tell him. We need to find a way to help Mom and Dad. I think they're in real trouble and are hiding it from us."

Kevin somberly nodded his agreement, thinking how when this all started, it was a cute and fun prank to pull on his dad. But now, not only was the worry he felt deepening, but worse was knowing that there was little he could do to help them, and that was the heaviest weight of all.

*****

It was midafternoon when Juky and Jim strolled into the Salty Anchor. Lobster season was in full swing, and the place was hopping. Both men stood amid the blare of the jukebox and the clamor of people talking and laughing while surveying the dining room for a place to take a seat. Abruptly, out of the din of sound and motion, a waitress whooshed by carrying a tray full of steaming crab claws and long-neck bottles of ice-cold beer calling out to them as she passed.

"There are two seats at the far side of the bar or at that table by the windows. Take your pick, boys."

Jim and Juky bobbed their heads around a moment trying to see where she was indicating with her quick head nod. Juky tapped Jim on the shoulder and pointed out the two open seats at the far end of the bar near the office door. Jim nodded and began quickly leading the way through the crowded dining room. They made it to the bar stools ahead of two sun-soaked tourists with the same intent, who, with a smile and a wave, simply shifted to the table by the windows.

Settling in, they sat taking in all the hustle and bustle. Leaning over to Juky, Jim spoke up. "Man, Cal and Donna must be doing pretty good. Look at how busy this place is."

"Yes, yes, it is vury busy, and so es de dive shop. In fact, de whole facility is crawling with people."

"Yeah, it gets this way every lobster season. All the islands get flooded with people from all up and down the east and west coast."

The bartender arrived unnoticed while they both were still looking around. Popping the thick wood bar top with the palm of his hand to get their attention, he loudly asked, "What are ya hav'n', boys, bottles or drafts?"

Startled, they quickly turned back around, each replying the opposite answer. The bartender raised one eyebrow and leaned on the bar with both hands. "So does that mean you want a draft and you want a bottle?" he asked, nodding to each.

Juky and Jim both nodded agreement to their preferences. The big hairy-armed bartender smiled and told them, "Got long-neck Bud as our afternoon special."

Jim quickly replied, "Then make mine a bottle too."

The burly bartender spun away while repeating the request out loud. "Two long-neck Buds it is."

Jim nudged Juky's shoulder nodding toward the office door as two ice-cold beers were set smartly down on paper coasters sporting the Salty Anchor's logo. Both men smiled watching a bit of beer foam and ice slurry drizzle down the sides of the frosty brown bottles.

Jim swooped up his bottle first while twisting halfway around holding it up for a toast; Juky quickly followed suit. Raising his bottle a bit higher, Jim said, "Here's to good times and here's to good beer. Let's not drink too much lest our butts get thrown outta here."

Letting go short laughs, they then took deep swigs letting a bit of foam drool onto their beard stubbled faces. Wiping their mouths with the back of their hands, they smiled broadly at each other.

Jim patted Juky on the back. "Well, we did it, mate. We helped Donna and that ole buzzard husband of hers get their precious sailboat back, now, didn't we?"

Juky's wide smile fell to little more than a smirk while staring down at the bar thinking about Jim's proclamation of success. He was about to express his reservations about the whole situation when someone called out Juky's name from off toward the office.

"Juky? Is that you? What are you doing here?"

Jim leaned back to look around Juky to see Kevin heading straight for them—his face held a look of concern and bewilderment as he quickly strode the short distance to stop behind them questioning Juky again. "What are you doing here? Juky, why aren't you with Mom and Dad on the *Donna Marie* helping to sail her home? What's going on?" Looking to Jim, he asked who he was.

"Oh, that's right. We've never met. I'm the guy who flew your crazy-ass dad all over southern Atlantic.

"So you're the one that about blew the roof off this place the other day."

"Yeah, that was me, but it was your dad's idea to get that low. But hey, have you heard from them, and are they on their way back?"

"They called last night saying everything was fine and that they would be heading home in a day or two after the waters settle down, which is a little puzzling."

Juky started to ask what he meant when Jim stopped him by pointing to the office door, saying, "Listen, can we go into your office, Kevin? It's too difficult to talk in here."

Kevin nodded agreement. Picking up their beers, Juky and Jim fell in behind Kevin. Halfway to the office, a shout came from behind, "Hey! You two! You gonna pay for those beers?"

Jim and Juky both stopped to look back to see the bartender leaning well over the bar top pointing a finger at them from his meaty, hairy-knuckled fist. Kevin stepped between them waving his hand in the air.

"It's all right, Liam. They're with me—the beers are on the house."

Liam gave a firm nod and wave. "Very good, sir, you be the captain of this ship."

Kevin pulled open the office door holding it for Juky and Jim to enter. Juky said as he entered the office, "I bet no one gets out of dis place without paying what dey owe, eh, Mista Kevin?"

Closing the door behind them, the clatter and noise of the dining room and bar instantly fell to a white-noise murmur. Kevin laughed a little. "Yeah, that's Liam Mahoney. We hired him maybe ten years ago, and boy, do the customers love him. He's big and brawny and has a ton of stories about Ireland. And in a little while, he'll have this whole place singing and dancing to old Irish folk songs."

Jim then said, "Man, I can't believe how quiet it got in here when you closed that door."

"Yeah, Dad fortunately had the good sense to heavily insulate the wall between the bar and the office, that plus this thick wooden door which came from a wrecked Spanish galleon that Dad found on an old house that was about to be torn down to make room for a condo. The contractor gave it to him." Kevin looked thoughtfully at the door for a moment, adding, "You should have seen him. You'd thought he had found a chest full of Spanish doubloons with the way he went on about this old door."

Kevin shook his head as if to clear his thoughts. Refocusing his attention on Juky and Jim, he asked, "What the heck is going on? Why are you here, what's happening with my mom and dad? They called last night and said they were fine—said they were in some place called Cockburn Town. They also said that they were waiting for waters to calm for a couple of days because of that tropical storm, which is bull. They have sailed in rough water before, and besides that, the *Donna Marie* can handle some pretty rough seas—she's not some little skiff."

Jim raised a hand, saying, "Wait, wait, they said they were where?"

"Cockburn Town. Why, what's up?"

Juky shot a worried look at Jim. "That es well south of de island of Mayaguana and Pirates Well where we found de sailboat."

Jim's cautious agreement didn't help to sooth Kevin's worries.

"Look, guys, you still haven't told me why *you* are here and Mom and Dad are not. What's going on?"

Jim gave a worried eye-cut at Juky then began, "We're *both* surprised to hear that they went farther south. Last we knew Cal was going to sail out of a narrow cut through a coral reef to avoid being seen by this guy called the Sawfish."

Smacking the palm of his hand down hard on the desk, Kevin's eyes flew open. "What? Who the hell is the Sawfish? And why on God's green earth did they have to avoid him?"

Jim rolled his eyes realizing that he wasn't doing the best job of reassuring him. "Look, Kevin, the important thing is that they called and said they were fine. If they're planning on returning a day or two later than expected, it sounds like everything is fine...right?"

Kevin looked at both men a long moment then grabbed the newspaper off the desk flipping through it until he found the weather report. Folding it back to the second page, he jabbed a finger on a black-and-white satellite image of the southern Caribbean.

Kevin somberly said, "Look at this! They don't have days to sit and wait. Another storm is out there."

Chapter 66

Cal and Donna had slept in late, a fact that Cal was still grumbling about at three in the afternoon. Donna paid little attention to his fussing, electing instead to simply enjoy going in and out of the small shops all along the waterfront and forgetting about their immediate situation for the day.

Cal had brief moments when he too got caught up in what they were doing rather than his concerns over how to leave the island unseen. He would smile and complement Donna on a sun hat she would try on or a floral print blouse she would hold up in front of herself asking his opinion. However, in the moments between his wife's ambling multishop fashion shows, his thoughts returned to how to get back home in one piece.

Without realizing it, they had walked a long way from the cottages where they had spent the night. The colorful tourist shops soon gave way to much-dingier structures that lined either side of the narrow shell road. They strolled past stacks of crab traps and the fish nets of commercial fisherman that hung from weathered wood drying racks, all of which tinted the air with a less than pleasant aroma. There were boat and auto repair shops, along with businesses with signs to let one know that they catered to the seedier side of human nature. This end of the island was solely about dealing with the local's daily lives and not the whims of tourists.

Cal took note of the stares from the men working in and around the eclectic mix of commerce going all around them. He began getting a bit nervous, for it was very apparent that they stuck out like a pair of rose bushes in a cactus patch. Donna was walking along with her eyes cast down recounting a story from her youth, one Cal had heard many times before but would never stop her from retelling it because he knew it made her happy to relive those memories.

Cal waited until she finished her story, which always ended with a little chuckle about how her sister's face looked when their dad had found out about their sneaking out one night to meet some boys. When she had finished telling her story, Cal suggested they return to their cottage. He had no sooner spoken when two men came from behind them and began walking with them, one on each side about an arm's length away.

The one next to Donna was tall and slender clad in a stained undershirt, cutoff jean shorts, and leather sandals. Dreadlocks dangled from under his multicolored knit cap. The other man walked to Cal's left just slightly behind. He was shorter and more muscular than the other man but was dressed in similar fashion. Cal slowed their pace to a stop. Donna moved in close to Cal when they stopped. Cal spoke before they did.

"Can I help you, gentlemen?"

Donna was again surprised at her husband's ability to not show any fear as the tall one spoke to his companion talking over their heads. "Do you hear? Dis one, 'e is asking if we need de 'elp." Fixing his eyes on Cal, he added, "Mah friend and me, we are thinking dat et es *you* who be needing de help. It appears that yo-ah lost."

Cal pressed his lips tight while thinking of how to handle the situation. Donna moved herself tight to Cal's side in an effort to put more distance between herself and the tall man. As she did this, Cal felt his wallet in the pocket of his cargo shorts, remembering the Interpol badge still pinned inside.

This gave him a little relief, but at the same time, he really didn't want to go pulling out a badge which didn't belong to him. He knew if things got ugly and the local authorities got involved, it would be he who went to jail instead of these two.

The huskier one took a step closer to Cal while saying, "Oh, I think he be right, ma friend. We do need de help. You see, our fishing was not good today, so maybe you could help me aund ma friend with some of your American dollars?"

Cal's facial expression and words conveyed irritation and sarcasm. "Oh, so you are robbing us, is that what this is?"

The tall man gave a menacing glare at Donna and a haughty laugh while replying, "Let us just say dat for a price, we will make sure you leave dis area with *all* dat you came with."

Cal's blood boiled seeing the way this cretin glared at Donna. He then did as he had done with the Russian. He took a deep breath and with an exasperated gaze upward, then back down to meet the smiling tall man's eyes. He reached in his pocket, saying, "Okay, fellas, let me get my wallet out." Both men began smiling broadly thinking he was about to start doling out some cash.

The two men moved together to conceal what they thought was going to be a big payoff. Cal watched both men's smiles grow even wider as he pulled his wallet out. Cal, as before, spoke with calm authority while flipping the wallet open. "Well, boys, today isn't your lucky day."

It took a second for the sun-glinted image of the badge to fully register with both men, and when it did, their broad smiles quickly melted away. However, Cal didn't get quite the response he was hoping to get. The tall man's expression went straight. Looking from the badge to Cal, he calmly said, "De badge, it does not even yo-ah odds. You see, people, deh disappear in de islands all de time, aund you are still just one maun."

Suddenly Donna spoke up. "Well, genius, maybe this evens things up a bit." Donna calmly nudged the barrel of a gun up just above the top of her big straw tote bag that hung from her shoulder.

Both men took a couple of rapid steps backward. Cal glanced down to see what Donna had done. Cal grinned seeing the gun barrel poking out his wife's handbag. Instantly he drew his attention back to both men, smoothly rolling with the change in situation.

"Like I said, gentlemen, today isn't your lucky day. Now you can move along and leave us be, or this lady here can pop two holes in each of you before you can say your sweet momma's name."

Both men remained still a moment, taking in what Cal had said when suddenly a voice called out from behind them, "It would be wise for you to do as ma friend here has suggested." Just then Cesar came along with two of his bodyguards stepping up beside Cal and Donna.

Both men gave each other fearful looks of recognition and immediately began backing away while making chatty excuses and apologies. Taking a couple more steps backward, they spun around and began hurriedly walking away taking quick looks back before disappearing around the corner of a dilapidated building.

Donna quickly shoved the gun back down in her tote, saying, "Oh, thank God you showed up."

Cal pocketed his wallet, adding, "Yeah, no kidding."

Cesar gave them both a big smile and laugh, telling them, "It appears as though you had things under control. You are vury convincing with dat badge you carry, Mista Cal."

"It wasn't the badge. It was Donna that got them backing up with the gun we keep on the boat."

"Miss Donna, I did not know dat you are proficient with a firearm."

"She's not," Cal quickly interjected.

"He's right. That was only the third time I've ever had a gun in my hand."

Cesar burst out with laughter while saying, "You two are quite de pair, I must say."

Cal smirked. "Yeah, we're a regular Starsky and Hutch."

"You two sure fit the part." His laughter quickly subsided, turning serious. He asked, "What are you two doing here? Dis is not de best place for tourists."

Rather than get into a long explanation, Cal simply said, "Guess we just didn't notice it."

Cesar gave them a pensive look then with a wave of his hand, he said, "C'mon, let's walk back de way you came. I have information dat may make you vury happy, but der are problems too."

Donna immediately asked, "What is it, is it that crazy Russian again?"

Cesar held up a halting hand. "Please, miss, let us leave dis area. Der are too many ears."

Donna cut her eyes around noticing all the people, mostly men standing in doorways or sitting on chairs leaned back against the walls of the sleazy-looking bars and brothels. A chill ran down her spine seeing all the eyes following them and remembering the inference made to Cal about her. Anxiously she asked, "Could we walk a little faster? I'm getting really uncomfortable."

Cal moved a little closer to her. Cesar, who was a good bit taller than both Cal and Donna, threw a quick gaze around. "Don't you worry, Miss Donna. Yo-ah safe. Now dat all of de eyes have seen you both with me, dey will not bother you anymore. You see, as I told you, a bad reputation can have its advantages."

They continued to walk in silence for a few minutes, and as the bright-colored buildings and smiling faces became more prominent once again, Cesar spoke up. Pointing ahead, he said, "See de two blue and white buildings up ahead? Der is a small path between dem where we shall go in and sit beneath a large tree while we talk."

A brick pathway led between two neat and well-kept wooden buildings, one a real estate office and the other a travel agency. The narrow brick path soon led them to a large courtyard with a huge Australian pine at its center. The sound of the ocean breezes sung loudly through its long wispy needles. Both Cal and Donna commented to Cesar on just how big and tall it was upon entering the courtyard.

"Yes, it es vury big, and it es de oldest tree on de whole island. Et es known as Le Gardienne.

"Why is it called 'The Guardian'?" Donna asked.

"Ah, so you know French, Miss Donna. She nodded in the affirmative as Cesar went to stand by the massive trunk. Patting it, he continued, "It es called this because it es said that some shipwrecked sailors lashed themselves to it to keep from being swept away during a great hurricane dat hit de island more dan a century ago."

The huge old pine was ringed with a continuous wooden bench spaced about three feet away from the trunk of the tree. Donna noted all the names and sayings that were carved in the bark in many different languages; some were quite high up the trunk of the tree.

"Yes, Miss Donna, der are many names and prayers and messages in the bark. But it es no longer allowed for fear of injuring de tree. But let us talk of now. I have good news and some bad news, so I must ask, which do you prefer first?"

Donna immediately said, "Give us the good news first. Has that grouchy old man finished the repairs to our boat quicker than he thought?"

Cesar gave a short chuckle. "Yes, he has already sewn up de holes in de sails, aund he's presently repairing the mast. But yo-ah vessel es not the only one being repaired." He looked to each of them, adding, "De *Akula*, de Russian's yacht, she has been dry docked for repairs. She hangs on a gantry boat lift down at the old navy pier. So you see, de Russian cannot chase after you now, which affords you a window of opportunity to escape without fear of pursuit."

Donna took in a long deep breath throwing her gaze up through the branches of the immense pine at the perfect blue sky. It was the first time since all of this started that she felt this was finally going to end and they could go home. Cal was glad to hear the news about the Russian; however, he knew there was bad news coming.

Giving Cesar a solemn look, he asked the obvious: "So what's the bad news, Cesar?"

Cesar drew a slow gaze up the trunk of the pine. "I'm afraid de breeze dat blows pleasantly through de boughs above us are giving a hint of what's coming."

Donna brought her gaze back down to look at Cal and Cesar just as Cal somberly said, "Another storm is coming, Donna."

Donna's face sank. "Are you sure? Are we going to try and ride it out here?"

"Miss Donna, I have a man at de weather station checking on the de situation, but I can tell you dis: It has not developed into a hurricane as of yet, but et es expected to do so in de next twenty-four to forty-eight hours. Dis dey are sure of. But de exact path es still not certain."

Cal asked, "How far away from here is it?"

"The eye is roughly about two days depending on de forward speed. But you both being from de Keys know about des storms, how dey can be vury unpredictable."

Cal nodded his agreement then asked, "When will your man return with an update?"

"Soon. De weather station es not far from he-ah. Why don't I walk with you back to where you are staying. We can discuss de options you 'ave. Antwan will remain he-ah and wait for my man. Where is it you are staying?"

Donna quickly replied, "The Sea's Edge."

Cesar let go a laugh while saying, "Dat es precisely de place I would have guessed you to stay. Vury well den, let us go." Cesar spoke to his man as they exited the courtyard telling him where they were going and to come quickly once the other man returned from the weather station.

Cal and Donna's pace was brisk and purposeful; Cesar understood their anxiousness. He knew also knew that Cal's silence as he walked meant he was already thinking about their options.

In short order, they arrived back at the cottage. Cal unlocked the door and held it open for Donna and Cesar to enter. Grabbing a towel from the bathroom, he dabbed the sweat from his face. Tossing it over the back of chair, he began to war game out loud their situation as he saw it.

"Okay, the first thing we need to do is go and find out how far along the repairs to the mast have gotten. We can't outrun a storm if we can't hang all the canvas and trim her for speed. We run the risk of being overtaken by the storm trying that."

"Perhaps, Mista Cal, there es de option of once de storm path es more certain, you can sail ninety degrees to its projected path."

"That's true, *if* it stays on a westerly course, but you know as well as I do that the closer these storms get to the States, they tend to turn northward. We could wind up right in its path anyway. To avoid that happening means sailing further to the east."

Donna remained quiet trying to take in all of what was being said. The last thing she wanted to do was head further from home. But she also knew that the stakes were very high, and getting caught in the middle of hurricane at sea would not likely end well.

During a silent moment, Donna asked, "Cal, what if it looks like it's coming our way, why don't we just fly home?"

"That's an option, I suppose. But I really don't want to leave the *Donna Marie* after going through all of this unless there is no other way."

Donna nodded, but it was easy to see the worry on her face. Cal was worried too, and frustrated. It seemed that every time it appeared as if they could simply sail for home, another roadblock changed their plans. Cal couldn't stand waiting any longer for word on the storm. "Okay, look, you two stay and wait for word on the storm. I'm going to go and see about the repairs to the *Donna Marie*, and maybe, just maybe, we'll get lucky on both fronts."

Donna and Cesar nodded their agreement. Cal opened the door to leave. Looking back, he said, "Donna, you go to the main office and check us out, then come back here and pack our stuff, because when I get back, we are either sailing or flying back home, but either way, we don't have time to waste."

Donna stood to follow Cal out of the door. Cal gave a quick glance to Cesar. "Sorry to leave you, old boy, but I have got to get this right."

"I understand completely. I'll be he-ah when you return, hopefully with better news about de storm."

Cal closed the door; it was a short distance to the motel office. Arriving at the office, he gave Donna a quick kiss, saying, "Don't worry, baby, we'll be all right. I'll be back as quick as I can."

Donna nervously nodded, telling him, "I love you. You be careful. I need you, Cal."

Cal saw her eyes moisten. He then pulled her in hugging her and telling her, "I love you too, sweetheart." Pulling back, he looked squarely in her eyes, adding, "Don't worry, if we do sail for home, with that Russian jackass out of the picture now, outrunning a storm will be a piece of cake."

Kissing the top of her head, he said, "Now go on in. I'll be back quick like a rabbit, okay?"

Donna swiped a small tear from the corner of her eye. "Yeah, okay, I'm fine. You know I get emotional first, but I'll be ready when you get back. You're bringing Johnny Mac back with you, right?"

Cal smiled broadly. "Of course. Heck, he's become like my personal barnacle, and I wouldn't scrape him off for nothing in the world." Donna smiled then opened the door to the motel office. As soon as the door closed, Cal shot off for the cove where the *Donna Marie* was moored. His hope was that all the repairs to the mast were complete. With no bullet holes in the mainsail now, the damage to cabin could wait until they got home.

Cal reached the row of small wooden structures that served as fish shacks for many of the local fishermen. The shacks and the boats that sat between them along with some tall weedy overgrowth hid the majority of the cove from his view as he approached. Reaching the end of a row of shacks, he turned the corner to where the end of the long pier that ran out to where El Jurakan's canvas shanty stood.

Stepping onto the dock, Cal suddenly froze. He stared for moment. El Jurakan's canvas shanty was there, all right, but the *Donna Marie* was not!

Chapter 67

The sound of Cal running thundered on the dock planks. Racing along, he hoped there was a logical reason for the *Donna Marie* being gone. Perhaps the repairs had been completed sooner than expected, and they had taken her out for a shakedown—this was his hope anyway.

Nearing the canopy, he began calling out, "J-Mac, are you in there?" He stopped to listen, but no there was no reply. Only the lap of water against the pilings and canvas rolling and flapping in the ocean breeze could be heard. Reaching for the flap of canvas, Cal folded it open and slowly stepped into the mysterious world of El Jurakan. Peering around, he called out again, "Johnny Mac? Hey, you guys in here?"

It was much darker inside, and it took a minute for his eyes to adjust to the small amount of light that slipped in under the bottom edge of the heavy canvas sides that draped down to the dock. Slowly, he crept farther inside, his eyes beginning to adjust to the dim light. Cautiously, he gazed around.

The dock had been widened out to one side of the pier to form a large twenty-foot square area. Old pallets had been stood on edge and stacked two high at the perimeter on the dock extension to make the walls over which the heavy tarps were draped and fastened.

Cal moved slowly around taking in the entirety of El Jurakan's world. A weathered wooden work bench ran along one side of the canvas wall closest to the pier. There were all manner of woodworking tools sitting on plywood shelves at the center of the room, with spools of heavy thread stacked next to them. Continuing toward the back of the makeshift structure, it appeared that this area was his living quarters, which consisted of a small bed and table with just one chair. To the right of that was a six-foot-long countertop holding a camp stove and a couple of small pots and cooking utensils. Underneath the table sat a large ice chest.

Cal shook his head seeing the meager existence this guy had and could not imagine what drove a man to live this way. Taking one last look around the twenty-foot square area, he noticed a canvas hanging down that partitioned off one corner. "That must be his luxurious bathroom," Cal stated out loud while walking toward it, more to satisfy his conclusions rather than to look for Johnny Mac or his grumpy shipwright.

He was about halfway there when he heard what sounded like a moan. Freezing in his tracks, he called out, "Johnny Mac?" Taking another slow step forward and listening intently, Cal saw the canvas partition move slightly. "Hey! J-Mac, is that you?"

It was then that a much louder moan came, this time accompanied by a foot pushing out from under the canvas! Cal shot forward upon recognizing Johnny Mac's leather sandal. Reaching the canvas, Cal snatched it partway open. There, lying side by side on the dock planks were both men tied up with tape over their mouths.

"Hey, you two! What happened?" Cal loudly questioned while removing the tape and rope from Johnny Mac first. Johnny Mac took in huge gulps of air while Cal untied him.

Johnny Mac spoke between breaths earnestly telling Cal to check on El Jurakan who wasn't moving. "Look after him—they knocked him out. He, uh...he...he tried to put up a fight."

Cal quickly moved to untie him and remove the tape. He tried rousing him for a moment or two. "J-Mac, he's starting to come around." Cal stood and hurried to the ice chest, reasoning that there might be some water in it. Sliding it from under a table, he lifted the lid and peered in. There, nestled in ice, were some eggs, fish fillets, a few vegetables, along with a quart-sized plastic jug of water. Snatching it out, he rushed back.

Shoving the canvas completely back out of the way this time, he saw that Johnny Mac had El Jurakan up to a sitting position. Cal kneeled on one knee in front of El Jurakan, offering the bottle of water to him. Silently and groggy, he grabbed the jug and took a short swig then dropped it down hard on the deck sloshing a little water out.

With his eyes still closed, he put the jug to his lips taking a deeper swig of the cool water. Swallowing, he shook his head. Pulling the plastic jug back, he opened his eyes wide staring at it with disgust. Dropping the jug hard on the deck again, he growled, "You gave me *water!* That's for cookin'. Whiskey's for drink'n', ya dang fool."

Cal rolled his eyes. Taking an exasperated breath, he sarcastically answered, "Well, it looks like you're okay." Cal earnestly questioned them. "What the hell happened? Who did this to you?"

Cal then focused all of his attention on Johnny Mac, who had leaned back against a dock post. Cal took the jug from El Jurakan, offered it to Johnny Mac. His hands shook as he reached to take the jug from Cal. He steadied it while Johnny Mac took a deep drink of the cool water.

Dropping the jug away from his face, Johnny Mac took a couple of deep breaths and cut his eyes to Cal. Haltingly, he spoke between breaths. "We...we tried to...to stop them...but...but there were three of them."

"Three of who, J-Mac, who took her?"

Johnny Mac took another drink of water. Setting the jug down, he shook his head trying to clear his mind. He then looked Cal straight in the eyes and gravely stated, "It was that Russian guy and two of his men."

Cursing out loud, Cal shot straight up. "Dammit! That son-of-bitch did it to me before I could do it to him...he baited *me!*"

Looking Johnny Mac straight in the eyes, he firmly questioned, "Can you stand? We need to get back and tell Donna and Cesar what's happened."

Johnny Mac shook his head no. "Look, you go ahead. I need a few minutes here to get my wits about me then I'll be along. Where will you be?"

Cal gave him an apprehensive look then said, "We are at the Seas Edge Cottages. It's on Front Street. Donna is checking us out now, so we can't hang out there, although I don't why. Nobody's going to be renting a cottage with a hurricane coming."

Hearing that, El Jurakan anxiously questioned, "There's a storm coming?"

"Not a hundred percent sure yet. One of Cesar's men is at the weather station getting the latest update."

Both men rose slowly to their feet. Johnny Mac told Cal he would stay with El Jurakan and to go on ahead. Cal nodded and turned to leave, stopping before pushing open the canvas. He threw a concerned look back at El Jurakan. "What about you? What are you going to do? What about all your stuff?"

Smashing his lips together, he looked quickly around at his meager existence, then flatly stated, "It was a damn storm that blew me in here, and I guess another one can blow me out."

Cal gazed at him in disbelief. "Suit yourself. But you may not be so lucky this time."

Somber and cold was his reply. "Who says I was lucky last time?"

Cal understood the implications of his comment but only gave him a short nod before flipping open the canvas flap. Calling back to Johnny Mac, he stated, "Don't be too long, it looks like we are going to try and fly out of here."

"Okay, I'm feeling better by the minute. The Sea's Edge Cottages, right?"

Cal answered as the flap fell closed behind him, "Right, but hurry up."

With the sound of Cal's trotted footfalls fading into the distance, Johnny Mac gazed over at El Jurakan, then while sweeping a hand around the entirety of El Jurakan's world, he asked, "You're not really going to ride out a storm in *this,* are you?"

"Well, mate, this ole dock crab has nowhere else to go."

Johnny Mac shot him a knowing gaze. "That's not quite true now, is it?"

Tinged with emotion, he replied, "I don't think I can go back to that life...not without her. I can't leave Ellie here. I just can't."

"But you won't be. You know that now."

"How can I be sure of that? Was it really her?"

Johnny Mac held a silent stare on him for a long moment then said, "I get no benefit from telling you these things. I've asked nothing from you, have I? What I've repeated to you is for you, Joel Harrington's benefit."

Casting a solemn look downward while shaking his head back and forth, El Jurakan said, "No one has called me by that name in a long, long time, so long now it seems as though that person died too."

Johnny Mac put a hand on his shoulder. "I understand that more than you know. But I also know that no one stays on the same path all their life. Frankly, I don't think we're supposed to."

"So what am I supposed to do now?"

Johnny Mac gave his shoulder a squeeze and a shake. "Well, for starters, getting blown away in a hurricane isn't an option. Now c'mon, grab whatever you think you need from in here, 'cause you're coming with us."

"What? But I…I *can't*. What about—"

"Stop it. She's telling you to get moving now!"

He shuddered hearing that, then drifting his eyes around at his meager existence then to Johnny Mac, he softly spoke. "I have only one thing I need from here." Taking a couple steps away, he bent and retrieved a small wooden box about six inches square from under his workbench. Clicking open a spring hasp and slowly raising the lid, he placed it carefully on the workbench.

Gently lifting a photograph and string of pearls, he showed them to Johnny Mac, telling him, "This is a picture of us taken down in St. Barts. It's the last one we ever took together." Holding up the string of pearls, he softly drifted his fingers down them, adding, "I bought these for her in St. Martin. They were to be an anniversary gift to her, but I never got to…before…before."

"Joel, look at me. I'm sure you've noticed the scars all over my face, hands, and arms. There are a lot more that my clothes hide. One thing I've learned though is a wound will never heal if you keep picking it open. It's time to let that wound heal."

Swallowing hard, he held his gaze on Johnny Mac. "But how?"

Johnny Mac threw him a warm smile. "For starters, getting out of the path of a hurricane would be a good move. C'mon, let's get going before we get left behind."

Exiting his bleak world, he turned back and removed from over the opening a foot-long weathered section of deck plank; scrawled in white was the name El Jurakan. He then confidently stated, "El Jurakan, *you* are no more." Grabbing it by one end, he drew back to toss it in the water but suddenly stopped. Instead, he held it in front of his face a moment and read the name out loud again.

He then looked to Johnny Mac and said, "You know, I think I might hang on to this. Might be good motivation to write a book about all of this someday."

Johnny Mac nodded his agreement but then empathically stated, "C'mon, we've got to hurry. It seems something big is about to happen."

"What? What is it?"

"I'm not sure, but I keep getting a sense of things reversing or turning around, and we are all in the middle of it." Both men began trotting the rest of the way down the dock to shore.

"The hurricane maybe?"

"Not sure. It just feels crazy and uncertain. I know we just need to hurry!"

Chapter 68

Cal slid to a stop at their cottage door. Twisting the handle, he thrust the door open practically shouting as he entered, "Its gone!" startling Donna and Cesar.

"Cal, Cal honey, slow down. What's wrong? What's gone?"

"That Russian bastard has taken the *Donna Marie*! That's what's wrong. I found Johnny Mac and El Jurakan tied up and gagged in that tent thing he lives in. He was knocked out too."

"Cal, calm down. Who was knocked out?"

Rolling his eyes, Cal took a deep breath and began telling them what happened. "Look, that Russian SOB went there early this morning. He had two of his men with him. They subdued Johnny Mac and El Jurakan, who put up some kind of fight, and they knocked El Jurakan out."

Donna looked worriedly at Cal. "Oh no! Are they both okay? Where is Johnny Mac?"

"Yeah, he and that old buzzard are okay. J-Mac should be here any minute. I told them about the storm too." Cal slammed his fist down on a small table by the door. "I guess that's it. She's gone, and we are flying back home without her. Damn it! I should have sailed for home as soon as that son-of-bitch turned tail and ran."

Cesar, who had been sitting in a chair taking in this new development, quietly asked, "Mista Cal, would you like my men to search de waters to see if they find her nearby?"

Cal pressed his lips in thought for a moment. His eyes widened as a thought occurred to him. Snapping his fingers, he exclaimed, "Wait a minute, you said his yacht was out of the water on a gantry crane getting repairs done—he's not going to leave that here."

Cesar stood abruptly. "That's right! Et was still der when I passed by a short while ago."

"C'mon, let's go! Let's grab our stuff. We've got to run!"

"Cal, wait, what are we doing? Where are we running to?"

Grabbing Donna by the shoulders, he implored, "Donna, two can play that game, but we have to hurry. If I'm right and we can pull it off, we can give that Ivan bastard a surprise he would never expect a couple of old farts like us to do."

Cesar began to laugh out loud. "Mista Cal, I find I like you more and more, aund you are right. Et es daring but not without danger. Two of his crew are der as well."

Cal grabbed his duffel bag and the larger of the two suitcases of Donna's. Opening the door, he again beseeched Donna to get moving. Cesar grabbed her other suitcase. "We must hurry, Miss Donna. We may still 'ave a chance to gain back what es yours."

"Cal, this is crazy! I know what you are thinking, but those guys have guns…big ones."

Cal started his way up the cobblestone path talking excitedly as he went with Donna following close behind. "That's right. They do have big guns, but they don't just walk around with machine guns hanging from their shoulders at a marina, which means those guns are likely still in that yacht.

"'E es right, Miss Donna. Look, 'ere comes my men now. We will 'ave information on both de storm aund de *Akula* too."

Cesar strode quickly around Donna and Cal to greet his men. He was twenty-feet ahead when they met and turned to walk with him. Cal and Donna watched as both men spoke alternately to him. Cesar slowed his pace to let Cal and Donna catch up. When they did, he stopped and turned to face them.

Cal set their things down as Cesar spoke up immediately. "Mista Cal, first let me tell you dat de *Akula* is being readied to be launched. Der es some good news with dat. Der are only two crew members dat wait for it to be placed in de water. Yo-ah assessment of der not having automatic weapon is also correct. However, dey are not unarmed—dey have handguns.

"So what do we do? We can't go in there with guns blazing like it's the OK Corral," Donna questioned.

"Dat es true. But Miss Donna, my men tell me dat de crewmen are not worried and are quite relaxed waiting for de crane operator to arrive."

Cal looked hopefully at Cesar. "Maybe we can use the late arrival of the operator to our advantage."

Cesar stared thoughtfully at Cal for a moment. "My man Antwan does know de man. Perhaps 'e can go and speak to 'em and tell 'em to delay es arrival further. 'E lives only a short walk from 'ere."

"So the guy gets here later, how does that help?" Donna queried.

Suddenly Antwan stepped forward. "Pardon my interruption, but 'ave you forgotten something?"

Cesar's brow furrowed in thought for moment, then a split second later, his eyes flew open wide with his deep laughter.

"Yes, yes, how could I 'ave forgotten? Yes, dat es right." Looking to both Cal and Donna, he patted Antwan on the shoulder while gleefully stating, "My man Antwan here use to operate dat vury crane before coming to work for me. 'E can operate de crane instead." Cesar gave Antwan a fifty-dollar bill, saying, "Tell de operator to stay home for an hour or so. Den hurry back here, understood?" Antwan nodded affirmatively. Cesar then waved his hand for Antwan to get going.

Watching Antwan retreat up the narrow street, Donna questioned, "So what about the crewmen, they are still going to be hanging around *with guns?*"

Cal glanced at Donna; she was of course right. He began to pace in a tight circle rubbing his chin and cheek with his hand in deep thought. Abruptly stopping, he looked at Donna and Cesar. "What if we could lure them away from the dock long enough for us to commandeer the *Akula* and haul ass with it?

Cesar gave Cal a thoughtful look then asked, "But what could make dese men abandon der post, Mista Cal?"

A big smile came to Cal's face as he said, "How about a direct order from their captain? You both remember the sweet young lady Anya who warned us about the Russian, right? What if she were to come and tell them that their crazy-ass captain is waiting for them in the cove where the *Donna Marie* was docked?"

Through a burgeoning smile, Cesar stated, "Mista Cal, dese men would never disobey an order, now would dey?"

"No, they wouldn't, especially from him."

"Cal, I don't like it," Donna interjected. "I don't want Anya involved. When they find out it was a trick, I worry about what they might do to her."

Cal pressed his lips tight in consideration of that possibility. He of course didn't want anyone getting hurt. Dropping his head in thought and pacing like a lion in a cage, his frustrations were building. Snapping his fingers, he ceased his pacing and faced Donna and Cesar once again. "What if…what if she simply delivers a note and says she was told to bring it to them. Then it won't be her telling them anything she's just doing as she was asked to do."

Still concerned for Anya's safety, Donna again dug deeper into the proposition. "Cal honey, won't they ask who gave her the note?"

Cal wanted her to stop finding problems with the plan, but knew she was right and was doing exactly what he should be doing, which was to see all the pitfalls. "Look, we don't have time to iron out every detail. I learned a long time ago that sometimes you just have to wing it, and I got a hunch that Anya is pretty good at that."

Donna gave little sideways nod. "Cal, I'm nervous about this. This is serious stuff here, and I don't want anyone to get hurt."

"Miss Donna, please don't worry. I have assets all through dese islands. I will make sure dat Anya is taken care of. You saw how dose men left you when I arrived. I have ways to make sure dat dey leave her alone."

Cesar glanced at his watch, and then waved his other man to come closer. He began addressing him as he approached. "Clovie, I need you to go to de Tradewinds bar and Grill aund tell de young lady Anya I need to see 'er immediately by Le Gardienne."

"What ef she cannot come because she is working?"

"Go to de owner. He knows me well, and tell hem I need Anya for a short time, maybe fifteen minutes." Cesar again reached into his pocket and produced a folded hundred-dollar bill. "Be sure aund give hem dis. Now go—you must 'urry, Clovie." With a sharp nod, Clovie took the money, turned, and raced away.

"Now let us go aund wait by de tree aund let our rosebud begin to blossom, shall we?"

They had taken only a few steps when Donna stopped dead in her tracks. Both Cal and Cesar turned to see what was wrong, but before either of them said a word, she worriedly asked, "Wait a minute, what about the storm? What did your man tell you about the storm?"

Cesar's eyes flew open realizing he had forgotten to tell them what was going on with the storm. "My goodness, I em so sorry. I got caught up in de moment. Yes, of course, de storm has slowed and is barely moving, so dat is buying us some time."

"That may buy us some time, Cesar, but you know as well as I do that when a storm slows, it can build in strength. Where is it from here, do you know?" Cal cautioned.

"Cal, de eye of de storm is northwest of Anguilla, which puts it roughly three 'undred aund fifty miles southeast of here."

Donna, sounding hopeful, said, "That's a good distance from here."

Cal cut his eyes to meet Donna's. "Donna, that is where the center of the storm is located." He then fixed his eyes on Cesar. "How big is the wind field, Cesar? And have they pinned down a direction yet?"

Cesar's expression and tone were serious. "Shipping communications aund de last satellite images indicate de tropical storm force winds extend out from de center for close to two 'undred miles."

Cal's eyes widened. "My god, that means its storm force winds are covering four hundred miles of ocean—this thing is becoming a monster. What about direction?"

"De slow movement makes it difficult to be accurate, but it seems to be moving due west. If et stays on dat course, we will see only squall lines passing over. However, even a small jog north could put much stronger winds sweeping over dis area. Come. Let us go and sit under Le Gardienne aund wait for Clovie aund Anya to return. Perhaps de wise old tree can tell us how best we should proceed."

Cal pawed his hand down his face in frustration; again, he was being presented with yet another life-or-death decision. Cesar urged both Cal and Donna to follow him along the short distance to once again sit beneath the singing needles of the old Australian pine. Nearing the brick path, they heard someone shouting out to them.

"Hey, hold up. We've been trying to find you!"

Stopping in their tracks, they looked to see both Johnny Mac and El Jurakan hurrying their way toward them.

Johnny Mac continued calling out to them as they drew near, "Me and Joel here have been looking all over for you. We didn't know if you two had already caught a flight outta here."

Cal waited until they were just a few feet away before responding to them. "No, as you can see, we are still here, but it looks like as a last resort, we may to have to catch a plane out of here now."

Johnny Mac shook his head and said something that would send a chill through them all. "No, I don't think you'll be doing that. We just came from the airport. The last plane out just left fifteen minutes ago."

Donna caught her breath, putting her fingers to her mouth. Worriedly she looked at Cal. "What are we going to do, Cal?"

Taking a deep breath, he tossed a stiff gaze around to each, then firmly stated, "Right now I'm going to sit under that big tree and wait for Anya to come, and then we are going to put to sea in that big ass yacht. That is what we are *going* to do. It's time to stop letting circumstances control what is happening. It's time we controlled the circumstances!"

Donna, in the quick moment before anyone else spoke again, looked straight to El Jurakan, exclaiming, "So your name is really Joel? What is your last name?"

Joel threw a damning look at Johnny Mac. Johnny Mac simply stated, "Joel, this is where one chapter stops and a new one begins."

Johnny Mac gave a worried look and the slightest of nods, he looked straight at Donna with the saddest eyes she thought she had ever seen and softly and simply said, "Yes, ma'am, the name's Joel Harrington, Joel Walker Harrington to be exact, ma'am."

Everyone turned to stare at him; no one spoke for a long moment. Finally, Cal ended the silence in classic Cal fashion. "Bullshit, everybody knows that guy's been dead for ten years. He and his wife went missing in the…the—" Cal stopped before he said "Caribbean" and stared at him again.

"Well, unfortunately, everyone has only been half right. I'm quite alive, but I have felt dead for these last ten years, and don't think I haven't considered making it so, more than a few times."

Cal then asked the obvious question, "But you are worth millions. Your investment firm is still going like nothing is wrong. It's like you never left."

"Well, I can thank my younger brother for that. He's the only other person in the world who knows I'm not dead. He found me here not long after it happened. He begged me to come back, but I just couldn't. He has refused to have me declared legally dead, even though the rest of the family has pressured him to do so. He still contacts me here so we can go over things concerning the business. He still tries to persuade come back."

Cal stared at him in amazement. Shaking his head to clear his mind and to refocus on the problem at hand, he firmly stated, "So what are you doing here?"

Joel gave Cal a pensive look then a sideways nod toward Johnny Mac. "He convinced me to go back, so I'm hoping to catch a ride with you."

Cal took a deep breath and exhaled while saying, "Okay, but I can't promise that you or any of us will make it back to the States in one piece."

Johnny Mac quickly interjected, "Hey, Cal, just roll with what you've been thinking. I think it's our best shot."

"You *think* it's our best shot?"

"Hey, like I've told you all before, in situations like this, none of what comes to me is written in stone."

"Well, let's hope that if it ever does get written in stone, it's not a headstone."

Donna suddenly smacked Cal on the shoulder. Speaking tersely to him, she admonished him, saying, "Caleb Arnold, would you stop being so negative? I haven't seen Johnny Mac be wrong yet, not even once, so whatever you have in that storm-clouded mind of yours, you spit out and do it now."

Cal threw a look around to all then simply stated, "I'm heading for the tree—it's where Anya is to meet us, plus I need to think on all of this some more. There is just too much riding on what we do next."

Cal turned on his heels and began heading for the courtyard. He needed desperately to settle his mind, and the sound of the wind blowing through that big tree was just the therapy he needed. His worry was that they might be walking into a trap; in fact, this whole thing smelled like a trap. If it was, he wanted that arrogant Russian to come up empty.

He had something spooling around in his mind, but to pull it off, he needed a little insurance that those crewmen could be dealt with quickly and without any gun play, but right now he needed to think, and the time waiting for Anya to arrive could just be enough for him to sort this all out. That and some good old-fashioned luck!

Chapter 69

Yuri paced the length of the *Donna Marie*'s deck; his mind was clouded with worry. He had them running on diesel power with the sails stowed to make it harder to be seen on the open water. He felt some bit of relief nearing their rendezvous point of Balfour Town on Salt Cay, which was only a short distance from Cockburn Town. There he would go aboard the *Akula* once again and leave three of his crew to do the work of sailing the *Donna Marie* across the Atlantic.

Still, he held a great deal of concern for having to change his original route for crossing the Atlantic at the last minute due to the storm. The plan *was* to take the *Donna Marie* the shortest route across the Atlantic by sailing southeast to Anguilla, then turn due east heading straight across the Atlantic to the coast of Africa, where they would then hug the African coast north to Lisbon. There he would meet with the intermediary.

The tropical storm had now forced him to take a longer route due east out of the Turks and Caicos adding more than five hundred miles to the trip. He knew well that this time of year in the southern Atlantic was not a good time to be attempting such a journey. The only solace he found in all of this was that the strong winds coming off the coast of the Western Sahara were driving the storms into the lower latitudes making them not take the usual turn northward.

While this was a good thing, he knew too that if those strong westerlies eased even a little, they could find themselves in the middle of the Atlantic Ocean with a hurricane bearing down on them with no safe port with which to seek harbor. Both vessels were capable of an ocean crossing, but a hurricane, *that* was a whole other matter.

Checking his watch, he gave the order to slow to a stop when they were a half mile off shore of Balfour Town. Glancing again at his watch, he thought, *The* Akula *should be back in the water by now.* Looking toward the small island of Salt Cay, he spoke low in English as if to make sure his adversary would understand. "Soon, cocky American, you will see who is da smarter one."

*****

Wordlessly they waited for Anya under the shade of Le Gardienne. A five-knot wind blew steady, with intermittent stronger gust that made a ghostly howl through the old pines' long needles, amplifying the feeling of dread that hung in the air. During this moment of tensioned, hushed silence, Cal had memories of times just like this during the war.

Times when battle plans had been drawn and gone over ad nauseam, only to be delayed because of weather or new information that affected those plans. It was the waiting to go into battle that was always the worst, because just like now, no one talked much, and when they did, it was low and somber. The words of the youngest among them were tinged with fear, the same fear they all had, but the battle-hardened managed to keep it at bay with their silence.

With these thoughts scrolling through his mind, he stared down at his feet shoved into his white canvas deck shoes, a far cry from the boondockers he wore during the war. He gave a small nod while staring at his feet, thinking, *You guys have carried me through a lot of stuff in my life.* Then just above a whisper, he said, "Feet, don't fail me now."

Donna, sitting right next to him, lost in her own thoughts, turned to stare at him upon hearing him say something so random and meaningless. "Why in the world did you say that?" she asked.

Cal turned his downcast stare up sideways to meet Donna's eyes. "Oh, just remembering something from a lifetime ago."

Donna could see it; she knew well that tone and facial expression. She had seen that look on his face now and again over the years. Occasionally he'd let slip out bits and pieces of that time in his life. She never questioned him about it for fear of the effects of his speaking life back into the memories of that retched war. Donna rolled a thoughtful smirk into one cheek, and then placing a hand over his, said, "Cal honey, I trust you, and I trust your judgment, and I'm with you no matter what. We can always stay right here and ride out the storm if it comes this way and, when it's over, fly home and go on with our lives. There's no score to settle and no scales to be balanced. And in the end, this is but one chapter in the whole of our life together." She patted his hand. "Okay?"

Cal held his gaze on her for a long moment then silently nodded and gave her hand a gentle squeeze, then said, "I suppose that's what I'm trying to pick between, the lesser of two evils. Stay here and risk being swept off an island by a hurricane or getting caught in one at sea."

Donna was about to comment back when Clovie and Anya came walking quickly from between the two offices straight into the courtyard, heading directly for Cesar. Donna held back her reply to Cal to see what Anya had to say, for if Anya had even the slightest hesitation about being involved in this, then she was going to tell Cal that they should stay on the island and take their chances here.

Clovie spoke up first. "Mista Cesar, Antwan is ready to lower the vessel as we speak. De two crewmen have waited so long in the pavilion dat both are lying on der backs on de tables—I think one may even be asleep."

Cesar threw a quick glance to Cal. Cal immediately thought, *This might be the luck we need.* He then quickly stated, "This could change things." Looking to Anya, he said, "Anya honey, we may need you. But I'm not sure yet how. Can you sit here a minute while we talk this over?"

Anya smiled broadly. "If it 'elps you to get yo-ah boat back, den count me in. I em ready to 'elp."

Donna immediately spoke up. "Anya, are you sure? This could be very dangerous. I don't want you getting hurt."

"Don't you worry about me. I 'ave grown up in dese islands. Anya knows how to 'andle herself. Besides, I 'ave de protection of de infamous Sawfish, de most feared man in the de islands, right, Mista Cesar?"

Cesar smiled and nodded. "Most assuredly, Anya." Looking to Cal, he added, "And now, Mista Cal, I suspect yo-ah forming a plan, are you not?"

Cal smiled broadly, saying, "Well, I *have* been sitting here thinking about times past, and now hearing that those two crewmen have let their guard down a bit has reminded me of a little thing called Operation Hailstone that I happened to be part of during the war. We managed to catch a good-sized portion of the Japanese navy with their collective pants down and sunk a bunch of their ships in Truk Lagoon."

Johnny Mac, who had been sitting quietly next to an equally silent Joel, suddenly spoke up. "Hey, I remember that being talked about in my fifth-grade history class. Truk was one heck of a navy battle, Cal."

Joel leaned away from Johnny Mac with his face scrunched in confusion and asked, "Wait, just hold on a minute. How could you be learning about that in history class? Aren't you two about the same age?" he asked, pointing from Johnny Mac to Cal.

Cal laughed out loud. Pointing to Johnny Mac, he said, "Hell, he's twenty years younger than me! He was in Nam, not World War Two."

Joel stared wide-eyed at Johnny Mac. "My god, man, what did they do to you? Was it that damn Agent Orange stuff?"

Johnny Mac tossed a quick glance to Cal and then back to Joel. "Look, Joel, I'll tell you about what happened to me over there some other time." Fixing his eyes on Cal, he asked, "Cal, what have you got swirling around in that head of yours?"

"Well, I figure it this way, J-Mac: If we hurry, I think we can catch those crewmen with their pants down just like we did the Japanese navy, *and* here's the kicker—we are going to make them take us right to the *Donna Marie*."

"Mista Cal, I think I know what you are planning, and me aund ma men are ready to help."

Cal nodded then said, "Good. We are going catch those guys off guard, but we need a little insurance." Looking to Anya, he asked, "When Antwan finishes lowering the yacht into the water, I need you to go and start talking to those two, but you need to do the hot chick, shy, coy way. Tell them how beautiful it is and how much you've always wanted see the inside of one. You know, stroke their male egos with how important they must be, you know, that kind of stuff."

Anya let go a giggle, saying, "Don't you worry. I know how to play dat game. I can make sure dey only pay attention to Anya."

"Good, but listen, don't get too close to them—stay back ten feet or so, because while their attention is on you, Cesar's men will subdue them from behind, so you have to stay just out of reach. We don't need any hostage situations here, got it?"

"Cal, I'm worried," Donna interjected. "About Anya—what if this doesn't go as planned? They could hurt her."

Before Cal could, Cesar answered her. "Miss Donna, my men are well trained for situations such as dis *aund* have done similar operations like dis in de past. My men will strike so fast dey will never see it coming."

"What about their guns?"

"Just watch, dey will be disarmed as dey are being subdued. Et es really something to see. Et happens vury fast. But we must act soon."

Cal looked at Donna first. She was clearly worried; however, he knew that once this started, she wouldn't let her worries interfere with anything. Giving Anya a quick look, he asked, "You ready? Remember to stay back but keep their attention on you, got it?"

"Oh, don't you worry. Dey will only be looking at me." With that, she tugged her V-neck T-shirt down a good bit. Cal smiled. "Anya, that looks like a good start to me."

"You can pop your eyeballs back in place, old man. I'm way more than you can handle."

Cal shot Donna a look of surprise then said, "Oh, don't go getting jealous, Donna, and whaddya mean calling me 'old man'?"

Joel suddenly interrupted them. "Hey as much as we'd all love to see you two do your Ralph and Alice Kramden routine, we need to get going with this if we're going to do it."

Cal flashed an annoyed look at him. "Yeah, okay. Look, everyone, he is right. Let's get a move on. Cesar, you and your men know what to do from here."

Cesar nodded then looked to Clovie. "You and Jaden go past de pavilion. Der are large boats dat sit in dry-dock next to it. Take up a position so dat you can see de crewmen aund Anya. Once she has fully engaged dem, both of you need to make your way quickly aund silently through de pavilion. Do not let yourselves be seen or heard. Remove your shoes so you don't crunch de small shells aund sand as you step."

Looking to Anya, he continued, "Anya, you must lead dem out from under de pavilion, but make sure de sun is at your back. It is vury sunny on de west side now. Dis will keep dem from seeing Clovie and Jaden's shadow as dey approach. Clovie will nod to you when dey are ready to make der move.

"Anya, de moment dey do, you must get out of de way. I 'ave surveyed dis well. You can find safety behind de office. Cal, all of you must wait by de crab traps dat are stacked close by the gantry crane's lifting slip. You all should be able to see everything dat is 'appening from dose vantage points. We will wait until Antwan has placed de *Akula* back in de water. Antwan will signal you, Clovie, to go when you are ready."

Looking around to all, he asked, "Do you all understand what you are to do?" Each nodded and replied affirmatively. "Good." Wordlessly, he nodded and pointed to Clovie and Jaden. The two men turned and quickly departed. "Anya, we will give dem three minutes to get into position. When dey are, dey will signal Antwan to lower de *Akula* down into de water. While dis is happening, Anya, you will make yo-ah way to de pavilion. Remember to lead dem out into de sun."

"All right then," Cal firmly stated. "Let's all head to the crab traps—that is our muster point." Cal turned to lead the way out. Donna followed right behind along with Johnny Mac and Joel; Cesar and Anya followed behind. Donna grabbed Cal's hand gripping it like never before. She was scared; she had never been involved in something so real and terrifying. She felt light-headed and didn't know how Cal and the others could seem so calm at a moment like this.

All she could think right at the moment was that all their lives could change dramatically in the next five minutes. She began saying a silent prayer focusing on every footfall. She just didn't want to see anyone get hurt, even the Russian crewmen whom she felt were just doing as they were told.

Reaching the huge stack of crab traps, they all huddled in close. Donna pinched her nose. The smell was so awful she didn't know how long she could take it, until finally she pulled the bottom of her T-shirt up over her nose. Peering through the slats of the wooden traps, they could see Antwan lowering the huge yacht slowly down. Clovie and Jaden had moved into position hiding behind two of the concrete columns that ringed the large open pavilion. And just as hoped, the crewmen's attention was on the yacht being lowered.

Donna felt a rush of adrenalin as the yachts' hull gently kissed the waters of the Caribbean Sea once again and began settling slowly into the warm waters until the massive straps fell slack—the *Akula* was afloat once again. This was it! Cesar tapped Anya on the shoulder and pointed for her to go around the end of the pavilion where the shipping office and restrooms were in order to block her approach from view. All eyes were on Antwan as he moved the giant gantry crane back away from the *Akula*. When the last lifting strap cleared the bow, he nodded to Anya who was waiting at the corner of the shipping office.

Anya acknowledged Antwan, gave her top another yank downward, took a deep breath, and stepped out. It was showtime!

Chapter 70

Jim glanced at Juky then down at his watch; they had been airborne for nearly two hours, having left Marathon around noon. They had told Kevin and Tammy they would fly down to Cockburn Town, find Cal and Donna, and fly them back home, tied up and gagged if they had to, but they weren't coming back without them.

Kevin had also contacted the FBI agent, telling him of the new developments. The agent assured Kevin that he would inform the State Department and the Coast Guard, although he made no promises of any direct involvement by either, because their parents were not government officials, nor had they been taken against their will. But he made it clear that he would pull every string he could to help out the situation.

During the flight, Juky kept a steady vigil out the cockpit windows at the ocean drifting past. Jim kept them at an altitude that was close enough to the water to make spotting the *Donna Marie* easier but not so low that avoiding other aircraft would become an even greater hazard than it already was. There was a lot of radio chatter from other pilots that were flying out of the path of the slow-moving storm.

Jim spoke out to Juky without taking his eyes from his constant scanning of the airspace around them. "You know this is crazy, what we're doing, right?"

Juky likewise answered without taking his eyes off the ocean below, "Yes, et es, but I could not live with myself if anything happened to dem, since dis es all my fault."

"What? Aw, come on, we both know it was Donna who pulled the trigger on this little operation."

"No, she only agreed to what I 'ad suggested we do. So you see, et es my fault."

"Look, don't go beating yourself up over this. Listen, that old cuss Cal could have walked away from all of this two days ago. If he had, he'd be selling bait shrimp and beer right now, not out there somewhere dodging hurricanes, for Pete's sake."

Suddenly Juky straightened up while leaning well forward. "Look, I believe dat es Cockburn Town, straight ahead."

Jim checked their coordinates. "Yup, that's it, all right. I'll circle the island to see if we can spot the *Donna Marie*. Hopefully we didn't miss them on the way here."

Nearing the island, Jim dropped them down to about five hundred feet and began two slow passes around the perimeter of the island. Juky left the cockpit and took up a position at the large bubbled-out observation windows on either side of the plane's tail section.

Finishing the second pass, Jim questioned Juky over the intercom. "See anything yet?" Juky's hollow reply of "no" amplified their frustrations. A moment more passed when Jim's voice crackled over the intercom again. "Hang on, Juky, I'm going to spin us back around the opposite way so I can make my final approach to land. I need to refuel and think of what our next move should be."

Juky acknowledged him, and then shifted his position to the opposite side of the plane so he could keep an eye on the waters below. Still hoping to see the *Donna Marie,* he settled on the small seat in front of the observation window. The Water Lily then began to lift and bank in a wide slow arc back to the opposite direction out past the southern tip of the island where the airport was located. Juky watched as the southern tip of Cockburn Town and the airport scrolled slowly into view.

Their path carried them out about five miles past the end of the island. Juky kept a hopeless vigil out the observation window; gazing down, he saw a small island pass by beneath them. As the small island slipped from view, Jim banked hard back to the northeast to make his final approach to land. This gave Juky a full-face view of the waters below.

The waves and the sunlight that shined on them was hypnotic, causing Juky to stare more than observe. Suddenly, as the plane began to level out, a familiar shape came rapidly into view and was gone just as fast. Juky jerked to attention, talking low to himself in disbelief. "Wait, I think dat's her. Dat's the *Donna Marie*!" Wide-eyed, Juky shouted up the gangway toward the open door to the cockpit. "I think I see 'er, Jim! Turn back around—I found dem!"

Chapter 71

Anya appeared from around the corner of the shipping office already fully engaged in a Paris runway model stomp toward the two crewmen. She caught their attention immediately when she began to speak. Her words saucy and light floated as though each was kissed away from her pooched lips. "Oh, de boat es so beautiful. You both must be vury important to 'ave such a powerful aund beautiful boat."

Both crewmen smiled broadly at each other then began walking toward her. Anya kept their attention squarely on her. Shading their eyes from the bright sunlight, the crewmen moved closer toward her. Anya peered past them to see Cesar's men silently easing their way up behind the crewmen. Now only a scant few feet behind them, Anya saw Clovie flick his head sideways toward the office. Instantly Anya did a back spin, disappearing behind the shipping office plastering herself against the wall.

In a flash, Clovie and Jaden were on the crewmen. Seizing each by the neck, their guns were snatched from their holsters and their legs swept from under them, landing both men hard, face down in the gravel with a knee in each of their backs.

Peering around the stack of crab traps, Cal and Donna were stunned at how quick and effortless Clovie and Jaden made it look. Cesar quickly trotted over to his men who now had the dust-covered crewmen up with one arm jacked up high behind their backs with guns jabbed in their ribs. Cal along with everyone else eased their way up to stand in the large pavilion.

"Turn them around," Cesar ordered. Cesar spoke to the crewmen as they were shoved around to face him. "Well, well, et es good to see you men again, and so soon. Tell me, where es yo-ah captain? I know he has taken my sailboat, and unless you two want to be made into fish bait, den you will tell me where yo-ah captain es."

One of the crewmen stared at Cesar with surly a contempt then spat on the ground in front of Cesar, holding a defiant glare on him but remained silent.

Cesar's face drew a broad, menacing, almost evil smile. Cesar's smile then rapidly disappeared. Looking past the Russian crewmen, he gave a small head nod to Antwan who was now standing a few feet behind the whole group. Antwan came around from behind to stand beside Cesar. Both crewmen dropped their eyes to see a large and very sharp machete hanging on Antwan's hip.

The one crewman who had been silent became very anxious and nervous and began talking nervously in Russian to his shipmate. His defiant shipmate angrily barked back at the nervous one. Cesar stepped up close to the defiant crewman glaring at him. His eyes narrowed, and his face was expressionless and rock-hard, as he spoke low and deep. "We shall soon see how deep yo-ah defiance runs."

Without taking his stare off the crewman, he sharply ordered, "Take dem aboard de *Akula*. Antwan, take de helm. We are putting to sea. We 'ave fish to feed!"

Donna had pressed herself tight to Cal's side wrapping both of her hands and arms around Cal's right arm. She trembled watching and hearing what was taking place right before her eyes. Her thoughts raced to what Cesar had told them, that his being known as the Sawfish was just a reputation he kept up. But the way he spoke, coupled with his body language, she was no longer sure what was true and what wasn't.

Watching as the two crewmen were marched aboard the *Akula*, Donna, quietly so only Cal could hear, said, "Cal, I'm scared. I'm really scared. What if Cesar has been lying to us all along?"

Cal looked down into his wife's tortured face, then back to Cesar, thinking, *What if he has been lying all along?*

*****

Jim radioed the control tower to abort his landing. The second it was acknowledged he rolled the Water Lily into a tight banking turn to line up over what Juky thought was the *Donna Marie*. Juky made his way back to the cockpit, and plopping down in the copilot's seat, he was already pointing out where he spotted the *Donna Marie*.

Leaning well forward, Juky searched the waters ahead. Suddenly he called out, "There! Over to our left. Yes, dat es her. Let's land in de water aund go find them."

"Now hold on just a second. I'm going to do a low pass by her to see if they are even aboard, 'cause I don't see a soul."

Juky watched as the *Donna Marie* swept by five hundred feet below; sure enough he saw no one on deck. "You are correct, Jim. I see no one. Maybe dey are asleep."

"I doubt that with a hurricane brewing not far south of here. My gut is telling me something isn't right." With that said, he throttled the engines up and began taking a course around the eastern tip of the small island, then headed straight out away from the island about two miles south.

Juky sat puzzled trying to figure out what he was doing, finally asking, "Jim, why do we fly away from de island?"

Jim glanced at Juky with a burgeoning smile and said, "Juky my friend, when I make the turn back toward that island, I'm going to line us up right on that sailboat and fly so fast and low over her that we'll rattle the eye teeth outta whoever's onboard."

Juky burst out laughing at the prospect of seeing Cal storming onto the deck shaking his fist at them. "Oh, Mista Jim, if Cal is on de boat, he will be so angry."

"Yeah, and it'll be funny as hell too." Laughing out loud, Jim began banking the Water Lily hard around to line her nose dead center of the small island, with the *Donna Marie* peacefully anchored just beyond.

Increasing their air speed, Jim took a quick glance over at Juky who was quite tense and looking for anything to hold on to. "What's the matter? Why you looking so scared?" Jim asked with a big smile.

"I 'ave never done anything like dis. What if something goes wrong?"

With a broad smile stretched across his face, Jim reached out and patted Juky hard on the shoulder, telling him, "Heck, don't worry—this, this is just a little barnstorming run. You oughta try this with a full rack of bombs and enemy fighter planes coming at you from every direction, all while dodging flack coming up from below. Now that, that can make a guy a tad jumpy."

"Mista Jim, I don't know 'ow et es you made it through all of dat." Juky never saw the smile melt rapidly away from Jim's face; his stare instead was on the fast approaching island. Jim's reply though caught his ear and his attention. "Juky my friend, I've often wondered that myself, why I made it through, and so many of my buddies didn't. Taking a deep breath, he glanced over to Juky, adding, "But I guess the old roulette wheel of life doesn't have favorites. When it's your time, it's your time."

Juky gave Jim a knowing nod; Jim, however, returned a devilish grin and wink, and then without warning, he shouted out, "Warp factor 10, Scotty, we're going in!" Reaching up, he jammed the throttles all the way forward, then pushed the nose of the big plane sharply downward. The engines roared, and the fuselage shook. Juky felt himself go light in the seat letting out a yell while grabbing for the instrument cowling. Seeing nothing but the island filling the cockpit windows, Juky was sure they were crashing!

Dropping three hundred feet in seconds, Juky was utterly terrified. Over the roar of the engines, he screamed out, "Pull up! Pull up!"

Jim though kept his eyes fixed straight ahead. Flicking his eyes to the instrument panel, he abruptly pulled sharply back on the flight control to bring them out of the dive. The engines screamed in protest; the controls shuddered in his hands. Juky could do nothing but claw onto the cowling and yell.

Jim held the flight controls back until the sound of the engines shifted from a howling scream to a low thundering roar whereupon he eased the flight control forward to bring the horizon rapidly back into view just as the island's shoreline whipped past below. Five hundred yards ahead, peacefully anchored, lay the *Donna Marie*.

Flying at top speed, the Water Lily quickly covered the distance roaring directly over the *Donna Marie* from bow to stern, just above the main mast. Instantly Jim broke out in raucous laughter while pulling gently back on the flight control and turning them back in long lazy arc toward the *Donna Marie*. Juky fell back hard in the copilot's seat gulping air and laying both hands over his chest. With his eyes closed, Juky hoarsely stated, "Don't...you...ev-ah do dat again!"

"Oh hell, what are you talking about? We didn't even crack any windows with that one. Hey, sit up now. We'll be passing by the *Donna Marie* here in a moment. Let's see if we woke Cal's old ass up."

Making the long arcing turn back toward the *Donna Marie* now a mile away, Jim glanced over at Juky who was slowly craning his head up to see out over the cowling. "Do you see what I see?" Jim asked, sporting a smile as big as all outdoors.

"Yes, I see hem. But..." Juky held his comment until they were closer. Jim flew them aft of the *Donna Marie*'s stern, low and a hundred yards out so they both got a good look at who stood shaking their fist at them. Juky said out loud, "Unless Cal has lost his hair and put on much weight, den I don't think dat is hem."

"Yeah, you're right, and *look,* there are two more dudes coming on deck now. This isn't looking good, Juky my man."

"What do we do, where could dey be?"

"We're not landing in the water, that's for sure. I don't have any idea where they could be, but we need to find out what is going on and fast. I need to refuel and get a lock on what that storm is doing too because *that,* my friend, is going to dictate whatever we do in the short term." Juky nodded agreement. Lifting the radio mike and keying it, he called again for clearance to land. Worry filled their minds as Jim flew out past the southern tip of Cockburn Town to make the turn for his final approach to land.

Wanting to ease their worry a little, Jim casually mentioned that he had flown in here during the war when it was a navy base. Juky replied, "Yes, I know. My father helped to build it." Looking down at the wharf below, he added, "And as you can see, we still use de huge crane to lif' de boats out for repair. In fact, it looks as though a beautiful yacht 'as just been launched. Der are people going aboard now." Juky looked back at Jim, saying with a smile, "It must be vury nice to have de money to own such a boat."

Jim gave a passing look at the yacht below; it took a few seconds for it to register. He then snapped his fingers. "Juky, wait just a damn minute. That's not just any yacht—that's the same one that was at Pirates Well, and the guys we saw on the *Donna Marie* were the same ones that were on that yacht."

"Are you sure, Mista Jim? We passed over so quickly."

"Yeah, I'm sure of it. I got to land this thing, and then we've got to hustle over to that wharf before they shove off.

Chapter 72

Jim had the Water Lily on the runway in short order, practically skidding her to a stop not far from the terminal. Doing a rapid shutdown check, Jim then sprang from his seat calling for Juky. "C'mon, we got to get moving."

"Okay, okay. But tell me, 'ow does a man yo-ah age have so much energy?"

"That's easy—good whiskey, better cigars, and faster women." Reaching the hatchway door, he released the latches and shoved the bifurcating door open. Glancing back at Juky before dropping the ladder down, he said with a laugh, "C'mon, Boy Wonder, we don't have the Batmobile, so we are going to have to hoof it over there." Dropping the ladder down, he stepped through the door, and he quickly disappeared.

Juky shook his head while talking to himself. "De man is over sixty, has all his hair with hardly any gray in it, is trim and fit, and has the energy of a twenty-year-old. Humpf, maybe der es something to 'is formula." Turning to descend the steps, Juky saw that Jim was already fifty yards away moving in a rapid trot. Juky, five years his junior, jokingly yelled out to Jim, "Wait for me, Mista Jim. I em not as young as you."

Jim made a big circular sweep of his arm, yelling back without looking, "C'mon, old man, there's a couple of those island bikes we can grab. Hurry up, man!" Juky took off running as fast as his legs would carry him, thinking as he ran, *Running, now biking, what's next, a two-mile swim?*

Jim was on one of the brightly painted bikes and waving for Juky to hurry up. Juky skidded to a stop gulping for air. He breathlessly pleaded, "Mista…Jim…please…" Juky gulped another breath. "Please let me catch my breath first."

"Nonsense, you can catch your breath while we hightail it over to the wharf." With that, Jim threw his leg over the bike and pushed off. Standing up, he began peddling hard away. Juky rolled his eyes, leaning the bike over and dropping his leg heavily over the bike, his foot landing hard on the upturned pedal. "He scares me to death *twice* in dat damn plane, aund now 'e tries to kill me in a marathon."

Wearily shoving down on the pedal, Juky shoved off to a shaky start but soon found himself coming around and able to get his breath back, but still thankful that the wharf was only a short distance away. Nearing the old navy docks, Juky saw that Jim had stopped and had dismounted his bike and was peering around the corner of the shipping offices at the end of the covered pavilion. The fenders and wire basket were rattling as Juky braked to a stop next to Jim, who was waving his hand behind him telling him to shush.

"I em sorry, Mista Jim, these island bikes do not get the best upkeep. What es going on? What do you see?"

"It looks like everyone is at the stern. Oh man, remember that Sawfish guy, Miss Ginger's cousin?" Juky nodded solemnly saying yes. "It appears he's taking over the yacht because his men are holding guns on a couple guys. And look, Cal, Donna, and that swami guy are on the yacht too. We got to get on that boat."

"But how? We can't just run up de gangway. De vessel is six feet above de dock, Jim."

Jim quickly scanned the length of the *Akula*'s hull but could see no easy way to gain access. Just then his eyes fell on the mooring ropes attached to the stern and bow deck cleats. Snapping his fingers, he looked back at Juky with a big smile, pointing to the bow. "Right there, my friend, we can tug on the bow rope to pull the bow closer to the dock and climb the rope to get on board, simple."

Juky's eyes widened. "Are you crazy, maun? I cannot do dat— my ribs are still painful from when Cal saved me from de sharks, plus de stitches from de cut on my leg are pulling apart."

Jim held his stare on Juky a moment. "Hey, yeah, I forgot about all that. Heck, with all that's happened lately, I'm not even sure what day of the week this is." Glancing back at the *Akula*, Jim thoughtfully spoke. "Look, you stay here just in case I need backup. I'll climb onboard and try and get a fix on what's happening. You just sit tight."

Juky nodded then asked, "Mista Jim, really how is it dat you can do all dis stuff at yo-ah age?"

Placing a hand on Juky's shoulder, he said, "Juky my man, it's like this. I absolutely love to fly, and I never want to stop. So at my age, if I don't stay in good physical shape, I could lose my pilot's license, and for me, that would be like dying. So I go to the gym three times a week and work out, and I keep an eye on what I eat."

Juky smiled then said, "So no whiskey, cigars, aund fast women den?"

Jim laughed, saying, "What do you think I do the other four days of the week?" Jim winked at him then added, "All right, now look, once I'm aboard, I'll ease my way back to the stern and try to figure out what the heck's going on."

"Yes, yes, okay. But what if dey see you?"

Pressing his lips tight, he then flatly stated, "Juky ole boy, we can only cross one bridge at a time." Patting him on the shoulder, he said, "Time to roll!" Taking a quick glance back at the stern to make sure everyone was still gathered there, he shot off for the dock piling. Jim's biggest concern right then was pulling the bow over slow enough that it didn't raise any suspicions.

Reaching the mooring cleat, he bent and grabbed the bowline. Looking back to Juky, he gave him a thumbs-up. Grabbing the thick rope, he kept his gaze down the length of the *Akula* and began easing the bow ever so slowly toward the dock. It took a little effort at first to get the big yacht to move. He had to do this just right; pulling too hard or not letting up at just the right moment would cause the bow to hit the dock.

Deftly Jim maneuvered the big yacht's bow as close to the dock as he dared. Looking back to Juky, he gave a short wave. Taking a cautious look toward the stern and seeing that no one was looking his way, he grabbed the thick rope and began climbing. Juky nervously watched as Jim climbed hand over hand up the rope quickly reaching the railing. He struggled a bit trying to get a good grip on the railing to pull himself up. Slipping a couple more times, he finally succeeded on his third attempt.

Juky whispered to himself, "That is one amazing man." He watched as Jim crouched low then disappear down the starboard side of the upper deck. Juky kept taking anxious glances to the rear of the yacht. There seemed to be a good deal of conversation going on, but about what, he couldn't imagine. Only a couple of tense minutes had passed when Jim came scurrying back hunched down low to the bow.

Fearfully, Juky watched Jim scamper over the deck railing and rapidly slid down the mooring rope. Hitting the dock, Jim raced over to Juky, exclaiming, "C'mon, we gotta go right now!"

"But why, what has happened?" Juky implored.

"Too many guns and us with none, and right now the guns are only pointed at those yacht crewmen we saw in Pirates Well. Doesn't look like Cal and Donna and the swami are in any immediate danger, but I think it's time to get the local authorities involved and quick. C'mon, let's move and fast!"

Chapter 73

Standing on the open rear deck of the luxurious yacht, Donna, were it not for the current situation, would have let herself be more impressed with her surroundings. For the *Akula* was beautiful, and it was huge. With eighty-five feet at the waterline, one hundred feet in total length, and a beam width of twenty-five feet, it was spacious. Cal too was taking in the vessel's magnificence as well noting the polished teakwood decks, and what wasn't stainless steel was polished brass. The dark navy-blue hull, white upper decks, and the cabins were a thing of beauty.

Cal shook his head trying to understand what that Russian nut would be doing on yacht like this while engaging in piracy; it made no sense. But whatever the reason, he had to figure out how to get the *Donna Marie* back and not get anyone hurt or killed. Antwan was the last one to board, retracting the gangway as he came aboard. He then went immediately to Cesar, who with Clovie and Jaden had formed a loose circle around the two Russian crewmen.

Cal told Donna and Joel to stay put but motioned Johnny Mac to follow him as he too went to where Cesar and his men stood. Stepping up behind Cesar, Cal and Johnny Mac remained quiet listening to what was being said to the crewmen.

With guns pressed in their ribs, Cesar questioned them. "Will you continue with yo-ah defiance to tell me yo-ah captain's location?"

The surly faced one looked sternly at his nervous shipmate then angrily barked in Russian, "Он вам ничего не говорит!"

Joel leaned toward Cesar, quietly saying, "He said, 'Tell him nothing!'"

Cesar glanced back at Joel. "You understand Russian?"

"A little, but not enough to trust getting all they might say right."

Johnny Mac stepped up right behind Cesar. Tapping him on the shoulder, he motioned for Cesar to lean in close. Johnny Mac whispered in Cesar's ear, "I believe he knows where his captain is." Cesar scrunched his face, and then whispered back, "You can read minds too?"

Johnny Mac gave a quick eye roll. "No, but I can sense that he is hiding something."

"And yo-ah sure about dis?" Cesar softly confirmed.

Johnny Mac winked. "As sure as pigs are made of bacon."

Cesar gave a slight smile then drew his attention back to the crewmen. He then began speaking out to all, "Well, since neither of dese mem prefers to communicate with us, it appears it's time to make some fish bait. Cal, would you aund Johnny Mac be so kind as to cast us off? Antwan here is quite capable of operating dis vessel. So, Antwan, if you will go and take de helm and prepare to leave harbor so we can take care business."

Cesar then stared hard at both crewmen. In a deep menacing tone, he said, "Et es too bad dat you choose not to cooperate with me, because I will tell you now to make peace with yo-ah maker, for you shall soon see hem. Clovie, Jaden, take dem to de stern and hold dem der."

Pushing the guns harder into their ribs, the two men were shoved toward the stern. Suddenly the nervous one began excitedly talking to his surly shipmate in Russian.

Abruptly, the surly crewman harshly replied through gritted teeth to his shipmate.

The nervous one yelled fearfully back, "No! Andros, I vill tell him what he vants to know. We both know of zis man. We know what he does to his enemies." He looked back at Cesar, then to his shipmate. "He will do zis to us too!"

Cesar immediately spoke out. "Ah, so you *do* speak English." Fixing his glare on the defiant crewman, Cesar added, "You should listen to yo-ah friend, Andros, while you still can. All I want is de sailboat, den you aund yo-ah captain may go yo-ah way unharmed.

If you choose otherwise, then none of you will see the next sunrise, including yo-ah captain. You see, I *own* dese waters, so et will take little time fo-ah me to find hem."

Andros, the defiant crewman, angrily answered his shipmate. He spat his words in English this time. "You are a fool, Sacha. He tries to make division between us. Our captain does not fear him. You know zis!"

Cal went back to stand next to Donna. She pressed herself tight into his side while they watched this high-stake chess game play out in front of them. Cal was impressed with Cesar's acting…at least he hoped it was an act. The thought did occur to him: what if Cesar *had* been using them all along? Using them to get both the *Donna Marie* and the *Akula*? Cal gave a short pensive look at Donna; he knew the next moments would be revealing.

Cesar turned away from the Russian crewmen to face the helm making a circular motion with his finger. Antwan gave a nod. In the next moment, the engines rumbled to life. Cesar again entreated Cal and Johnny Mac to cast off the mooring lines. Cal shot a worried look at Cesar. He understood but said nothing, only giving him a slight smile, wink, and a nod. Cal understood that to mean Cesar was taking his bluff the whole way.

Cal took a breath and headed for the bow to cast off. Donna went with him. She was very nervous and found she wanted and needed to stay by Cal's side, plus she wanted to get his thoughts on what was playing out right in front of her. Reaching the bow, Cal bent and lifted the looped end of the thick mooring line, tossing it onto the dock.

Turning back to face Donna, he saw the anxiety etched on her face. She was scared, and understandably so, she had never experienced anything like this in all her life. He, on the other hand, had been in tight squeezes many times before; however, this one held some big unknowns, the biggest one being if the two crewmen decided to call Cesar's bluff, then what? It all seemed to depend on which Cesar they were dealing with, the notorious Cesar, known as the Sawfish, or the undercover Cesar who worked with the police.

Donna took the opportunity of their being alone to question Cal. "Sweetheart, what do you think is going to happen? I'm really scared. I love our sailboat, but I'm not going to be a party to murder."

Cal placed a hand on her shoulder. "Donna, baby, he's not going to make these guys into fish bait. Well, I'm ninety-nine percent sure anyway."

"Cal, how can you be so sure? He seems so different now. It gave me a chill seeing and hearing how he spoke to those crewmen."

"Look, Donna honey, I've had a moment while walking up here to think about all of this. I'm pretty sure he has something up his sleeve. I doubt that he is going to do anything to those crewmen, fish bait-wise anyway.

"But you saw and heard him, and now we are going to be heading to God only knows where so he can, can..." She shuddered, unable to finish saying what she was thinking.

"Donna, listen to me. He is not going to do what you're thinking. One reason I believe this is, he has too many witnesses aboard this yacht. He'd have to whack us all."

"How do know he won't do that? Look, he will have this yacht *and* our sailboat. That would be a huge payday for him and his henchmen."

Cal let go a little laugh at her referring to them as henchmen. "Look, Donna, all I can tell you is I don't believe he is going to do anything to them or us."

"And just what are you hanging that belief on, Mr. Arnold?"

Cal looked his worried wife straight in the eyes. "He gave me a smile a wink and nod just now."

Donna's eyes flew wide open. In a hushed yell, she lit into Cal. "What? That's it? A smile, wink, and a damn nod is what you are betting our lives on? Are you crazy?"

"Shhh, Donna, calm down. Listen to me, please. He's not going to whack us or those crewmen. My gut is telling me that."

"Your gut? The only thing that gut of yours has ever told you is when it's hungry!"

"C'mon, you tell me all the time about your gut telling you this or that, so why can't my gut do the same?"

"First of all, my *gut* doesn't tell my anything. It's my woman's intuition, and right now it's screaming at me to get off this damn yacht!"

Suddenly they became aware they were moving! Both looked toward the dock to see that they were already fifty yards away. They had been moving out the whole time they squabbled about what to do.

Cal tossed a sideways glance at Donna who just stared at the retreating dock and shoreline. "Guess we are going to find out pretty soon just which Cesar we have onboard now."

Donna replied without looking, "I just pray that gut of yours is right about something besides food this time."

Both stood and watched as the bow slowly spun away from the wharf to point out toward the open sea. A strong gust of warm tropical air swirled past them ruffling their clothes and hair, reminding them that their suspicions about Cesar was not the only storm that was brewing for them.

Cal and Donna returned aft to stand in a covered portion of the rear deck for some shade and to stay out of the wind. They saw that Cesar had taken a seat in one the comfortable deck chairs sitting a few feet away and directly in front of the two crewmen. He calmly sat sipping on a cold Coca-Cola, smiling and commenting on what a refreshing drink it was. He then gave them a menacing smile and spoke directly to them.

"Et was very thoughtful of yo-ah captain to have this vessel so well stocked for-ah me. You must remind me to thank hem for his unintended generosity. Although, when I find hem, I am quite sure his mood will not be a good one, and you, gentlemen, will no doubt be the focus of his ire for letting his beautiful yacht fall into, shall we say, de wrong hands."

Then Sacha started to speak but was elbowed in the ribs by Andros. Cesar took note of this and continued speaking to them directing his comments more to Sacha. "Your-ah shipmate does not seem to care that you both are in a dire position. His insistence that you remain silent on yo-ah cooperating with me would be commendable in the military. However, it is a silly position to take in this instance, for there is no flag nor county for which to sacrifice one's self.

"Yo-ah deaths, sadly, will mean nothing to yo-ah captain, nor will yo-ah bravery be noted in history books. Songs will never be written of the boldness with which you met yo-ah fates. But et does not have to end dis way. I ask but one thing from you: tell me where yo-ah captain is, aund you both may go on with yo-ah lives to whatever life has in store for you."

Sacha stared fearfully back at Cesar. Desperately, he wanted to tell him what he wanted to know. Nevertheless, the fear of his captain ran deep keeping him frozen in terror.

*****

The actions of the mysterious plane that buzzed him earlier along with the fact that he had not heard anything from his crewmen aboard the *Akula* had Yuri angry and nervous. He worried that his plans had somehow been corrupted. The plane made him nervous because although it didn't say U.S. Air Force on it, it still carried the Air Force colors and the national star emblem on its flanks.

Maybe, he thought, that overconfident windbag really was a drug enforcement agent. There was only one way to find out, and that was to leave Salt Cay to a point just offshore of the wharf at Cockburn Town. Yuri stood on the cabin roof and peered through binoculars methodically searching for the *Akula*, and at the moment, he was missing the height of the *Akula*'s flying bridge.

Frustrated with his vantage point, he could only wonder if she was still docked, and if so, why? Abruptly snatching the binoculars away, he ended his search, deciding instead to try something different. Tersely, he spoke to the crewman standing just behind him. He gave orders to raise the *Akula* on the ship-to-shore radio and to relay new coordinates to meet and for them to come immediately. The crewman gave only a sharp nod, quickly departing to do as instructed.

If the crewman he had left with the *Akula* answered a radio call, this would at least confirm that nothing was drastically wrong.

If so, they would meet up and immediately set sail for Lisbon. All he wanted right now was to be back aboard the *Akula* and to get out of these waters as fast as he could. He knew one thing: Once back aboard the *Akula*, if it became necessary, he would sink this damn sailboat and anyone on it.

*****

The nervous crewman inched his way farther from his shipmate. The defiant one quickly spoke angrily to him in Russian. Johnny Mac and Joel stood a few feet behind Cesar. They, like Donna and Cal, remained silent, listening and watching the high-stakes poker game being played out right in front of their eyes. Joel caught the gist of what was being said by the defiant crewman. "He thinks you are lying. Told him to be quiet."

The nervous crewman's eyes darted crazily around to all. Suddenly he fixed his stare on Cesar, taking a deep breath to speak, but before a single word left his lips, the ship-to-shore radio crackled to life. "Акула…вызова де Акула вы читаете…прийти в Акулу это срочно вы отвечаете." The nervous crewman then simply said, "He calls us." Cesar stood abruptly and threw a harsh stare at the nervous crewman. "It seems fate is giving you one last opportunity to see old age. Make yo-ah choice a wise one."

Chapter 74

Antwan ran his eyes over the dials on the control console to make sure all the needles were sitting where they should be. Satisfied that all was well, he placed his hand on the throttles and slowly began throttling up the engines. Donna, still sitting in the deck chair next to Cal, felt her heartbeat increase. She knew well that they might be heading into a situation that neither Cal nor anyone else could BS their way out of, but the die had been cast.

She reached over and placed her hand on top of Cal's and squeezed, startling him from his own thoughts. Turning to her, he cupped her hand under his and squeezed back, quietly saying, "It'll be okay. I promise."

"Cal honey, I've never been so tense or worried. There are so many things that can go wrong."

"Yes, there are, but there are just as many that can go right too. That's the strange thing about the unknown. People always tend to focus on what might go wrong in tough situations, and you should to a point. But focusing only what could go wrong only keeps you from seeing the right path."

Giving him a tight smile, she said, "Cal, this why I need you. Every time life has troubled the waters, you have been the rock I can climb on to get above them."

Cal though held his gaze on his wife; the intense worry on her face showed, and he didn't like what he saw. He had adored her ever since the very first time they met. Thinking about that and what they were about to attempt, and over what, brought a completely different focus to the situation. Softly patting her hand, he abruptly stood. She questioned him about what he was doing, and he was about to tell her when Cesar came up to them smiling and saying, "I 'ave good news. We 'ave located what we believe is yo-ah sailboat on the radar."

"How do you know it's the *Donna Marie*?"

"Well, sir, et es all but certain. For one thing, et es sitting at de approximate coordinates just given by de Russian, aund et es de only vessel showing on de screen for two miles."

Cal tossed a quick look to Donna then back to Cesar. "That's all well and good, Cesar, but I've decided to run this tub straight for Ramrod Key. She's just not worth the risk. Besides, that Russian is going to lose more than us. This yacht is worth a hell of a lot more than our sailboat."

Donna quickly spoke out. "That's not true, Cal. Monetary value is not the only thing we have wrapped up in the *Donna Marie*. We have years of memories in her. She has become part of the Salty Anchor too. How many couples have been married on her decks? Some of those couples still come back every year to celebrate their anniversaries with sunset cruises on her that you and I take them on."

"Look, Donna, I understand that, but just now I saw what the weight of this is doing to you. I didn't like what I saw, and I can't and I won't risk yours or anyone else's life over money and memories, Donna."

Cesar gave a disappointed look to both. "I can call this operation off if you so desire. I will understand, but I must say we do 'ave de upper hand—'e will be surrounded, aund I suspect dat 'e desires to 'ave es vessel back as much, if not more, dan you want yours. But say de word aund it will be done."

Donna kept her gaze on Cal; while she was terrified about what might happen going forward with their plans, hearing what Cesar had just said instilled some confidence in her to the point she hoped Cal wouldn't call things off.

Cal could read her like a book. He knew she was conflicted, so was he; however, the thought of someone getting killed over this just wasn't worth the risk. Cal turned to face Cesar and somberly said, "Kill it. It's just not worth the risk."

Donna's shoulders sank. She wanted to speak but found she couldn't find the words. Cesar simply said, "Very well, as you wish." Just then Sacha was heard calling out to them from the helm. They turned to see him hurrying toward them heading directly for Cesar as he approached. "Captain, Captain, de boat, der is something strange happening with it. You must come see radar screen. Please hurry, come now please!"

They made rapid questioning glances to each other, then hurried to follow Sacha who kept turning back to wave them on while practically running toward the helm. Trotting up to the console and stepping to the side, Sacha excitedly began pointing to the screen. "See, look, de vessel is behaving oddly. Come see."

Cesar strode up to the radar console. Cal and Donna stopped on either side of him. With the glow of the screen illuminating their faces, they all peered down at the screen in silence. Nobody spoke for a moment or two. Cesar spoke up first. "It looks like she's turning in wide slow circles."

Cal kept his eyes focused on the green blip that blinked on in a slightly different position with each pass of the radar's sweep. Suddenly he spoke out. "Hold on, guys, she appears to be moving sideways now, but how…" Cal stopped and looked to Cesar and Donna. "I think she's adrift. These wind gusts are just spinning and pushing her all over."

Cesar leaned over the screen, holding his stare on it for a moment, then lifting his eyes to meet Cal's, he spoke, his voice low and serious, "It would appear so, but why?"

"Maybe he had someone pick him up and take him back to Cockburn Town," Donna suggested.

"Maybe, but why?" Cal questioned.

Johnny Mac and Joel appeared from the cabin still eating the last of their sandwiches. Johnny Mac asked, "What's going on, why all the long faces? Somebody lose something?"

Cal took a step back from the radar console. Pointing to the screen, he stated, "It's the *Donna Marie*. It looks like she's been set adrift."

Johnny Mac took step closer. Leaning in, he stared at the screen while shoving the last bite of his ham sandwich in his mouth; talking while he chewed, he curiously said, "Huh, that does look weird."

"Yeah, it is, and what I can't figure out is why that crazy Russian bastard would be doing that, especially after tersely giving his men the coordinates they were to come to, which by the way he is rapidly drifting away from."

Johnny Mac thoughtfully said while swiping the back of his hand across his mouth then on the back of his shorts. "Maybe nobody's onboard."

"What? C'mon, of course he is, and likely a couple of his men too. Where could they go way the hell out here?"

Johnny Mac smirked while checking the back of his hand for the mustard he had wiped from his face then confidently stated, "Have you all forgotten where we are?"

Getting a little irritated, Cal snapped, "Of course I know where we are, but what has that got to do with the *Donna Marie* twirling around haplessly in the Caribbean Sea?"

"That's right, we are in the Caribbean Sea, which means we are also smack dab in the middle of the Bermuda Triangle, the Devil's Triangle. This kind of thing happens rather frequently out here. Heck, they once found a huge freighter adrift that still had all its cargo, no damage at all, but the entire crew was gone. Plates of food were still on the table in the galley, and all the crew's things were still in their quarters. So yeah, maybe the Triangle got them."

"Oh, c'mon, J-Mac, you don't really expect me to believe that the Bermuda Triangle magically made that Russian a-hole just disappear off the *Donna Marie* do you?"

"I'm not saying that *is* what happened, but remember me saying I couldn't get a feel for anything, that it seems like everyone is talking at once?"

"Yeah, so what's that got to do with our sailboat appearing to be abandoned?" Cal retorted.

"Look, being in the Devil's Triangle could be the reason I can't get a read on anything. Maybe it's because of where we are and not everyone's emotions. This area is known to have strange magnetic anomalies. Ship's compasses go haywire, airplane instruments go all whacky. Maybe that's what is happening to me. I've been sitting quiet for the last forty minutes struggling to clear my head. It's really starting to bother me, and the sooner we get out these waters, the better. That's all I'm saying."

Cesar suddenly interjected, "I 'ave to say, Mista Cal, de islands are full of such stories. Planes 'ave gone down in clear weather, aund many boats 'ave washed ashore in de same condition as 'e says." He nodded toward Johnny Mac.

"So what we are supposed to do now? Just run right up to her and climb aboard?" Donna asked.

Cal looked to Donna, then to Cesar. "No, we continue with our original plan but approach with extreme caution, Devil's Triangle or not. If she is adrift, we need to figure out why, and don't forget this could be a trick."

Cesar gave Cal a huge smile, then turned to Antwan. "Antwan, radio de other boats with de current coordinates, aund apprise dem of de situation. Oh, aund tell dem to 'old back a few 'undred meters until we will approach first. Any sign of trouble dey are to come immediately, understood?"

"Yes, absolutely."

Turning to Cal and Donna, he said, "Good. Now let us go over just what we will do as we approach."

Cal gave a look to Sacha then to Cesar, then with a small smile, he said, "Friends and neighbors, I've got an idea that could let us draw right alongside the *Donna Marie*, and if that crazy-ass Russian *is* still aboard, he might just show his hand first.

Chapter 75

Cal's idea of putting Sacha on the flying bridge to pilot the *Akula* was so that he could be easily seen and hopefully make all seem completely normal, and so far it appeared to be working. The *Donna Marie* was in sight now only quarter a mile away, and no sign of the Russian or anyone else yet. Cal was suspicious and felt the Russian to be cunning and shrewd. Their effort at normalcy was to make him show himself first.

Drawing near to the *Donna Marie,* they all peered in silence out the cabin windows. No damage was evident, her sails were neatly stowed, and other than appearing abandoned, nothing seemed out of place. It was a disturbing scene for Cal and Donna seeing their beloved sailboat floating free. Watching it moving aimlessly on the rolling sea cast an eerie pall over her. The pitch and yaw of her graceful hull in unison with the hot winds that spun through her rigging created a sound that clattered across the waves and sang in harmony with the ghostly howl of her mast and spar lines.

Everyone settled back away from the windows. Though they were all quiet, their minds and emotions were anything but; Johnny Mac, however, sat the furthest away from everyone cross-legged on a small couch with his head down looking like a Tibetan shaman in deep meditation.

The tension was made even more intense when the *Akula's* engines were throttled down to barely above an idle; a gentle rumble and vibration now pulsed through her hull. At fifty yards distance, Sacha brought the *Akula* to a full stop to make a call on the radio to his former captain aboard the *Donna Marie.* If this was some kind of trick by his former captain, Sacha was to draw him out in the belief that everything was okay. It would all come down to Sacha's ability to convince him that all was normal. If any questions arose concerning where his shipmate was, Sacha was to tell him he had gotten sick on something he had eaten and was in the crew's quarters recuperating.

Cal gazed slowly around the cabin; he had tried to take into account every angle with regard to how he believed this would go down. If the Russian was onboard and believed what he was seeing and hearing, Cal felt certain that he would want to be right back on the *Akula*. The best-case scenario was a peaceful exchange, with everyone going their own way with no gunfire. Cal knew too that the crazy Russian's temper was the one random element he couldn't calculate for, and that was what could make this all go south in a very bad way.

Donna let go a slight yelp as Sacha's voice suddenly erupted over the *Akula's* intercom causing everyone to jerk a little and breaking their moment of tense silence. Sacha had keyed the yacht's intercom so they could hear what was going on while he tried to raise someone on the *Donna Marie's* radio.

All remained frozen, just listening to a second call to his former captain, then a third, still with no reply. Cal gave Cesar a look of concern. Talking barely above a whisper, Cal said, "I don't like this, Cesar. He *has* to be on that damn sailboat. Where would he have gone? This makes no sense."

Speaking very low, Cesar replied, "'E is a man with, I suspect, many enemies, Cal. Perhaps 'e 'as encountered one out here. What do you wish to do now, Mista Cal?"

Cal dropped his head to stare at the floor for a moment, then while nodding, lifted his head, saying, "She's my boat, and I'm her captain, so I'm going onboard to check things out, and if it's all clear, we are hightailing it for home. That's what we do now."

Donna immediately protested this, as did Cesar. However, Cal stood up while waving a hand in the air in front of himself, firmly stating, "Nope, not another word from anyone. I'm going onboard, armed of course, but I'm going alone, and that's all there is to it, all right!"

"No, not all right, Captain Bligh. I'm going with you, and if you say one word to try and stop me, I'll put my foot somewhere that'll make you wish you were born a woman. Do you hear me, Walter Caleb Arnold?" Donna forcefully commanded.

Cal stared at his wife in silence. Drawing in a deep breath, holding it a second or two, he let it go. "Donna, this goes way against my better judgment, but okay, you can come with me, only because I know that you'd come onboard soon I as was out of sight anyway, so it's better for me to know where you are rather than to accidently shoot you not knowing you're onboard."

Cesar quickly spoke to both of them. "See 'ere, you two, I can send Clovie to go onboard to check things out. We are more familiar with dese sorts of things."

Cal put a hand on his shoulder, saying, "Cesar, I know, but I'd rather you were our backup if needed, so as soon as we are onboard, bring in your other men. You'll have him surrounded, so what's he going to do? At worst, it'll be some kind of weird ocean-going Mexican standoff. Besides, there aren't many places he can hide on her."

Cesar held his stare on the two of them then shook his head. "Okay, if dat es de way you want it."

Just then Sacha spoke low over the intercom. "Shall I try him on the radio again, Captain?"

Cesar made his way to the intercom panel. Grabbing the mike, he looked back to Cal and Donna standing side by side, truly admiring them as a couple. A worried look followed by a warm smile drifted across his face. He then quietly said, "Sacha, bring us slowly alongside and pay close attention to the timing of these wind gusts. Try to time it to come alongside during their slack, do you understand?"

"Yes, sir. Most certainly I do, Captain."

"Very well, meet me at de helm on the main deck as soon as you 'ave us alongside of de *Donna Marie*."

Turning to face the whole group, Cesar somberly stated, "You all understand de risk we are taking 'ear. Know dat me aund my men will do everything we can to secure yo-ah safety, but der are no guarantees. De Russian, as we 'ave seen, can be quite unpredictable. If 'e remains onboard, 'e most certainly will not be alone. Further, they may shoot first. Mista Cal aund Miss Donna, I cannot express de amount of care you must exercise once aboard yo-ah boat. Hopefully he has abandoned et, and you all can return home safely. Dat es my wish."

Cal smiled broadly at Cesar. "Thanks, Cesar, we'll be all right. Besides, the only person who cares more about my old ass is this girl right here. I can't let anything happen to her because nobody else will have me."

Donna elbowed him in the side, saying. "Have you? You mean put up with you, ya ornery old goat."

Joel, who had been sitting in the background staying quiet watching all this unfold and wondering just what he had gotten himself into, abruptly spoke up from behind them, causing them all to turn to face him. "Look, I don't know what I've gotten into here, but I've got a small score to settle with the SOB that clocked me on the head." Fixing his eyes on Donna, he added, "I'll go with your husband. A lady shouldn't be putting herself in danger like this. Besides, I can handle a gun. What I can't handle is seeing something bad happen to you. Neither of you want to live with what I have had to for the last ten years." With a smirk, he added, "Besides, nobody will miss me. Heck, far as the world knows, I'm already dead."

Donna's eyes met Cal's. "What about it, Donna, will you stay here while we check things out? He's right, and I would feel a whole lot better if you remained onboard."

Donna's face showed the reluctance of what she was going to say before a word crossed her lips. "Yeah, okay. But promise me you will be very, very careful. Our future grandbaby will need a grandpa just like you, okay?"

Cal gave her a kiss on the cheek and said, "Don't worry, I'll be fine. Besides, I've been looking forward to the day when I could start spoiling kids instead of raising them."

Cal then looked toward the front of the cabin. "Johnny Mac, you have been quiet like Joel here. You wanna go on this little recon mission with us?"

Looking up, he stared intently at Cal a moment then replied. "No, I think I'd just be in the way. Some of the confusion I've been experiencing is subsiding. But listen to me, Cal. To win, you must lose what you hold in your hands."

Everyone gawked at Johnny Mac a moment trying to figure out what the heck he was talking about. Cal finally asked, "J-Mac, what the hell are you saying? Lose what?"

Straight-faced he replied, "Just what I said." He then dropped his head down in silence, leaving everyone else shaking theirs.

Just then they felt the *Akula*'s forward motion came to a stop. This was it. Cal tensed a little as they stepped out onto the deck. All the craziness of the last few days was coming down to this one moment, a moment he desperately hoped ended well for everyone, even that crazy Russian.

Cal and Joel stood side by side waiting for Sacha to maneuver close enough for them to make the jump onto the *Donna Marie*. For the moment the winds had calmed; however, the sea still rolled with three-foot swells, making the jump from one moving deck and onto another a challenge. The *Akula* edged closer and closer to the *Donna Marie*. Both Cal and Joel knew this was a tricky maneuver; if they misjudged and landed in the water, they could be crushed between the hulls.

All eyes were focused on the *Donna Marie*. Cesar stood just behind them. Everyone anxiously studied the pitch and roll of the *Donna Marie* now a mere five feet away, then four, three. "Jump now!" Cesar roared. Cal and Joel leapt into the air. Just as their feet cleared the edge of the *Donna Marie*'s deck, a strong gust of wind and rain raced across the water catching them and blowing them backward, dropping them just shy of the *Donna Marie*'s deck.

Dropping down between the boats, both instinctively clawed for the deck railing, catching it as they dropped past, jerking them both to a swift stop. Joel, however, hung precariously by only one hand, struggling to grip with the other. Cal instantly reached for his flailing arm, grabbing hold of it just as he lost his grip with the other hand.

A painful yell erupted from Cal who strained mightily to hold onto Joel and the portside railing while being repeatedly dropped and lifted form roiling waters. With each up and down cycle, Cal's one-handed grip slipped more and more. Time seemed to freeze yet race by in the few seconds Joel's body flailed wildly down and backward to the *Donna Marie*'s hull. Another dredge through the water threatened to wash them into the turbulent waters that boiled between the two vessels.

Donna screamed out helplessly, seeing the gap between the *Akula* and the *Donna Marie* rapidly tightening. Cesar shouted out, "Back us away! Back us away!" Immediately, the *Akula*'s reverse thrust boiled the sea into swirling turbulence. Just then above all the commotion, a deep voice boomed out over the wind and engine noise. "Quickly, grab zem! Bring zem aboard!"

Chapter 76

In the next instant, Cal felt his forearm being tightly gripped. With Joel barely clinging to Cal's left arm, they were quickly hoisted over the railing and unceremoniously hurled onto the deck, soaking wet and out of breath.

Pawing the rain and seawater from their faces, they found themselves looking down the barrel of guns pointed directly at their heads. Standing just behind the armed crewmen was Yuri smiling and laughing; in his hand was the fake package of cocaine that Johnny Mac had made with pancake mix and powdered sugar. "Vell, vell, look who vee have here, ze arrogant American. I must say, American, you *did* fool Yuri with this. It is not easy to fool Yuri, but you did. But now, now ze tables have turned, have they not, American?"

Cesar's men, as instructed, slowly approached the *Donna Marie* taking widely separated positions on her portside. Sacha held a parallel position on her starboard side, effectively sandwiching the *Donna Marie* between them. Cal slowly tucked his legs under and pushed himself up to stand all the while the gun was kept trained on him. Facing Yuri, Cal pawed his hand down his face again then quite calmly stated, "No, Ivan, they have not. The place and the setting may have changed a little, but your situation is the same as before. You are outmanned and outgunned. Look around you."

Yuri stared at Cal a moment then cautiously turned partway around to see Cesar's men approaching on three boats, each with three men on board. Yuri tuned back to face Cal showing a defiant smile. He then coldly stated, "And you think zis gives you ze upper hand? I think not, for I have you, and as a bonus," pointing to Joel, he added, "a second hostage, although I don't think anyone vill miss him."

Cal began to tap into his abilities of persuasion once again. While the situation was different than their first meeting, he decided their best chance was to key off some of what Sacha had told them about this guy and try and convince him that he would be better served to let everyone go their merry way. Just exactly what is he going to do or say wasn't on the tip of his tongue at the moment.

As Cesar's men moved within a hundred feet, they quickly took positions at the *Donna Marie's* bow, midsection, and stern, with two Uzi-armed men standing on the bow of all three boats.

Yuri laughed out loud. "So many guns, and you think Yuri is afraid now, yes?"

Cal steadied himself on the sea-tossed deck. "No, Yuri, I don't. A man like you is never afraid, even sometimes when he should be. What I want to see though is if you are smart or not. Sure, you can shoot me and him," Cal calmly said, pointing to Joel, who had stood up next to him. "*But* if you do, you *know* what will happen next? That's right, lead will be flying all over this boat, most of it at you. So the outlook isn't good for either one of us, a fact that I'm sure won't play well with your, shall I say, financial sponsor back home at the Gosbank. Yes, that's right, I know about your little operation."

Yuri's expression went instantly straight. "So you 'ave beaten my men for information, I see."

"No, it appears you do all the beating. We, just like my country does, offered freedom instead of oppression."

Yuri scoffed. "You imperialists, always believing in your own false righteousness and perfection."

"No, not perfect, but we are free to strive for it. Look, we can stand here all day extolling the virtues of our two counties, but we have a little standoff here, and in case you haven't noticed, we may have a hurricane bearing down us, so what are we doing here? You know the sea can get really ugly really quick as that storm approaches."

Yuri looked around taking stock of his situation; if that storm was headed their way, he thought, he would much prefer to be aboard the *Akula*. Looking back at Cal, he considered just what to do. He was right about trying to shoot things out. He worried too about how this all would play out back home with his contacts, for he was also engaging in activities they knew nothing about and was well beyond the smuggling of information and sensitive materials to and from Cuba. He was about to ask Cal what he thought would be a good solution to this deadlock, when his mind flashed to a deck of cards in the forward cabin. A smile drifted across his face at what he was considering.

Taking a deep breath and with great confidence, he spoke out. "American, it occurs to Yuri dat you are ze sporting type of man, one who takes a gamble now and again, are you not?"

Cal's mind whirled wondering just where he was going with all of this. Cautiously, he answered, "I've been known to take a chance or two now and then. What are you suggesting?"

A stiff breeze blew across them. Yuri looked up into the graying skies then drew his stare back to Cal. "Let us return to ze island, secure our vessels, and while we wait out zis storm, you and I shall play a game of cards, yes?"

Cal couldn't believe what he was hearing, but before agreeing, he cautiously asked, "What game, and what are the stakes?"

Yuri threw a glance up and down the length of the *Donna Marie* and then along the *Akula*. Laughing a bit, he firmly stated, "Poker, and de winner takes all, do you agree?"

Cal dropped his head thinking quickly. They would be much safer back on the island, avoiding both the risk of being shot or maybe drowning at sea. Turning halfway around to look back at the *Akula,* he saw Donna staring back him. He doubted she could hear much of what was being said or what was going on, so he gave her a devilish grin, and then made a hand gesture in front of his stomach so Yuri couldn't see. Scrunching her face, she couldn't believe what she was seeing or why.

Yuri shouted out, drawing Cal's attention back to him by demanding, "Vhat about it, American? Do you feel lucky today?"

Cal nodded as he stated, "Lucky or not, losing a card game beats the hell out of losing a gunfight, wouldn't you say?"

Yuri laughed out loud. "Yes, yes, zat is much better for you, American, I agree." Cal just stared at him, watching him laugh, and glance around to his stone-faced men. Cal though was glad that his arrogance kept Yuri seeing things from his perspective of superiority.

Cal recalled that his easiest marks were always the overconfident ones. Still though, he felt he had to be very careful how he handled himself. Poker was his game, and he seldom ever lost, *and* he didn't plan on losing now; there was just too much at stake. The real trick was to make himself appear to be an average player of poker and got lucky on just the right hand. If Yuri suspected Cal to be better at the game than he let on, Cal was sure it would go straight to guns and bullets again.

Suddenly, Yuri raised both his arms up high while shouting out, "Everyone, lower your weapons. Zer will be no shooting today!" Then to Cesar, he continued, "You, Sawfish, you vill toss a tow line to my men. Ze *Akula* vill tow us back to port so we all arrive at za same time."

Cesar nodded his understanding and called to Clovie to ready a line. He then directed Sacha to bring the *Akula* around to the *Donna Marie*'s bow. Donna stepped over to Cesar, asking, "What the *heck* is going on, what are we doing?"

"I em not sure, Miss Donna, but from de grin yo-ah man just showed, it would seem dat he and de Russian 'ave struck a deal."

A half smile came to Donna while mouthing the word *deal*. She had seen Cal give that devilish grin many times before, and anytime she saw it, she knew he was feeling pretty confident about something, and most times it centered on some silly little bet he had with some of the staff or a regular customer at the Salty Anchor. Suddenly it hit her. She shuddered at the thought. The hand gesture he made with his hand, showing four fingers spread then curling them in with a thumbs-up, was his sign for royal flush. He did this any time he thought he had the winning hand. "Oh my god, he's going to play a game of poker. He's going to try and win the *Donna Marie* back by gambling for her!"

Chapter 77

Encountering little wind, the sea still rose and fell in large rolling swells on their return to Cockburn Town. The *Akula*, with the *Donna Marie* in tow, plied the waters with relative ease; approaching the leeward side of the island, the swells subsided, which made docking and securing both vessels at the old navy supply dock far less burdensome.

Cal and Joel had remained aboard the *Donna Marie* for the return to Cockburn Town. Yuri's demeanor had changed somewhat, becoming more affable, offering them something to drink and granting Cal's request to go into the cabin to change into some dry clothes. Both Joel and he were allowed to go one at a time with one of Yuri's armed crewmen.

Returning to the helm, Cal thanked Yuri. "Hey, ah, thanks. It feels much better being out of those wet clothes."

"Yes, yes, zat is good. A man is not at his best if he is uncomfortable. Yuri prefer to win ze game with a man who has no excuse for ze losing."

Cal smiled half-heartedly. Yuri stood a few feet away sporting a big grin while palming the pack of cards he had found in the *Donna Marie's* sleeping quarters. Seeing the cards being rolled and tossed up and down in Yuri's hand, Cal's eyes suddenly widened with his grin. It was his own deck of cards, and not just any deck, his own marked deck! He had forgotten they were even onboard. This certainly bent things dramatically in his favor.

Feeling a good deal of relief, he decided to stoke up ole Yuri's bravado a bit more while at the same time playing down his own abilities at the game of poker. "Hey, ah, Yuri, ah, you don't mind if I call you by that do you?" Yuri enthusiastically answered affirmatively. Cal continued, "Okay, good. Listen, poker can be such a long game to play. What say we play blackjack, a best seven outta ten. Still winner takes all, what do ya think?"

Yuri ceased his fumbling with the pack of cards and just stared straight-faced at Cal a moment then cautiously spoke. "So you vant to play different game, maybe ze man's game of poker es too much for you, so you vant to play little boy's game now?"

"No, I'm, uh, I'm okay with poker, just thinking we could settle things much quicker, you know with this storm looming south of us."

Yuri let go a deep laugh then broadly smiled while firmly stating, "Yuri not worried about storm. Ve have all ze time to play game and see who es better at man's game of cards. Maybe you say zis because you not good at game of poker, yes?"

Cal gave him a doubtful look, then replied, letting his words be tinged with the same doubt, "Well, of, of course I know *how* to play poker. Sure, I mean what kind of man doesn't? My…my dad showed me the game when I was a kid. Heck, me and my buddies, we, uh, we get together a couple times a year to play, you know just us guys."

Yuri again laughed out loud. "Zen der es nothing to worry about. Yuri not, uh, uh, how say, ze, ze card shark. Yuri just like you, see, so ve are equals. Zat is good, yes?"

Cal gave him his best scolded puppy look. "Yeah, yeah, I suppose so. Poker it is then."

Arriving in the harbor, the *Akula* slowed. Letting the tow line fall slack to the *Donna Marie*, which was quickly unwound from the bow cleat, her diesel engine fired up; she was under her own power once again. It was decided to let her enter the huge three-sided docking slip and bring the *Akula* in behind her for additional protection from the wind and waves should the storm come their way.

Donna stood with Cesar and Johnny Mac listening to the latest update on the storm which appeared to be good news for the most part anyway. U.S. satellites and hurricane hunter aircraft were putting the forecast track of the storm's eye wall well to the west of Cockburn Town. That was the good news; the not so good news was that the strong side of the storm would be on its eastern side. This meant that the outer bands of this very large storm would likely be passing right over the island, some of which could reach near hurricane force.

Returning her attention to look out the windows of the main deck helm, she watched her man acting like nothing was wrong, even assisting with securing the *Donna Marie*. She smiled watching him do something they had done many times back home in Ramrod Key. The second she thought of home, she felt a knot in her stomach. It was then that she realized that she hadn't thought about the kids, the Salty Anchor, or her future grandbaby. Suddenly she wanted nothing more than to get off this boat and run to make a call home. She knew that they must be worried sick about their crazy parents.

The *Akula* was brought in behind the *Donna Marie* and secured. For the time being, both vessels were pulled to one side of the docking slip. The slip had been constructed with one side lower than the other so as to be able to handle the different size ships that the navy would dock here during the war.

Once each vessel was secured, Yuri turned back to face the *Akula*. Placing his hands on either side of his mouth, he shouted to Cesar who now stood on the *Akula*'s bow. "Let us all meet in de pavilion to discuss vhat we are doing. None of our men, just us. Yes, do you agree?"

Cesar nodded, then gestured toward the open pavilion. Donna, who was standing now a few feet behind Cesar, immediately and firmly stated, "I'm going with you."

Cesar turned to face her showing a broad smile. "I would expect nothing less from you, dear lady."

Walking past his men, Cesar told both Antwan and Clovie that if trouble broke out to cut the mooring lines and to leave immediately with the *Akula* and take it a mile off shore and wait for instructions. As Donna and Cesar began making their way to the pavilion, she abruptly stopped, having decided to let Cesar know what she thought was happening. Cesar stopped two steps beyond and turned back to face her.

"Cesar, you know when my husband turned back to face us with that big smile, he also made a hand gesture to me."

"I remember. I meant to ask you about et."

"Yes, well, that is his little signal that he has a winning hand."

"A winning hand—you mean like when playing a game of cards?"

"Yeah, it means he has a royal flush. He will flash that at me whenever he has some silly little bet going with someone back home. That's why I think that he and the Russian are going to play a game of poker for possession of the *Donna Marie*."

"Really? But isn't dat how he obtained yo-ah sailboat in de first place?"

Rolling her eyes at the memory of it, she gave a short, sardonic reply, "Yes, it is."

Throwing his head back, Cesar let go a boisterous laugh. "Ahh, Miss Donna, I must say de both of you are quite de couple, but what if yo-ah man loses? De Russian will gain possession of yo-ah beautiful boat."

Donna simply shook her head no and said, "Cal doesn't lose, well, not much anyway. He learned the game as a kid, and he used his winnings to help support the family after his father disappeared under mysterious circumstances."

"I see, so yo-ah not worried den about him losing?"

"No, Cesar, I'm not. I'm worried as hell about him winning."

Cesar scrunched his face in thought for a moment, then thoughtfully said, "Umm, yes, yes, I see what you mean. De Russian is most unpredictable, and after seeing his earlier display of temper, I em sure he will not take lightly to losing."

Turning to Donna, he gestured with a leading hand while saying, "We shall go now aund he-ah what de Russian has in mind."

*****

Descending the steps to the weather station, Jim, Juky, and the police captain were met by one of his officers. "Captain! Captain!"

"Yes, yes, what is it.?"

"De boats aund de men Mista Abbot spoke of, dey are at de navy docks, aund der are several people heading to de cargo pavilion."

Jim quickly spoke up. "Well, Captain, doesn't look like you need *me* now, but I still need you and your men. My friends are not with that Russian or that Sawfish guy by choice, that's for sure."

"No, I em sure dey are not. But we must be careful so dat we do not bring unintended harm to yo-ah friends."

"What do you suggest?"

"We need to know more about what's going on, so I will send two of my men in civilian clothes. Several of de locals are 'elping de fisherman to secure traps, nets, aund der vessels. Don't forget de satellite image showed a large squall line being spun off from de storm. We 'ave maybe two hours before it arrives."

"Yeah, I know. Looks like I have only two choices now: fly the hell out of here or secure my bird and stay here to help my friends and hope that squall line loses some of its punch before it gets here."

The captain gave Jim an empathetic smile. "Mista Abbot, it would appear to me dat you 'ave but one choice."

Jim pressed his lips tight while fixing his eyes on the captain. "Yup, it would seem so. Listen, I know the airport was built during the war. I'm pretty sure there are tie-down cleats for planes built into the tarmac. What I don't have is rope. Is there any way you can help with that?"

"Most certainly." Looking past Jim, he pointed and shouted out to a group of his men standing nearby. "Marcus, take two men with you aund assist dis man with securing his aircraft. Get him whatever 'e needs. When finished, come back he-ah straight away."

Jim reached and excitedly shook the captain's hand, then tossed a harried look to Juky. "Listen, why don't you hang back here and see what is going on with Cal and Donna. I should be back here shortly, okay?"

"Okay, I can help he's men with de surveillance, if dat es okay," Juky answered.

"Yes, yo-ah welcome to assist with our efforts."

Jim was already hustling away when he called back to Juky. "Okay then, get a move on. I have a feeling that something big is about to go down."

Chapter 78

Donna and Cesar walked along in silence both watching Cal and Yuri strolling side by side like two old buddies. It was obvious they were conversing back and forth, about *what,* she could only imagine. Cesar finally broke their brief silence. "Yo-ah husband certainly appears relaxed, like nothing at all es wrong."

"Cesar, from some of the stories that man has told me of his past, what he is doing right now is baiting a trap. He has a story about how he tricked two cops into drinking a magic elixir he was brewing in the woods back home."

"A magic elixir?"

"Yeah, he spun one heck of a tale that had them believing that it could make them live longer and be more manly, if you know what I mean. *But* all they were really drinking was just white lightning—moonshine. He got 'em both drunker than Cooter Brown. When they passed out, he then left them there to go and find who it was that had ratted him out to those cops, and that's where Juky enters the picture."

Cesar let go a deep laugh while saying, "Miss Donna, when dis is over, I must come to de Salty Anchor to 'ear more stories of dis man you married. You know they should make a movie about his escapades. De people would love it, I em sure."

Donna joined his laughter, adding, "Oh, heck no, we'd have to change our names after that." Just then their brief moment of escape was broken by the sound of Cal calling back to them to hurry up. Donna and Cesar turned their attention from each other to see Cal and Yuri were already standing in the pavilion both waving for them to pick up their pace.

"Looks like we need to get a move on. I know my husband. He seems calm on the outside, but on the inside, he has one thing on his mind, and that's beating the pants off that arrogant Russian."

Starting into a trot, they quickly covered the remaining distance to the pavilion. Arriving, Yuri began speaking. "Finally, it is good to meet the one whose name graces the beautiful sailboat that everyone is so interested in." Looking to Cesar, he added, "And you, Sawfish, what is your continued interest in dis vessel? Certainly you have other matters zat bear your attention more?"

"Let's just say dat I 'ave a deep interest in der safety—one I hope you share as well."

"Ahh, so you think I will harm them. No, no, no, zat is not my intention. You see. Sawfish, me and uh..." Yuri cut his eyes to Cal. "Cal is correct, yes?" Cal nodded. "Yes, good, Cal. You see, men like Cal and myself, ve have agreement. Ve settle zis like men, no guns, no shooting, no fighting, not today. Today will be settled with de turn of a card!" It was then that Yuri, like a magician, deftly rolled the deck of cards seemingly out of nowhere into the palm of his hand.

This magician-like maneuver was clearly meant to intimidate Cal. And it did leave him wondering a bit about his adversary's true talent at poker and perhaps shed some light on just how intense this game could get. Cal felt he may have underestimated Yuri's prowess at cards. However, he was not going let his little sleight of hand carry more weight than it should.

"Hey, uh, Yuri, where shall we play our little game of poker?" Before he could answer, Cal continued, "How about this, since the *Donna Marie* is really what's at stake here, let's settle this onboard her. I think it will be more satisfying for the victor, wouldn't you say?"

Caught off guard a bit, but quickly recovering, Yuri rubbed his chin in consideration of Cal's suggestion. Cal though figured he was taking a moment picturing himself victorious standing on the deck of the *Donna Marie*.

"How 'bout it? I'm man enough for it, are you?"

Yuri threw Cal a stern glare, then barked, "That is good place. We play der, just you and me, yes?"

"Ah, not quite, we—"

Yuri tersely interrupted Cal. "Vhat? Zat is vhat you just said."

"Now hold on, let me finish. Yes, we will play on the *Donna Marie*, but it won't be just you and me. We need a witness and a dealer, one we both can agree on."

Yuri pursed his lips while thinking a moment. Cal then made a suggestion. "What about that ornery old cuss that I paid to fix all those damn bullets holes you shot in my boat? I don't think he particularly likes anybody here. Hell, I don't think he likes anybody, for that matter."

Yuri again rubbed his chin. "Hmm, I don't know, vhy vas he aboard ze *Akula* with you?"

"Well, fact is, I was dragging his ass back with me so he could finish what he had started. We had a business deal, that's all, pure and simple."

Yuri nodded while thinking; perhaps the old skinny shipwright might not like Cal so much, especially after nearly getting him crushed between two boats. Suddenly he slapped his thigh with the deck of cards, loudly stating, "Okay! De skinny shipwright vill deal."

"Great! Then let's get going."

Yuri took one step in front of Cal then abruptly stopped. Holding up a hand, he said, "No, vait, one more thing. The game may be long, so your woman, she vill come aboard to serve us drinks and food so ve don't leave de table."

Cal shot a rapid look in Donna's direction; seeing her swallow hard, Cal figured she was about to give Yuri a good old-fashioned tongue-lashing for referring to her like some slave girl. But surprisingly, she replied in a quiet, almost supplicating tone, "I will be happy to serve you both."

Cal stared wide-eyed at his wife thinking he could be knocked over with a feather right then. "Good, good, and here Yuri believe all American woman push de men around. Yuri see you have trained zis one vell, yes?"

Cal saw Donna's nostrils flare and knew she was holding back a big one. He figured one more insulting remark like that and there would be no need to play a game of poker, because Donna would burn him down to the ground right where he stood. Cal inhaled and exhaled a deep cleansing breath as if to try and blow out the searing gaze she held on Yuri's back, but in that split second of silence, the devil in him, as it often did, wouldn't let this moment pass without giving his wife a little good-natured prodding. Sure, he'd pay for it later, but he just couldn't help himself.

Tossing an arm around Yuri's shoulders, he started them walking up the docks again. He gave a rapid look and devilish grin back at Donna. Turning back, he said, "You know, Yuri, my father once told me that a man should keep a tight rein on his woman, that a man's word should always be respected *and* obeyed by his woman. And by golly, my woman knows her place."

Yuri, oblivious to Cal's schoolboy-like poking at his wife, replied with great approval, "Yes, yes, zis is true, and she listen good."

Cal needn't look back; he could feel her hot glare on the back of his neck. Smiling to himself, he hoped that his winning the *Donna Marie* back and the time it would take to do so would give her time to cool down, that is unless Yuri kept up with the Slavic sexism—all bets were off on how that would all go.

Coming up next to the *Donna Marie*, Cesar commented, "Yo-ah man, he does know how to play someone—those two appear to be best friends now."

Donna just stared at Cal a moment watching them stroll away. "Yes, he does, Cesar, he sure does." She briefly thought of all the times over the years he would poke at her like this. She would never let him get away with any of it, but at the same time, she always understood what he was doing. In his own quirky way, he was confirming that he had indeed married a strong and independent woman; however, she thought, she was going to have to come up with a pretty good return volley for this one.

Chapter 79

Cesar and his men along with Yuri's men were to wait in the pavilion's offices, unarmed. All weapons were left in their respective boats. The cargo pavilion's office ran the full width of the large expansive cargo loading area and was the best place to ride out a storm. This rectangular facility was built by the U.S. Navy and, in typical governmental fashion, overbuilt. The offices were constructed of eight-inch-thick solid concrete walls. The open pavilion likewise had massive steel beams and columns supporting a steel roof that hovered over the open-sided loading area, covering ten thousand square feet.

The windows were few and rather small. Cesar, as did one of Yuri's men, sat at the only large window, one that faced the docks. They had a perfect view of the *Donna Marie* and the *Akula* from this vantage point. They wordlessly watched Yuri, Cal, Joel, and Donna disappear into the *Donna Marie's* cabin.

Cesar looked over to the man sitting to his right. "Well, ma friend, et would appear dat dis matter will soon be settled."

The stoned-faced man gave a small nod. "Yes, et will be. My captain, he not lose. He win all za time."

Cesar returned a knowing nod electing not to say any of what he knew about Cal's abilities. Instead he decided that he would work to get more information from the Russian crew, by drawing on his known reputation in these waters.

"Yes, I can see dat yo-ah captain es very smart aund capable maun. Tell me what was es his intention for de vessel once he wins her?"

The crewman narrowed his stare at Cesar. "Vhy should I tell you?"

Cesar smiled before standing. Taking a couple steps away, he spoke out into the open room, his deep voice echoing off the gray concrete walls. "No reason really, just curious if he was going to do de same thing I would have had *I* seized her before yo-ah captain outwitted us all."

"And vhat would zat be, Sawfish?"

Cesar turned back to face the crewman. "Myself, I had plans to put de word out of ets availability among des islands and perhaps take de highest bidder, is dis not what yo-ah captain had planned?"

With a mocking laugh, the crewman looked away briefly and then back to Cesar. "Zat is sure way to have authorities catch you. Our captain not do such stupid thing as zis. No, we have contact in Lisbon. Zis is where we go after captain win easily game with ze stupid American."

"Ahh, I see, yo-ah quite correct. De taking of dis vessel was a, shall we say, new endeavor for me aund my men. Perhaps I should reconsider how to best to handle such activities in de future. Tell me, does de contact in Lisbon, will deh deal with others or only yo-ah captain?"

The crewman studied Cesar before he answered, taking a moment to consider his own future with his captain. He well knew the harshness of his captain's command; things could degrade in ways that might make taking up with the Sawfish a more desirable alternative. Deciding to leave his options open, he calmly stated, "Yes, ze contact has others he deals with, but he is cautious. He deal only with ze people he has checked out."

"By his people?"

"Yes, he have many people around ze world."

Cesar's eyes widened. "Dis contact is dealing with dat many boats?"

Feeling more relaxed, the crewman laughed while looking away from the window he had been staring out of, fixing his eyes on Cesar. "No, no, not just de expensive boats, no. He deal in many, many items of high value. From paintings, rare jewels, even antiques. I even see him deal with old, ah, ah, de, uh, dinosaur bones, taken from museum in France. Zat one was big, big money."

461

Finally, one of the other crewmen spoke out harshly in Russian. "Grigori! Вы слишком много говорите."

Grigori shot a resentful glare toward the crewman then growled, "I talk too much! You, Lev, you butt in too much! Speak so all can understand, or do you have no spine for zat. Lev, you, you forget too much my rank in our little navy. I not tell who de contact is. You know, like me, ze contact, he pay good money for new sources, so maybe we get money for, for us now. Za captain gets much for himself. How much do we get? We get de change what spills from his pockets. And Yuri, he eats za best food and drinks za best wine and vodka."

Lev kept a hot hateful glare on Grigori for a short moment then turned sharply away saying nothing.

Cesar eased slowly back to a long table where his men quietly sat. He couldn't believe what he was hearing. He remembered reading about many of the stolen things the crewman spoke of. The realization that he and his men might be on the verge of breaking open an international ring of thieves had his mind racing.

Looking to his men then to Grigori, Cesar spoke up, his words careful and low. "You know, et es a well-known fact that many of the world's wealthy have such items as you describe, among des islands great works of art, rare jewels, and many other things of great value are littered throughout des islands. It would seem to me dat perhaps our little group he-ah could come to some type of agreement and share in de profits gained by de careful, shall we say, harvesting of such items."

Lev suddenly spoke up, this time so all understood. "Do not listen to hem, Grigori. I do not trust hem."

"No, Lev, you listen! You know how Yuri treat us, like slaves. He throw a few rubles at us while he fills his pockets with much cash. I know. I see what he does. He think Grigori do not see, but I do. His contact at Gosbank, dey both grow rich while we grovel for de crumbs dat fall from de table, so yes, maybe we make deal with de Sawfish." Tossing a rapid look at Antwan, he barked, "You, how long you work for de Sawfish? How does your captain treat you?"

Surprised by the question, Antwan looked to Cesar. Cesar quickly said, "Go ahead, Antwan, speak freely. If we are to make a deal with des men, dey need to know who dey are dealing with."

Antwan nodded. Facing Grigori, he confidently stated, "I 'ave been with de Sawfish many years now. Our captain es vury good to us. We are paid well. Our families live in good homes, we 'ave plenty to eat, aund much, much more. Before, we barely had enough food. De Sawfish is good to us all."

"Do you see, Lev, zis men are happy to work for der captain, while we, we have to grovel like dog before ours."

"Grigori, listen to me. You know what za punishment will be for us if Yuri learns of our even talking about zis. Ze gulags are filled with people who have been sent der as traitors to za people."

"We are a long way from ze gulags, Lev. Destiny has brought us a chance to live better lives. I say we deal with zis man."

Cesar spoke out quickly. "Yo-ah man here is correct. Yo-ah crewmate Sacha has already joined my crew, so he will suffer no longer at de will of yo-ah captain."

Hearing this, Grigori quickly ran with this new information. "You see, Lev, you know well how badly Sacha has been treated. Even if he go back to Soviet Union, he will have nothing. He will live like rat in ze communal apartments as we all do. We have five families in my apartment. Many others have more. Zey promise us zat if we do ze smuggling to Cuba, we will get better food, better apartment, but I do not trust zem."

Gesturing toward the window, he angrily added, "Za poorest bastard of des islands lives better zin we do back home. At least zey are free to fish for za food zey need, while we, we wait in long lines for hours just to get crumbs. So, Lev, I tell you zis: I 'em not going with de captain. If Sacha have de guts to leave"—he smacked his chest with the palm of his hand—"zen so does Grigori."

Lev stood, stepping close to Grigori. His eyes narrowed. Pointing a ridged finger in his face, he warned, "Den Grigori, you better pray de captain loses."

Cesar watched with great interest the standoff between the two men; there was only one other crewman now that Cesar didn't know where his loyalties lay. Cesar decided to try and redirect and cool the emotions of everyone, easing his way back to the large window. Stepping up close, he spoke out to no one in particular.

"Gentleman, et would seem dat all of our fates now hang on de turn of a single card." Turning back to face them all, he added, "Let us hope et es not de Tower card."

Chapter 80

A rush of warm tropical air swirled in as Jim pushed open the door to the police station causing him to have to shove the door closed behind him. "Dang, it's getting rough out, gentlemen. That wind is pretty stiff out there now."

Captain de la Rosa looked up from a weather report he was reviewing and nodded. "Et appears that et may get much worse before et gets better."

Pulling off his ball cap, Jim asked while using his shirttail to wipe the sweat from his face, "Why, what's going on? Has that storm changed direction?"

The captain stood up from his desk and spoke while offering the report to Jim. "Mista Abbot, et appears der es a ridge of high pressure dat es moving south over de Gulf of Mexico which es blocking de storm from its northwest track. Further, it may begin to steer de storm closer to our location, maybe even right over us!"

"What?" Jim hurried around the counter separating them. Reaching for the weather report, he anxiously spoke out, "Hell, thirty minutes ago we were just getting some squalls. This could change everything." The captain outlined the situation while Jim quickly read through the report.

"Dis es de most recent update. What we saw earlier, Mista Abbot, was six hours old. De U.S. hurricane hunter aircraft just flew through de storm an hour ago. Dis just came across de wire. Dis is a preliminary report. A more detailed one will follow."

Looking up from the report, Jim exclaimed, "This says that the future course is unclear, but what's not unclear is that it's gaining strength, that it could be a cat 4 by as early as tomorrow morning!"

Juky, who had been sitting at a desk listening to these new developments, asked out loud to no one in particular, "So what do we do now? I'm sure Mista Cal and Donna, dey do not know any of dis information."

"Gentlemen, I em quite sure you can see dat my priorities have changed now as well. I have to see to de welfare of de citizens of Cockburn Town now, so whatever es going on with yo-ah friends and de Russian will have to be dealt with later."

Jim raked the palm of his hand over his head then snapped his ball cap back on. Turning his attention to Juky, he spoke out like the flight commander he used to be. "I'll tell you what we are going to do. We are going over there and get those nutcase friends of ours and fly their asses outta here whether they like it or not, and that sailboat of theirs be dammed!"

"But Mista Jim," Juky cautioned, "dose men, dey 'ave guns, aund we 'ave none."

Jim smiled while producing his chrome Smith & Wesson 44 pistol from his back. The captain's eyes widened as he immediately spoke up. "Now wait just a moment, Mista Abbot, I em not going to have you start a shoot-out with those men. I have enough to deal with already. My men along with Juky have reported to me what they have seen with yo-ah friends, aund I must say I don't understand et at all. However, et appears to me dey are in no immediate danger."

"They're not? How can you be so sure?"

"Well, sir, for one thing, de only occupants on the sailboat are an older man, a woman, the Russian, and for reasons I don't know, a man who lives here who is known only as El Jurakan."

"What about that Sawfish guy, where is he?"

"He along with his men aund de Russian crew are all waiting in de old navy shipping offices. Obviously one of dem has a contact with de owners of de facility to be allowed in der."

"So what about my friends? Is that Russian and that, that El Jurakan cat holding them hostage?"

The captain's face held a perplexed expression while letting go a laugh. "Mista Abbot, I believe Mista Juky can best inform you of what he saw when he crept aboard the sailboat."

Jim turned sharply toward Juky. "What's up, big guy, what's going on?"

Juky raised his brow and factually stated, "Believe et or not, dey were playing a game of cards, enjoying some drinks and food, and seemed quite happy. So you see, der is no need to go in der and start brandishing dat weapon of yo-ahs."

Totally frustrated, Jim spun around on his heels while yanking off his hat once again to palm a hand over his head. "This is the craziest shit I've been involved in since I flew bombers over Nuremburg. I should load my ass up in the Water Lily and make for home."

"Mista Jim," Juky solemnly began. "While I have not known you long, der is one thing I do know about de guys like you who were in de great war."

"Yeah, and just what would that be, Juky?"

"Dat you don't abandon your fellow soldiers."

Jim held his stare on Juky for a moment then quietly, almost apologetically replied, "Well, they're not soldiers."

Juky's reply was soft but hit hard. "No, dey are not. Dey are more. Dey are yo-ah friends."

Jim rubbed his forehead then shot Juky a condemning glare. "Okay, okay, you're right. So let's go over there and tell them what's going on with the storm. Then they can decide what they want to do." Pointing a finger at Juky, he added, "But listen, if them knuckleheads decide they want to stay, or sail that tub for home, that's on them, not me, understood!"

Juky nodded. "But of course, as et should be."

Jim turned his attention to the captain. "Listen, I'm not going over there to start any trouble, but if something goes down, I'd like to know you and your men have got our six."

The captain gave a twist of the head as he replied, "As I said, my immediate duty is to the residents of Cockburn Town. However, if you have trouble, we will do what we can, which of course depends on the immediate situation. You understand, of course."

"Yeah, sure, it's probably something goofy anyway. Heck, if they're eat'n', drink'n', and play'n' cards, what could be the problem, right?"

"Most certainly, Mista Abbot, I'm sure der es a reasonable explanation for what es going on."

Jim arched his brow high. "Well, if there *is* something reasonable going on, it will be the first reasonable thing that I've seen since I got involved in this wacky boat chase." Glancing to Juky, Jim nodded toward the door. "What's say we go give a weather report, Juky old man."

Chapter 81

It was agreed to play five hands of poker they also agreed on just three rounds of betting before showing their hands. This kept games from being overly long and drawn out. Having lost the first hand, Cal slowly laid his cards on the table. Yuri peered over his to see what Cal had laid down. Yuri's eyes squinted from a big smile. "Ah, nice, three of a kind—a good hand." He then slowly and purposely laid his cards on the table. "However, I believe de straight is de better hand, yes?"

Cal simply gave a stone-faced nod. Yuri let go a big laugh. "Cal my friend, do not be so serious. Yes, you must win ze next hand, zis es true, but do not let et pressure you so much. Yuri can see you are good at zis game."

Donna gave Cal a curious look wondering just what he could be planning. She had never seen him lose two hands back-to-back. They had agreed to play five hands, however, and if Yuri won the next hand, it was over; he would have three wins. There was no coming back from that, and their sailboat would be gone. Cal saw her look of concern but gave her no indication of what he was planning to do. Donna, however, knew that there was no way he would lose the next hand, at least she hoped he wouldn't.

Cal looked to Joel and chose to use his acquired moniker of El Jurakan to keep any suspicions Yuri had of their familiarity at bay. "El Jurakan, shuffle 'em up. Let's have another go at it." Scooping the cards from the table, Joel folded the cards in with the deck deftly shuffling them up tapping them on the table. He then began dealing the third hand, he looked to each man then to Donna. He then simply stated, "Good luck, gentlemen," then began dealing the cards.

Outside the wind had picked up and was holding a steady twelve knots, with occasional gusts reaching twenty. Donna took the occasion to take a peek out the widows. What she saw though gave her a good deal of concern, not for what she was seeing but rather for what she wasn't, for she saw almost no one. The stack of crab traps had all been placed on the ground in a single layer with the fishing nets laid over them and tied to stakes driven in the ground. The few buildings she could see were boarded up; hardly a soul was seen, and those that were scurried in and out of sight.

She had seen this kind of behavior back home any time a storm was coming. She looked back to Cal and Yuri. She knew the Russian would just blow off anything she might say about what she was seeing or thinking. Cal though was another matter; he knew well the dangers that these storms bring. She was about to comment on it when Yuri barked at her, "Cal's wife, you vill bring us more beer. I vish to make toast before we play za next hand."

Rolling her eyes, she went to retrieve two bottles of beer and briefly considered cracking him on the head with one but figured it wouldn't even dent that Neanderthal skull of his. Placing the bottles on the table, she did take the opportunity to mention that things were getting much cloudier and windier.

Cal saw the look of real concern on her face; she was not a woman given to overreaction when it came to things of this nature. "What's going on, Donna?"

"To begin with, it appears to me that everyone is preparing for a lot more than just a single squall line coming over us." She began to describe what she had seen, but Yuri interrupted her.

"Please, Cal, tell your woman not to worry so much. Our agreement could end with zis hand—surely ze storm can wait."

Cal looked from Yuri to Donna, then said, "Donna, if there is something else going on with that storm, it's already too late for us to do anything but ride out whatever is coming. So for now we may as well see what happens with this next hand."

Cal had no sooner stopped talking when a hard wind-driven downpour swept over them. Cal turned to Yuri. "I need to start the engine. It drives a mechanical bilge pump so the battery-powered one isn't overwhelmed."

Cal started to get up when Donna tersely stated, "Just stay seated there, Wild Bill Hickok. I know how to take care of that. I want you to play that damn hand, so get to it."

Yuri gave Cal a look of consternation as Donna left to go to the engine room. "Your woman has a fiery tongue. You do not address zis with her?"

Cal gave Yuri a crooked smile and then thoughtfully stated, "Yuri, sometimes fires are better left to burn themselves out."

Yuri let go a deep laugh then raised his bottle of beer. Cal followed suit raising his bottle high. "Let us toast," Yuri commanded. "My great-grandfather would say, I have a vish to buy a house, but I have no means. I have ze means to buy a goat, but I have no vish. So let us drink to have all our vishes match our means! Salute!"

Clacking their bottles together, they each took deep swigs of beer as the *Donna Marie*'s diesel engine rumbled to life. Donna returned to the main deck in time to see they had indeed begun the next hand. A knot built in her stomach wondering just what was going to happen. She had to steady herself as a sudden gust blew hard against their starboard side causing them to list a few degrees to port. Cal tossed a quick look toward Donna, and then to the windows; nothing but a wall of rain could be seen. They both knew that the mooring lines were keeping her from listing more; likewise, each knew that deck cleats and rope do have their limits.

The *Donna Marie* was capable of handling rough weather and seas, but rough is one thing, and extreme is a whole other ball game, and sitting broadside to the wind wasn't helping matters either. All of this was making it harder for Cal to stay focused on the game as he should be. While looking out the window, he had missed seeing the backs of Yuri's cards; his big thick hands covered all but one card completely, and the one Cal could see was a king of hearts.

Somehow, he needed to get Yuri to reveal the upper half of his remaining cards. Cal stared at Yuri's hands a moment. He was about to just move ahead and see and raise Yuri when he focused on the two large rings Yuri wore, one on each hand.

Picking up the chips, he hesitated while asking Yuri about the rings. "Those rings you have look pretty special there, Yuri. They military?"

Yuri immediately dropped his cards down from in front of his face to reveal a big smile. He then rolled his hands slightly toward himself glancing over the cards at his rings. "Oh, yes, zis one," he said, shifting the cards to his left hand, "is for…for ze, how you say, ze, uh, valor during battle, yes."

Cal smiled and nodded and then asked, "And the other? It looks *very* special."

Yuri, now in full boast mode, quickly shifted his cards to his right hand while holding his ringed finger closer for Cal to see. "Zis one was given to me by Brezhnev himself for leading ze first battalions into Kabul."

Cal feigned interest while looking past the prominent hammer and sickle on the ring to the cards now haplessly clutched in Yuri's hand. The broad smile Cal showed wasn't for the ring but rather for the hand Yuri held. The king was his high card; his other cards were a two of spades, a four of clubs, five of hearts and a three of diamonds. Right now, Cal was sitting with the makings of a straight but knew he could and should better his hand. He wasn't taking any chances that Yuri might somehow dig out of the hole he was in. Cal knew he would try and bluff his way out, and true to form, that is precisely what Yuri began doing.

Expressionless, Cal likewise called Yuri's bet and raised him two chips and took a draw. Unknown to Yuri, *his* attempt at a poker face was failing him. Cal had noted during their first hand that Yuri kept pressing the right side of his mouth ever so slightly into his cheek whenever he was dealt cards he didn't like. He noticed too that it ceased when his hand improved during play. This unconscious facial tick made it easy to see the cards being dealt him were not to his liking. This almost made playing with a marked deck unnecessary.

The card Cal picked up and folded into his hand was good, very good, for he was now holding a full house. The best Yuri was holding was a king and two sevens. It was now time to reveal their hands. Clearly unhappy with his hand, Yuri laid his cards down with a thump revealing what he had.

Cal stared at his hand a split second trying to figure out what Yuri's reaction might be by losing this hand so convincingly, but right then he didn't care. Cal needed to win the next hand, this would put all the pressure on Yuri big time. And that was just where he was steering the big Russian oaf. Cal slowly laid his cards on the table. Yuri's whole posture instantly stiffened, but then just as quickly, he shifted to hollow congratulator exuberance. "Look at you, you come back strong yes, *but* Yuri will not let you win zat easy on ze next hand, zis is for sure."

Upon seeing Cal's hand, Donna finally let go the breath she had been holding for what felt like an eternity, practically gulping in the next. She decided to go forward and sit on a built-in couch that folded out into a bed. Between what was going outside and the drama unfolding inside, she felt as though every nerve in her body was on fire and wanted to tell Cal to just give him the damn boat so they could go home. But that seemed highly improbable now.

The rain positively roared for several unnerving minutes, then suddenly, like a faucet being shut off, it ceased. The wind dropped off to a far more tolerable level as well. Donna hoped that was the expected squall line and things would now begin to settle down, leaving her with only this damnable card game to worry over. Turning around, she peered out through the large front cabin windows; the sun brightly shone like it was just another typical sunny day in the Caribbean.

Turning back to face Cal and Yuri, she took a deep cleansing breath. Exhaling it slowly, she let herself relax a little. Joel had already dealt the next hand. She studied them as they perused their respective hands. She held her attention on Cal for a long moment wondering what her crafty husband might be up to by losing the first two hands. She knew just as he did that the game of poker is much more than just the mechanics of playing the game; the really great players understood the psychology and nuances of body language during the game. Cal was that kind of a player, that she knew. Yuri was another matter; his level of skill was completely unknown.

In this moment of calm, it appeared as though this could all be over in the next thirty minutes…or less if Cal lost this fourth hand. She prayed he wouldn't lose. She then gazed around the entirety of the *Donna Marie*'s cabin. Shaking her head a bit, she couldn't believe this gorgeous sailboat was again the ante in a game of poker and that *she* was now a part of it this time.

She decided that what she needed right then was a beer. Standing up from the couch, she eased her way to the refrigerator. Reaching to its open the door, she jumped as a sharp banging came at the cabin door accompanied by a panicked voice. "Hey, open up. it's me!" Yuri shot an angry look toward to door and yelled out to shut up and go away. The banging and yelling stopped for a second, and then a louder but calmer voice came. "Cal, open up. it's me, Jim. A hurricane could be coming straight for this place. Now open this damn door!"

Chapter 82

Donna's eyes immediately met Cal's. Cal then nodded for Donna to open the door. Jim was making another more earnest appeal when Donna swung the cabin door wide open. Jim stood there a second staring wide-eyed at Donna. He then surveyed the cabin with Juky peering over his shoulder. "Well, just don't stand there, come on in," Cal ordered. Jim cautiously entered closely followed by Juky. Taking another hasty look around the cabin, he repeated his earlier warning as Juky moved to stand beside him.

Yuri slammed his cards face down on the table, loudly demanding, "What es going on here? Who are zese men, and vhy are zey here? Zis es a trick you make on Yuri!"

Suddenly everyone burst out loudly talking which rapidly disintegrated into yelling. Cal shouted for everyone to shut up, while Juky was shouting out to Donna about what was happening, with her screaming back that she couldn't hear him. All the while Yuri kept loudly demanding that Jim and Juky immediately leave. Joel, annoyed with the whole situation, rolled his eyes, then abruptly snatched a copy of *Life* magazine off a chair next to him. Rolling it tight, he shot to his feet while slapping the magazine down hard on the table causing everything on it to leap up in the air. "Shut the hell up! All of you!" He punctuated the demand with an even harder a slam of magazine.

The cabin fell instantly silent. All eyes were squarely on Joel. He then pointed the rolled-up magazine at Jim. "Don't anyone say a word. You," he said, pointing at Jim, "I don't know who you are, but what the hell are you talking about? That storm was supposed to be sending a squall line over us, which it just did."

"That is what I am trying to tell you. The latest weather report has it becoming potentially a cat 4 storm that could get steered in this general direction by a high-pressure ridge."

Cal spoke up. "How did you find us?"

"Your phone call home, that's how. Juky and me, we stopped by the Salty Anchor to plan a welcome home party for you two. But when your son Kevin told us you had gone further south to Cockburn Town, well, Juky and I thought that maybe that Sawfish guy had something to do with it. That's when Kevin told us about the storm. So me and Juky hightailed it here to try and find you two and fly you straight back home. Now come on, we have a narrow gap in the weather right now. I can fly us out of here, but we have to go now!"

Cal shook his head like he was trying clear smoke away from his face and started to speak, but Yuri cut him off. "Just one minute, nobody go anywhere, not before we finish ze game. Ve have agreement, so it es you who must leave."

Jim threw a hard glare at Yuri. "Hey, pal! I don't know who you are, but I don't take orders from you or anyone else. Look, I don't know what's going on here, and I don't care about any game or agreements you two have, but if that storm starts heading this way, this damn sailboat ain't going to be the place to be, especially if it ramps up to a category 4." Looking to Cal and Donna, he asked, "Now are you two coming with me and Juky or not?"

Cal dropped his head, staring at the floor a moment. Giving a sideways look up to Yuri, he calmly spoke while lifting his head and turning to face him. "Yuri, yes, we have an agreement, that's true, but I don't see how we can complete the game now. The risks are too great." Cal then cut his eyes to Donna standing a couple of steps behind Yuri; it was easy to see she had had enough and was ready to go home. Cal brought his attention back to Yuri. "Look, if you want my sailboat this bad, take it. I'm done risking people's lives over it."

Yuri studied Cal's face a moment while taking in what he had said. Looking back to Donna, he saw the utter dejection written all over her. He had never been in a situation like this before; in fact, these were the first Americans he had ever met face-to-face. And Cal's willingness to just give up the *Donna Marie* had him thinking maybe not all Americans were the imperialist monsters he had always been told they were.

Cal spoke up again. "What about it, Yuri?"

Yuri turned back to face Cal. This is not how he wanted this to go; all his life it had been drilled into him that "to the victor go the spoils." To him there was no honor in taking this vessel in this way. Who could he ever brag to about his conquest? No one. In fact, he felt like it would dishonor him to acquire it in this way, never mind that his original intent was to abscond with it through piracy. However, right now, all his skewed sense of morals kept telling him was that he had to obtain it through some sort of conquest.

Donna solemnly spoke out into the tormented silence. "Cal honey, are you sure about this?"

"Donna, I'm not going keep risking people getting killed over this boat. I can replace a sailboat, but I can't replace people."

Joel abruptly added to Cal's sentiment, "He's right, missy. You don't want him or anybody living with what I live with every day."

Standing in the eight-foot gap that separated Cal and Donna, Yuri's head dropped slightly, turning only part way to face her. He was desperately trying to think of something he could say that would keep Cal there to finish the game. At the moment he was coming up with nothing more than simply demanding they stay and finish what they started. Just as he was about to make his demand, he caught sight of the perfect answer. Donna saw a smile suddenly push into his thick beard-shadowed cheek.

Suddenly he bellowed out while pointing out the cabin to the windows behind. "Look! Zat es where we finish za game. In ze shipping offices. We have perfect place to go. You see, Yuri have answer to problem, yes?"

All turned to look out the window. Cal took a couple of steps towards a window while speaking out loud. "He might be right. I came here a time or two during the war—that building is built like a fort. It has endured God only knows how many storms. Look, we can't stay here no matter what, so why not go where we can finish the game? That way if the storm does come our way, we'll be safe."

Donna's shoulders slumped; taking a deep breath, she turned back from the window to face Cal. With a disheartened smirk pushing into one cheek, she simply stated, "Let's do it."

Suddenly, Yuri let go a deep laugh that bellowed out filling the cabin. "Ah, zis es very good, yes. Now we finish game like men. Come, let us hurry."

Cal threw a look to Joel. "You heard the man. Let's roll."

Jim suddenly spoke out to all. "Hold on just a damn minute! You all understand that when I step off this boat, I'm flying for home? This is your last chance to get out of the path of that storm."

Cal immediately shot a look to Donna. Instantly she knew why and just as rapidly called him on it. "Oh no you don't, buddy boy. Come hell or high water, I'm staying right here."

Jim shook his head at them while affirming Donna's comment. "Well, you two just might get exactly that." He then added, "Look, no matter what, when that storm gets out of the picture, I'll shag my ass right back here." He then ominously added, "That is if there is still a *here* to fly to."

Cal, annoyed with the ominous overtones, spoke to no one in particular. "Look, enough of all that. Let's all just go do what we think is best and let the cards fall where they will—no pun intended." Everyone remained frozen, then Cal barked, "Let's go!

Chapter 83

The group walked quickly along the dock. The cloudless sunshine heated the humidity-laden air to lay upon on them like a wet blanket, and the light warm breeze that blew was the only thing keeping it from being completely intolerable.

Reaching the door to the shipping office, Yuri entered first. Pulling it briskly open, he stepped inside; his men, surprised by his sudden appearance, immediately stood giving stiff nods and addressing him as entered. "Капитан!"

"Sit, sit," Yuri gestured. "I will speak ze English for ze benefit of all here, so all vill understand, yes?"

Yuri waited until everyone was inside. Cal was the last to enter, as the heavy steel door banged closed behind him. Cal noted that all the seats were taken by Yuri and Cesar's men. "Hey, uh, Yuri, I'm sure you've noticed that the only place we can finish our game is at that lunch table that your men are occupying."

Yuri held up a hand while nodding and fixing his eyes on his men. "Yes, yes, I see zis, and my men will go back aboard ze *Akula*. She takes heavy weather good."

Cal looked to Cesar. "And what about you and your men?" Cesar stood while answering, "It seems things have changed with de storm. Cal, we have a safe place dat is close by." Tossing a look at Yuri, he added, "It's vury close by."

Yuri let out a short laugh. "Sawfish, you needn't worry about zese people, especially while we are here on ze island. I have but one interest here, to win zis game and take vhat es mine. Zat es all."

Cesar kept a stone-faced stare on Yuri then questioned, "Aund ef you lose?"

Yuri's face hardened upon hearing any reference to his not being the victor. "I do not anticipate zat being ze outcome, but ef it is, so be it. I vill honor ze agreement."

Cesar turned to Cal and Donna. "You both are truly okay with dis?"

Donna cut her eyes to meet Cal's; both wordlessly held each other's gaze a long moment. Donna then gave Cal a small nod; Cal did likewise. Without looking away from Donna, he simply stated, "Yeah, we're both okay with this."

Yuri let go a deep laugh. "Zer, you see, Sawfish, ef Cal and his woman es good with zis, zen you have nothing to worry about."

Donna scrunched her face as all the men filed past her exiting the shipping office. She then turned to Cal. "Where is Johnny Mac?"

Cal glanced around the room then back to Donna. Shaking his head, he declared, "I don't know. I thought he had come here with everyone else. He was on the *Akula* the last I saw of him."

Stopping at the office door, Cesar said, "Do not worry. I shall send one of my men for em, aund he may stay with us. Good luck with yo-ah game, Mista Cal."

Cal simply nodded as Cesar exited the office. Cal turned to face Joel. "Well, let's get this party started, shall we?" Joel said nothing, only giving a small nod, then headed for the square four-place table at far end of the open office. Taking a seat, he entreated both Cal and Yuri to take the seats to his left and right.

Donna watched as Cal and Yuri sat down. Both took a moment to move and adjust the metal folding chairs. The shipping office was Spartan, to say the least, a far cry from either the *Donna Marie* or the *Akula*. Joel looked to Cal and to Yuri. "Okay, shall we pick up where we left off?"

Yuri spoke up, his voice low, his words guarded. "You do vell. Are you prepared for ze bad outcome for you zis next hand?"

Cal sensed that Yuri was bothered by losing far more than he was letting on and felt it was time to turn up the psychological heat a little more. Holding a steeled stare straight in Yuri's narrow-set eyes, Cal calmly and confidently stated, "Yuri, I cut my teeth on turning bad outcomes into conquest, so I'm really not worried. Let's get to it."

Donna positively stared in amazement at her husband, for in that bare moment of time, she got a true glimpse of the man Cal used to be. She shuddered to think of how many times he had been in similar situations, surrounded by men of a much lower caliber than the guns they likely carried. She was pretty sure he was not going to lose, and this ran an immediate chill through her. For sitting across from the man she loved more than life itself was a man she knew didn't take well to losing.

The fourth hand went mercifully quick for Donna. But the win came with a good deal of trepidation for Cal and Donna, for it was clear that Yuri was struggling against his ill-tempered nature Her only comfort though was that it was three against one in this office. And if Yuri lost the last hand and chose to react as he did while attempting to commandeer Donna Marie, then she would fight him like a crazed wildcat if that's what it took.

Suddenly Joel's voice broke Donna from her thoughts of the past and future. "All right, gentlemen, this is the deciding hand. The outcome will be final *and* binding, agreed?"

Cal held his stare on Yuri, firmly stating, "Agreed."

Joel nodded at Yuri. "And you?"

Yuri cut his eyes to Joel then back to Cal, followed by the merest moment of hesitation before answering, then blurted out, "Yes, yes, agreed!" Cal caught the tension in his voice but met his answer with emotionless silence and a small nod.

Donna elected to take a seat at a small manager's desk near the center of the room by the south wall. This vantage point allowed her to keep an eye on the main office door to her right and still watch the goings-on at the table to her left.

At the moment, Joel was doing a long and thorough job of shuffling the cards. Yuri finally barked at him about it. "Zat is good enough. Time to deal."

Not one to be intimidated or barked at, Joel gave it right back. "Keep your shirt on already. I'm not going to be accused of doing a poor job by whoever loses this game, so back off!"

Cal watched Yuri struggle against his nature to hit back when hit by offering what he was sure was a rare apology. "Yes, yes, of course. Please continue. Certainly ve vaunt you to do your best. Please forgive me. Proceed."

"Good, more talk like that and I'm outta here, and you two can arm wrestle for that damn sailboat for all I care. All right, here we go, and as before, may the best man win." Joel looked to each man, then called them to ante up. The moment the first card hit the table, Donna again found herself holding her breath and thinking, *Just breath normal, woman. You don't need to be passing out.* Struggling against her emotions, she focused on the game like a bystander with nothing at stake.

As the moments passed, her anxiety eased somewhat, reasoning that the way it had been going, it wouldn't be long, and this would all be over, and Cal would be the winner, she hoped. Then they could put all of this behind them and head for home.

The thought of going home had no sooner came to mind when a low thrumming drone drew nearer and nearer until a thundering roar zoomed directly overhead. She knew without looking it was the Water Lily. Suddenly her anxiety returned full force. *There goes the last plane out,* she worried.

Chapter 84

Walking away from the shipping pavilion, Grigori asked Cesar where he and his men were going to ride out the storm. "We will go to a friend's house not far away."

Grigori took a rapid look around at the buildings that ran along the shore and queried him further. "Ze structures here, zey do not appear to be strong for to hold against hurricane."

Cesar gave him a quick sideways glance and smile then said, "Et may surprise you, but many of dese buildings you see have been he-ah for fifty or sixty years aund have endured many storms. Some say et es because dey don't fight de wind but move with it."

Grigori gave a nod, replying, "Yes, ve have similar saying. It say a sapling will bend with ze wind and survive, while ze oak resists and breaks."

"Ah, yes," Cesar thoughtfully began. "Der es a lot to be said for being pliable. However, de trick is knowing when to be pliable aund when to be strong. I believe you aund yo-ah fellow crewmen are facing just such a choice."

"Sir, you should perhaps come aboard ze *Akula* until ve see who wins ze game."

Lev suddenly snarled, "Grigori! Again, you take liberties with your position!"

Grigori spun around putting a sharply pointed finger just under Lev's nose. "Zen if et worries you, I suggest you go now and inform your glorious captain. Don't forget in ze gulags, snitches have short lives, but ze confines of a filthy cell es not always necessary for zis to happen."

Lev glared hard at his finger for a second. His eyes narrowed. He then furiously slapped Grigori's hand sharply away. "Then I do exactly zat. You have crossed me for ze last time, Grigori. You vill see."

Grigoris's jaw hardened, his nostrils flared in rage, and in a flash, he grabbed Lev by his shirt collar drawing it tight around his neck practically lifting him off the dock. "You, you are no different zan your father, and his father too. Zey help Stalin's spies find, murder, and imprison ze poor and hungry of ze villages all over Russia! Yes, I know of your family's treacherousness and vhat they do to make sure zey had food while ze neighbors starved."

Grigori, his face twisted and purple with rage, squeezed Lev's collar even tighter to the point of cutting off his breath. Suddenly, he felt a big hand on his shoulder. "Let 'em go!" Cesar firmly ordered. "Dis es not de place or time to vent yoah anger on dis man. Ef what you say es true, den without redemption, all of their fates are sealed by God, aund der is no escaping dat fate."

Grigori held Lev seconds more, his face dark red as he gasped for air. Grigori then violently threw him down hard on the dock as he spat out a last rage-infused invective at the gasping man lying at his feet. "Zer! Lev, you now have yet another soul you are indebted to, for zis man just saved your worthless life, and by God and all of his mercies, I pray you never seek his redemption!"

Lev lay on his back rubbing his neck taking gulps of air and glaring up at Grigori. Grigori shook his head, and then in a final show of the contempt, he stepped over Lev while saying, "Leave zis trash where it lays."

The whole group was twenty feet away when Lev rose to his feet shouting back at the group, "You believe you are tough now, Grigori! But you vill see! I vill be rewarded, and you…you vill starve to death in gulag, but not before you are beaten every day for vhat you do here zis day!"

No one acknowledged his shouts in any way. Arriving at the *Akula*'s gangway, Lev watched as one by one they went aboard. When the last man stepped aboard, he turned and began walking briskly up the dock toward the shipping offices, rubbing his neck and muttering to himself, "They will see, and Grigori he vill pay like dog."

This group of unlikely shipmates gathered in a loose circle at the stern; Cesar stood in the middle of the group. "Gentlemen, et would appear we are to spend a little more time together. Et es my hope dat we can remain civil to one another while we await de outcome of de card game." Looking to Grigori, he asked, "Is there anything you need from my men to ready de *Akula* for de storm should et come our way?"

"Zer es good protection from ze wind here, and ze *Akula*, she has very powerful pumps to deal with much water. Ve need only to secure ze deck hatches."

Cesar nodded. "Vury well den, please take care of dose things as you see fit to do."

Standing with the Russian crewman was Andros, the defiant one whom Cesar had ordered to be tied up before. He had been released when Yuri had sent them all to the shipping offices earlier. However, he had remained oddly silent after being released, only watching and listening to all that had occurred in the shipping offices and just now on the docks with Lev.

Sacha had been ordered to remain onboard the *Akula* to monitor all the yacht's functions. Andros had attempted to alert Yuri to Sacha's personal mutiny; however, Yuri had stopped him from speaking, telling him that he had no time to listen to small matters.

Andros found himself conflicted, for he knew what Grigori had said in the shipping offices about Yuri was true, but his struggles now were compounded by what Grigori had revealed about Lev essentially being a spy for party officials back in Moscow. He knew too that there was a very real chance that Yuri didn't even know this about Lev; it was how things worked. No one ever kept secrets long from the state, and the state trusted no one.

Andros had also paid close attention to the things the Sawfish had said. He felt too that there was something about the man that made him begin to doubt all the stories he had heard of him. Having been a guard in a gulag, he was no stranger to the heartlessness that some men are capable of; it was held in their eyes. And this man

485

known as the merciless Sawfish did not have the hollow coldness in his stare that he saw in the gulags.

He decided it was best to see what was going to happen when all these factions finally played their hand; he felt a lot was going to be revealed, and very soon.

Chapter 85

A crisp knock came at the shipping office door. Donna craned her head to try and see who it might be. She was about to stand up when a second knock came, this time accompanied by a panicked voice calling out in Russian. Donna stood and looked toward Cal and Yuri. Upon hearing a third harder knock, Yuri threw a furious glare at the door then to Donna. "Go! Open ze door!"

Donna was taken aback by the dynamite-like explosiveness of the command. She hesitated only a second before he repeated the command practically shouting at her. Cal smacked his hand hard on the table. "Hey! Watch who you're yelling at. That's my wife, not one of your thick-skulled crew!"

Hearing Cal's rebuke, Yuri, while still very upset by this unexpected interruption, quickly fought to tamp down his anger. Taking a deep breath, he spoke with as much calm as he could muster. "Forgive me please, please. Sit and I vill deal with zis interruption." Yuri stood and started for the door keeping his cards in his hand.

Reaching the door, he slid the dead bolt back hard. Twisting the doorknob, he thrust open the door nearly hitting Lev, startling him. Nervously, speaking Russian, Lev immediately began apologizing, his words firing like bullets from his mouth. Yuri listened for the briefest moment, and then in a voice that thundered the room, "Лев, закрой рот сейчас!" ("Lev, shut your mouth now!")

Instantly falling silent, he stepped back, giving a short nod. Electing to speak so all could understand, Yuri tersely questioned him about his reasons for interrupting. "Lev, you ver told to go aboard the *Akula*. Vhy did you not go aboard?"

Lev gulped, then began replying in Russian. "Stop, Lev! Speak so all can understand. I vill not be accused of planning something by zese people."

Taking nervous rapid peeks around Yuri, he gulped again. "Et es Grigori. He has let ze Sawfish and his men come aboard ze *Akula,* and."

Suddenly Yuri loudly barked, "Enough! You have interrupted vith more of your squabbling with Grigori! I grow tired of zis. Now go. I vill deal vith you both later."

"Captain, please, zer es more. He es—"

"Enough I say! Ef I lose zis game now, et vill be you I blame! Do you hear, Lev?" Yuri then leaned in close. With an arrow-straight finger under Lev's chin, he added, "And I promise you et vill not be good for you upon our return to Moscow, do you understand? Now go!"

Lev cast his eyes down at Yuri's rock-hard finger, then back up to meet the hollow coldness of his captain's eyes. Lev meekly replied, "Yes, my captain." His words had barely left his lips when the door was slammed closed and bolted. Yuri, with his head down, remained facing the door a moment just breathing in and out in an attempt to calm himself before returning to the game. Donna, Cal, and Joel wondered just what was coming next; Joel though was growing tired of all of this.

"All right, Captain Bligh, are you forfeiting the game or not?" Yuri's head instantly snapped up. He spun around giving his answer as he did so. "No! Ve finish ze game!" Returning to his seat, he grumbled to no one in particular, something that shed a fragment of light on life back home in Russia. "You should all be glad for vhere you have your lives. Life is very hard when zer is no trust to be had in ze people you live among."

Donna stared at Yuri a long moment wondering just what life must be like in the Soviet Union. She of course had read newspaper stories of the wheat shortages of the '70s and of Russian citizens having to wait hours in long lines to get food items, many times taking whatever they could get. Joel spoke up, drawing her attention back fully on the game.

"All right, Cal, I believe you had seen his bet and raised four chips. It's to you now, Yuri."

Yuri stared intently at his hand, and then placed five chips in the center of the table. Cal stared at the chips then up to Yuri's face, then back to the cards he held, studying them. Yuri's hand was good, a club straight, jack high. Cal then cut his eyes to the deck in front of Joel. Playing with a marked deck was helpful, but the hand he held had nothing to do with a marked deck and everything to do with stupid good luck.

Seeing how tense Yuri had become and knowing how volatile he could get, Cal had concerns about what to do next. After all, they had taken each other's word that they were not armed. In the few seconds he pondered all of this, he suddenly remembered Johnny Mac's odd admonition before leaving the *Akula*: "In order to win, you must lose what you hold in your hands."

Cal gave a quick side glance to Donna; deep worry clearly lay upon her face. Leaning his cards slightly back, he stared again at the hand he held. Abruptly Joel spoke up. "What's it gonna be, Cal? This is the last hand, so call, raise, or fold?"

Cal brought his eyes to meet Yuri's, remembering what Johnny had said about winning and losing. *Hope this is what you meant, Johnny Mac.* Taking a deep breath, he exhaled while saying, "I fold." He then laid his cards all face down on the table, folding both hands on top.

Yuri stared in disbelief at Cal and the cards for a brief moment. Suddenly his eyes flew open wide at the realization of what had just happened. Yuri shot up to stand, throwing his cards down on the table face up. "Zer! Now you see zat I am ze better man. My straight has crushed you. Ze sailboat es now mine to take, just as ve agreed, yes?"

Donna stared at Cal with mouth agape. She was dumbfounded and couldn't believe what had just happened. She wanted to speak but was unable to utter a single word. Joel was likewise dumbstruck a second or two, and then could only weakly state the obvious, "Yuri, looks like you are the winner."

Yuri stood, positively bursting with pride and bravado then demanded to see Cal's hand, to which Cal firmly replied, "Nope, I believe in a gentleman's game. It's not required that I show my hand."

Joel quickly chimed in, "He's right. It saves further embarrassment to the loser."

"Yes, yes, I know zis, but I only vant to see how close ze game was, you understand, don't you?"

Cal shook his head no, saying, "Look, Yuri, it wasn't even close. You won. You now have our sailboat, and I should think you could understand that we have suffered enough embarrassment already."

"Yes, I know, but et...et..." Yuri stopped and looked into Cal and Donna's faces seeing their utter dejection. His wide smile melted slightly. Staring down at the cards on the table, he gave a short nod. "All right, et es as you vish. I have won!"

Wanting to cut all this short, Cal stood. "Look, we want to go and gather our personal effects from the *Donna Marie*. It won't take long, and then...and then I guess she's yours."

Yuri's disposition now shifted to one of being the magnanimous victor. "But of course, take your time. I can have some of my men assist you if you like."

"No, that won't be necessary. There's not very much. We'll be twenty minutes or so."

"Vury well, I vill vait here for you to do as you say."

Cal looked to Donna. "Let's go. I want to get this over as quick as we can. I don't want to drag it out."

Donna stood, but her legs felt like rubber and would collapse from under her at any moment; she held her arms out for Cal. It was easy to see she was not handling this well, so Cal moved swiftly to her side. He put his arm around her waist and urged her toward the office door. Donna's first steps were shaky. Reaching the door, Cal twisted the knob and shoved it open and eased Donna through. Joel stayed behind with Yuri, figuring he may as well wait out the storm where he was.

The humidity outside seemed worse than before they walked in silence as they made their way back to the *Donna Marie*. Donna kept her gaze downward at her feet; she didn't want to look over at the *Donna Marie* for fear she would burst into tears. Each footstep felt heavier and heavier as though she were walking to the gallows.

She was taking this far harder than Cal thought she would. He knew that she loved that ole sailboat—he did too. But at the moment, he had the oddest feeling that this wasn't over yet, and the only thing he could hang that on was Johnny Mac's comment, which didn't make sense when he said it, and frankly, it didn't now. Soon they were standing next to the *Donna Marie.*

Cal knew he would have to be the one to step aboard first. He took a short breath, then stepped onto the gunwale and then down onto the deck. He quickly turned and held out a hand to assist Donna onboard. Donna didn't move at first. The sadness she felt positively enveloped her. She held her eyes on Cal for a brief moment then looked the full length of the *Donna Marie*'s graceful hull, trying to absorb as much of it as she could, wanting to lock it away in her mind where no one could ever steal it away.

Cal's heart broke for her. Touching her hand, he gently clasped it and urged her onboard, saying, "C'mon, sweetheart, we don't have much time. I want to get this over with. We don't want to be here when *he* steps aboard her."

Donna looked down at Cal. She knew this was killing him too, but in typical Cal fashion, he was trying to be strong for her. She gave him a tight smile and then stepped onboard. She stepped up close to him reaching for both of his hands. As she held her eyes in his, her expression lost all the anguish she was feeling. She then leaned into him, kissing him softly. Pulling back a bit, she quietly said, "Let's turn this page together."

Chapter 86

Donna and Cal managed to shake off some of their somber mood and went about gathering their belongings first from the main cabin. Cal retrieved a screwdriver from a drawer and began taking down the personal photos that were in various places around the cabin, many of which were of people who had been married on the *Donna Marie*. It was a melancholic moment for them both because the photos held such happy memories.

Donna stood for a moment just holding and staring at one of the framed photos Cal had handed to her to place in a small box. He then went to the far corner to take down the last photo. She spoke out to Cal while still holding her gaze on the photo before placing it in the box. "Sweetheart, I'm so, so sorry that I caused all this to happen. I never meant for things to go like this. I just wanted to put a little adventure into your…our lives, to spend a little time away from the Salty Anchor. I was hoping to kill two birds with one stone, I guess."

Lowering the photo into the box, she turned to face him. Cal remained silent, sensing that what his wife needed right now was to express her feelings about all this. Looking at each other from opposite sides of the cabin, she continued with her moment of confession. "I just thought that…that if you got away for a while, you'd begin to miss being at the Salty Anchor, and maybe even miss the craziness that comes with owning a marina in the Florida Keys."

Cal put down the screwdriver and eased his way to where Donna stood. Stepping up close, gently placing both hands on her shoulders, he gazed into her eyes. "Donna, first, you don't have a thing to be sorry about. I understand what you were trying to do. It was a great plan. I do miss the craziness of the Salty Anchor." Cal smirked. "And frankly, the craziness we have been through for last few days makes the Salty Anchor look like a monastery by comparison. Besides, look at all the new stories we have to entertain all our customers."

Donna knew he was trying to put the best spin on this to ease her guilt but couldn't help but point out the giant fly in the ointment. "That's all true, honey, but we won't have the *Donna Marie* anymore. She's been like one of the family for years now. All of our regulars, they expect to see her there. I don't want to forever be seen as the one who caused us to lose the *Donna Marie*."

Hearing that, Cal immediately put a finger up in front of her. "Now hold on just a darn minute. I lost the card game, remember? So you didn't lose anything.—I did, got it?"

"Yes, but I set all this into motion. I put you in that position. None of this would have happened were it not for my stupid plan. And while we're on it, how did you lose that hand of poker, or should I say *why*? I can count the number of times I've seen you lose and not hit double digits."

Donna kept her intense stare on Cal who remained silent. Abruptly her eyes flew open. "Did you...did you lose on purpose?"

Cal held his hands up in front of himself. "Now look, Donna, hear me out. Yes, I threw the game, but I had a good reason."

"A good reason? What kind of damn reason could you have had that would make you willingly lose a very expensive sailboat to that Russian jerk?"

Cal stood looking at his fired-up Irish wife and knew that what he was going to say next wasn't going to make things any better. "Well, I...I, uh, I did it because of what Johnny Mac had said before we left the *Akula*."

"What? I don't remember his saying anything so profound that would make you want to lose the *Donna Marie* on purpose. What could he have possibly said that would make you do something that stupid?"

Cal thought, *Crap, she is going to go full nuclear on me now.* In a much calmer tone, he began, "Donna, sweetheart, don't you remember him telling me that in order to win, I must first lose. Don't you remember we both looked at him trying to figure out what the hell he meant? Well, as I held that last hand, it hit me: I had to lose the poker match in order to win—that is what he meant…at least I hope that's what he meant."

"You *hope*? Cal, dammit, I was ready to do whatever we had to save the *Donna Marie* from that Russian oaf, and right now he's the only one I see doing the winning."

Cal was about to try and explain when they felt the boat dip on one side accompanied by someone yelling. In the next instant, Yuri exploded into the cabin yelling loudly. "You! You cheated Yuri!" Throwing the whole deck of cards at Cal, Cal slapped them away sending cards flying in every direction. "You cheated me of a true win!" Yuri bellowed again. Cal shot right back, "I did no such thing. You won, I lost. I didn't cheat you!"

"After you left, I look at de cards on ze table. You held a diamond straight, ace high. Zat beats ze hand I held. Zer is no honor in zis for me!"

Cal cut him off. "Yeah, yeah, I got it, so what! You won, so take the damn boat. It's yours!"

Yuri's face turned purple with rage as he screamed out, "No! I vill not be insulted like zis! Yuri not a spoiled child zat must be bribed!" Suddenly he drew back his fist and charged at Cal. Cal couldn't believe what he was seeing. Reflexively he ducked as Yuri's big fist swooshed over his head. Cal instinctively brought his fist up hard into Yuri's midsection staggering him back, causing him to fall backward over the box they had been packing.

Donna began screaming for them to stop as Yuri sprang to his feet again charging at Cal with open hands reaching to grab him by the throat. Cal though shot two rapid-fire punches, landing one square on his chin and the other right on his throat. Yuri staggered back again coughing and choking. Cal had been a trained boxer in the Navy, and technique has its advantages, but Yuri was younger, bigger, and stronger.

Cal yelled at him, "Knock it off. This is stupid. You won, asshole!"

Yuri wiped some blood from the corner of his mouth, glanced at it, and then shot Cal a hateful glare. "Not yet, I haven't."

Cal backed up a few steps. The look on Yuri was that of a madman. Donna screamed again at Yuri. "What's wrong with you! Stop it!" Cal began turning a slow circle, edging his way toward the cabin door, where he hoped to draw him out onto the open deck. Yuri's back was now to Donna. Cal saw Yuri's nostrils flare. This was it!

Yuri let out a wild banshee-like scream before charging Cal. Abruptly the bedroom door flew open behind Donna with Johnny Mac shouting out loudly, "Donna, catch!"

Spinning halfway around, she caught what was somersaulting through the air and instantly spun back, swinging like she was going for the game-winning homer. She landed a smashing blow on the right side of Yuri's head and reversed, landing an even harder hit to his left side.

Yuri froze a second, then staggered forward a couple more steps. He turned on one foot to see Donna poised to take another swing. "You...you hit Yuri with a...a..." Not another word left his mouth as his eyes rolled back in his head, and he crumpled to the floor with a resounding thud.

Cal looked down at Yuri, motionless on the floor, then up to his wife, still holding a batter's stance. Cal trailed his eyes along what she held poised over her shoulder. Suddenly he burst out laughing. Through the laughs, Cal asked her, "Donna, do...do you even know what you hit him with? Look at what you are holding over your shoulder, Mickey Mantle."

Donna gave Cal a puzzled look then dropped her eyes down to see what was tightly clutched in her hands. The second she did, she let out a yelp seeing a foot jutting out of her hands, dropping it instantly. The wooden mannequin leg tumble to the floor bouncing a couple of times before coming to a rest.

Johnny Mac moved up beside her. "Wow! Now that's a drop-kick he won't soon forget."

Cal stepped over Yuri next to Donna, and Johnny Mac, looking down at Yuri and then to the mannequin leg. Johnny Mac observed, "See, I knew that leg would come in handy one day. Oh, and by the way, Donna, you have one helluva swing, and that back spin thing was amazing, very Bruce Lee of you."

"Thanks, I owe the swing to my college softball days and the Bruce Lee move to a self-defense class I took."

A moan emanated from Yuri; he was beginning to regain consciousness. They all looked to see to his legs beginning to shift. "Shit!" Cal blurted out. "Johnny Mac, there's some duct tape in the storage closet, go and get it. I don't want him getting up." Just as Johnny Mac went for the tape, a shadow fell across the open cabin doorway. "Hey, es everyone all right in he-ah?"

Cal and Donna both snapped their attention to the cabin door to see Juky stepping into the cabin. Both let out a collective sigh while calling out his name. Cal quickly motioned him over. "Juky, quick, come and help me secure this guy before he comes to."

"E's dis what all de screaming and yelling was about? I could hear et from a long way off."

"Yes, yes, now help me roll him onto his back. J-Mac, where's that tape you used the other day? Go get it and bring it here. He's starting to move more."

Johnny Mac quickly retrieved the tape and knelt down beside Cal handing him the tape. "Hope there is enough left. I used a good bit on that fake packet of cocaine."

Cal glanced at the roll. "We'll put the majority around his wrists. Juky, cross his hands."

Cal worked quickly to bind Yuri's wrists; they then did the same to his ankles, finally using the last bit of tape to cover his mouth. Cal had no sooner finished smoothing the tape over Yuri's mouth when he began blinking his eyes struggling to hold them open. Finally, his eyes open wide. He stared straight up at first and then rapid glances around the cabin.

He then looked downward at his tightly taped wrist and ankles. Becoming fully aware of his situation, a muffled yell came as he tried to free himself. Cal stood up and backed a couple of steps away. Looking directly at him, he flatly stated, "Yuri, you should have quit while you were ahead. I'm taking my damn sailboat back. Now all I have to do is figure out what to do with you."

Juky tapped Cal on the shoulder and, with a big toothy grin, said, "I think I know just who can take care of 'em fo-ah you. I have recently made de acquaintance of de police captain who has expressed a deep interest in dis maun."

Cal gave an approving nod. "Good, hey, but wait a minute. What are you doing here? I thought you flew out with Jim."

"No, I only went to help untie his plane. He tried to get me to go with hem, but dese islands are my home. I cannot leave when der es trouble. Besides, I had a feeling you were going to have need of me before dis was over."

"Looks like you were right." Looking down at Yuri, he added, "Yuri old buddy, looks as though you are going to meet a new friend. I think he'd be very interested in knowing that you are running a piracy operation in his waters."

Yuri struggled and snorted hard against his bindings, letting out another muffled roar. Juky smiled, patted Cal on the shoulder, and stood to leave. "I will be back with de captain. He will be most interested in what you have to say, Mista Cal."

Juky hurried to leave. Reaching the cabin doorway, Cal called after him, "Hey, listen, see what you can find out about that damn storm too. I don't like how humid it's getting—not a good sign."

Juky nodded. "Okay, I'll see what I can find out. De captain may know something by now. I'll be back as quick as I can."

Cal nodded then turned his attention to Donna and Johnny Mac who stood across the room. "Johnny Mac, when did you get on the *Donna Marie*? Last we saw of you, you were on the *Akula*."

"Yeah, well, I figured you were going to win the card game, so I didn't want get left here when you two left for Ramrod Key."

"It's a good thing you did. It looks like our troubles are over. And as soon as we know what's going on with that storm, we can make plans for sailing home."

Donna gave Cal an anxious look. "At this point, I'd be willing to sail right through a hurricane if it meant it could blow us home faster."

Johnny Mac spoke out. "Well, you know what they say about being careful what you wish for." Immediately Cal and Donna glared at him. Johnny Mac scrunched his face, answering their unasked question, "Hey, look, you two, can't a guy quote an old saying without triggering a panic?"

In unison, they responded, "No!

Chapter 87

While waiting for the police to arrive, the three of them went about straightening up from the fight. Being physically and emotionally drained, neither talked and just went about it quietly. In fact, the whole island was eerily quiet. Yuri lay watching them. The whole time he watched he could feel the tape pulling loose from one side of his mouth. He began working his jaw to speed the process. Soon he felt it let go.

Stretching his mouth wide, the tape pulled loose to hang from one cheek. Grinning, he took a breath to speak, his deep booming voice startled them. "Yes, good, you clean what is mine." Cal spun around fearful that he had somehow freed himself but was relieved to see him still bound up. Yuri saw look of relief on Cal's face.

Holding up his arms in front of himself, he warned, "Yes, ze tape holds for now. However, zis humid air makes me perspire, so I feel my freedom coming little by little." Glancing at the floor, he spied the empty tape roll. "And too bad for you, you have no more tape."

Cal pressed his mouth tight while holding his stare on Yuri a moment, then turned and spoke as he walked to the galley where Donna's purse sat. I don't need any more tape. I have something even better, a gun." Nearing the counter, about to thrust his hand in to grab the gun, someone yelled from the cabin doorway.

"Stop! Stop right ver you are!" Cal spun around to see the same man who had interrupted their game earlier now pointing a machine gun straight at him. "Lucky for me, I remember et being thrown aboard your vessel. Now I, Lev, can help my captain take vat es his."

With his back to the cabin door, Yuri called out loudly, "Yes! Lev, come quick and free me. Zey have sent for ze police."

"All of you stand together by ze table. Do not try stop me. I vill shoot you, even ze woman, do you hear?"

Doing as ordered, they watched in frustration as the tape was unwound from Yuri's wrists, who took the gun from Lev. Holding it on the three of them, he waited while Lev bent to remove the tape from around his ankles. Seconds later he stood, his face hardened into a hate-filled glare focused squarely on Cal. "And now I vill deal with you ze vay I should have from ze beginning."

Cal quickly spoke up. "Hold on, take the boat, I don't care. I'll sign a paper. You can do whatever you want with it, just let us go."

"I don't need paper, and I don't need your permission. I vill take what I vant. Now move! We all go aboard ze *Akula*." No one moved at first. Shouting out his order again, he pointed the gun right at Cal's head. "I said, move now!"

"Look, Yuri, your beef is with me. Take me but let my wife and J-Mac go," Cal beseeched.

Bringing the gun's aim to bear on Donna, one guttural word was growled through Yuri's gritted teeth, "Move!"

Cal felt a hot flash rush through his entire body. "Okay, okay, we're going, we're going."

A small smile shown grew on Yuri's face as they filed past him. "Remember, I have ze gun aimed right at your lovely wife's back, so go quickly and no tricks."

Nearing the doorway, Cal simply waved his hand, repeating, "No tricks."

Cal began a slow pace up and out of the cabin. Stepping out onto the deck, he stopped before continuing onto the dock. He stared into the distance hoping to see Juky returning with police, but to his extreme dismay, he saw no one. Taking a breath, his thoughts raced trying to figure out what to do.

They only had the time it would take to walk to the *Akula*. Their only chance, he felt, was if they could take off running for the center of town. Nearing the *Akula*, he finally landed on the only thing he could think of doing. Turning to face the gangway onto the

Akula, he looked around to Johnny Mac and Donna; their eyes met. Cal gave her only the slightest eye-cut toward town. She knew in an instant that her husband was seconds away from trying something. Yuri, annoyed by Cal's pace and hesitation at the gangway, barked, "Stop your stalling and go aboard."

Cal threw a sullen glare back at him. This was it. He had to do something and do it now! Placing a foot on the gangway, he abruptly stopped. One more bluff, he thought. Snapping his head up, he looked across the docking slip to the pavilion, yelling out while pointing, "It's the police. They're coming!"

Yuri and Lev both looked to see where Cal was pointing. The second they did, Cal looked back to Donna and Johnny Mac, yelling out, "Run!" Instantly Yuri reached back to try and grab Donna by the arm, but as he made his move, she back-spun away, bringing her leg up and back down hard on Yuri's arm. The machine gun flew from his hands landing and skidding a few feet away.

Yuri yelled out in pain and whirled back to face her; Cal charged him like a linebacker driving his shoulder solidly into his stomach, launching him backward off his feet, landing them hard on the ground. For a split second, everyone froze seeing the gun five feet from Yuri's outstretched hand. A mad scramble then erupted for the gun.

Lev kicked Donna's feet out from under her causing her to fall short of grabbing the gun. Scrambling, he leapt over her, crashing hard on his side and scooping up the gun up in one motion. Folding his legs under, he quickly stood. "Stop now or I shoot! Stop now!" he screamed while alternately pointing the gun at Cal then Donna.

Cal slowly stood up off Yuri. Donna likewise slowly stood shaking her hair from her face. Yuri struggled to stand, coughing and rubbing his wrist as did so. Lev, his face covered in dirt, held a hollow stare. He again felt the same power he had known as a guard in the gulags. "You vill move now, or I swear I vill shoot you vhere you stand, do you hear me?"

Cal moved in front of Donna; Lev backed up a couple of steps. Yuri eased his way to Lev's side, saying as he went, "I suggest you do as he says."

Hearing all the ruckus, Yuri's men along with Cesar and his men exited the *Akula*'s cabin, gathering on the rear deck. Yuri called out to Cesar, "You and your men vill leave my vessel, or Lev here vill do exactly as he said and shoot your friends. You see, zer is no one around to see, and all your weapons are on your boats."

Suddenly an echoed voice rang out from the direction of the pavilion. "No one move! Aund put down your weapons! Yo-ah all under arrest." Everyone slowly turned to see Juky leading several police officers rapidly moving through the pavilion with guns drawn and running toward them. Arriving quickly, eight officers surrounded the entire group, with one stepping forward. "I am Captain de la Rosa. You will all come with me to the station house."

Yuri, not one to be intimidated, stepped out in front of everyone. "I vill do no such thing. You cannot arrest me. I have diplomatic immunity."

The captain merely smiled and walked toward him, speaking as he went, "E's dat so? I seem to 'ave no record of any diplomats visiting our fair island, which is required by our laws. But ef et es as you say, we can clear it all up vury quickly, but you must accompany me to the station house. I would prefer yo-ah cooperation. Otherwise, I shall have to handle de situation differently, and dat, I'm afraid, will complicate matters for you aund yo-ah men."

Lev suddenly stepped out from behind Yuri, still holding the machine gun. Nervously he looked around. "Ve don't have to listen to him. Zey vill not shoot us. It vould cause big problem for zem with Kremlin and give zem much trouble."

Growing tired of the standoff, Captain de la Rosa firmly commanded, "Sir, if you do not hand over yo-ah weapon to me now, et will be you who will 'ave de big problem."

Lev glared at the captain. "No! I vill not!" He began to raise the gun up, but in the next instant, Grigori tore across the gangway leaping on top of Lev driving him hard into the ground. His fists tightly clenched, he began landing rage-filled rapid-fire blows at Lev's head and chest. He then grabbed him by the hair and slammed his face into the ground knocking him unconscious.

Captain de la Rosa snapped his fingers in the air. "Take dem!" Four armed men rushed forward with their automatic rifles pointing straight forward. "Everyone on yo-ah knees. Clasp yo-ah hands behind yo-ah heads. You too, sir," de la Rosa ordered, pointing directly at Yuri. Yuri took a threatening step toward the captain but instantly felt the barrel of a gun shove into his back by one of the officers. "Handcuff hem tightly," de la Rosa firmly stated.

Cal and Donna, thinking he meant for them to kneel as well, started to comply but was stopped by the captain who smiled. "No, no, yo-ah not under arrest. Yo-ah friend Juky has explained de situation to me." Donna, Cal, and Johnny Mac stood back to watch as all of Yuri's men were marched off single file toward the police station.

Captain de la Rosa looked to Cesar, questioning his involvement. "Sawfish, what role do you 'ave in all of dis? Are you and yo-ah men working a case he-ah?"

Cesar responded while stepping up to de la Rosa, "Well, Captain, it didn't start off dat way, but de fact is we were attempting to help de owners of de sailboat to keep it out of de Russian's hands," pointing to Yuri and his men.

"He lies!" Yuri bellowed as he walked away.

"Do not worry, sir, we shall see who lies and who es truthful." De la Rosa then sharply nodded to his men, saying, "Lock dem in de large cell in de back. I do not want to he-ah de big one's mouth until I question 'em."

Captain de la Rosa waited until Yuri and his men were out of earshot. Smiling, he turned back to Cesar and his men. "Cesar, you and yo-ah men may have just helped to break up not only a piracy ring but an espionage ring as well. It seems Interpol has been looking for a reason to search de Russian's yacht aund question hem fo-ah quite some time now. Aund it appears we have good reason now. A charge of piracy, aund now we can add a kidnapping charge to go along with it. Well done, sir."

Cesar shook his head and laughed a little as he replied, "Captain de la Rosa, me and my men had vury little to do with es capture. It was all dem," he said, nodding toward Cal, Donna, and Johnny Mac.

De la Rosa turned around to face them. "E's dis so? We arrived after de fight between you all had begun."

Cal put his arm around Donna, smiling like a Cheshire cat. "Captain, my little wife here kicked that loudmouth Russian's ass twice in the last twenty minutes, and that's a fact," he said, giving her a tight sideways hug and a kiss on top of her head.

"Really. Well, now we must all go to my office. I simply must he-ah dis whole story."

Cesar laughed out loud. "Certainly, aund let me say et es one heck of a story."

They all began walking in a group. Nearing the door to the shipping office, it suddenly swung open wide, and out staggered Joel, rubbing the back of his head and cussing. Cal called out to him. "Hey, what the hell happened to you? You missed all the action!"

Captain de la Rosa gave Cal a wide-eyed look, and then to Joel, asking, "El Jurakan? What es *yo-ah* part in of all dis?"

Rubbing the back of his head, he groused, "Apparently, it's to be a damn punching bag. The crazy-ass Russian shoved me backward when I tried to keep him from picking up your cards, Cal. I fell and hit my head on the desk, knocking me out!"

Captain de la Rosa nodded, saying, "Et appears our ill-tempered Russian now has an assault charge against him. This will make his claimed diplomatic immunity defense of little value now."

Joel groused, "Hell, that SOB did this to me twice!"

Captain de la Rosa assured all, "Do not worry. I shall press every charge I can against him aund his men."

Chapter 88

Three days had passed since leaving Cockburn Town. The hurricane that had threatened to come their direction had fortunately worked its way westward along the frontal boundary and was heading for the middle of the Gulf of Mexico and the Yucatan Peninsula.

Captain de la Rosa was amazed by the testimony given by everyone involved. Cal, Donna, and Johnny Mac's determination and resourcefulness impressed him, considering the nature of the men they were up against. Sacha, Grigori, and Andros requested and were given temporary asylum until their cases could be reviewed.

This left only Yuri and Lev to face the charges of piracy and kidnapping. Captain de la Rosa did warn that due to the complexity of the case, they may not be able to get a conviction and instead be left with only a permanent expulsion from the island and the surrounding waters. He promised that he would notify them of the outcome of the proceedings.

The goodbyes that came were heartfelt and tearful, especially for Donna. Joel and Juky had elected to stay behind. Juky decided to take up with Cesar and his men, and Joel felt he could do more good staying than being in a boardroom. He planned to sell off his shares of the company and use the money to build a school, among other philanthropic endeavors, and all of it done in his wife's name, the name only he used: Ellie.

Cal and Donna had called home before departing Cockburn Town to let Kevin and Tammy know when they expected to be back. And even though they were all excited, the recent events kept an air of uncertainty hovering over them. It was late afternoon when they passed under the arch of the Niles Channel Bridge. As the shadow of

the bridge drew across the *Donna Marie*, it seemed surreal to be seeing the shoreline of Ramrod Key passing a few hundred yards away,
amplifying the anxiousness they all were feeling.

Now only minutes away from being able to dock the *Donna
Marie* right back where she belonged, at the Salty Anchor, Cal
stepped away from the ship's wheel and said, "Here, Donna, you
take over. Johnny Mac and me need get these sails lowered." Donna
gave him a solemn look and took the wheel.

Cal took a quick look at Donna and then to Johnny Mac and
knew they were experiencing the same incredible feelings of repressed
exuberance as he was. Returning home had never felt so good or
strong before. Watching the shoreline drift by, Cal tried to imagine
how sailors three hundred years ago must have felt returning home
after being gone for months or even years, thinking they must have
been out of their minds with anticipation.

Cal and Johnny Mac made quick work out of lowering and
stowing the sails. Donna fired up the diesel to help maintain their
course. Nearing the entrance to the long canal that led right up to the
back side of the Salty Anchor, Donna offered the helm back to Cal.

Cal kissed her forehead, saying, "No, you take her in. You saved
her. It's only right."

"Cal honey, I'm so wound up right now I'm afraid I'll make a
mistake—that turn to the dock is pretty tight."

"Just take a deep breath and pretend you're kicking the shit out
of that Russian again."

Johnny Mac chimed in, "Hey, don't forget the home run she
made on his head with the leg."

Cal leaned away from Donna a little. Scrunching his face, he
asked, "By the way, just how long have you been able to do all those
karate moves anyway?"

Slowing the *Donna Marie*, she kept her attention locked on
bringing them smoothly alongside the dock, answering him without
looking at him, "Oh, about ten years now I guess."

"Ten years! Boy, I'm glad I never made you mad enough to use
that shit on me."

She gave him an impish grin. "Who says you didn't, and if you don't stop cussing like that, Mr. Arnold, I might just start now."

Donna eased them down the length of the canal then slowed to make the turn at the end. She worked the throttle while spinning the ship's wheel right, then left, carefully easing them up to the dock with the slightest bump. She took a deep breath as tears began rolling down her cheeks and falling on her bare feet. She shut down the motor. They were home!

Cal was about to compliment her on a perfect docking, but before he could get a word out, the doors of the restaurant suddenly flew open wide. A huge throng of people began pouring out of the restaurant, streaming toward them, yelling and cheering, and holding up glasses of beer and whiskey. They poured onto the dock, with some spilling onto the *Donna Marie*'s decks. Leading the whole procession was Kevin, Tammy, and the whole Salty Anchor crew.

In an instant, Kevin had his arms around both his parents' necks, pulling them in close, hugging them like he never had before. Tammy squeezed her way to Donna, grabbing her. She began hugging and crying, repeatedly pulling back to look into her face and then hugging her again.

Cal shouted out over all the commotion of laughter and jubilation, "Hold on, hold on! Everyone hush up a minute, please. Hush up, I want to say something!"

Cal stepped up onto roof of the cabin to address everyone. Holding up his hands, he quieted everyone again. "Hush up, everyone, hush, please. First, I can't tell you all how happy we are to be back home with our family, and believe me when I say the Salty Anchor *is* our home and you *all* are our family, I mean it." Shouts and cheers erupted again. Cal quieted the crowd once again. "Please, quiet down, I've one more thing to say." A hush once again fell over all. Cal then pulled Donna to his side. Putting his arm around her, he gave her the sweetest look and then continued.

"Thirty-five years ago, I married this lady, and now all these years later I know now more than ever that I could not have married a better woman, or *apparently* a more dangerous one. 'Cause let me tell you, this girl can fight!"

Everyone exploded in cheers and shouts. Over all the noise and confusion, Cal turned to face Donna leaning in close so only she could hear what he said. "Looks like we both have some wild stories to tell now." Gazing warmly at her, he added, "I love you, baby." He then pulled her deep into his arms kissing her long and hard.

9 781684 984824